THE COSMOLOGICAL EYE

HENRY MILLER

THE COSMOLOGICAL EYE

NEW DIRECTIONS

ISBN: 0-8112-0110-4

TENTH PRINTING

TABLE OF CONTENTS

Peace! It's Wonderful!

It was only the other night while entertaining an American writer who had come to visit France after a long absence that I realized poignantly what has happened to me since I left my native land. Like all my compatriots who come to see me he asked quite naturally what it was that had kept me here so long. (It is seven years since I am living in Paris.) I felt that it was useless to answer him in words. I suggested instead that we take a stroll through the streets. We started out from the corner of the Rue de la Gaîté and the Avenue du Maine where we had been sitting; I walked him down the Rue de l'Ouest to the Rue du Châ-

1

teau, then over the railroad bridge back of the Gare Montparnasse down the Boulevard Pasteur to the Avenue de Breteuil and thence to a little café facing the Invalides where we sat in silence for a long while. Perhaps that silence which one finds in the streets of Paris at night, perhaps that alone was a sufficient answer to his query. It is something difficult to find in a big American city.

At any rate, it was not chance which had directed my footsteps. Walking with my friend through the deserted streets I was reliving my first days in Paris, for it was in the Rue de Vanves that my new life really began. Night after night without money, without friends, without a language I had walked these streets in despair and anguish. The streets were everything to me, as they must be to every man who is lost in a big city. Walking through them again with my countryman I congratulated myself silently that I had begun my life in Paris behind the scenes, as it were. If I *had* led a Bohemian life, as some imagine, it was through bitter necessity. A *Bohemian life!* What a strange phrase that is when you think of it! There is so little that is Bohemian about it. In any case, the important thing is that in the Rue de Vanves I touched bottom. Like it or not, I was obliged to create a new life for myself. And this new life I feel is mine, absolutely mine, to use or to smash, as I see fit. In this life I am God, and like God I am indifferent to my own fate. I am everything there is—so why worry?

Just as a piece of matter detaches itself from the sun to live as a wholly new creation so I have come to feel about my detachment from America. Once the separation is made a new orbit is established, and there is no turning back. For me the sun had ceased to exist; I had myself become a blazing sun. And like all the other suns of the universe I had to nourish myself *from within*. I speak in cosmological terms because it seems to me that is the only possible way to think if one is truly alive. I think this way also because

2

it is just the opposite of the way I thought a few years back when I had what is called hopes. Hope is a bad thing. It means that you are not what you want to be. It means that part of you is dead, if not all of you. It means that you entertain illusions. It's a sort of spiritual clap, I should say.

Before this inward change came about I used to think that we were living in extraordinarily difficult times. Like most men I thought that our time was the worst possible time. And no doubt it is—for those, I mean, who still say "our time." As for myself, I've thrown away the calendar by which one reckons the lean and the fat years. For me it is all gravy, one continuous, marvellous stream of time without beginning or end. Yes, the times are bad, permanently bad—unless one becomes immune, *becomes God*. Since I have become God I go the whole hog always. I am absolutely indifferent to the fate of the world: I have my own world and my own private fate. I make no reservations and no compromises. I accept. *I am*—and that is all.

That is why, perhaps, when I sit at my typewriter I always face East. No backward glances over the shoulder. The orbit over which I am travelling leads me farther and farther away from the dead sun which gave me birth. Once I was confronted with a choice—either to remain a satellite of that dead thing or create a new world of my own, with my own satellites. I made my choice. Having made it there is no standing still. One becomes more and more alive, or more and more dead. To get a piqûre is useless; a blood transfusion is useless. A new man is made out of the whole cloth, by a change of heart which alters every living cell of the body. Anything less than a change of heart is sure catastrophe. Which, if you follow the reasoning, explains why the times are always bad. For, unless there be a change of heart there can be no act of will. There may be a show of will, with tremendous activity

3

accompanying it (wars, revolutions, etc.), but that will not change the times. Things are apt to grow worse, in fact.

Over many centuries of time a few men have appeared who, to my way of thinking, really understood why the times are permanently bad. They proved, through their own unique way of living, that this sad "fact" is one of man's delusions. But nobody, apparently, understands them. And it is eminently right that it should be thus. If we want to lead a creative life it is absolutely just that we should be responsible for our own destiny. To imagine a way of life that could be patched is to think of the cosmos as a vast plumbing affair. To expect others to do what we are unable to do ourselves is truly to believe in miracles, miracles that no Christ would dream of performing. The whole social-political scheme of existence is crazy—because it is based on vicarious living. A real man has no need of governments, of laws, of moral or ethical codes, to say nothing of battleships, police clubs, high-powered bombers and such things. Of course a real man is hard to find, but that's the only kind of man worth talking about. Why talk about trash? It is the great mass of mankind, the mob, the people, who create the permanently bad times. The world is only the mirror of ourselves. If it's something to make one puke, why then puke, me lads, it's your own sick mugs you're looking at!

Sometimes it almost seems that the writer takes a perverse delight in finding the times out of joint, finding everything awrack and awry. Perhaps the artist is nothing more than the personification of this universal maladjustment, this universal disequilibrium. Perhaps that explains why in the neutral, sterilized countries (Scandinavia, Holland, Switzerland), so little art is forthcoming, or why in the countries undergoing profound social and political changes (Russia, Germany, Italy), the art products are of negli-

4

gible value. But, whether there is little art or bad art, art, it should be understood, is only a makeshift, a substitute for the real thing. There is only one art which, if we practised it, would destroy what is called "art." With every line I write I kill off the "artist" in me. With every line it is either murder in the first degree or suicide. I do not want to give hope to others, nor to inspire others. If we knew what it meant to be inspired we would not inspire. We would simply *be*. As it is we neither inspire nor aid one another: we deal out cold justice. For myself I want none of this stinking cold justice; I want either warm-hearted magnanimity or absolute neglect. To be honest, I want something more than any man can give me. I want everything! I want everything—or nothing. It's crazy, I know, but that's what I mean.

Is it good here in France? It's wonderful. Marvellous. For *me* it's marvellous, because it's the only place in the world I know of where I can go on with my murder-and-suicide business—until I strike a new zodiacal realm. For a French writer it may be bad here, but then I am not a French writer. I should hate to be a French or a German or a Russian or an American writer. It must be hell. I am a cosmological writer, and when I open my trap I broadcast to the whole word at once. (Like Father Divine: *Peace! It's Wonderful!*) Acting as I do I am apt to get it in the neck. I am apt to get sucked good and proper, and I know it. But that's my temperament, and I'll stand or fall by it. Eventually I shan't even bother to be a cosmological writer: *I shall be just a man.* But first there's a lot of slaughtering to be done.

Every man who aspires to be a good French writer (or a bad one), or a (good or bad) German writer, or a (good or bad) Russian writer, any man, I mean, who hopes to make a living by giving regular doses of medicine to his sick countrymen, helps to perpetuate a farce which has been going on since the beginning of

5

history. Such writers, and they are practically all we have, it seems, are the lice which keep us from knowing Paradise or Hell. They keep us in a perpetual Purgatory where we scratch without let. Whereas even the earth wobbles on its axis, or will change its axis from time to time, these blokes keep us forever on an even keel. In every great figure who has flashed across the horizon there is, or was, a large element of treachery, or hatred, or love, or disgust. We have had traitors to race, country, religion, but we have not yet bred any real traitors, *traitors to the human race*, which is what we need. The chances are slim, I know. I mention it merely to show how the wind blows.

As I say, one needs either a heaven or a hell in which to flourish —until one arrives at that Paradise of his own creation, that middle realm which is not a bread-and-butter Utopia of which the masses dream but an interstellar realm in which one rolls along his orbit with sublime indifference. Dante was the best cartographer of the soul which Europe ever produced, everything clear as a whistle and etched in black and white; but since his time not only Europe, but the whole universe, has moved into new spiritual dimensions. Man is still the center of the cosmos, but having stretched the cosmos almost to the bursting point—the scientists actually predict that the universe will explode!—man himself is practically invisible. Artificial wings won't help, nor artificial eyes, nor escalators, nor pemmican. The whole damned universe has to be taken apart, brick by brick, and reconstructed. Every atom has to be rearranged. Perhaps just to sit quiet and take deep breathing exercises would be better than popping one another off with slugs of dynamite. Because the strange thing is that just doing nothing, just taking it easy, loafing, meditating, things tend to right themselves. As it is we are all terrified by the thought of losing our freedom. And yet it is freedom, *the idea of freedom*, which is what we dread most. Freedom means the strict inner precision of a Swiss watch—combined with absolute recklessness. Whence gayety and indifference, at present non-existent. Of course only lunatics dream of such a condition. And so we all remain sane and bite into one another like lice. And the lousier it gets the more progress we make. *Peace! It's Wonderful!*

I should say that ever since the dawn of history—all through the great civilizations, that is to say—we have been living like lice. Once every thousand years or so a man arises who is not a louse— and then there is even more hell to pay. When a MAN appears he seems to get a stranglehold on the world which it takes centuries to break. The sane people are cunning enough to find these men "psychopathic." These sane ones seem to be more interested in the technique of the stranglehold than in applying it. That's a curious phenomenon, one that puzzles me, to be frank. It's like learning the art of wrestling in order to have the pleasure of letting someone pin you to the mat.

What do I mean to infer? Just this—that art, the art of living, involves the act of creation. The work of art is nothing. It is only the tangible, visible evidence of a way of life, which, if it is not crazy is certainly *different* from the accepted way of life. The difference lies in the act, in the assertion of a will, and individuality. For the artist to attach himself to his work, or identify himself with it, is suicidal. An artist should be able not only to spit on his predecessor's art, or on all works of art, but on his own too. He should be able to be an artist all the time, and finally not be an artist at all, but a piece of art.

In addition to the deep breathing exercises perhaps mercurial inunctions ought also to be recommended—*for the time being.*

Max

THERE ARE SOME PEOPLE whom you call immediately by their first name. Max is one of them. There are people to whom you feel immediately attracted, not because you like them, but because you detest them. You detest them so heartily that your curiosity is aroused; you come back to them again and again to study them, to arouse in yourself a feeling of compassion which is really absent. You do things for them, not because you feel any sympathy for them, but because their suffering is incomprehensible to you.

I remember the evening Max stopped me on the boulevard. I

8

remember the feeling of repugnance which his face, his whole manner inspired. I was hurrying along, on my way to the cinema, when this sad Jewish face suddenly blocks my way. He asked me for a light or something—whatever it was it was only an excuse, I knew. I knew immediately that he was going to pour out a tale of woe, and I didn't want to hear it. I was curt and brusque, almost insulting; but that didn't matter, he stuck there, his face almost glued to mine, and clung like a leech. Without waiting to hear his story I offered him some change, hoping that he would be disgusted and walk off. But no, he refused to be offended; he clung to me like a leech.

From that evening on it almost seems as if Max were dogging my steps. The first few times I ran into him I put it down to sheer coincidence. Gradually, however, I became suspicious. Stepping out of an evening I would ask myself instinctively—"where now? are you sure Max won't be there?" If I were going for a stroll I would pick an absolutely strange neighborhood, one that Max would never dream of frequenting. I knew that he had to maintain a more or less fixed itinerary—the grand boulevards, Montparnasse, Montmartre, wherever the tourists were apt to congregate. Towards the end of the evening Max would disappear from my mind completely. Strolling home, along an accustomed route, I would be entirely oblivious of Max. Then, sure as fate, probably within a stone's throw of my hotel, out he'd pop. It was weird. He'd always bob up head on, as it were, and how he got there suddenly like that I never could figure out. Always I'd see him coming towards me with the same expression, a mask which I felt he had clapped on expressly for me. The mask of sorrow, of woe, of misery, lit up by a little wax taper which he carried inside him, a sort of holy, unctuous light that he had stolen from the synagogue. I knew always what his first words would be and I would laugh as he uttered them, a laugh which he always interpreted as a sign of friendliness.

"How are you, Miller!" he would say, just as though we hadn't seen each other for years. And with this *how are you* the smile which he had clapped on would broaden and then, quite suddenly, as though he had put a snuffer over the little wax taper inside him, it would go out. With this would come another familiar phrase—"Miller, do you know what has happened to me since I saw you?" I knew very well that *nothing* had happened in the interim. But I knew also, from experience, that soon we would be sitting down somewhere to enjoy the experience of *pretending* that something had happened in the interim. Even though he had done nothing but walk his legs off, in the interim, that would be something new that had happened to him. If the weather had been warm, or if it had been cold, *that* would be something that had happened to him. Or if he had managed to get a day's work that too would be something. Everything that happened to him was of a bad nature. It couldn't be otherwise. He lived in the expectation that things would grow worse, and of course they always did.

I had grown so accustomed to Max, to his state of perpetual misfortune, that I began to accept him as a natural phenomenon: he was a part of the general landscape, like rocks, trees, urinals, brothels, meat markets, flower stalls, and so on. There are thousands of men like Max roaming the streets, but Max was the personification of all. He was Unemployment, he was Hunger, he was Misery, he was Woe, he was Despair, he was Defeat, he was Humiliation. The others I could get rid of by flipping them a coin. Not Max! Max was something so close to me that it was just impossible to get rid of him. He was closer to me than a bedbug. Something *under* the skin, something in the blood-stream.

When he talked I only half-listened. I had only to catch the opening phrase and I could continue by myself, indefinitely, ad infinitum. Everything he said was true, horribly true. Sometimes I felt that the only way to make known this truth would be to put Max flat on his back on the sidewalk and leave him there spouting out his horrible truths. And what would happen, should I do that? Nothing. Nothing. People have a way of making cute little detours, of stuffing their ears. People don't want to hear these truths. They can't hear them, for the reason that they're all talking to themselves in the same way. The only difference is that Max said them aloud, and saying them aloud he made them seem objective, as though he, Max, were only the instrument to reveal the naked truth. He had gotten so far beyond suffering that he had become suffering itself. It was terrifying to listen to him because he, Max, had disappeared, had been swallowed up by his suffering.

It's easier to take man as a symbol than as a fact. Max to me was a symbol of the world, of a condition of the world which is unalterable. Nothing will change it. Nothing! Silly to think of laying Max out on the sidewalk. It would be like saying to people —"Don't you see?" See what? The world? Sure they see. The world! That's what they're trying to escape, trying not to see. Every time Max approached me I had this feeling of having the whole world on my hands, of having it right under my nose. The best thing for you, Max, I often thought to myself as I sat listening to him, is to blow your brains out. Destroy yourself! That's the only solution. But you can't get rid of the world so easily. Max is infinite. You would have to kill off every man, woman and child, every tree, rock, house, plant, beast, star. Max is in the blood. He's a disease.

I'm talking all the time about Max as about something in the past. I'm talking about the man I knew a year or so ago, before he went to Vienna—the Max I ran out on, the Max I left flat. The last note I had from him was a desperate plea to bring "medicaments." He wrote that he was ill and that they were going to throw him out of the hotel. I remember reading his note and laughing over the broken English. I didn't doubt for a minute that everything he said was true. But I had made up my mind not to lift a finger. I was hoping to Christ he would croak and not bother me any more. When a week had passed, and no further word from him, I felt relieved. I hoped he had realized that it was useless to expect anything more of me. And supposing he had died? It made no difference to me either way—I wanted to be left alone.

When it seemed as if I had really shaken him off for good and all I began to think of writing about him. There were moments when I was almost tempted to look him up, in order to corroborate certain impressions which I intended to exploit. I felt so strongly about it that I was on the point several times of paying him to come to see me. That last note of his, about the "medicaments," how I regretted having given it away! With that note in my hands I felt I could bring Max to life again. It's strange now, when I think about it, because everything Max had ever said was deeply engraved in my memory . . . I suppose I wasn't ready to write the story then.

Not long after this I was obliged to leave Paris for a few months. I thought of Max only rarely, and then as though it were a humorous and pathetic incident in the past. I never asked myself—"is he alive? what can he be doing now?" No, I thought of him as a symbol, as something imperishable—not flesh and blood, not a man suffering. Then one night, shortly after my return to Paris, just when I am searching frantically for another man, whom do I run smack into but Max. And what a Max!

"Miller, how are you? Where have you been?"

It's the same Max only he's unshaved. A Max resurrected from the grave in a beautiful suit of English cut and a heavy velour hat with a brim so stiffly curved that he looks like a mannikin. He gives me the same smile, only it's much fainter now and it takes longer to go out. It's like the light of a very distant star, a star which is giving its last twinkle before fading out forever. And the sprouting beard! It's that no doubt which makes the look of suffering stand out even more forcibly than before. The beard seems to have softened the look of absolute disgust which hung about his mouth like a rotten halo. The disgust has melted away into weariness, and the weariness into pure suffering. The strange thing is that he inspires even less pity in me now than before. He is simply grotesque—a sufferer and a caricature of suffering at the same time. He seems to be aware of this himself. He doesn't talk any more with the same verve; he seems to doubt his own words. He goes through with it only because it's become a routine. He seems to be waiting for me to laugh, as I used to. In fact, he laughs himself now, as though the Max he was talking about were another Max.

The suit, the beautiful English suit which was given him by an Englishman in Vienna and which is a mile too big for him! He feels ridiculous in it and humiliated. Nobody believes him any more—not in the beautiful English suit! He looks down at his feet which are shod in a pair of low canvas shoes; they look dirty and worn, the canvas shoes. They don't go with the suit and the hat. He's on the point of telling me that they're comfortable nevertheless, but force of habit quickly prompts him to add that his other shoes are at the cobbler's and that he hasn't the money to

13

get them out. It's the English suit, however, that's preying on his mind. It's become for him the visible symbol of his new misfortune. While holding his arm out so that I may examine the cloth he's already telling me what happened to him in the interim, how he managed to get to Vienna where he was going to start a new life and how he found it even worse there than in Paris. The soup kitchens were cleaner, that he had to admit. But grudgingly. What good is it if the soup kitchens are clean and you haven't even a sou in your pocket? But it was beautiful, Vienna, and clean—so clean! He can't get over it. But tough! Everybody is on the bum there. But it's so clean and beautiful, it would make you cry, he adds.

Is this going to be a long story, I'm wondering. My friends are waiting for me across the street, and besides, there's a man I must find . . .

"Yes, Vienna," I say absent-mindedly, trying to scan the terrasse out of the corner of my eye.

"No, not Vienna. Basle!" he shouts. "*Basle!*"

"I left Vienna over a month ago," I hear him saying.

"Yes, yes, and what happened then?"

"*What happened?* I told you, Miller, they took my papers away from me. I *told* you, they made a tourist out of me!"

When I hear this I burst out laughing. Max laughs too in his sad way. "Can you imagine such a thing," he says. "I should be a *tourist!*" He gives another dingy chortle.

Of course that wasn't all. At Basle, it seems, they pulled him off the train. Wouldn't let him cross the frontier.

"I says to them—what's the matter, please? Am I not *en règle?*"

All his life, I forgot to mention, Max has been fighting to be *en règle.* Anyway, they yank him off the train and they leave him there, in Basle, stranded. What to do? He walks down the main drive looking for a friendly face—an American, or an Englishman at least. Suddenly he sees a sign: *Jewish Boarding House*. He walks in with his little valise, orders a cup of coffee and pours out his tale of woe. They tell him not to worry—it's nothing.

"Well, anyway, you're back again," I say, trying to break away.

"And what good does it do me?" says Max. "They made me a tourist now, so what should I do for work? *Tell* me, Miller! And with such a suit like this can I bum a nickel any more? I'm finished. If only I shouldn't look so well!"

I look him over from head to toe. It's true, he does look incongruously well off. Like a man just out of a sick bed—glad to be up again, but not strong enough to shave. And then the hat! A ridiculously expensive hat that weighs a ton—and silk-lined! It makes him look like a man from the old country. And the stub of a beard! If it were just a little longer he'd look like one of those sad, virtuous, abstract-looking wraiths who flit through the ghettoes of Prague and Budapest. Like a holy man. The brim of the hat curls up so stiffly, so *ethically*. Purim and the holy men a little tipsy from the good wine. Sad Jewish faces trimmed with soft beards. And a Joe Welch hat to top it off! The tapers burning, the rabbi chanting, the holy wail from the standees, and everywhere hats, hats, all turned up at the brim and making a jest of the sadness and woe.

"Well, anyway, you're back again," I repeat. I'm shaking hands with him but he doesn't drop my hand. He's in Basle again, at the Jewish Boarding House, and they're telling him how to slip across the border. There were guards everywhere and he doesn't know how it happened but as they passed a certain tree and since no one came out it was safe and he went ahead. "And like that," he says, "I'm in Paris again. Such a lousy place as it is!

In Vienna they were clean at least. There were professors and students on the bread line, but here they are nothing but bums, and such lousy bums, they give you bugs right away."

"Yes, yes, that's how it is, Max," and I'm shaking his hand again.

"You know, Miller, sometimes I think I am going mad. I don't sleep any more. At six o'clock I am wide awake already and thinking on what to do. I can't stay in the room when it comes light. I must go down in the street. Even if I am hungry I must walk, I must see people. I can't stay alone any more. Miller, for God's sake, can you see what is happening to me? I wanted to send you a card from Vienna, just to show you that Max remembered you, but I couldn't think on your address. *And how was it*, Miller, in New York? Better than here, I suppose? No? The *crise*, too? Everywhere it's the *crise*. You can't escape. They won't give you to work and they won't give you to eat. What can you do with such bastards? Sometimes, Miller, I get so frightened . . ."

"Listen, Max, I've got to go now. Don't worry, you won't kill yourself . . . not yet."

He smiles. "Miller," he says, "you have such a good nature. You are so happy all the time. Miller, I wish I could be with you always. I would go anywhere in the world with you . . . anywhere."

This conversation took place about three nights ago. Yesterday at noon I was sitting on the terrasse of a little café in an out of the way spot. I chose the spot deliberately so as not to be disturbed during the reading of a manuscript. An *aperitif* was before me—I had taken but a sip or two. Just as I am about half-way through the manuscript I hear a familiar voice. "Why

16

Miller, how are you?" And there, as usual, bending over me is Max. The same peculiar smile, the same hat, the same beautiful suit and canvas shoes. Only now he's shaved.

I invite him to sit down. I order a sandwich and a glass of beer for him. As he sits down he shows me the pants to his beautiful suit—he has a rope around his waist to hold them up. He looks at them disgustedly, then at the dirty canvas shoes. Meanwhile he's telling me what happened to him in the interim. All day yesterday, so he says, nothing to eat. Not a crumb. And then, as luck would have it, he bumped into some tourists and they asked him to have a drink. "I had to be polite," he says. "I couldn't tell them right away I was hungry. I kept waiting and waiting for them to eat, but they had already eaten, the bastards. The whole night long I am drinking with them and nothing in my belly. Can you imagine such a thing, that they shouldn't eat once the whole night long?"

To-day I'm in the mood to humor Max. It's the manuscript I've been reading over. Everything was so well put . . . I can hardly believe I wrote the damned thing.

"Listen, Max, I've got an old suit for you, if you want to trot home with me!"

Max's face lights up. He says immediately that he'll keep the beautiful English suit for Sundays. Have I an iron at home, he would like to know. Because he's going to press my suit for me . . . *all my suits*. I explain to him that I haven't any iron, but I may have still another suit. (It just occurred to me that somebody promised me a suit the other day.) Max is in ecstasy. That makes *three* suits he'll have. He's pressing them up, in his mind. They must have a good crease in them, his suits. You can tell an American right away, he tells me, by the crease in his trousers. Or if not by the crease, by the walk. That's how he spotted me

17

the first day, he adds. And the hands in the pockets! A French-man never keeps his hands in his pockets.

"So you're sure you'll have the other suit too?" he adds quickly.

"I'm fairly sure, Max . . . Have another sandwich—and another demi!"

"Miller," he says, "you always think of the right things. It isn't so much what you give me—it's the way you think it out. You give me courage."

Courage. He pronounces it the French way. Every now and then a French word drops into his phrases. The French words are like the velour hat; they are incongruous. Especially the word misère. No Frenchman ever put such misère into misère. Well, anyway, courage! Again he's telling me that he'd go anywhere in the world with me. We'd come out all right, the two of us. (And me wondering all the time how to get rid of him!) But to-day it's O. K. To-day I'm going to do things for you, Max! He doesn't know, the poor devil, that the suit I'm offering him is too big for me. He thinks I'm a generous guy and I'm going to let him think so. To-day I want him to worship me. It's the manuscript I was reading a few moments ago. It was so good, what I wrote, that I'm in love with myself.

"Garçon! A package of cigarettes—pour le monsieur!"

That's for Max. Max is a monsieur for the moment. He's looking at me with that wan smile again. Well, courage, Max! To-day I'm going to lift you to heaven—and then drop you like a sinker! Jesus, just one more day I'll waste on this bastard and then bango! I'll put the skids under him. To-day I'm going to listen to you, you bugger . . . listen to every nuance. I'll ex-tract the last drop of juice—and then, overboard you go!

"Another demi, Max? Go on, have another . . . just one more! And have another sandwich!"

"But Miller, can you afford all that?"

He knows damned well I can afford it, else I wouldn't urge him. But that's his line with me. He forgets I'm not one of the guys on the boulevards, one of his regular clientèle. Or maybe he puts me in the same category—how should I know?

The tears are coming to his eyes. Whenever I see that I grow suspicious. Tears! Genuine little tears from the tear-jerker. Pearls, every one of them. Jesus, if only I could get inside that mechanism for once and see how he does it!

It's a beautiful day. Marvellous wenches passing by. Does Max ever notice them, I wonder.

"I say, Max, what do you do for a lay now and then?"

"For a what?" he says.

"You heard me. For a lay! Don't you know what a lay is?"

He smiles—that wan, wistful smile—again. He looks at me sidewise, as though a little surprised that I should put such a question to him. With his misery, his suffering, should he, Max, be guilty of such thoughts? Well, yes, to tell the truth, he does have such thoughts now and then. It's human, he says. But then, for ten francs, what can you expect? It makes him disgusted with himself. He would rather . . .

"Yes, I know, Max. I know exactly what you mean . . ."

I take Max along with me to the publisher's. I let him wait in the courtyard while I go inside. When I come out I have a load of books under my arm. Max makes a dive for the package —it makes him feel good to carry the books, to do some real work.

"Miller, I think you will be a great success some day," he says.

19

"You don't have to write such a wonderful book—sometimes it's just luck."

"That's it, Max, it's sheer luck. Just luck, that's all!"

We're walking along the Rue de Rivoli under the arcade. There's a book shop somewhere along here where my book is on display. It's a little cubby-hole and the window is full of books wrapped in bright cellophane. I want Max to have a look at my book in the window. I want to see the effect it will produce.

Ah, here's the place! We bend down to scan the titles. There's the *Kama Sutra* and *Under the Skirt, My Life and Loves*, and *Down There* . . . But where's my book? It used to be on the top shelf, next to a queer book on flagellation.

Max is studying the jacket illustrations. He doesn't seem to care whether my book is there or not.

"Wait a minute, Max, I'm going inside."

I open the door impetuously. An attractive young Frenchwoman greets me. I give a quick, desperate glance at the shelves. "Have you got the *Tropic of Cancer*?" I ask. She nods her head immediately and points it out to me. I feel somewhat relieved. I inquire if it's selling well. And did she ever read it herself? Unfortunately she doesn't read English. I fiddle around hoping to hear a little more about my book. I ask her why it's wrapped in cellophane. She explains why. Still I haven't had enough. I tell her that the book doesn't belong in a shop like this—it's not that kind of book, you know.

She looks at me rather queerly now. I think she's beginning to doubt if I really am the author of the book, as I said I was. It's difficult to make a point of contact with her. She doesn't seem to give a damn about my book or any other book in the shop. It's the French in her, I suppose . . . I ought to be getting along. I just realize that I haven't shaved, that my pants are not pressed and that they don't match my coat. Just then the door opens and a pale, aesthetic-looking young Englishman enters. He seems completely bewildered. I sneak out while he's closing the door.

"Listen, Max, they're inside—a whole row of them! They're selling like hot-cakes. Yes, everybody's asking for the book. That's what she says."

"I told you, Miller, that you would be a success."

He seems absolutely convinced, Max. Too easily convinced to suit me. I feel that I must talk about the book, even to Max. I suggest we have a coffee at the bar. Max is thinking about something. It disturbs me because I don't want him to be thinking about anything but the book for the moment. "I was thinking, Miller," he says abruptly, "that you should write a book about my experiences." He's off again, about his troubles. I shunt it off quickly.

"Look here, Max, I *could* write a book about you, but I don't want to. I want to write about myself. Do you understand?"

Max understands. He knows I have a lot to write about. He says I am a *student*. By that he means, no doubt, *a student of life*. Yes, that's it—a student of life. I must walk around a great deal, go here and there, waste my time, appear to be enjoying myself, while all the time, of course, I am studying life, studying people. Max is beginning to get the idea. It's no cinch being a writer. A twenty-four hour job.

Max is reflecting on it. Making comparisons with his own life —the difference between one kind of misery and another. Thinking of his troubles again, of how he can't sleep, thinking of the machinery inside his bean that never stops.

Suddenly he says: "And the writer, I suppose he has his own nightmares!"

21

His nightmares! I write that down on an envelope immediately.

"You're writing that down?" says Max. "Why? Was it so good what I said?"

"It was *marvellous*, Max. It's worth money to me, a thought like that."

Max looks at me with a sheepish smile. He isn't sure whether I'm spoofing him or not.

"Yes, Max," I repeat, "it's worth a fortune, a remark like that."

His brain is beginning to labor. He always thought, he starts to explain, that a writer had first to accumulate a lot of facts.

"Not at all, Max! Not at all! The less facts you have the better. Best of all is not to have any facts, do you get me?"

Max doesn't get it entirely, but he's willing to be convinced. A sort of magic's buzzing in his brain. "That's what I was always thinking," he says slowly, as if to himself. "A book must come from the *heart*. It must *touch* you . . ."

It's remarkable, I'm thinking, how quickly the mind leaps. Here, in less than a minute, Max has made an important distinction. Why, only the **other** day Boris and I we spent the whole day talking about this, talling about "the living word." It comes forth with the breath, just the simple act of opening the mouth, *and being with God*, to be sure. Max understands it too, in his way. That the facts are nothing. Behind the facts there must be the man, *and the man must be with God*, must talk like God Almighty.

I'm wondering if it might not be a good idea to show Max my book, have him read a little of it in my presence. I'd like to see if he gets it. And *Boris!* Maybe it would be a good idea to present Max to Boris. I'd like to see what impression Max would make on him. There'd be a little change in it, too, no doubt.

Maybe enough for the both of us—for dinner . . . I'm explaining
to Max, as we draw near the house, that Boris is a good friend
of mine, another writer like myself. "I don't say that he'll do
anything for you, but I want you to meet him." Max is perfectly
willing . . . why not? And then Boris is a Jew, that ought to
make it easier. I want to hear them talking Yiddish. I want to
see Max weep in front of Boris. I want to see Boris weep too.
Maybe Boris will put him up for a while, in the little alcove
upstairs. It would be funny to see the two of them living to-
gether. Max could press his clothes and run errands for him—
and cook perhaps. There's lots of things he could do—to earn
his grub. I try hard not to look too enthusiastic. "A queer fel-
low, Boris," I explain to Max. Max doesn't seem to be at all
worried about that. Anyway, there's no use going into deep ex-
planations. Let them get together as best they can . . .

Boris comes to the door in a beautiful smoking jacket. He
looks very pale and frail and withdrawn, as though he had been
in a deep reverie. As soon as I mention "Max" his face lights
up. He's heard about Max.

I have a feeling that he's grateful to me for having brought
Max home. Certainly his whole manner is one of warmth, of
sympathy. We go into the studio where Boris flops on the
couch; he throws a steamer blanket over his frail body. There
are two Jews now in a room, face to face, and both know what
suffering is. No need to beat around the bush. Begin with the
suffering . . . plunge right in! Two kinds of suffering—it's mar-
vellous to me what a contrast they present. Boris lying back on
the couch, the most elegant apostle of suffering that ever I've
met. He lies there like a human Bible on every page of which
is stamped the suffering, the misery, the woe, the torture, the

anguish, the despair, the defeat of the human race. Max is sitting on the edge of his chair, his bald head dented just below the crown, as if suffering itself had come down on him like a sledge-hammer. He's strong as a bull, Max. But he hasn't Boris' strength. He knows only *physical* suffering—hunger, bedbugs, hard benches, unemployment, humiliations. Right now he's geared up to extract a few francs from Boris. He's sitting on the edge of his chair, a bit nervous because we haven't given him a chance yet to explain his case. He wants to tell the story from beginning to end. He's fishing around for an opening. Boris meanwhile is reclining comfortably on his bed of sorrow. He wants Max to take his time. He knows that Max has come to suffer for him.

While Max talks I snoop about looking for a drink. I'm determined to enjoy this seance. Usually Boris says immediately— "what'll you have to drink?" But with Max on hand it doesn't occur to him to offer drinks.

Stone sober and hearing it for the hundredth time Max's story doesn't sound so hot to me. I'm afraid he's going to bore the pants off Boris—with his "facts." Besides, Boris isn't keen on listening to long stories. All he asks for is a little phrase, sometimes just a word. I'm afraid Max is making it all too prosaic. He's in Vienna again, talking about the clean soup kitchens. I know it's going to take a little while before we get to Basle, then Basle to Paris, then Paris, then hunger, want, misery, then full dress rehearsal. I want him to plunge right into the whirlpool, into the stagnant flux, the hungry monotony, the bare, bedbuggy doldrums with all the hatches closed and no fire escapes, no friends, no *sortie*, no-tickee-no-shirtee business. No, Boris doesn't give a damn about continuity; he wants something dramatic, something vitally grotesque and horribly beautiful and true. Max will bore the pants off him, I can see that. . . .

24

It happens I'm wrong. Boris wants to hear the whole story, from beginning to end. I suppose it's his mood—sometimes he shows an inexhaustible patience. What he's doing, no doubt, is to carry on his own interior monologue. Perhaps he's thinking out a problem while Max talks. It's a rest for him. I look at him closely. Is he listening? Seems to me he's listening all right. He smiles now and then.

Max is sweating like a bull. He's not sure whether he's making an impression or not.

Boris has a way of listening to Max as if he were at the opera. It's better than the opera, what with the couch and the steamer blanket. Max is taking off his coat; the perspiration is rolling down his face. I can see that he's putting his heart and soul into it. I sit at the side of the couch glancing from one to the other. The garden door is open and the sun seems to throw an aureole around Boris' head. To talk to Boris Max has to face the garden. The heat of the afternoon drifts in through the cool studio; it puts a warm, fuzzy aura about Max's words. Boris looks so comfortable that I can't resist the temptation to lie down beside him. I'm lying down now and enjoying the luxury of listening to a familiar tale of woe. Beside me is a shelf of books; I run my eye over them as Max spins it out. Lying down this way, hearing it at full length, I can judge the effect of it better. I catch nuances now that I never caught before. His words, the titles of the books, the warm air drifting in from the garden, the way he sits on the edge of his chair—the whole thing combines to produce the most savory effect.

The room is in a state of complete disorder, as usual. The enormous table is piled with books and manuscripts, with pencilled notes, with letters that should have been answered a month ago. The room gives the impression somehow of a sudden state

25

of arrest, as though the author who inhabited it had died suddenly and by special request nothing had been touched. If I were to tell Max that this man Boris lying on the couch had really died I wonder what he would say. That's exactly what Boris means too—*that he died*. And that's why he's able to listen the way he does, as though he were at the opera. Max will have to die too, die in every limb and branch of his body, if he's to survive at all . . . The three books, one next to the other, on the top shelf—almost as if they had been deliberately arranged that way: The Holy Bible, Boris' own book, the Correspondence between Nietzsche and Brandes. Only the other night he was reading to me from the Gospel according to Luke. He says we don't read the Gospels often enough. And then Nietzsche's last letter—"*the crucified one.*" Buried in the tomb of the flesh for ten solid years and the whole world singing his praise . . .

Max is talking away. Max the presser. From somewhere near Lemberg he came—near the big fortress. And thousands of them just like him, men with broad triangular faces and puffy underlip, with eyes like two burnt holes in a blanket, the nose too long, the nostrils broad, sensitive, melancholy. Thousands of sad Jewish faces from around Lemberg way, the head thrust deep into the socket of the shoulders, sorrow wedged deep between the strong shoulder blades. Boris is almost of another race, so frail, so light, so delicately attuned. He's showing Max how to write in the Hebrew character; his pen races over the paper. With Max the pen is like a broomstick; he seems to draw the characters instead of inscribing them. The way Boris writes is the way Boris does everything—lightly, elegantly, correctly, definitively. He needs intricacies in order to move swiftly and subtly. Hunger, for instance, would be too coarse, too crude. Only stupid people worry about hunger. The garden, I must say, is also re-

mote to Boris. A Chinese screen would have served just as well
—better perhaps. Max, however, is keenly aware of the garden.
If you gave Max a chair and told him to sit in the garden he
would sit and wait for a week if necessary. Max would ask noth-
ing better than food and a garden . . .

"I don't see what can be done for a man like this," Boris is
saying, almost to himself. "It's a hopeless case." And Max is
shaking his head in agreement. Max is a case, and he realizes it.
But *hopeless*—that I can't swallow. No, nobody is hopeless—not
so long as there is a little sympathy and friendship left in the
world. The *case* is hopeless, yes. But Max the man . . . no, I can't
see it! For Max the man there is still something to be done.
There's the next meal, for example, a clean shirt . . . a suit of
clothes . . . a bath . . . a shave. Let's not try to solve the case:
let's do only what's necessary to do immediately. Boris is think-
ing along the same lines. Only differently. He's saying aloud, just
as though Max were not there—"of course, you could give him
money . . . but that won't help . . ." *And why not?* I ask myself.
Why not money? Why not food, clothing, shelter? *Why not?*
Let's start at the bottom, from the ground up.

"Of course," Boris is saying, "if I had met him in Manila I
could have done something for him. I could have given him work
then . . ."

Manila! Jesus, that sounds grotesque to me! What the hell has
Manila got to do with it? It's like saying to a drowning man:
"What a pity, what a pity! If you had only let me teach you
how to swim!"

Everybody wants to right the world; nobody wants to help his
neighbor. They want to make a man of you without taking your
body into consideration. It's all cockeyed. And Boris is cockeyed
too, asking him *have you any relatives in America?* I know that

27

tack. That's the social worker's first question. Your age, your name and address, your occupation, your religion, and then, very innocent like—*the nearest living relative, please!* As though you hadn't been all over that ground yourself. As though you hadn't said to yourself a thousand times—"I'll die first! I'll die rather than . . ." And they sit there blandly and ask for the secret name, the secret place of shame, and they will go there immediately and ring the door-bell and they will blurt out everything—while you sit at home trembling and sweating with humiliation.

Max is answering the question. Yes, he had a sister in New York. He doesn't know any more where she is. She moved to Coney Island, that's all he knows. Sure, he had no business to leave America. He was earning good money there. He was a presser and he belonged to the union. But when the slack season came and he sat in the park at Union Square he saw that he was nothing. They ride up on their proud horses and they shove you off the sidewalk. For what? For being out of work? Was it *his* fault . . . did he, Max, do anything against the government? It made him furious and bitter; it made him disgusted with himself. What right had they to lay their hands on him? What right had they to make him feel like a worm?

"I wanted to make something of myself," he continues. "I wanted to do something else for a living—not work with my hands all the time. I thought may be I could learn the French and become an *interprète* perhaps."

Boris flashes me a look. I see that that struck home. The dream of the Jew—*not to work with the hands!* The move to Coney Island—another Jewish dream. From the Bronx to Coney Island! From one nightmare to another! Boris himself three times around the globe—but it's always *from the Bronx to Coney Island*. Von Lemberg nach Amerika gehen! Yea, go! On, weary

28

feet! On! On! No rest for you anywhere. No comfort. No end to toil and misery. Cursed you are and cursed you will remain. *There is no hope!* Why don't you fling yourself into his arms? Why don't you? Do you think I will mind? Are you ashamed? Ashamed of what? We know that you are cursed and we can do nothing for you. We pity you, one and all. The wandering Jew! You are face to face with your brother and you withhold the embrace. That is what I can't forgive you for. Look at Max! He is almost your double! Three times around the globe and now you have met yourself face to face. How can you run away from him? Yesterday you were standing there like him, trembling, humiliated, a beaten dog. And now you stand there in a smoking jacket and your pockets are full to bursting. *But you are the same man!* You haven't altered an iota, except to fill your pockets. *Has he a relative in America?* Have you a relative in America? Your mother, where is she now? Is she down there in the ghetto still? Is she still in that stinking little room you walked out of when you decided to make a man of yourself? At least you had the satisfaction of succeeding. You killed yourself in order to solve the problem. But if you hadn't succeeded? What then? What if you were standing there now in Max's shoes? Could we send you back to your mother? And what is Max saying? That if only he could find his sister he would throw his arms around her neck, he would work for her until his dying day, he would be her slave, her dog . . . He would work for you too, if you would only give him bread and a place to rest. You have nothing for him to do—I understand that. But can't you *create* something for him to do? Go to Manila, if needs be. Start the racket all over again. But don't ask Max to look for you in Manila three years ago. Max is here now, standing before you. *Don't you see him?*

29

I turn to Max. "Supposing, Max, you had your choice . . . I mean suppose you could go wherever you like and start a new life . . . where would you go?"

It's cruel to ask Max a question like that, but I can't stand this hopelessness. Look here, Max, I'm running on, I want you to look at the world as if it belonged to you. Take a look at the map and put your finger on the spot you'd like to be in. What's the use? *What's the use?* you say. Why just this, that if you want to badly enough you can go anywhere in the world. Just by wanting it. Out of desperation you can accomplish what the millionaire is powerless to accomplish. The boat is waiting for you; the country is waiting for you; the job is waiting for you. All things await you if you can but believe it. I haven't a cent, but I can help you to go anywhere you wish. I can go around with the hat and beg for you. Why not? It's easier than if I were asking for myself. Where would you like to go—*Jerusalem? Brazil?* Just say the word, Max, and I'll be off!

Max is electrified. He knows immediately where he'd like to go. And what's more, he almost sees himself going. There's just a little hitch—the money. Even that isn't altogether impossible. How much does it take to get to the Argentine? A thousand francs? That's not impossible . . . Max hesitates a moment. It's his age now that worries him. Has he the strength for it? The *moral* strength to begin afresh? He's forty-three now. He says it as if it were old age. (And Titian at 97 just beginning to get a grip on himself, on his art!) Sound and solid he is in the flesh, despite the dent in the back of his skull where the sledge-hammer came down on him. Bald yes, but muscles everywhere, the eyes still clear, the teeth . . . Ah, the teeth! He opens his mouth to show me the rotting stumps. Only the other day he had to go to the dentist—his *gencives* were terribly swollen. And do you know what the dentist said to him? Nervousness! Nothing but nervousness. That scared the life out of him. How should the dentist know that he, Max, was nervous?

Max is electrified. A little lump of courage is forming inside him. Teeth or no teeth, bald, nervous, cockeyed, rheumatic, spavined, what not—what matter? A place to go to, that's the point. *Not Jerusalem!* The English won't let any more Jews in —too many of them already. *Jerusalem for the Jews!* That was when they needed the Jews. Now you must have a good reason for going to Jerusalem—a better reason than just being a Jew. Christ Almighty, what a mockery! If I were a Jew I would tie a rope around my neck and throw myself overboard. Max is standing before me in the flesh. Max the Jew. Can't get rid of him by tying a sinker around his neck and saying: "Jew, go drown yourself!"

I'm thinking desperately. Yes, if I were Max, if I were the beaten dog of a Jew that Max is . . . What then? Yeah, *what?* I can't get anywhere imagining that I'm a Jew. I must imagine simply that I am a man, that I'm hungry, desperate, at the end of my tether.

"Listen, Boris, we've got to do something! *Do* something, do you understand?"

Boris is shrugging his shoulders. Where's all that money going to come from? He's asking *me!* Asking *me* where it's going to come from. All that money. *What* money? A thousand francs . . . two thousand francs . . . *is that money?* And what about that dizzy American Jane who was here a few weeks ago? Not a drop of love she gave you, not the least sign of encouragement. Insulted you right and left—every day. And you handed it out to her. Handed it out like a Croesus. To that little gold-digging bitch of an American. Things like that make me wild, furiously wild. Wouldn't have been so bad if she had been a plain whore. But she was worse than a whore. She bled you and insulted you. Called you a dirty Jew. And you went right on handing it out. It could happen again to-morrow, the same damned thing. Anybody can get it out of you if only they tickle your vanity, if only they flatter the pants off you. You died, you say, and you've been holding one long funeral ever since. But you're not dead, and you know you're not. What the hell does spiritual death matter when Max is standing before you? Die, die, die a thousand deaths —but don't refuse to recognize the living man. Don't make a problem of him. It's flesh and blood, Boris. *Flesh and blood.* He's screaming and you pretend not to hear. You are deliberately making yourself deaf, dumb and blind. You are dead before the living flesh. Dead before your own flesh and blood. You will gain nothing, neither in the spirit, nor in the flesh, if you do not recognize Max your true brother. Your books on the shelf there . . . they stink, your books! What do I care for your sick Nietzsche, for your pale, loving Christ, for your bleeding Dostoievski! Books, books, books. Burn them! They are of no use to you. Better never to have read a line than to stand now in your two shoes and helplessly shrug your shoulders. Everything Christ said is a lie, everything Nietzsche said is a lie, if you don't recognize the word *in the flesh.* They were foul and lying and diseased if you can derive a sweet comfort from them and not see this man rotting away before your very eyes. Go, go to your books and bury yourself! Go back to your Middle Ages, to your Kabbala, to your hair-splitting, angel-twisting geometry. We need nothing of you. We need a breath of life. We need hope, courage, illusion. We need a penny's worth of human sympathy.

We're upstairs now in my place and the bath water is running. Max has stripped down to his dirty underwear; his shirt with the false front is lying over the arm-chair. Undressed he looks like a gnarled tree, a tree that has painfully learned to walk. The man of the sweat shop with his dickey slung over the arm-chair. The powerful body twisted by toil. From Lemberg to America, from the Bronx to Coney Island—hordes and hordes of them, broken, twisted, spavined, as though they had been stuck on a spit and the struggle useless because struggle or no struggle they will sooner or later be eaten alive. I see all these Maxes at Coney Island on a Sunday afternoon: miles and miles of clear beach polluted with their broken bodies. They make a sewer of their own sweat and they bathe in it. They lie on the beach, one on top of the other, entangled like crabs and seaweed. Behind the beach they throw up their ready-made shacks, the combination bath, toilet and kitchen which serves as a home. At six o'clock the alarm goes off; at seven they're in the subway elbow to elbow, and the stench is powerful enough to knock a horse down.

While Max is taking his bath I lay out some clean things for him. I lay out the suit that was given to me, the suit which is too big for me and which he will thank me for profusely. I lie down to think things over calmly. The next move? We were all going to have dinner together over in the Jewish quarter, near St. Paul. Then suddenly Boris changed his mind. He remembered an engagement he had made for dinner. I wangled a little change out of him for dinner. Then, as we were parting, he handed Max a little dough. "Here, Max, I want you to take this," he said, fishing it out of his jeans. It made me wince to hear him say that—and to hear Max thanking him profusely. I know Boris. I know this is his worst side. And I forgive him for it. I forgive him easier than I can forgive myself. I don't want it to be thought that Boris is mean and hard-hearted. He looks after his relatives, he pays his debts, he cheats nobody. If he happens to bankrupt a man he does it according to the rules; he's no worse here than a Morgan or a Rockefeller. He plays the game, as they say. But *life*, life he doesn't see as a game. He wins out in every sphere only to discover in the end that he's cheated himself. With Max just now he won out handsomely. He got off by squeezing out a few francs for which he was handsomely thanked. Now that he's alone with himself he's probably cursing himself. To-night he'll spend twenty times what he gave Max, in order to wipe out his guilt.

Max has called me to the bathroom to ask if he can use my hairbrush. Sure, use it! (To-morrow I'll get a new one!) And then I look at the bath tub, the last bit of water gurgling through the drain. The sight of those filthy cruds floating at the bottom of the tub almost makes me puke. Max is bending over the tub to clean the mess. He's got the dirt off his hide at last; he feels good, even if he must mop up his own dirt. I know the feeling. I remember the public baths in Vienna, the stench that knocks you down . . .

Max is stepping into his clean linen. He's smiling now—a different sort of smile than I ever saw him give. He's standing in his clean underwear and browsing through my book. He's reading that passage about Boris, about Boris being lousy and me shaving his arm-pits, about the flag being at half-mast and everybody dead, including myself. That was something to go through —and come out *singing*. Luck! Well, call it that if you like. Call it luck if it makes you feel any better. Only I happen to know differently. Happens it happened to me—*and I know*. It isn't that I don't believe in luck. No, but it isn't what I mean. Say I was born innocent—that comes nearer to hitting the mark. When I think back to what I was as a kid, a kid of five or six, I realize that I haven't altered a bit. I'm just as pure and innocent as ever. I remember my first impression of the world—that it was good, *but terrifying*. It still looks that way to me—good but terrifying. It was easy to frighten me, but I never spoiled inside. You can frighten me to-day, but you can't make me sour. It's settled. It's in the blood.

I'm sitting down now to write a letter for Max. I'm writing to a woman in New York, a woman connected with a Jewish newspaper. I'm asking her to try to locate Max's sister in Coney Island. The last address was 156th Street near Broadway. "*And the name, Max?*" She had two names, his sister. Sometimes she called herself Mrs. Fischer, sometimes it was Mrs. Goldberg. "And you can't remember the house—whether it was on a corner or in the middle of the block?" No, he can't. He's lying now and I know it, but what the hell. Supposing there was no sister, what of it? There's something fishy about his story, but that's his affair, not mine.

It's even fishier, what he's doing now. He's pulling out a photograph taken when he was seven or eight—a photograph of mother and son. The photograph almost knocks the pins from under me. His mother is a *beautiful* woman—in the photograph. Max is standing stiffly by her side, a little frightened, the eyes wide open, his hair carefully parted, his little jacket buttoned up to the neck. They're standing somewhere near Lemberg, near the big fortress. The whole tragedy of the race is in the mother's face. A few years and Max too will have the same expression. Each new infant begins with a bright, innocent expression, the strong purity of the race moistening the large, dark eyes. They stand like that for several years and then suddenly, around puberty often, the expression changes. Suddenly they get up on their hind legs and they walk the tread-mill. The hair falls out, the teeth rot, the spine twists. Corns, bunions, calluses. The hand always sweating, the lips twitching. The head down, almost in the plate, and the food sucked in with big, swishing gulps. To think that they all started clean, with fresh diapers every day . . .

We're putting the photograph in the letter, as an identification. I'm asking Max to add a few words, in Yiddish, in that broomstick scrawl. He reads back to me what he has written and somehow I don't believe a word of it. We make a bundle of the suit and the dirty linen. Max is worried about the bundle—it's wrapped in newspaper and there's no string around it. He says he doesn't want to be seen going back to the hotel with that awkward looking bundle. He wants to look respectable. All the while he's fussing with the bundle he's thanking me profusely. He makes me feel as if I hadn't given him enough. Suddenly it occurs to me that there was a hat left here, a better one than the thing he's got on. I get it out and try it on. I show him how the hat should be worn. "You've got to turn the brim down and pull it well over your eye, see? And crush it in a bit—like that!" Max says it looks fine on me. I'm sorry I'm giving it away. Now Max tries it on, and as he puts it on I notice that he doesn't seem enthusiastic about it. He seems to be debating whether it's worth the trouble to take along. That settles it for me. I take him to the bathroom and I set it rakishly over his right eye. I crush the crown in even more rakishly. I know that makes him feel like a pimp or a gambler. Now I try the other hat on him—his own hat with the stiffly curled brim. I can see that he prefers that, silly as it looks. So I begin to praise the shit out of it. I tell him it becomes him more than the other. I talk him out of the other hat. And while he's admiring himself in the mirror I open the bundle and I extract a shirt and a couple of handkerchiefs and stuff them back in the drawer. Then I take him to the grocer at the corner and I have the woman wrap the bundle properly. He doesn't even thank the woman for her pains. He says she can afford to do me a service since I buy all my groceries from her.

We get off at the Place St. Michel. We walk towards his hotel in the Rue de la Harpe. It's the hour before dark when the walls glow with a soft, milky whiteness. I feel at peace with the world. It's the hour when Paris produces almost the effect of music upon one. Each stop brings to the eye a new and surprising architectural order. The houses actually seem to arrange themselves in musical notation: they suggest quaint minuets, waltzes, mazurkas, nocturnes. We are going into the oldest of the old, towards St. Severin and the narrow, twisting streets familiar to Dante and da Vinci. I'm trying to tell Max what a wonderful neighborhood he inhabits, what venerable associations are here stored away. I'm telling him about his predecessors, Dante and da Vinci.

"And when was all this?" he asks.

"Oh, around the 14th century," I answer.

"That's it," says Max, "before that it was no good and after that it has been no good. It was good in the 14th century and that's all." If I like it so well he'd be glad to change places with me.

We climb the stairs to his little room on the top floor. The stairs are carpeted to the third floor and above that they are waxed and slippery. On each floor is an enamel sign warning the tenants that cooking and washing are not permitted in the rooms. On each floor is a sign pointing to the water closet. Climbing the stairs you can look into the windows of the hotel adjoining; the walls are so close that if you stuck your mitt out the window you could shake hands with the tenants next door.

The room is small but clean. There's running water and a little commode in the corner. On the wall a few clothes hooks have been nailed up. Over the bed a yellow bulb. Thirty-seven francs a week. Not bad. He could have another for twenty-eight francs, but no running water. While he's complaining about the size of the room I step to the window and look out. There, almost touching me, is a young woman leaning out of the window. She's staring blankly at the wall opposite where the windows end. She seems to be in a trance. At her elbow are some tiny flower-pots; below the window, on an iron hook, hangs a dish-rag. She seems oblivious of the fact that I'm standing at her side watching her. Her room, probably no larger than the one we're standing in, seems nevertheless to have brought her peace. She's waiting for it to get dark in order to slip down into the street. She probably doesn't know anything about her distinguished predecessors either, but the past is in her blood and she connects more easily with the lugubrious present. With the darkness coming on and my blood astir I get an almost holy feeling about this room I'm standing in. Perhaps to-night when I leave him Max will spread my book on the pillow and pore over it with heavy eyes. On the flyleaf it is written: "To my friend Max, the only man in Paris who really knows what suffering is." I had the feeling, as I inscribed these words, that my book was embarking on a strange adventure. I was thinking not so much of Max as of others unknown to me who would read these lines and wonder. I saw the book lying by the Seine, the pages torn and thumb-marked, passages underlined here and there, figures in the margin, coffee stains, a man with a big overcoat shoving it in his pocket, a voyage, a strange land, a man under the Equator writing me a letter: I saw it lying under a glass and the auctioneer's ham-

38

mer coming down with a bang. Centuries passing and the face of the world changing, changing. And then again two men standing in a little room just like this, perhaps this very room, and next door a young woman leaning out of the window, the flower pots at her elbow, the dish-rag hanging from the iron hook. And just as now one of the men is worn to death; his little room is a prison and the night gives him no comfort, no hope of relief. Weary and disheartened he holds the book which the other has given him. But he can take no courage from the book. He will toss on his bed in anguish and the nights will roll over him like the plague. He will have to die first in order to see the dawn . . . Standing in this room by the side of the man who is beyond all help my knowledge of the world and of men and women speaks cruelly and silently. Nothing but death will assuage this man's grief. There is nothing to do, as Boris says. It is all useless.

As we step into the hall again the lights go out. It seems to me as if Max were swallowed up in everlasting darkness.

It's not quite so dark outdoors though the lights are on everywhere. The Rue de la Harpe is thrumming. At the corner they are putting up an awning; there is a ladder standing in the middle of the street and a workman in big baggy trousers is sitting on top of it waiting for his side-kick to hand him a monkey-wrench or something. Across the street from the hotel is a little Greek restaurant with big terra cotta vases in the window. The whole street is theatrical. Everybody is poor and diseased and beneath our feet are catacombs choked with human bones. We take a turn around the block. Max is trying to pick out a suitable restaurant; he wants to eat in a *prix fixe* at 5.50 frs. When I make a face he points to a de luxe restaurant at 18 francs the meal. Clearly he's bewildered. He's lost all sense of values.

We go back to the Greek restaurant and study the menu pasted on the window. Max is afraid it's too high. I take a look inside and I see that it's crowded with whores and workmen. The men have their hats on, the floor is covered with sawdust, the lights are dingy. It's the sort of place where you might really have a good meal. I take Max by the arm and start dragging him in. A whore is just sailing out with a toothpick in her mouth. At the curb her companion is waiting for her; they walk down the street towards St. Severin, perhaps to drop in at the *bal musette* opposite the church. Dante must have dropped in there too once in a while— for a drink, what I mean. The whole Middle Ages is hanging there outside the door of the restaurant; I've got one foot in and one foot out. Max has already seated himself and is studying the menu. His bald head glistens under the yellow light. In the 14th century he would have been a mason or a joiner: I can see him standing on a scaffold with a trowel in his hand.

The place is filled with Greeks: the waiters are Greek, the proprietors are Greek, the food is Greek and the language is Greek. I want egg-plant wrapped in vine leaves, a nice patty of egg-plant swimming in lamb sauce, as only the Greeks know how to make it. Max doesn't care what he eats. He's afraid it's going to be too expensive for me. My idea is to duck Max as soon as the meal is over and take a stroll through the neighborhood. I'll tell him I have work to do—that always impresses him.

It's in the midst of the meal that Max suddenly opens up. I don't know what's brought it on. But suddenly he's talking a blue streak. As near as I can recall now he was visiting a French lady when suddenly, for no reason at all, he burst out crying. Such crying! He couldn't stop. He put his head down on the table and wept and wept, just like a broken-hearted child. The French lady was so disturbed that she wanted to send for a doctor. He was ashamed of himself. Ah yes, he remembers now what brought it about. He was visiting her and he was very hungry. It was near dinner time and suddenly he couldn't hold back any longer—he just up and asked her for a few francs. To his amazement she gave him the money immediately. A French lady! Then suddenly he felt miserable. To think that a strong, healthy fellow like himself should be begging a poor French lady for a few sous. Where was his pride? What would become of him if he had to beg from a woman?

That was how it began. Thinking about it the tears came to his eyes. The next moment he was sobbing, then, just as with the French lady, he put his head on the table and he wept. It was horrible.

"You could stick a dagger into me," he said, when he had calmed himself, "you could do anything to me, but you could never make me cry. Now I cry for no reason at all—it comes over me like that, all of a sudden, and I can't stop it."

He asks me if I think he's a neurasthenic. He was told it was just a *crise de nerfs*. *That's a breakdown, isn't it?* He remembers the dentist again, his saying right away it's nothing, just nervousness. How could the dentist tell that? He's afraid it's the beginning of something worse. Is he going mad perhaps? He wants to know the truth.

What the hell can I tell him? I tell him it's nothing—just nerves.

"That doesn't mean you're going buggy," I add. "It'll pass soon as you get on your feet . . ."

"But I shouldn't be alone so much, Miller!"

Ah, that makes me wary. I know what's coming now. I ought to drop in on him oftener. Not money! No, he underlines that continually. But that he shouldn't be alone so much!

41

"Don't worry, Max. We're coming down often, Boris and I. We're going to show you some good times."

He doesn't seem to be listening.

"Sometimes, Miller, when I go back to my room, the sweat begins to run down my face. I don't know what it is . . . it's like I had a mask on."

"That's because you're worried, Max. It's nothing . . . You drink a lot of water too, don't you?"

He nods his head instantly, and then looks at me rather terrified.

"How did you know that?" he asks. "How is it I'm so thirsty all the time? All day long I'm running to the hydrant. I don't know what's the matter with me . . . *Miller, I want to ask you something*: is it true what they say, that if you're taken sick here they do you in? I was told that if you're a foreigner and you have no money they do away with you. I'm thinking about it all day long. What if I should be taken sick? I hope to God I shouldn't lose my mind. *I'm afraid, Miller* . . . I've heard such terrible stories about the French. You know how they are . . . you know they'll let you die before their eyes. They have no heart! It's always money, money, money. God help me, Miller, if I should ever fall so low as to beg them for mercy! Now at least I have my *carte d'identité*. A *tourist* they made me! Such bastards! How do they expect a man to live? Sometimes I sit and I look at the people passing by. Every one seems to have something to do, except me. I ask myself sometimes—*Max, what is wrong with you?* Why should I be obliged to sit all day and do nothing? It's eating me up. In the busy season, when there's a little work, I'm the first man they send for. They know that Max is a good presser. *The French!* what do they know about pressing? Max had to show them how to press. Two francs an hour they give me, because I

42

have no right to work. That's how they take advantage of a white man in this lousy country. They make out of him a bum!"

He pauses a minute. "You were saying, Miller, about South America, that maybe I could start all over again and bring myself to my feet again. I'm not an old man yet—only *morally* I'm defeated. Twenty years now I've been pressing. Soon I'll be too old . . . my career is finished. Yes, if I could do some light work, something where I shouldn't have to use my hands . . . That's why I wanted to become an *interprète*. After you hold an iron for twenty years your fingers aren't so nimble any more. I feel disgusted with myself when I think of it. All day standing over a hot iron . . . the smell of it! Sometimes when I think on it I feel I must vomit. Is it right that a man should stand all day over a hot iron? Why then did God give us the grass and the trees? Hasn't Max a right to enjoy that too? Must we be slaves all our lives—just to make money, money, money . . . ?"

On the terrasse of a café, after we've had our coffee, I manage to break away from him. Nothing is settled, except that I've promised to keep in touch with him. I walk along the Boulevard St. Michel past the Jardin du Luxembourg. I suppose he's sitting there where I left him. I told him to stay there awhile instead of going back to the room. I know he won't sit there very long. Probably he's up already and doing the rounds. It's better that way too—better to go round bumming a few sous than to sit doing nothing. It's summer now and there are some Americans in town. The trouble is they haven't much money to spend. It's not like '27 and '8 when they were lousy with dough. Now they expect to have a good time on fifty francs.

Up near the Observatoire it's quiet as the grave. Near a broken wall a lone whore is standing listlessly, too discouraged even to make a sign. At her feet is a mass of litter—dead leaves, old news-

43

papers, tin cans, brushwood, cigarette stubs. She looks as though she were ready to flop there, right in the dung heap, and call it a day.

Walking along the Rue St. Jacques the whole thing gets confused in my mind. The Rue St. Jacques is just one long picturesque shit-house. In every wormy little shack a radio. It's hallucinating to hear these crooning American voices coming out of the dark holes on either side of me. It's like a combination of five-and-ten-cent store and Middle Ages. A war veteran is wheeling himself along in a wheel chair, his crutches at his side. Behind him a big limousine waiting for a clearance in order to go full speed ahead. From the radios, all hitched up to the same station, comes that sickening American air—*"I believe in miracles!"* Miracles! Miracles! Jesus, even Christ Almighty couldn't perform a miracle here! *Eat, drink, this is my body broken for thee!* In the windows of the religious shops are inexpensive crosses to commemorate the event. A poor Jew nailed to a cross so that we might have life everlasting. And haven't we got it though . . . cement and balloon tires and radios and loud-speakers and whores with wooden legs and commodities in such abundance that there's no work for the starving . . . *I'm afraid that I should be alone too much!* On the sixth floor, when he enters his room, the sweat begins to roll down his face—*as if he had a mask on!* Nothing could make me cry, not even if you stuck a dagger in me—*but now I cry for nothing!* I cry and cry and I can't stop myself. *Do you think, Miller, I am going mad?* Is he going mad? Jesus, Max, all I can tell you is that the whole world's going mad. You're mad, I'm mad, everybody's mad. The whole world's busting with pus and sorrow. Have you wound your watch up? Yes, I know you still carry one—I saw it sticking out of your vest pocket. No matter how bad it gets you want to know what time it is. I'll tell you, Max, what time it is—

44

to the split second. *It's just five minutes before the end.* When it comes midnight on the dot that will be the end. Then you can go down into the street and throw your clothes away. Everybody will pop into the street new-born. That's why they were putting up the awning this evening. They were getting ready for the miracle. And the young woman leaning out of the window, you remember? She was dreaming of the dawn, of how lovely she would look when she would come down amidst the throng *and they would see her in the flesh.*

MIDNIGHT

Nothing has happened.

8.00 A. M. It's raining. A day just like any other day.

Noon. The postman arrives with a pneumatique. The scrawl looks familiar. I open it. It's from Max, as I thought . . .

"To My Dear friends Miller and Boris—I am writing to you these few lines having got up from bed and it is 3 o'clock in the morning I cannot sleep, am very nervis, I am crying and cant stop, I hear music playing in my ears, but in reality I hear screaming in the street, I suppose a pimp must have beaten up his hur—it is a terrible noise, I cant stand it, the water tape is running in the sink, I cant do a wink of sleep I am reading your book Miller in order to quieten me, its amusing me but I have no patience I am waiting for the morning I'll get out in the street as soon as daylight breaks. A long night of suffering though I am not very hungary but I am afraid of something I don't know what is the matter with me—I talk to myself I cant control myself. Miller, I don't want you to help me any more. I want to talk to you, am I a child? I have no courage, am I losing my reason? Dear Miller really don't think I need you for money, I want to talk to you and to Boris, no money, only moral help I need. I am afraid of my room I am

45

afraid to sleep alone—is it the end of my carrier? It seems to me. I have played the last cart. I cant breed. I want morning to come to get out in the street. I am praying to God to help me to pass quigly this terrible night, yes it is a night of agony. I cant stand the heat, and the atmosphere of my room. I am not drunk believe me while I'm writing this—only I pass the time away and it seems to me that I'm speaking to you and so I am finding a little comfort but I am afraid to be alone—what is it, it is just raining outside and I'm looking out of the window, that does me good, the rain is talking to me but morning wont come—it seems to me that night will never end. I am afraid the french will do me away in case of sickness because being a forinner is that so? Miller, tell me is it true—I was told that if a forinner is sick and has nobody they do him away quigly instead of curing him even when there is a chance. I am afraid the french shouldn't take me away, then I shall never see daylight. Oh no, I shall be brave and control myself but I don't want to go out in the street now, the Police might take a false statement, else I should go out now of my Room out in the street, for I cant stay in my Room, but I'm much afraid every night, I'm afraid. Dear Miller, is it possible to see you? I want to talk to you a little. I don't want no money, I'm going crazy. Sincerely yours, Max."

The Golden Age

At present the cinema is the great popular art form, which is to say it is not an art at all. Ever since its birth we have been hearing that at last an art has been born which will reach the masses and perhaps liberate them. People profess to see in the cinema possibilities which are denied the other arts. So much the worse for the cinema!

There is not one art called the Cinema but there is, as in every art, a form of production for the many and another for the few. Since the death of avant-garde films—*Le Sang d'un Poète*, by Cocteau, was I believe the last—there remains only the mass production of Hollywood.

47

The few films which might justify the category of "art" that have appeared since the birth of the cinema (a matter of forty years or so) died almost at their inception. This is one of the lamentable and amazing facts in connection with the development of a new art form. Despite all effort the cinema seems incapable of establishing itself as art. Perhaps it is due to the fact that the cinema more than any other art form has become a controlled industry, a dictatorship in which the artist is dominated and silenced.

Immediately an astonishing fact asserts itself, namely, that the greatest films were produced at little expense! It does not require millions to produce an artistic film; in fact, it is almost axiomatic that the more money a film costs the worse it is apt to be. Why then does the real cinema not come into being? Why does the cinema remain in the hands of the mob or its dictators? Is it purely an economic question?

The other arts, it should be remembered, are fostered in us. Nay, they are forced upon us almost from birth. Our taste is conditioned by centuries of inoculation. Nowadays one is almost ashamed to admit that he does not like this or that book, this or that painting, this or that piece of music. One may be bored to tears, but one dare not admit it. We have been educated to pretend to like and admire the great works of art with which, alas, we have no longer any connection.

The cinema is born and it is an art, another art—but it is born too late. The cinema is born out of a great feeling of lassitude. Indeed lassitude is too mild a word. The cinema is born just as we are dying. The cinema, like some ugly duckling, imagines that it is related in some way to the theatre, that it was born perhaps to replace the theatre, which is already dead. Born into a world devoid of enthusiasm, devoid of taste, the cinema functions like a eunuch: it waves a peacock-feathered fan before our drowsy eyes.

48

The cinema believes that what we want of it is to be put to sleep. It does not know *that we are dying*. Therefore, let us not blame the cinema. Let us ask ourselves why it is that this truly marvellous art form should be allowed to perish before our very eyes. Let us ask why it is that when it makes the most heroic efforts to appeal to us its gestures are unheeded.

I am talking about the cinema as an *actuality*, a something which exists, which has validity, just as music or painting or literature. I am strenuously opposed to those who look upon the cinema as a medium to exploit the other arts or even to synthetize them. The cinema is not another form of this or that, nor is it a synthetic product of all the other this-and-thats. The cinema is the cinema and nothing but. And it is quite enough. In fact, it is magnificent.

Like any other art the cinema has in it all the possibilities for creating antagonisms, for stirring up revolt. The cinema can do for man what the other arts have done, possibly even more, but the first condition, the prerequisite in fact, is—*take it out of the hands of the mob!* I understand full well that it is not the mob which creates the films we see—not technically, at any rate. But in a deeper sense it *is* the mob which *actually* creates the films. For the first time in the history of art the mob has dictated what the artist should do. For the first time in the history of man an art is born which caters exclusively to the masses. Perhaps it is some dim comprehension of this unique and deplorable fact which accounts for the tenacity with which "the dear public" clings to its art. The silent screen! Shadow images! Absence of color! Spectral, phantasmal beginnings. The dumb masses visualizing themselves in those stinking coffins which served as the first movie houses. An abysmal curiosity to see themselves reflected in the magic mirror of the machine age. Out of what tremendous fear and longing was this "popular" art born?

I can well imagine the cinema never having been born. I can imagine a race of men for whom the cinema would have been thoroughly unnecessary. But I cannot imagine the robots of this age being without a cinema, *some kind of cinema*. Our starved instincts have been clamoring for centuries for more and more substitutes. And as substitute for living the cinema is ideal. Does one ever remark the look of these cinema hounds as they leave the theatre? That dreamy air of vacuity, that washed-out look of the pervert who masturbates in the dark! One can hardly distinguish them from the drug addicts: they walk out of the cinema like somnambulists.

This of course is what they want, our worn-out, harassed beasts of toil. Not more terror and strife, not more mystery, not more wonder and hallucination, but peace, surcease from care, the unreality of the dream. But *pleasant* dreams! *Soothing* dreams! And here it is difficult not to restrain a word of consolation for the poor devils who are put to it to quench this unslakable thirst of the mob. It is the fashion among the intelligentsia to ridicule and condemn the efforts, the truly herculean efforts, of the film directors, the Hollywood dopesters particularly. Little do they realize the invention it requires to create each day a drug that will counteract the insomnia of the mob. There is no use condemning the directors nor is there any use deploring the public's lack of taste. These are stubborn facts, and irremediable. The panderer and the pandered must be eliminated—*both at once!* There is no other solution.

How speak about an art which no one recognizes as art? I know that a great deal has already been written about the "art of the cinema". One can read about it most every day in the newspapers and the magazines. But it is not the art of the cinema which you will find discussed therein—it is rather the dire, botched embryo as it now stands revealed before our eyes, the still-birth which was mangled in the womb by the obstetricians of art.

For forty years now the cinema has been struggling to get properly born. Imagine the chances of a creature that has wasted forty years of its life in being born! Can it hope to be anything but a monster, an idiot?

I will admit nevertheless that I expect of this monster-idiot the most tremendous things! I expect of this monster that it will devour its own mother and father, that it will run amok and destroy the world, that it will drive man to frenzy and desperation. I cannot see it otherwise. There is a law of compensation and this law decrees that even the monster must justify himself.

Five or six years ago I had the rare good fortune to see "L'Age d'Or", the film made by Luis Bunuel and Salvador Dali, which created a riot at Studio 28. For the first time in my life I had the impression that I was watching a film which was pure cinema and nothing but cinema. Since then I am convinced that L'Age d'Or is unique and unparalleled. Before going on I should like to remark that I have been going to the cinema regularly for almost forty years; in that time I have seen several thousand films. It should be understood, therefore, that in glorifying the Bunuel-Dali film I am not unmindful of having seen such remarkable films as:

The Last Laugh (Emil Jannings)
Berlin
Le Chapeau de Paille d'Italie (René Clair)
Le Chemin de la Vie
La Souriante Madame Beudet (Germaine Dulac)
Mann Braucht Kein Geld
La Mélodie du Monde (Walter Ruttmann)
Le Ballet Mécanique

Of What Are the Young Films Dreaming (Comte de Beaumont)
Rocambolesque
Three Comrades and One Invention
Ivan the Terrible (Emil Jannings)
The Cabinet of Dr. Caligari
The Crowd (King Vidor)
La Maternelle
Othello (Krause & Jannings)
Extase (Machaty)
Grass
Eskimo
Le Maudit
Lilliane (Barbara Stanwyck)
A Nous la Liberté (René Clair)
La Tendre Ennemie (Max Ophuls)
The Trackwalker
Potemkin
Les Marins de Cronstadt
Greed (Eric von Stroheim)
Thunder Over Mexico (Eisenstein)
The Beggars' Opera
Mädchen in Uniform (Dorothea Wieck)
Midsummer Night's Dream (Reinhardt)
Crime and Punishment (Pierre Blanchard)
The Student of Prague (Conrad Veidt)
Poil de Carotte
Banquier Pichler
The Informer (Victor MacLaglen)
The Blue Angel (Marlene Dietrich)
L'Homme à la Barbiche
L'Affaire est dans le Sac (Prévert)

Moana (O'Flaherty)
Mayerling (Charles Boyer & Danielle Darrieux)
Kriss
Variety (Krause & Jannings)
Chang
Sunrise (Murnau)

nor

Three Japanese films (ancient, mediaeval and modern Japan)
the title of which I have forgotten;

nor

a documentaire on India

nor

a documentaire on Tasmania

nor

a documentaire on the death rites in Mexico, by Eisenstein

nor

a psychoanalytic dream picture, in the days of the silent film,
with Werner Krause

nor

certain films of Lon Chaney, particularly one based on a novel
of Selma Lagerlof in which he played with Norma Shearer

nor

The Great Ziegfeld, nor Mr. Deeds Goes to Town

nor

The Lost Horizon (Frank Capra), the first significant film out
of Hollywood

nor

the very first movie I ever saw, which was a newsreel showing
the Brooklyn Bridge and a Chinaman with a pigtail walking over
the bridge in the rain! I was only seven or eight years of age when
I saw this film in the basement of the old South Third Street

53

Presbyterian Church in Brooklyn. Subsequently I saw hundreds of pictures in which it always seemed to be raining and in which there were always nightmarish pursuits in which houses collapsed and people disappeared through trap-doors and pies were thrown and human life was cheap and human dignity was nil. And after thousands of slap-stick, pie-throwing Mack Sennett films, after Charlie Chaplin had exhausted his bag of tricks, after Fatty Arbuckle, Harold Lloyd, Harry Langdon, Buster Keaton, each with his own special brand of monkey shines, came the chef d'œuvre of all the slap-stick, pie-throwing festivals, a film the title of which I forget, but it was among the very first films starring Laurel and Hardy. This, in my opinion, is the greatest comic film ever made—because it brought the pie-throwing to apotheosis. There was nothing but pie-throwing in it, nothing but pies, thousands and thousands of pies and everybody throwing them right and left. It was the ultimate in burlesque, and it is already forgotten.

In every art the ultimate is achieved only when the artist passes beyond the bounds of the art he employs. This is as true of Lewis Carroll's work as of Dante's "Divine Comedy", as true of Laotse as of Buddha or Christ. The world must be turned upside down, ransacked, confounded in order that the miracle may be proclaimed. In "L'Age d'Or" we stand again at a miraculous frontier which opens up before us a dazzling new world which no one has explored. "Mon idée générale," wrote Salvador Dali, "en écrivant avec Bunuel le scénario de "L'Age d'Or", a été de présenter la ligne droite et pure de conduite d'un être qui poursuit l'amour à travers les ignorables idéaux humanitaires, patriotiques et autres misérables mécanismes de la réalité." I am not unaware of the part which Dali played in the creation of this great film, and yet I cannot refrain from thinking of it as the peculiar product of his collaborator, the man who directed the film: Luis Bunuel.

Dali's name is now familiar to the world, even to Americans and Englishmen, as the most successful of all the Surrealists to-day. He is enjoying a temporal vogue, largely because he is not understood, largely because his work is sensational. Bunuel, on the other hand, appears to have dropped out of sight. Rumor has it that he is in Spain, that he is quietly amassing a collection of documentary films on the revolution. What these will be, if Bunuel retains any of his old vigor, promises to be nothing short of staggering. For Bunuel, like the miners of the Asturias, is a man who flings dynamite. Bunuel is obsessed by the cruelty, ignorance and superstition which prevail among men. He realizes that there is no hope for man anywhere on this earth unless a clean slate be made of it. He appears on the scene at the moment when civilization is at its nadir.

There can be no doubt about it: the plight of civilized man is a foul plight. He is singing his swan song without the joy of having been a swan. He has been sold out by his intellect, manacled, strangled and mangled by his own symbology. He is mired in his art, suffocated by his religions, paralyzed by his knowledge. That which he glorifies is not life, since he has lost the rhythm of life, but death. What he worships is decay and putrefaction. He is diseased and the whole organism of society is infected.

They have called Bunuel everything—traitor, anarchist, pervert, defamer, iconoclast. But lunatic they dare not call him. True, it is lunacy he portrays in his film, but it is not of his making. This stinking chaos which for a brief hour or so is amalgamated under his magic wand, this is the lunacy of man's achievements after ten thousand years of civilization. Bunuel, to show his reverence and gratitude, puts a cow in the bed and drives a garbage truck through the salon. The film is composed of a succession of images without sequence the significance of which must be sought for below the threshold of consciousness. Those who were deceived because they could not find order or meaning in it will find order and meaning nowhere except perhaps in the world of the bees or the ants.

I am reminded at this point of the charming little documentaire which preceded the Bunuel film the night it was shown at Studio 28. A charming little study of the abattoir it was, altogether fitting and significant for the weak-stomached sisters of culture who had come to hiss the big film. Here everything was familiar and comprehensible, though perhaps in bad taste. But there was order and meaning in it, as there is order and meaning in a cannibalistic rite. And finally there was even a touch of aestheticism, for when the slaughter was finished and the decapitated bodies had gone their separate ways each little pig's head was carefully blown up by compressed air until it looked so monstrously life-like and savoury and succulent that the saliva flowed willy-nilly. (Not forgetting the shamrocks that were plugged up the ass-holes of each and every pig!) As I say, this was a perfectly comprehensible piece of butchery and indeed, so well was it performed, that from some of the more elegant spectators in the audience it brought forth a burst of applause.

It is five years or so ago since I saw the Bunuel film and therefore I cannot be absolutely sure, but I am almost certain that there were in this film no scenes of organized butchery between man and man, no wars, no revolutions, no inquisitions, no lynchings, no third degree scenes. There was, to be sure, a blind man who was mistreated, there was a dog which was kicked in the stomach, there was a boy who was wantonly shot by his father, there was an old dowager who was slapped in the face at a garden party and there were scorpions who fought to the death among the rocks near the sea. Isolated little cruelties which, because they were not woven into a comprehensible little pattern, seemed to shock the

56

spectators even more than the sight of wholesale trench slaughter. There was something which shocked their delicate sensibilities even more and that was the effect of Wagner's "Tristan and Isolde" upon one of the protagonists. Was it possible that the divine music of Wagner could so arouse the sensual appetites of a man and woman as to make them roll in the gravelled path and bite and chew one another until the blood came? Was it possible that this music could so take possession of the young woman as to make her suck the toe of a statued foot with perverted lascivi-ousness? Does music bring on orgasms, does it entrain perverse acts, does it drive people truly mad? Does this great legendary theme which Wagner immortalized have to do with such a plain vulgar physiological fact as sexual love? The film seems to suggest that it does. It seems to suggest more, for through the ramifications of this Golden Age Bunuel, like an entomologist, has studied what we call love in order to expose beneath the ideology, the mythol-ogy, the platitudes and phraseologies the complete and bloody machinery of sex. He has distinguished for us the blind metabo-lisms, the secret poisons, the mechanistic reflexes, the distillations of the glands, the entire plexus of forces which unite love and death in life.

Is it necessary to add that there are scenes in this film which have never been dreamed of before? The scene in the water-closet, for example. I quote from the program notes:

"Il est inutile d'ajouter qu'un des points culminants de la pureté de ce film nous semble cristallisé dans la vision de l'héroïne dans les cabinets, où la puissance de l'esprit arrive à sublimer une situa-tion généralement baroque en un élément poétique de la plus pure noblesse et solitude."

A *situation usually baroque!* Perhaps it is the baroque element in human life, or rather in the life of civilized man, which gives to

57

Bunuel's works the aspect of cruelty and sadism. Isolated cruelty and sadism, for it is the great virtue of Bunuel that he refuses to be enmeshed in the glittering web of logic and idealism which seeks to mask from us the real nature of man. Perhaps, like Lawrence, Bunuel is only an inverted idealist. Perhaps it is his great tenderness, the great purity and poetry of his vision which forces him to reveal the abominable, the malicious, the ugly and the hypocritical falsities of man. Like his precursors he seems animated by a tremendous hatred for the lie. Being normal, instinctive, healthy, gay, unpretentious he finds himself alone in the crazy drift of social forces. Being thoroughly normal and honest he finds himself regarded as bizarre. Like Lawrence again his work divides the world into two opposite camps—those who are for him and those who are against him. There is no straddling the issue. Either you are crazy, like the rest of civilized humanity, or you are sane and healthy like Bunuel. And if you are sane and healthy you are an anarchist and you throw bombs. The great honor which was conferred upon Luis Bunuel at the showing of his film was that the citizens of France recognized him as a true anarchist. The theatre was taken by assault and the street was cleared by the police. The film has never been shown again, to my knowledge, except at private performances, and then but rarely. It was brought to America, shown to a special audience, and created no impression whatever, except perplexity. Meanwhile Salvador Dali, Bunuel's collaborator, has been to America several times and created a furore there. Dali, whose work is unhealthy, though highly spectacular, highly provocative, is acclaimed as a genius. Dali makes the American public conscious of Surrealism, and creates a fad. Dali returns with his pockets full of dough. Dali is accepted—as another world freak. Freak for freak: there is a divine justice at work. The world which

58

is crazy recognizes its master's voice. The yolk of the egg has split: Dali takes America, Bunuel takes the leavings.

I want to repeat: "L'Age d'Or" is the only film I know of which reveals the possibilities of the cinema! It makes its appeal neither to the intellect nor to the heart: it strikes at the solar plexus. It is like kicking a mad dog in the guts. And though it was a valiant kick in the guts and well aimed it was not enough! There will have to be other films, films even more violent than Luis Bunuel's. For the world is in a coma and the cinema is still waving a peacock-feathered plume before our eyes.

Wondering sometimes where he may be and what he may be doing, wondering what he *could* do if he were permitted, I get to thinking now and then of all that is left out of the films. Has anybody ever shown us the birth of a child, or even the birth of an animal? Insects yes, because the sexual element is weak, because there are no taboos. But even in the world of the insects have they shown us the praying Mantis, the love feast which is the acme of sexual voracity? Have they shown us how our heroes won the war —and died for us? Have they shown us the gaping wounds, have they shown us the faces that have been shot away? Are they showing us now what happens in Spain every day when the bombs rain down on Madrid? Almost every week there is another News Reel theatre opened up, but there is no news. Once a year we have a repertoire of the outstanding events of the world given us by the news getters. It is nothing but a series of catastrophes: railroad wrecks, explosions, floods, earthquakes, automobile accidents, aeroplane disasters, collisions of trains and ships, epidemics, lynchings, gangster killings, riots, strikes, incipient revolutions, putsches, assassinations. The world seems like a mad-house, and the world is a mad-house, but nobody dares dwell on it. When an appalling piece of insanity, already properly castrated, is about to be presented a warning is issued to the spectators not to indulge in demonstrations. Rest impartial! that is the edict. Don't budge from your sleep! We command you in the name of lunacy—*keep cool!* And for the most part the injunctions are heeded. They are heeded willy-nilly, for by the time the spectacle is concluded everybody has been bathed in the innocuous drama of a sentimental couple, plain honest folks like ourselves, who are doing exactly what we are doing, with the sole difference that they are being well paid for it. This nullity and vacuity is dished up to us as the main event of the evening. The hors d'œuvre is the news reel which is spiced with death and ignorance and superstition. Between these two phases of life there is absolutely no relation unless it be the link made by the animated cartoon. For the animated cartoon is the censor which permits us to dream the most horrible nightmares, to rape and kill and bugger and plunder, without waking up. Daily life is like we see it in the big film: the news reel is the eye of God; the animated cartoon is the soul tossing in its anguish. But none of these three is the reality which is common to all of us who think and feel. Somehow they have worked a camouflage on us, and though it is our own camouflage, we accept the illusion for reality. And the reason for it is that life as we know it to be has become absolutely unbearable. We flee from it in terror and disgust. The men who come after us will read the truth beneath the camouflage. May they pity us as we who are alive and real pity those about us.

Some people think of the Golden Age as a dream of the past; others think of it as the millennium to come. But the Golden Age is the immanent reality to which all of us, by our daily living, are either contributing or failing to contribute. The world is what we make it each day, or what we fail to make it. If it is lunacy that we have on our hands to-day then it is we who are the lunatics. If you accept the fact that it is a crazy world you may perhaps succeed

60

in adapting yourself to it. But those who have a sense of creation are not keen about adapting themselves. We affect one another, whether we wish to or not. Even negatively we affect one another. In writing about Bunuel instead of writing about something else I am aware that I am going to create a certain effect—for most people an unpleasant one, I suspect. But I can no more refrain from writing this way about Bunuel than I can from washing my face to-morrow morning. My past experience of life leads up to this moment and rules it despotically. In asserting the value of Bunuel I am asserting my own values, my own faith in life. In singling out this one man I do what I am constantly doing in every realm of life—selecting and evaluating. To-morrow is no hazardous affair, a day like any other day: to-morrow is the result of many yesterdays and comes with a potent, cumulative effect. I am to-morrow what I chose to be yesterday and the day before. It is not possible that to-morrow I may negate and nullify everything that led me to this present moment.

In the same way I wish to point out that the film "L'Age d'Or" is no accident, nor is its dismissal from the screen an accident. The world has condemned Luis Bunuel and judged him as unfit. Not the whole world, because as I said before, the film is scarcely known outside of France, outside of Paris, in fact. Judging from the trend of affairs since this momentous event took place I cannot say that I am optimistic about the revival of this film to-day. Perhaps the next Bunuel film will be even more of a bomb-shell than was "L'Age d'Or". I fervently hope so. But meanwhile—and here I must add that this is the first opportunity, apart from a little review which I wrote for "The New Review", I have had to write about Bunuel publicly—meanwhile, I say, this belated tribute to Bunuel may serve to arouse the curiosity of those who have never heard the name before. Bunuel's name is not unknown to Hollywood, that I know. Indeed, like many another man of genius whom the Americans have gotten wind of, Luis Bunuel was invited to come to Hollywood and give of his talent. In short, he was invited to do nothing and draw his breath. So much for Hollywood . . .

No, it is not from that quarter that the wind will blow. But things are curiously arranged in this world. Men who have been dishonored and driven from their country sometimes return to be crowned as king. Some return as a scourge. Some leave only their name behind them, or the remembrance of their deeds, but in the name of this one and that whole epochs have been revitalized and recreated. I for one believe that, despite everything I have said against the cinema as we now know it, something wondrous and vital may yet come of it. Whether this happens or not depends entirely on us, on you who read this now. What I say is only a drop in the bucket, but it may have its consequences. The important thing is that the bucket should not have a hole in it. Well, I believe that such a bucket can be found. I believe that it is just as possible to rally men around a vital reality as it is around the false and the illusory. Luis Bunuel's effect upon me was not lost. And perhaps my words will not be lost either.

Reflections on "Extasy"

EVERY TIME I have seen the film, and I have seen it four or five times, the reaction of the audience is the same—cheers and applause mingled with groans and catcalls. The hostility, I am convinced, has nothing to do with the alleged immorality of the film. The audience is not shocked, but indignant. The feeling is, so far as I can determine, that they have been let down, or rather that they, the spectators, have been left hanging in mid-air. As a matter of fact "THEY" are right, but right as usual in the wrong way.

Each time I view the film I am more impressed; each time I go I discover new marvels in it. And each time I understand better why, even if there had never been a question of censorship, *Extase* would create antagonisms. Even in its best moments the film is bound to produce a feeling of discomfit for the ordinary movie-goer, for like all of Machaty's films *Extase* is a flagrant violation of that unwritten code which dictates that the movie-goer shall not be allowed to fall asleep. (Drugged, yes, but no sleeping!)

Extase induces fatigue just as the opening pages of Proust's great work inevitably induce fatigue. This *lenteur*, from an intelligent standpoint, is precisely the great virtue of Machaty's technique. It means that he has succeeded in creating, through the medium of the film, a space condition altogether unique. Employing the medium itself as a mobile, plastic thing, Machaty allows it to expand beyond the known borders and limitations of cinema, thereby creating the illusion of an extra-temporal world the nearest approach to which is the world of music. This marvellous unfolding space in which the characters and events are bathed almost recreates for us the time-destroying element of thought itself. Those who are acquainted with Machaty's previous films are aware that the technique here employed is not a new discovery of his. But in *Extase* it reaches a degree of perfection which was only hinted at in the other films. And it is just this approach to perfection, to a purity in the use of his medium, which creates the general confusion observed at each seance.

By use of what, for lack of a better term, we might call "slow motion" the spectator is obliged to forego his cherished grip on plot and action; he is forced, whether he will or no, to swim in the very essence of Machaty's creation. It is difficult not to become abstruse in attempting to seize the grand motif of this film; it has a pulsation which springs from a cosmic sense of rhythm. Aside from a superficial external resemblance, Machaty's technique has scarcely anything in common with what is known as slow motion.

Slow motion, as we know it, has been employed up to the present almost exclusively as a stunt, as one more device or trick to tickle the public's jaded sensitivity. In *Extase* however this technique is brought over into the realm of consciousness; it comes not as shock or novelty but as the very vehicle of expression, and it remains so throughout the film, pervading the mind inexorably.

This question of slow motion technique is in my mind bound up with another question. I am puzzled, for instance, by the fact that despite the number of times I have reviewed the film the name of the author of the story escapes my memory. Was it ever given, I wonder? Is Machaty director and author both? It is difficult for me to believe that. Whether he realized it or not I have the impression that Machaty has given it. No doubt this is my own peculiar interpretation. Nevertheless to me it seems undeniable that not only the scenario, but the mode of expression and the philosophy behind this mode of expression, emanated directly from D. H. Lawrence. For it is undoubtedly a metaphysic which inspired the technique of this film. To be sure I cannot say that there exists a specific tale of Lawrence's to which the scenario of this film corresponds. I will say, however, that if Lawrence had ever written a story expressly for the films *Extase* would have been a most worthy example of his talent, and Machaty moreover would undoubtedly have been his choice of director. That Machaty may never have heard of D. H. Lawrence's work is unimportant. This is a Lawrencian theme and Machaty is the one man in the movie world capable of giving adequate expression to Lawrence's ideas.

Let me revert again to the very definite expression of hostility aroused by each showing of the film. I consider it a phenomenon of some importance, something which demands explanation. Parenthetically, be it observed please, that no one—not even its detractors—is immune to the beauty of the film. The curious thing is

65

that discussion of the film usually seems to center about the question of "immorality". And yet, as I mentioned previously, it is not a question of morality or immorality at all which disturbs the public. It is the presence of a new and dangerous element which is the upsetting factor. Beneath the public's hostility is the grudging admission of the presence of a superior force, a disturbing force. It is this force which Lawrence is constantly suggesting to us whenever he deals with "blood-consciousness". It is a force, as he himself has said, which resides in the solar plexus, an astral force which is located there behind the stomach in the great nexus of nerves which unite the upper and lower nerve centers. The rhythm dictated by this ganglia of nerves and blood-vessels is in direct opposition to the rhythm which we have set up through our tyranny of mind and will. This rhythm elevates to its former prestige and glory the hegemony of the instincts; it regards the mind as a tool. This is body rhythm, blood rhythm, as opposed to the masturbative rhythm of the intellect. The recognition of this rhythm involves not a new technique but a new way of living. Once again I repeat that the hostility provoked by Machaty's film arises not so much through dissatisfaction with a "weak ending", but through the silent menace, the challenge, of a new life-mode. Those who have already grasped the significance of this new attitude towards life have little quarrel with the deficiencies of the plot, with what is really the "technical" aspect of the film. When once we enter into life as real beings, as individuals, all this art of story which has now become an obsessional mania with editors and public will fade into insignificance. The terrible emphasis to-day upon plot, action, character, analysis, etc.—all this false emphasis which characterizes the literature and drama of our day—simply reveals the lack of these elements in our life. We want plot because our lives are purposeless, action because we have only an insect activity, character development because in turning in upon the mind we have discovered that we do not exist, mystery because the dominant ideology of science has ruled mystery out of our scope and ken. In short, we demand of art a violence and drama because the tension of life has broken down; we do not find ourselves opposed to one another in any primal sense, *certainly not as individuals.*

A strange lacuna in the critical attitude of public and reviewers alike, as concerns the film, is the seeming unawareness of, or indifference to, the motivating idea. No one seems at all concerned with the IDEA behind the film. This idea, I need hardly say, is the dominating idea back of all Lawrence's writings . . . the idea of an automatic death, a DEATH IN LIFE. Not once has this word "death" cropped up. For the French this word is more peculiarly abhorrent than for the Anglo-Saxon even. And yet it was to make this clear to the world that Lawrence sacrificed his life.

To make this more clear . . . As the story is related to the public by the critics the husband is always referred to as an "old man". Now it is true that the husband is considerably older than the wife, but he is decidedly not an old man. He is, in fact, from a sane point of view a man decidedly at the peak of life, a middle-aged man whose powers should now be revealed in all their fulness. From the statistical point of view he is, to be sure, an old man. That is to say, he has done his bit for home and country. But from any sane, normal standpoint this man is not an old man. He is something much worse than an old man—*he is a dead man.* To miss this is to miss everything. Machaty has given us a living man who in the very prime of life has gone dead. It is true Machaty has seized upon this corpse-like quality of the husband with extraordinary relish. Machaty overdoes it, in fact. But, let it be remembered that Machaty is a Czech and that the Czechs have still a glimmering of the meaning of "soul". They know that life springs not from the interstitial glands, but from the soul.

Every one who is acquainted with Lawrence's work must realize the enormous effort he made to establish an autonomy of life based on that irreducible ghost which we call at different periods by different names, but which is never anything other than primordial man. An illusion, to be sure, but one of the most tenacious, the most fructifying, that man has made use of. Always in Lawrence's work there is this reducing down to some primitive, mystic, obscene creature, half goat, half man, in whom there exists the feeling of unity—the preconscious individual who obeys the voice of the blood. Whenever such a literature appears it passes beyond all the artificial frontiers of the intellect. Such a literature also brings about a great confusion. Values are either overlooked or misunderstood. What sweeps it on, with overpowering illogicality, is the basic life impulse, the innate chaos out of which it emerges and to which it appeals with all its fecundating lure.

In the Machaty film the engineer does not function as engineer, nor is the young girl, the wife, merely the personification of a bourgeois ideal. They are stripped down, in typical Lawrencian fashion, in order to gravitate towards each other as man and woman. They would meet inevitably, no matter what barriers existed between them. Naturally, where they represent opposing worlds, the attraction is augmented: it is part of the Lawrencian theory of tension, of dynamic counterpoint. Characteristic also is the insistence on making the woman the aggressor; her fundamental predatory nature is thus emphasized. With Lawrence's theory of the loss of polarity between the sexes it follows logically that the female *must* take the initiative. The male is hopelessly bogged in the morass of false cultural values which he has established. The male is emasculate, epicene.

68

Certainly neither of the protagonists is conscious of the destined character of his behavior. Their meeting is that of pure bodies, their union is poetic, sensual, mystical. They do not question themselves—they obey their instincts. The drama of conjugal adjustment, on which so much of modern tragedy is erected, did not interest Lawrence. That is superficial drama, the study of the irrelevant, the inconsequential.

In *Extase* the drama is one of life and death, life impersonated by the two lovers, death by the husband. The latter represents society as it is, while the lovers represent the life force blindly struggling to assert itself.

It seems to me that Machaty was keenly aware of all this and that when he is accused of dramatizing it is not quite understood *what* he is dramatizing. Certainly the man who chose so slight a story, who suppressed all those extraneous details which give the unusual life adventure its exciting element of plot, certainly this man was aware of the theatricality of the husband's death. But was not Lawrence always theatrical in the presentation of his ideas? Are not ideas in and of themselves theatrical? Lawrence outlines his characters in a cultural form; he moves these living statues by pulling his ideological wires. What he omitted from his dramas is the entire area of what is called "the human equation". This human problem was killed off. Lawrence began with the assumption that it was already dead. The new "human" element represented, for him, an unknown quantity, or quality, rather. It would evolve in the test-tubes of his ideological stew. The drama that he hands us is laboratory drama; it has all the glamour for this age which the bacteriological drama has for the scientist. When a moment ago I used the word "pure" in connection with the two bodies I meant to inject into the common notion of carnality an element of the mysterious bio-chemical activity which brushes

69

away the obscurity embedded in the old language of sensuality. Lawrence's animal natures, just because of their irreducible obscenity, are the purest bodies in our current literature. Animated by a metaphysical conception they act through obedience to fundamental laws of nature. Of these laws Lawrence admits his complete ignorance. He created his metaphysical world by faith; he proceeds only by intuition. He may have been utterly wrong, but he is absolutely consistent. He reflects, furthermore, the hunger and desperation of an age seeking a *vital* reality. This in itself would justify a possible "error".

It will be recalled that in the very beginning of the film there is contrasted the slow, plant-like movements of the girl's body as against the mechanical, rigid, corpse-like gestures of the husband. The effect of contrasts is continued throughout the film. The husband *kills* the insect which annoys him when reading the paper; the lover *liberates* the insect which has accidentally fallen into his hands. But the most remarkable example of contrasts is given us in the scene where the girl lies on the marriage bed dreamily regarding her fingers; the merest sensation of movement seems to awaken in her a sense of wonder, of the mystery of life boundless and manifold. This scene is, in its implications, one of the most profound and subtle which Machaty has given us. This dreamy blood-stirring, this sensual apathy so vitally different from the husband's apathy, makes us aware with terrific intensity of a world of sensation which the ordinary films studiously ignore. To the sensitive observer there is more potent drama in this idle, listless stirring than in all the terror and soul struggle of the Russian propagandist film with its gigantic wheel of society in the background and the loom of quotidian pain and misery on which the characters are crucified. This drama of mute fingers reveals all the inexpressible longing and pain of the individual; society is not directly implicated, but its presence is felt. It is not a passive denial, but a most vital apprehension; the eternal conflict of individual versus society is here echoed through the tremors of the end organs.

In his use of symbols Machaty is perhaps less crude, less tasteless than the Russians, but one feels nevertheless that his symbolism did not develop out of the organic material of his film. His symbols are often excrescences. Such are the eye-glasses, the statues, the horses, etc. They cut through the expanding medium of reality in which his images usually float. They are too solid, too precise, too thought-contained. They mar the dream, they tear it, blunt it, obsess it. Here, in a fairly conventional handling of the screen, the use of image and symbol is false. It has the same artificial quality as the interior dialogue in literature. It is an attempt to exploit material inappropriate to the particular technique adopted. It is bad taste.

The eye-glasses, of course, might well be regarded as symbolical of the modern way of seeing things. They might well represent the stigma of knowledge, of the obsessive pursuit of dead things, of the fetichism which produces life-blindness. The husband falling dead with the glasses in his hand is typical of the plight of the modern man who lives entirely by artificial sight and even in death persists in clinging to his false vision. He is born with glasses and he dies with them—the thick colored glasses which the optometrist, society, provides him with when still in the womb. He has never truly gazed upon life, and it may well be questioned whether he will ever know death. Life passes him by, and death too. He lives on, immortal as the cockroach.

In the race with death Machaty again reveals his awareness of the theme song. This incident is another of those incidents which the critics dismiss as theatrical—or as a cliché. But one has only to bear in mind how differently the cliché is handled in *Extase* to realize the keenness of Machaty's insight. The high moment comes, it will be remembered, when the husband's only contact with a vital reality has been destroyed. The loss of his young wife, which he suddenly and fatally accepts, urges him to end the protracted death which he had been enjoying. It is the first sign of life in him—of will, of individual act. Prior to this, though we know little of his actual life, we sense that he has been functioning as a cog in the vast machine world to which he belongs. He is a rubber stamp with a *fondé de pouvoir*, a man who says Yes to everything because he has not the power to say NO. And so, in the moment when he grips the steering wheel, we have the expression of his extreme affirmation, expressed in the Will To Die. Here for the first and only time there is injected into the film an element of speed. Contrast again. Here, profoundly and accurately, Machaty reveals the true meaning of the modern craze for speed; prime symbol of our suicidal mania, he makes it appear as the apotheosis of the senseless activity of the human insect and his inhuman machinery, of movement by tropism rather than by choice and direction. The thrill of the race lies not in the possibility of escape, but rather in the certainty of catastrophe. The suicide takes place in the machine, in the death race, and not upstairs at the inn, with pistol and eyeglasses. The scene in the inn, where the actual death occurs, was dictated by the hackneyed exigency of plot; the lover, who was in the car with the husband, had to be preserved from a fortuitous end in order to reveal the true outlines of the major conflict. For the real conflict is not between the husband and the wife, as I have remarked before, but between life, represented by the pair of lovers, and death the husband.

It was in the car, nevertheless, that the husband really met his end. The outward elements of disaster which were only fleetingly disclosed—a momentary swerve, the rush of the train, a tree brought up close—all these are minimized in order to give force to the inner struggle. One can actually feel, in this mad race with the machine, the husband giving up the ghost. And this surrender of the Holy Ghost is contrasted with the surrender of self which the girl makes when she offers herself to the engineer in his cabin. They are both death struggles. To read into the girl's anguish a mere physical immolation is to destroy the real meaning of the drama. The girl surrenders to the man the great female principle of life which she represents. She sacrifices not her virginity, her pride, her bourgeois ideals, etc., but her very self, her female incarnation. It is the great act of submission which Lawrence so often stresses in his books; it forms the cornerstone of his religious edifice.

That the drama ultimately concludes with the woman's desertion of her lover is no contradiction of this view. The important thing, from the Lawrencian standpoint, is the recognition of the sacred aspect of sex, of life through sex. For her the moment of illumination was the supreme thing. That is why the seeming trend of fulfillment, the rendezvous with the lover in the inn, falls flat. It falls flat purposely. It is inserted merely to indicate the eventuality ahead. The brimming champagne glasses, the bubble, the overflow, the effervescence which the union symbolizes, enables us to focus again upon the eternal character of this drama. The life quality is preserved by symbol and ritual. It is a gush and overflow, a breaking of bounds and limits, and it stands out forcefully in contrast to the husband's cautious, measured, analytical movements. The girl may eventually desert the man she loves, but the spark remains, is passed on.

The very last scene, in which the audience usually groans and howls, shows us the lover abandoned on the bench at the railway station. The lover is left sleeping on a bench while the semaphores fade out and the train, with his mistress aboard, pulls out of the station. To a French audience this is the last straw in a lack-logic concatenation of events. As I said in the beginning, they feel tricked, let down. And in the bottom of their hearts they are right, for the despair and the ennui which sends them back to the cinema night after night must be based, I suppose, on the hope of a denouement to this farce which all of us are leading. Is it possible, in this rage which overtakes them at the end of the film, that in the lover who is left fast asleep on the bench at the railway station they see themselves? Is there perhaps the flicker of a suspicion in their addled pates that life is passing them by? I notice that the resentment is largely confined to the male members of the audience. Could one read into that a Freudian story of bankruptcy?

Scenario

(A Film With Sound)

This *Scenario* is directly inspired
by a phantasy called *The House
of Incest* written by Anaïs Nin.

I

NIGHT. A tropical garden filled with pebbled paths. In the center of the garden a small pond out of which rises a huge bowl filled with gleaming gold-fish. The heavy face of Alraune hovers over the garden like a mask. The face grows larger and larger until it fills the screen. Her mouth is clouded with smoke which ascends in spiral curves. The eyes roll upward; they have the fixed stare of a drug addict. They grow round, large, glassy, then troubled, then wild. They twitch like the eyes of a Javanese dancer. They grow calm and fixed again, dreamy, like the eyes of an opium smoker.

As Alraune's face fades out the wind stirs the leaves in the garden, gently at first, then more agitatedly, until it reaches the violence of a tornado. Over an endless desert a simoun wind blows. The sand piles up in huge drifts. Alraune's mask-life face lies in the sand, the wind sweeping over it, covering it with two huge mounds shaped like a woman's breasts.

As the wind dies down the two huge mounds of sand appear as the domes of a mosque; from the interior of the mosque there comes the sound of Arab music, a ceaseless rise and fall, a dreamlike wandering in strange keys. Flashes of the interior of the mosque—angles and curves, glittering panels, chequered slabs. A brief flash of an Arab sitting with legs crossed on the tesselated floor, followed immediately by the hollow music of the quena.

Through a casement of the mosque the sky is seen and hanging upside down in the sky are fabulous cities. The hollow chanting music changes suddenly to a dance rhythm, the sand begins to whirl, the clouds bulge. The rhythm beats faster and faster, the clouds balloon like whirling skirts; women with bare backs are whirling with flaring skirts. A woman with a strong spine gyrating like a top; up close the spine changes to a mountain ridge. Kaleidoscopic flashes of the Andes, a strong spine, then the quena, accompanied by a hollow chant, then a skull, the desert, bones bleaching in the white sand, a skull of rock crystal, the lines converging to infinity, the desert, space, sky, infinity, monotony.

II

The garden again. A door opens and out of the white Moorish house steps Mandra, a slender Spanish woman. She walks pensively along the gravel path towards the huge bowl of gold-fish. She walks with the undulating rhythm of a dancer to the muted beat and chant of Arab music. The gold-fish are swimming lazily in the glass bowl. She presses her face close to the bowl and stares at them. Her image is reflected about the whole perimeter of the bowl and in the water where the gold-fish are lazily churning. She stares in fascination as the fish swim through her eyes. Flash of the crystal skull again, the infinite stretch of desert, the ridge of the Andes, the sacrificial altar of Quetzalcoatl with its interlaced serpents.

Mandra walks thoughtfully, head down, towards the garden wall. Same undulating walk as before, same airy tread. She stops before the wall and picks a pomegranate; the seeds burst open in her hand. Simultaneously there comes a burst of clangorous music followed by the frenzied ringing of church bells—a wild alarum interspersed with shots of steeples and belfries, the slits of the belfries opening and closing like shutters, the bells swinging violently, the clappers of the bells pounding furiously. Then one huge bell swinging slowly back and forth, the clapper smiting the bell with a vibrant ring. Like a mouth opening and shutting.

As the last deafening toll dies out there is heard the faint tinkle of the door bell and at the same moment the garden door opens silently, mysteriously, as if moved by unseen hands. Mandra looks towards the garden door expectantly, hesitates a moment, then walks swiftly forward in time to greet the mysterious woman enveloped in a loose-flowing black cape who is entering the garden.

Alraune and Mandra greet each other as if there were a secret understanding between them. Arm in arm, their feet crunching the gravel in even rhythm, they walk towards the house in the rear of the garden. As they approach the huge bowl in the center of the garden they exchange glances and then gaze up at the bowl. They take up positions on opposite sides of the bowl and, peering through the glass, they stare at each other. For a moment their images, slightly distorted, are shown reflected in the rippling water. The stars too are reflected in the bowl and the stars are dancing on

77

their wavering images. The water becomes tranquil and only the face of the moon floats now on the surface of the water.

The smooth, moon-lit surface breaks, the water becomes agitated, filled with flashing ripples and broken waves. The gold-fish move faster and faster, they leap and dive, then revolve at terrifying speed. Mandra and Alraune smile at each other from opposite sides of the bowl. Their smiles are churned and mangled by the splashing fish. They look like two hags leering and grinning at each other.

The bowl is entirely filled now with the reflection of the moon, the moon as seen through a telescope. The pale dead surface of the moon crumbles and as the familiar vague image of the lady in the moon dissolves there remains distinctly only the sockets of her eyes. From these cold, dead sockets there now bubble two cauldrons of lava which fill the bowl with columns of thick smoke. As the smoke clears away we see the craters of volcanoes—Fujiyama, Vesuvius, Aetna, Mauna Loa. The craters belch forth fire and smoke, the lava streams out in a thick black mass which pours down the sides of the volcanoes, destroying homes, villages, forests. Everything alive and standing is mowed down by the molten stream of lava.

The women smile at each other through the bowl, the agitated surface of the water calms down. Their faces look natural again, even more enchanting than before. There is a mysterious look in their eyes, a look of love, of gratitude, of mutual understanding.

III

A room in the house, furnished in Moorish style. Mandra is seated in a gorgeous high-backed chair, like a throne. Alraune is pacing back and forth. There is a huge divan with heavy, billowy pillows. The light is splintered by the Moorish grill of the lamp

78

suspended from the ceiling. Tabarets, foot-stools, crystal ash-bowls, arched windows. Heavy, saturated air of smoke and incense, of passion, of luxury, indolence, drugs.

Alraune is dressed in a long flowing sheath-like gown which gleams like patent leather and which reveals the heavy curves of her body. Her pantherish strides are emphasized by the sweeping spread of her gown which encircles the richly-brocaded carpet in voluptuous waves. The circular sweep of her dress over the rich pattern of the carpet alternates with flashes of the sea breaking against the shore, the waves pounding, eddying back and forth, staining the sand. The steady splash and moan of the breakers, quicker and quicker transitions from dress to beach, from beach to dress, the waves pounding, the eddies flowing back and staining the sand—all synchronized with Alraune's feverish bounds, her insistent animal thrusts, her sexual advance and retreat upon Mandra.

Taut, somewhat terrified, but with cold, majestic dignity Mandra sits upon her throne chair. She looks small and frail, like a temple dancer, or a carved idol. Close up her features betray an astounding sensibility. Every movement, every gesture of Alraune is re-reflected in her subtly changing features. The mobility of her features contrasts with the taut stiffness of her posture, with the bizarre, geometric ornamentation of the throne chair. Successive, kaleidoscopic flashes of the inlaid work of the chair, of Mandra's mobile features, of richly ornamented idols, of temple dancers, of the goddess Isis, of a fan, of a peacock's plume, of Alraune's pantherish strides, of the circular sweep of her dress, of the eddying waves, of the stains they leave on the sand, of the brocaded carpet.

Both Alraune and Mandra are loaded with barbaric ornaments. Over her gleaming sheath-like gown Alraune wears a heavy, steel necklace. As she plunges back and forth, in and out of shadow, the sea breaking, the waves running out, we get the accompanying rise and fall of her heavy steel necklace, its flash and jingle. We get again the instrument called the quena, made of a human skull, and Mandra's delicately chiselled fingers plaintively caressing it. The rock crystal skull flashes again over the endless desert, followed by the flash of piano strings and then the flash of steel girders, of the skeletons of skyscrapers, of acetylene torches on steel rails. And Alraune bounding about more and more pantherish, her body enveloped in mail, her nude body thrashing in a flail of hail. The clash of men in armor, their swords hacking through coats of mail, the sound of rivets driven into steel girders, the piano again and a hand pounding the keys, the strings rattling and whizzing. The movement of machines in jagged rhythm, a motor whirring, cogs jigging and meshing. The press of a newspaper at full speed, a saw cutting through hard wood, a steel rail bored through by acetylene torches. The skeletons of the skyscrapers, miles and miles of them, all toppling, buckling, crashing to earth with an overwhelming din.

Contrasted with the glitter and violence of Alraune's movements we have the grave, sedate poise of Mandra, dressed like a Javanese idol. An inscrutable smile lights up the passive Oriental face as she manipulates a pair of cotton-tipped sticks. The instrument on which she plays resembles the cymbalon. As she performs there is heard the music of the lute, the desert chant, the tinkling, ingratiating sound of bracelets clinking, the rustle of beaded curtains parting on bare legs. The skull flashes again, with smoke issuing from the hollow sockets, followed by the mournful, melancholy music of the flute and the flash of bleached bones lying in the desert, of sumptuous divans and voluptuous nude women smothered in the pillows, the pounding of surf, the moan of the wind, a woman lying in the sand, her breasts exposed, the two huge mounds of sand, the domes of the mosque, Mandra's long, tapering fingers caressing a woman's breasts, the swirl of dancing dresses, only the dresses flowing and swirling—no faces, no bodies, just the swelling and dying of flowing skirts, with the crash of surf, the waves eddying back towards the sea, leaving stains in the sand.

Alraune now pounces on Mandra hungrily. Unclasping her heavy steel bracelet she fastens it upon Mandra's wrist. As the bracelet closes about her wrist Mandra's eyes glow ecstatically. They seem to be flooded with a supernatural light. Suddenly the walls of the room give way and the line of Mandra's vision leads us through caves and grottoes cluttered with brilliant stalagmites—one cave leading into another through a labyrinthine maze. The light diminishes rapidly. We are in the garden again and the bowl is shown close up; the moon, reflected in the churning water, is spitting fire from its dead craters. The gold-fish flash again; they leap like flying fish, like sharks and sword-fish, their flaming fins brilliant as jewels. In fury and ecstasy they charge against the glass and as they strike the glass the sparks fly, and intermittently as they dash against the bowl there flashes a man with a revolver firing point-blank at another man, the bullets splattering against the skull, tearing the flesh away until there is nothing left but a gleaming multi-faceted diamond. Simultaneously the bowl falls to pieces and to the incessant crashing of glass from a great height there rises a flood of molten lava which drowns out villages and forests, cattle, men, women, children. From the sunken pond where the bowl originally stood there rises the sacrificial altar of Quetzalcoatl alive with hissing serpents, their tongues spitting fire, their bodies wriggling and shimmering, inextricably intermingled. This convulsive mass changes gradually into the rock crystal skull with lines converging to infinity of desert.

81

Alraune, heavy and naked, is moving with groans and spasms, her contortions reminiscent of the writhing movement of the serpents. She dances with the despair of one who is insatiable, her eyes rolling over, her mouth twitching, her torso jumping and quivering as if it were being lashed by a thousand whips. As she dances there are flashes of men bound to the earth, their bodies being tattooed, boys being circumcised with sharp flints, fanatics gouging themselves with knives, dervishes whirling like tops, and as they whirl and slash and gouge they fall one by one and they lie on the ground and squirm and foam at the mouth like epileptics. All this to the accompaniment of groans and wails, of blood-curdling shrieks and hair-raising screams. A continuous succession of primitive dances executed by savages with long, matted hair, their faces blue, their torsos streaked with chalk. Men and women dancing frenziedly, rubbing their genitals together, performing the most grotesque, obscene gestures. Dancing to the frenzied beating of drums, a continuous roll of deep drums that makes the hair stand on end. They dance in the shadow of a great fire, and as the din increases the animals which were hidden in the depths of the forest are seen rushing from their lairs and bounding through the flames. Lions, wolves, panthers, jackals, hyenas, boars—leaping through the flames as if they had gone mad. The screen is filled with terrified beasts: they leap through the bamboo walls of the huts, through the sides of circus tents, through glass windows, through furnaces of molten steel. They rush in troupes over the sides of precipices—deer, chamois, antelopes, yaks. Troupes of wild horses rushing madly over burning pampas, hurling themselves into craters. Monkeys, gorillas, chimpanzees scrambling from the limbs of burning trees. The earth is aflame and the beasts of the earth are running mad.

Meanwhile, amidst the pandemonium, Alraune continues her

orgiastic dance. She is surrounded by a cluster of naked savages who clasp an enormous bracelet about her body. The bracelet tightens about her body like a vise. A boy is lying on the ground; they are bending over him with sharp instruments, tattooing eyes all over his body. He lies very quiet, terrified. The voodoo men have long, matted hair, dirty nails, disfigured faces, and their bodies are smeared with ashes and excrement. Their bodies are grotesquely emaciated. As they tattoo the young man's beautiful strong body the eyes are seen to open, one after the other; they wink, blink, twitch, roll from side to side.

The bracelet around Alraune's squirming body is unloosed; she recommences her obscene movements, the drums beat again, and the rhythm of the drums works up to an even more tremendous climax than before. The young man's body writhes and squirms; it is fastened to the ground by heavy stakes. The tattooed eyes open convulsively; they shudder and twitch. We see the eyes up very close, the veins stand out taut. Alraune's body flashes more convulsively; her vulva looks like a tattooed eye. The boy squirms and twists, the veins so taut and swollen that finally they burst. As they burst Alraune flashes in her most obscene pose, the vulva twitching, the eyes bursting. This keeps on and on until there gushes from her body a flood of blood, whereupon suddenly, abruptly, we see the huge bowl in the garden, the water calm, the glass intact, the gold-fish swimming lazily.

IV

The bed-room of Mandra's home. Spacious, luxurious, heavily Moorish. Mandra frail, idol-like, lies in the center of an enormous bed. She is dressed in exotic costume, again suggestive of the Javanese. The bed-posts are richly studded, inlaid with ebony and ivory and precious gems. The windows are made of stained glass and throw an intricate pattern upon the bed. The bodies of the two women are splintered with light and color.

Alraune bends over Mandra tenderly and places beside her a marionette. The face is that of a skulking rake, a lout, a degenerate. Alraune is clothed in her tight-fitting black sheath-like gown that glitters and ripples. She hugs the marionette passionately before placing it beside Mandra. In laying it on the bed she is obliged to disengage the marionette's wooden arm which has slipped down her bosom. One full round breast is exposed.

It is high noon and the sun beats golden through the heavy stained glass windows. The room is flooded with light, the bed glitters, the atmosphere is radiant, joyous, almost holy. Alraune crouches beside Mandra like a tigress and with great deliberation hands her a pack of worn playing-cards . . . fortune-telling cards. The pack is spread out on the bed like a fan; the colors of the figures are beautifully faded and weave harmoniously with the hue of the richly stained glass windows.

The women handle the cards as if they were performing a sacred ritual. The figures on the cards are fantastic in design. As Mandra languidly gathers up the cards, one by one, with her extraordinary tapering fingers her face reveals a subtle variety of expression. She has a cruel, cunning, ancient look, almost stone-like—so much so that beside her Alraune now appears childish, innocent, elf-like. Alraune looks timid, frightened, mystified.

On one of the cards lying face up there appears the oval face of a woman with eccentric coiffure, as in a Japanese print. The woman holds a mirror to her face. As we look at the card the engraved mirror becomes a real mirror with a gorgeously studded handle of green bronze. We see Mandra's face in the mirror— with that cruel, cunning, ancient expression as before. And then there flashes in the mirror scene after scene—the streets of Lahore, the gardens of Babylon, the Taj Mahal, the temples of Greece, the slave market in Alexandria, the mosques of Mecca, the harems with their houris—one after the other, one dissolving into the other, like water dissolving into smoke.

Alraune peers over Mandra's shoulder with increasing amazement. She stares at Mandra's image with glowing, worshipful admiration. Mandra's face appears again in the mirror; it changes back slowly, subtly, from the ancient stone-like mask to the face of youth, the head classically shaped, exotic, like a face etched in copper. A strange, haunting face with large dewy eyes.

And now Mandra hands the mirror to Alraune with a mysterious, significant gesture—and Alraune gazes into it. Alraune's eyes open in even greater amazement than before. She shudders and then looks more closely, more intently. We see in the mirror not the face of Alraune, but the face of Mandra, and as we regard it intently the face of Alraune glides over Mandra's like the moon passing over the face of the sun; there is a blur and then the faces fuse and we have a composite face of Mandra and Alraune. This changes back again to the cruel, cunning, ancient, mask-like face of Mandra, as before.

Now the frame of the mirror focuses attention; we see that it is a playing card whose edges are slightly torn. This curled, frayed edge we see now in various guises—as the edge of a wave, the edge of a crater, the edge of a cruel mouth, the edge of a scimitar, the prow of a boat, the leaf of a tree, the rim of a cloud, the fin of a fish, a hundred and one objects whose contours have a surprising quality of edge.

Mandra gathers the cards together and hands them to Alraune. Alraune shuffles the cards and spreads them fan-wise on the bed. A card drops on the floor face down. Alraune bends over to pick it up, looks at it in consternation. The picture of a man with a long white beard, his eyes closed, his hands clasped and pointed towards heaven, his lips mumbling a prayer. Mandra gathers the cards together, shuffles them, spreads them out fan-wise on the bed. A card drops to the floor face down. She bends over to pick it up; the edge of the card becomes the frame of a door which opens slowly, revealing a long, narrow cell, narrow as a slit, narrower, narrower; at the end of the corridor is an old man with a bald head who sits before an illuminated globe which is slowly revolving. He chants in a deep guttural voice and makes the holy signs with his fingers. The globe glows with a mystical blue light. The man and the globe draw nearer. Now the man's head is in the globe; the latitudinal bars form a vizor in which his head is imprisoned. His fingers cease twitching; they are encased in steel gloves. His whole body is encased in a suit of armor, but the mystical blue globe with his head inside goes on revolving. Finally it stops turning and the steel helmet opens. Opens and shuts repeatedly. Each time it opens the man's head is thrust forward, but always too late. The last time it opens a homunculus springs out. Larger and larger it grows, until it reaches the ceiling. The man in the armor is terrified. The head begins to revolve at lightning speed, the light changes from blue to violet, then sputters out. And as it does so there comes the clang of metal against metal, a tense, vibrant ring that echoes through the long dim corridor and reverberates and reverberates. In the dull glow we see a huge sledge-hammer come crashing down on the steel mask. The suit of armor falls apart and out rolls an embryo, a half-grown foetus with one eye, the body doubled up, the arms and legs twisted in long mats of hair. With this the noise recommences, louder and louder, more and more resonant, thunderous, terrifying, and with it comes the roar of frenzied

86

human voices, a sea of fear which rolls up under the thunder of clanging anvil strokes.

V

The open street and the sound of terror rumbling through it like an angry sea. Above the tumult, the frenzy, the screams, the curses rises the wild clangor of bells, thousands of bells all of different intonation, all ringing Alarum! The street is choked with people spilling out of the houses, all screaming Alarm! Alarm! They fall over one another as if blown down by a hurricane, their clothes flung over their heads, the very stones unloosed by their mad rush. Some run with their necks thrust forward like geese and the veins in their necks burst like grapes. The windows of all the houses are flung open frantically. Naked and half-dressed they jump from the windows on to the heads of the stumbling, crazy mob below. Some are frantically trying to open the windows and can't, paralyzed by fear. Some smash the windows with chairs and fling themselves after the chairs head first. Some open the windows and pray. Some are singing, singing like lunatics, and beating their breasts. And all the while the bells are ringing, thousands and thousands of them, and the mob below is milling and charging and the houses tremble so with the impact of their feet that the shutters fall off their hinges and people run with broken shutters around their necks. And as the din increases the wind sweeps through the street with greater fury. The air is filled with flying shutters, with torn clothes, with arms and legs and scalps and false teeth and bracelets and chairs and dishes.

Suddenly in the window of the astrologer's house a blue light shows, and at the same moment it begins to hail. The hail comes down like huge china eggs that ricochet from wall to wall with the rat-a-tat-tat of machine guns. Three times the light flashes in the astrologer's window. Then he is seen to open a black box.

Now the most incredible things happen. It is like a nightmare. It is daylight, but the sky is full of stars. The hail has ceased but there is the steady hissing noise of rain falling in torrents somewhere in the distance. A noise like tin sliding over tin. The houses have disappeared. There is only a great black terrain filled with dead trees and from the roots of the trees huge fat snakes issue forth spitting fire. The people are dancing among the flaming tongues of the snakes, their bodies covered with blood, their eyes rolling deliriously.

While over the black heath the witches' dance goes on, the trees forked with flaming tongues, the naked bodies smeared with blood, the astrologer sits before the open window peering into his black box. A profound, uncanny silence envelopes his dwelling. In the black box is the blue bowl, the globe that slowly revolves. The globe is spangled with stars and the stars arranged in constellations after the pattern of the zodiac. He sits by the window in a deep reverie, his head sunk on his chest. The maid comes and pushes a little table before him over which she throws a tablecloth. Then she lifts the blue bowl out of the box and places it on the little table in front of him.

The scene divides in two. On the one side is the astrologer's window, the little table and the blue bowl. On the other side is the black heath with the witches' revel in full swing, the stars shining vividly, the sun beating down with an orange effulgence, the trees livid and twisted with flame-tongued snakes. The astrologer sits in peace and absent-mindedly puts his hand in the bowl which is now filled with gold-fish. One by one he pulls them out and swallows them. Meanwhile the revellers are making merry on the heath. They gather up the blue china eggs and pelt one another. The stars glow more and more brilliantly and the air turns blue and then green. The air is green as grass. The stars cluster thickly and glow with a fierce brilliance. The stars seem to be closing in on the earth and the light they shed is so intense that the trees burst open. Out of the dead trees there pours a stream of animals and the animals are pure white, every one of them. The revellers commence to fornicate with the animals. After they have fornicated they commence to kill the animals; then they fall on one another and with knives and teeth and nails they tear one another apart. The earth becomes one huge vomit of blood.

And when the ground is strewn with white mangled bodies, when there is no stopping them any more, suddenly the astrologer picks up his flute and, blowing a mournful note, he points significantly to the stars. At the same moment the blue bowl is transformed into a human skull and suddenly from the skull there issues a weird chant, a melody which is harrowing and unearthly. The scene changes back again to a street at the end of which is the astrologer's house. Again the street is filled with a surging mob, a sea of human bodies, of panic-stricken faces, of men without arms, of women with scalps torn loose. From the little house at the end of the street comes the weird music of the quena.

Not a sound comes from the street except this weird unearthly chant. The people are rushing by like ghosts, making no sound except a moaning as of the wind. The skull which was in the window has become a door, a pear-shaped door with two little petals in the center. Mandra and Alraune are fleeing before the mob, their capes flying, their hair streaming wild. As they reach the door the little petals open up and they are sucked in.

The petals close, the door becomes a skull, the skull changes to the face of the astrologer. The face of the astrologer grows round with fright, with wonder, with consternation. The face becomes like a dead moon in which there is no nose or mouth—just two big craters for the eyes.

VI

The astrologer's den is filled with books and bottles. The astrologer himself resembles a living automaton made entirely of metals. He sits in a swivel-chair oiling a mechanism in his chest. The mechanism is made of little wheels, like the inside of a watch. In the thorax is a big pendulum which swings slowly back and forth. He seems unaware of the presence of Mandra and Alraune. He bends over his green bottles and pours an amber fluid from one into the other. He gets down a book and pulling a few words out of the page he spills them into a green bottle. The words begin to smoke and then suddenly they turn to ash and fall to the bottom of the bottle. He repeats the experiment a number of times. The words always smoke and then fall to the bottom of the bottle like ash. He goes back to the chair and again he oils the mechanism in his chest. He puts on a pair of dark spectacles, then a dunce cap, then a pair of horns. He gets down on his knees and searches for something on the floor. The floor is like a geography book, stained with continents and seas, rivers, lakes, mountains. On his hands and knees he wanders from one continent to another until he comes to a little purple island. The island is surrounded by a blue sea on which there sails a silver ship and in the prow of the ship, straight as a rudder, stands Mandra, her hair flown back in stiff waves. The ship is very small and Mandra is smaller still. She stands at the prow of the ship singing. The astrologer bends down still closer to hear her. It sounds like a human voice. He stretches out full length and holding the little ship in the palm of his hand he listens to her as if enchanted. And as he listens the books open of themselves and the words come down out of the books and dance about the room like motes in a sun-beam. And now the words which had fallen like ash to the bottom of the bottle, the words rise up in smoke and they curl up through the thin neck of the bottle in spirals and whirl about the astrologer's head. His body is no longer made of metal parts, but of skin and bones, and the blood glows faintly through the transparent white skin.

The voice of Mandra now grows more distinct. Her song rises, ever louder, ever higher, until the room glows with a violet light. With a long beautifully-shaped forefinger she traces a circle over the astrologer's heart. The circle bursts into a flame and then, as the flame dies down, we see a cross engraved in his heart. On the cross appears a Christ crucified, his neck broken, his side pierced by the lance. The cross fades out and there is a statue of Venus, immediately replaced by another statue, that of Pallas Athena. This fades out and there is left instead of the statue the cross, the flaming circle, the mechanism with wheels. For a minute or two the wheels revolve like a dynamo at full speed, then suddenly the mechanism comes to a stop. At this moment the astrologer throws up his arms and shouts like a maniac: *Biskra! Mahratta! Valjevo! Cienfuegos!*

Above the last shout rises the voice of Mandra, a shrill piercing song that splits the sails of the ship. The room with its books and bottles, the blue bowl, the swimming continents, slowly dissolves, blurs out like the edge of a dream. Mandra stands at the prow of the ship, her eyes bandaged, the scales in her right hand. The ship slowly sinks beneath the waters and as it sinks the astrologer is seen leaving his house with arms outstretched

91

and moving like fins. He walks through the thick fog like a man walking on the bed of the ocean. He walks with arms outstretched, swimming through the fog. He is walking under the sea, across a lost continent inhabited now by a race of men and women born under the water, men and women with water-veiled eyes. He stumbles blindly among the ruins of ancient cities, the buildings swaying like reeds, the colors melting one into another as if a rainbow had sputtered out in the icy black depths of the sea. About him move the denizens of a lost world: their bodies glow with a sulphurous transparency, they sway on their feet, light and boneless as ballet dancers. Through the belfries of the cathedrals huge scintillating fish drift like weeds, their fins gently swaying the bells. What looks like a solid city reeling under the broken light of a rainbow is fluid and transparent as the dream. With swimming stride the inhabitants walk through the walls, leaving no rent or tear, no jagged edges. Their water-veiled eyes gleam like emeralds, their voices are faint from the deafening sound of bells. Nothing is difficult for them. Nothing bruises them. All is drift and change, the ease of yawning, or opening one's fist. A perpetual feast of color, like living inside a diamond. A perpetual feast, as if the storms above were ordained to provide them manna. Everything tumbles down through the diamond light of the depths. The bed of the ocean is littered with the treasures of the earth; the sea swarms with the riches that were plucked from the earth. Here nothing is accomplished by effort. One has only to open his mouth and drink. One has only to relax and dream. Over the reeling, undulating city with its transparent walls and the bells constantly tolling plays a flood of diffracted light, the continuous guttering of the rainbow, the mist and brilliance of the diamond's hard core. Here is the joy of the body released from the prison of matter. The joy of rubbing against silken caresses, the silken brush of plants swaying, of gum branches, of golden fins electric with life. The joy of ceaseless orgasm, of swaying in a hammock endlessly. The joy of sound penetrating the pores like light. The joy of seeing through and beyond and around. The joy of gleaming phosphorescence, of perpetual radiation, of night, of endless night pierced with stars. The joy of endless spiral movement, of endless ecstasy, of endless song.

VII

A room in a hotel. Mandra lies on an iron cot with an opium pipe beside her. The room is very small and the ceiling is covered with cobwebs. Mandra lies absolutely still, her eyes closed. Her feet protrude from beneath the sheets—two perfectly shaped feet, white as marble, the blue veins showing like streaks of mercury. Each toe is perfect, the nails are perfect. Never were there two more perfect feet.

Mandra lies there in a trance. From the body of this Mandra issues another Mandra with the face of Alraune. There are two Mandras in the room—one lying prostrate with feet exposed, the other standing at the foot of the bed and smiling. The one with the smile has gold-red jungle eyes, eyes that seem to glow from the depths of a cavern. The eyes of a lizard basking in the sun, the cold, slippery eyes of a snake with a forked tongue. The eyes gleam like gems under the lapidary's wheel. The eyes of an idol burning in the depths of the jungle.

The room is like an iron cage. From the ceiling there is suspended the corpse of a man who was hanged. He hangs by his feet and his lifeless hand clutches a huge bell-shaped flower with thick, tangled roots. The body of the man sways slowly to and fro above the prostrate figure of Mandra whose eyes are closed.

93

To and fro the lifeless body sways. As if the heavy perfume of the flower were penetrating her drugged body Mandra stirs slightly. The movements of dream. The room changes as in the dream. The room grows smaller and smaller, the walls sweat. From invisible beings there rises a thick vapor, like the steam in a laundry. The air is filled with the smoke of cigarettes. Nothing is visible except the body of Mandra lying on the cot, stirring fitfully in dream.

The sound of human voices, of weeping, of low hysterical moans, of sobs, of shrieks and gales of laughter. In the darkness the cigarettes glow, the smoke curls upward in spiral rings. Above the body of Mandra appear two dormer windows and reflected in the windows are the faces of frog-like men with long green hair and flesh the color of cigars. They laugh and weep, they gnash their teeth, they gibber and wail, they howl with laughter. They cluster around the window like flies attracted by the light. The rain beats down on them, but they are not wet. The rain soaks through the fibres of the hair and drips inside the brain. Only the brains show through the windows now—coils and coils of gray-white brains through which the rain slowly drips. Snow falls and the brains freeze. A naked woman walks through the frozen brains with a sword between her legs. The icicles cut through her flesh, her feet are bleeding. The woman falls through a fissure in the ice. She falls on to a cot in the same room and it is night. She stirs slightly, as if dreaming. Her feet protrude from beneath the sheets, just as before. Two perfect feet, white as marble, the veins cast with a mercurial blue. In the long silence of the night she hears a dog barking. She opens her eyes for a moment and there, in the window above, is the man she loves gashing his way through the frozen brains. He carries the sword which she had let fall in her wandering. He hacks and slashes until she screams with joy. There is the thud of a body falling and the corpse which was suspended from the ceiling falls to the ground. Again the room is filled with laughter, wild, shrill, hysterical screams, long blood-curdling shrieks. Laughter, laughter, as if all the insane asylums had turned loose their victims.

Mandra opens her eyes in terror. At the foot of the bed stands Alraune. Her features are indistinguishable except for the eyes which gleam now like two jewels stuck in an idol. Mandra puts forth her arms imploringly. The room grows smaller. The room is choked with cobwebs; they form a thick canopy over the bed. At the same time the hysterical laughter dies down, changes imperceptibly into soft, crooning negro voices, as if coming from a radio. The bed on which Mandra lies is filled with gravel. From the ceiling is suspended a huge pair of scissors which open and close, which cut away the cobwebs. But fast as the scissors cut the cobwebs reform. One cannot see the body of Alraune clearly but one can see her gesticulations, her frantic efforts to extricate herself from the webs in which her arms are pinioned. Mandra lies under the canopy of webs stretching forth her arms imploringly. Her eyes are fixed on Alraune's mouth from which there issues the sound of crooning negro voices. She gazes ecstatically at Alraune whose face is indiscernible except for the large voluptuous mouth out of which there pours a cascade of flowers and jewels and finally a stream of liquid fire. We see again the scissors overhead opening and closing, the cobwebs forming, the gravel on the bed, Mandra's arms outstretched, her neck taut, her eyes fixed ecstatically. Where Alraune stood a moment ago is now suspended a huge coin with the Mona Lisa face engraved. The features fade away, leaving only the inscrutable smile. Again the eyes gleam forth, gold-red jungle eyes, the eyes of an idol buried in the forest. Mandra stretches forth her arms in anguish.

Above the webbed canopy appears a procession of figures, one by one, all waving farewell to her. Wraiths which come and go. All waving farewell. A long procession of men and women floating through the cobwebs, then cut away by the huge scissors which open and close.

Mandra falls back on the bed weeping. Her eyes close. Her feet protrude from under the sheets, as before. The bed changes to a ship of sapphire sailing over a coral sea. Mandra is standing at the prow singing. From the distant shore comes the sound of lutes. The Alhambra flashes, the cool gardens with jets of liquid fire running through the corridors, peacocks strutting over the marble slabs, the lacquered walls panelled with jewels. The ship sails on over the coral sea, the sails swelling with the breath of Mandra's song. Against the swelling sails is pitted a sky of pearl-like clouds. The song rises, the sails swell, the clouds bulge, the ship scuds on a dangerous keel. Earth and sky reel. Mandra stands upright, her hair flown back, her eyes radiant. The ship rises and falls on waves of spun glass. The voice flows like jets of liquid fire. The sails burst, the clouds break. The edges of the sails, the edges of the clouds burn away like cloth ignited. Over the horizon line is a huge sea shell in the hollow of which is the figure of Venus. The lines are clearly revealed: they trace a never-ending spiral. Above the horizon line is the sea shell with its endless spiral whorl. Below is a rainbow in reverse, as if reflected in the sea. The rainbow breaks, the colors spill and run. The ship is scudding on her keel. The ship slowly submerges beneath the spun glass waves. The coral sea becomes a brilliant light, as if the stars had suddenly plunged into the sea. A city made entirely of coral rises from the ocean bed. Again the fish with electric fins, the wavering, teetering walls, the belfries with their huge bells slowly swinging.

And now from every nook and cranny in the walls, from the

windows, doors and belfries there swims forth a sea of men with water-veiled eyes. They swim towards the ship in which Mandra stands lashed to the mast. The ship is still slowly sinking. It sinks in a shower of pollen which opens miraculously into myriad flowers. The shimmering city of coral, dazzling with light, with broken colors, with flying fish, is now garlanded with flowers. The mast to which Mandra is lashed changes to the form of a mandrake, the mandrake changes to a huge purple flower with a bell-shaped corolla. For a moment everything fades but the huge bell-shaped flower whose mouth opens and closes. Then two petals such as were in the astrologer's door. The petals change to the lips of a vulva. The lips of the vulva become elongated, hang down like an apron. A naked woman is dancing, a savage woman with brass bracelets. A torso writhing, the purple apron, the lips of the vulva, the flower with its bell-shaped corolla, the belfries with their slow-swinging bells, the scintillating sword fish, their electric fins, the shimmering walls, the rainbow light, the swarm of men with water-veiled eyes, the mast like a phallus, the pollen miraculously bursting into flower, the coral city garlanded with flowers, the ship slowly descending to the ocean floor and Mandra standing at the prow, her hair flown back, her eyes filled with ecstasy, her mouth opened in song.

Mandra stands now on the coral bed in the center of a fish-bowl filled with gold-fish lazily churning the water. The figure of Mandra is very tiny, the gold-fish are enormous. The city ceases to waver, the lines harden, the walls become a coral plant in the fish-bowl. Mandra looks about her with large round eyes which change from wonder to alarm. She is standing on a rock in the midst of a black sea filled with hissing serpents which lash about the rock and hypnotize her with their great bulbous eyes. Outside the bowl in which she stands there swarms a flock of sea-gulls with manuscripts in their beaks. They fly around the globe, flapping their huge wings. Mandra frantically tries to read the hieroglyphs which are stamped on the manuscripts. The characters are in all forms of writing, none of which Mandra can decipher. The bowl is plastered with these strange characters which Mandra vainly tries to read. Mandra stands helplessly on the rock, imprisoned in the glass bowl. The rock becomes the purple island which the astrologer had found on his hands and knees. The island is very green now and filled with glass palm trees which keep throwing off new shoots made of spun glass. Amidst the palm trees there now appears a white path edged with cactus. Mandra flees down the white path, her flesh torn by the spiny cactus. The breeze she creates in her flight causes the trees to tinkle, a sound as of beaded curtains parting.

She flees down the white road towards a little house shaped like an egg. There are no windows in the house and the carpet is made of cotton-batting. The walls are made entirely of soft down. The tinkle of the glass leaves changes to the music of a street organ, a muffled melody which is drowned in the soft white down of the walls. There is a soft knock at the door. Mandra puts her hands to her ears as if she heard the deafening thunder of machinery. The knock comes again. Mandra swoons. Against her forehead is pressed a band of steam rivets which throb violently. The riveting machines are breaking through an asphalt bed from which there pours a stream of gravel. The riveters are plunging red hot bolts into Mandra's forehead. The forehead bursts open and we see again the coils of gray-white brains. For a moment the brains seems like a coral bed; then gradually they change to steel girders, to skeletons of buildings through which walk human skeletons. They walk towards a huge searchlight which makes their bones gleam like phosphorus. They walk in and out of the steel girders to the sound of deafening riveting machines. The organ plays . . . the street organ. The music is wild, ferocious. The skeletons become animated. There is the noise of glass breaking, the sound of wheels crunching the glass, the bark of wolves. Then suddenly silence. The astrologer appears with the little mechanism in his chest and the dunce cap on his head, green spectacles over his eyes. The mechanism slows down, then dies out altogether. With this the astrologer throws up his arms and, dancing like a maniac, he yells: *Biskra! Mahratta! Valjevo! Cienfuegos!*

VIII

The corridor of a hotel. A maid walking down the corridor with a towel in her hand. She comes to room No. 35 and knocks. There is no response. She opens the door and walks into a huge cobweb which envelops her like a fish-net. She drops the towel and runs out of the room screaming.

Mandra is sitting on the bed naked, gazing into a long oval-shaped mirror on the wall. She has the eyes of a Siamese cat, with two fine slits down the center of the iris. She smiles at herself as if she were smiling at a stranger. She talks to her image without recognizing herself. On the bed her face is sad; in the mirror it is smiling. She talks loudly, angrily, she gesticulates, but the face in the mirror smiles with a sad, inscrutable smile. She gets up and approaching the image in the mirror she makes mocking gestures which are reflected by the grotesque, wooden gestures of a marionette. She laughs aloud, hysterically, but her image responds with the same grave smile. She tears her hair in agony. The image in the mirror solemnly dislocates its arms, then wrenches one arm out of its socket and drops it on the floor. One arm hangs limply, as if dead; the arm on the floor commences to gesticulate, as if it were manipulated by an invisible string.

99

Terrified Mandra bends down to pick up the arm. In doing so her head crashes against the mirror and the glass cracks. When she raises herself she sees two women joined together, like the Siamese twins. The two are trying to tear apart from each other. They cling to the frame of the mirror and pull and twist and squirm. As they struggle to break apart the mirror begins to revolve. The room whirls with arms and legs, with truncated bodies, with decapitated heads. The mirror stops turning.

Mandra is walking through a forest of decapitated trees. Some of the trees are lying down, like tombstones; others are standing upright, partially carved into human form. Some are huge blocks shaped like skulls with many facets. Some are standing on torsos and their arms are cut off above the elbow. Some have two faces, one concave, the other convex. The ones lying down look like saints; the wood is rotting and the worms are crawling over their bodies.

As Mandra moves among the figures the trees come to life. The forms which were partially carved are swallowed up by the growth of the trees; they are buried alive in the trunks of the trees. Mandra sees nothing of this because the miracle occurs only in her wake. Ahead of her is always the same tangled mass of half-human trees, of dead trunks, of arms and legs and torsos. Behind her springs up a forest with magnolias and birches and elms and spruces, all in full foliage. In the trunks of the trees are dimly recognizable the half-grown forms which Mandra had seen; they seem to be dreaming in the trees. Mandra stumbles on magically opening the veins of the forest. Half the forest is in sunlight, the other half in gloom.

At the edge of the forest the sky hangs down like a brocaded dress. The sky is spangled with dazzling stars out of which shoots a profusion of leaping greyhounds. The sky trembles like a veil in the wind and across the glittering veil the greyhounds pass with long sweeping strides, with fantastic leaps. Mandra stands at the edge of the forest with a bundle of quivers in her girdle and a bow in her hand. She draws the bow and lets fly the piercing arrow. One arrow after another until the sky is sewn with bleeding dogs. And when all the arrows are gone the veil falls and the earth is strewn with a magic carpet over which sullen-faced gypsies are dancing, their dresses glittering with spangles, their elbows bursting the jingling tambourines. As they swirl about on the brocaded carpet, their feet painted like roses, Mandra rushes amongst them, scanning their faces eagerly. Soon she is in the center of them and her feet are moving in the same rhythm. She dances with her eyes shut, her body moving lasciviously. From the girdle around her waist there hangs the purple flower with the bell-shaped corolla and the thick roots. It dangles between her legs. Her dance becomes obscene. She dances over a sword, her legs bending, her torso squirming and twisting. Her movements are like a succession of orgasms. The eyes open but they show only the whites.

In the reflection of a thousand mirrors Mandra continues her dance, the eyes rolled back, the whites showing. The mirrors are studded with glistening faces, with dilated nostrils, with heavy open mouths, with bulging eyes. The purple flower dangles above the pointed tip of the sword. The sword gleams with the brilliant reflections of the mirrors. Between the legs of Mandra dancing the faces jiggle, the gaping mouths, the bulging eyes, the dilated nostrils. The faces broaden and bulge, the bodies dwindle until they seem like frogs. The eyes in the mirrors seem to be floating, like flowers drowning in a heavy sea. Mandra is stretching out her hands, her eyes still capsized. She touches the faces in the mirrors and there is the sound of glasses falling, of glasses being shattered to bits. Now the faces take on all varieties of expression—torture, mockery, contempt, jeers, supplication. Some look wounded, some look somnolent, some smile, some implore, some curse, some ridicule, some are brazen, some defiant, some insolent. Mandra moves about with arms outstretched, her fingers searching for the eyes. The eyes die out, like cigarettes. Mandra moves among the blank mirrors from which not even her own image is reflected. She moves in agony, as if her limbs had been racked. Her pain is insupportable, but there is no image of it in the mirrors.

And now there comes again the weird, mournful sound of the quena and in the single oval mirror before which Mandra stands we see the sky filled with low-hanging clouds. The wind tears the clouds to tatters, the light takes on a sulphurous hue. The clouds disappear and we see the crater of Vesuvius belching fire and brimstone. Quickly, in rapid succession, there passes the vision of ruined cities, of Babylon, of Nineveh, of Pompeii, of Carthage, of Alexandria, of Rome, of the buried cities of Yucatan, of Jerusalem, of Bagdad, of Samarkand. City after city buried beneath the ashes. Then for a moment the altar of Quetzalcoatl, then the Chinese Wall, then the Wailing Wall of Jerusalem, the temple of Angkor, the Parthenon, the gate of Damascus, the mosque of Suleiman, the great volcanic monuments of Easter Island, the Maori masks, the old Swedish coins shaped like keys, the labyrinth at Knossus, the nine cities of Troy, one beneath the other, the Trojan horse, the dolmens and menhirs at Stonehenge, the mosques at Stamboul, the Alhambra, the battlements of Carcassonne, the campanile of St. Mark, the prayer-wheels of Thibet, the city of Lahore, the temple dancers in Bali, the whirling dervishes in Egypt, the ruins of Memphis, the temple of Isis, the Inca pyramids with their sacrificial altars, the beach at Waikiki, the wave by Hokusai, a deck of cards with torn edges, an oval mirror with a bronze han-

102

dle, the face of Alraune, heavy, fleshy, smiling with an inscrutable smile. The eyes of Alraune are half-closed, the lids are seagreen. Her hair hangs loosely, the color of violet. She opens her eyes slowly, very wide, round, gazing into space with a hypnotic stare.

Mandra approaches the image in the mirror as if hypnotized. About the forehead of Alraune is a band of precious jewels. The jewels are bleeding. From her nostrils there issues a thin stream of smoke. Alraune smiles now with the smile of a whore, her lips parted, her face heavy, drugged, yet glowing effulgently. Mandra puts her lips to the mirror and kisses the heavy, sensual mouth of Alraune. The lips glue together, the faces merge. For a moment the composite face of Alraune and Mandra takes on a leaden, ashen color. The quena sounds again, the faces dissolve into a grinning skull, the lava bubbles out of the crater of Vesuvius, the ruins flash again, more rapidly now, kaleidoscopically: there is the brocaded carpet, the sullen faces of the gypsies dancing, the greyhounds leaping through the air, the flying fish, the belfries under water, the wavering, undulating walls, the silver ship on a sapphire sea, the coral island, the mystic blue bowl, the gold-fish churning lazily, the gravel path, the white road, the little house like an egg, the glass palm trees, the tinkle of beaded curtains parting, the sound of the lute, a donkey braying, a woman sobbing.

SILENCE

Alraune and Mandra sitting side by side in a gold chariot which is aflame. Alraune and Mandra exchanging amorous glances, touching each other lightly, their lips heavily rouged, their eyes painted. Alraune and Mandra bending over each other voluptuously in a long drawn-out kiss. Alraune and Mandra in each other's arms, pressing each other lasciviously, their hair entangled, their feet entwined. Alraune and Mandra sitting in the chariot ecstatically, their hair swarming with moths and butterflies, their bodies enveloped in a transparent veil of peacock plumes. The flames mount, the flames lick their bodies; they writhe convulsively in each other's arms, their bodies unscorched, their eyes ecstatic. The flames become a lashing sea of fire, the chariot a silver ship tossing to and fro. From the tip of the mast there issues a stream of smoke. The mast splits, the sails rip.

Mandra and Alraune are lying on a beautiful couch beneath a canopy studded with stars. They are lying naked, face to face, breathing into each other's mouth. The sun beats through the open window in long oblique shafts of powdered gold. There is the music of the lutes, soft, distant, incessant as rain.

IX

The same scene except that the room is suspended in an enormous bowl flooded with an intense blue light. The bed sways gently to and fro as if it were a hammock. At the top of the bowl a few dead gold-fish are floating face up. A hand reaches into the bowl and removes the dead fish one by one. Mandra, who has been asleep, slowly opens her eyes, and, seeing the enormous hand above her, the fingers closing round the dead gold-fish, she opens her mouth and screams—but there is only a faint echo of her voice. Alraune lies beside her, on her back, her legs slightly parted. The purple flower with the fleshy roots is planted between her legs. From the long bell-shaped corolla protrudes a pistil bursting with seed. Mandra bends over the body of Alraune and examines the flower attentively. She gazes and gazes until her eyes seem ready to pop out of her head.

The body of Alraune gradually changes color, the limbs stiffen, the half-opened mouth settles into a rigid grimace. As the color of her body changes, from flesh-pink to the dull black of a meteor, the heavily charged pistil bursts and the seed spills over the bed.

The scene alternates now from bed to garden, back and forth incessantly. We see the maid walking down the gravel path towards the pool in the center of the garden. She carries the dead gold-fish in a basket trimmed with palmetto leaves. She gets down on her knees and, lifting a plug from the bottom of the pool, she lets the water drain away. At the bottom of the pool is a jewel box. She opens the box, which is lined with satin, and deposits the gold-fish therein. Then she walks to a corner of the garden and, digging a hole, she buries the casket, making the sign of the cross when she is through. As she walks back towards the house, the gravel crunching beneath her feet, she moves her lips as if in prayer. The face is that of an idiot. She is cross-eyed, her hair unkempt, the tears streaming down her face, her lips moving mechanically. As she mounts the steps leading to the door her dress suddenly bursts open in back, exposing her bottom. She stands a moment on the steps, perplexed, makes the sign of the cross again and turns the door knob. As she does so two white doves fly out of her rectum.

The bed-room again. Over the empty bed swings the body of a man, head down, his hand clutching the purple flower—as in the hotel room. The room is flooded with a dazzling light. The two white doves are fluttering frantically, blinded by the light. They collide against the walls of the globe, fall on the bed with broken wings. The corpse which has been dangling above them falls and crushes them. Simultaneously the body of the dead man commences to swarm with maggots. The body is like a honey-comb. The maggots take on wings, scaly, scintillant, transparent wings, like the wings of dragon-flies. The swarm writhes and twists, like a woman in labor, and then suddenly the whole mass rises on wings and disappears through the top of the bowl. The last few look like angels.

And now from the bottom of the bowl, in magic prismatic formation, there rises up a coral island, a fantastic city of coral whose leaping growth seems to be inspired by a giant fish with a magnificent tail. As the fish dives the radiance of its tail illuminates the fibrous pores of the coral, revealing a prismatic structure of endless geometric figures, one within the other, luminous, substanceless, denominated only by sharp lines which intersect like a diamond web. The web expands, like ice forming on a window-pane. The pattern revolves in a blinding light. In the middle of a blazing sun is a black spot; the spot grows larger and larger, until it resembles a dead moon swimming in the fire of the sun. The black moon grows larger and larger, until there is only a thin rim of fire glowing at the periphery of the moon. When it is one huge black ball suddenly there is a gleam of light in the center. The black mass becomes agitated, as if it were boiling lava, and slowly it takes form and substance. The edges shrivel and curl in towards the center, the streaks which looked like canals, appear as limbs. Finally, as a dull, normal daylight breaks over it, we can distinguish the form of a foetus curled up in the womb.

The foetus fades out abruptly and we see Mandra climbing out of an enormous bed, her hands to her throat, as if she were choking. She runs to the oval mirror hanging on the wall and opening wide her mouth she coughs. She coughs again and again, as if something were stuck in her throat. Finally she feels it coming and she holds out her hands to catch it. She coughs again and there falls into her hands a tiny little heart, about the size of a pigeon's egg.

The Universe of Death

from

"The World of Lawrence"

IN SELECTING Proust and Joyce I have chosen the two literary figures who seem to me most representative of our time. Whatever has happened in literature since Dostoievski has happened on the other side of death. Lawrence apart, we are no longer dealing with living men, men for whom the Word is a living thing. Lawrence's life and works represent a drama which centers about the attempt to escape a living death, a death which, if it were understood, would bring about a revolution in our way of living. Lawrence experienced this death creatively, and it is because of his unique experience that his "failure" is of a wholly different order from that of

Proust or Joyce. His aborted efforts towards self-realization speak of heroic struggle, and the results are fecundating—for those, at any rate, who may be called the "aristocrats of the spirit".

Despite all that may be said against him, as an artist, or as a man, he still remains the most alive, the most vitalizing of recent writers. Proust had to die in order even to commence his great work; Joyce, though still alive, seems even more dead than Proust ever was. Lawrence on the other hand, is still with us: his death, in fact, is a mockery of the living. Lawrence killed himself in the effort to burst the bonds of living death. There is evidence for believing, if we study for example such a work as *The Man Who Died*, that had it been given him to enjoy the normal span of life he would have arrived at a state of wisdom, a mystic way of life, in which the artist and the human being would have been reconciled. Such men have indeed been rare in the course of our Western civilization. Whatever in the past may have operated to prevent our men of genius from attaining such a state of perfection we know that in Lawrence's case the poverty, the sterility of the cultural soil into which he was born, was certainly the death-dealing cause. Only a part of the man's nature succeeded in blossoming—the rest of him was imprisoned and strangled in the dry walls of the womb. With Proust and Joyce there was no struggle: they emerged, took a glance about, and fell back again into the darkness whence they come. Born creative, they elected to identify themselves with the historical movement.

If there be any solution of life's problems for the mass of mankind, in this biological continuum which we have entered upon, there is certainly little hope of any for the individual, i. e., the artist. For him the problem is not how to identify himself with the mass about, for in that lies his *real* death, but how to fecundate the masses by his dying. In short, it is his almost impossible duty now to restore to this unheroic age a tragic note. This he can do only by establishing a new relationship with the world, by seizing anew the sense of death on which all art is founded, and reacting creatively to it. Lawrence understood this, and it is for this reason that his work, however conventional it may appear extrinsically, has vitality.

The fact remains, nevertheless, that not even a Lawrence was able to exercise any visible influence upon the world. The times are stronger than the men who are thrown up. We are in a dead-lock. We have a choice, but we are unable to make it. It was the realization of this which impelled me to end my long introduction to *The World of Lawrence*, of which this is the final section, with the title *Universe of Death*.

So far as the creative individual goes life and death are of equal value: it is all a question of counterpoint. What is of vital concern, however, is how and where one meets life—or death. Life can be more deadly than death, and death on the other hand can open up the road to life. It is against the stagnant flux in which we are now drifting that Lawrence appears brilliantly alive. Proust and Joyce, needless to say, appear more representative: they reflect the times. We see in them no revolt: it is surrender, suicide, and the more poignant since it springs from creative sources.

It is in the examination, then, of these two contemporaries of Lawrence that we see the process all too clearly. In Proust the full flower of psychologism—confession, self-analysis, arrest of living, making of art the final justification, but thereby divorcing art from life. An intestinal conflict in which the artist is immolated. The great retrospective curve back towards the womb: suspension in death, living death, for the purposes of dissection. Pause to question, but no questions forthcoming, the faculty having atrophied. A worship of art for its own sake—not for man. Art, in other words, regarded as a means of salvation, as a redemption from suffering, as a compensation for the terror of living. *Art a substitute for life.* The literature of flight, of escape, of a neurosis so brilliant that it almost makes one doubt the efficacy of health. *Until* one casts a glance at that "neurosis of health" of which Nietzsche sings in *The Birth of Tragedy*.

In Joyce the soul deterioration may be traced even more definitely, for if Proust may be said to have provided the tomb of art, in Joyce we can witness the full process of decomposition. "Whoso", says Nietzsche, "not only comprehends the word Dionysian, but also grasps his *self* in this word, requires no refutation of Plato or of Christianity or of Schopenhauer—*he smells the putrefaction*". *Ulysses* is a paean to "the late-city man", a thanatopsis inspired by the ugly tomb in which the soul of the civilized man lies embalmed. The most astoundingly varied and subtle means of art are herein exploited to glorify the dead city. The story of *Ulysses* is the story of a lost hero recounting a lost myth; frustrated and forlorn the Janus-faced hero wanders through the labyrinth of the deserted temple, seeking for the holy place but never finding it. Cursing and vilifying the mother who bore him, deifying her as a whore, bashing his brains out with idle conundrums, such is the modern Ulysses. Through the mystery-throngs he weaves his way, a hero lost in a crowd, a poet rejected and despised, a prophet wailing and cursing, covering his body with dung, examining his own excrement, parading his obscenity, lost, lost, a crumbling brain, a dissecting instrument endeavoring to reconstruct the soul. Through his chaos and obscenity, his obsessions and complexes, his perpetual, frantic search for God, Joyce reveals the desperate plight of the modern man who, lashing about in his steel and concrete cage, admits finally that there is no way out.

In these two exponents of modernity we see the flowering of the

Hamlet-Faust myth, that unscotchable snake in the entrails which, for the Greeks, was represented by the Oedipus myth, and for the whole Aryan race by the myth of Prometheus. In Joyce not only is the withered Homeric myth reduced to ashes, but even the Hamlet myth, which had come to supreme expression in Shakespeare, even this vital myth, I say, is pulverized. In Joyce we see the incapacity of the modern man even to doubt: it is the simulacrum of doubt, not its substance, that he gives us. With Proust there is a higher appreciation of doubt, of the inability to act. Proust is more capable of presenting the metaphysical aspect of things, partly because of a tradition so firmly anchored in the Mediterranean culture, and partly because his own schizoid temperament enabled him to examine objectively the evolution of a vital problem from its metaphysical to its psychological aspect. The progression from nerves to insanity, from a tragic confrontation of the duality in man to a pathologic split in the personality, is mirrored in the transition from Proust to Joyce. Where Proust held himself suspended over life in a cataleptic trance, weighing, dissecting, and eventually corroded by the very scepticism he had employed, Joyce had already plunged into the abyss. In Proust there is still a questioning of values; with Joyce there is a denial of all values. With Proust the schizophrenic aspect of his work is not so much the cause as the result of his world-view. With Joyce there is no world-view. Man returns to the primordial elements; he is washed away in a cosmological flux. Parts of him may be thrown up on foreign shores, in alien climes, in some future time. But the whole man, the vital, spiritual ensemble, is dissolved. This is the dissolution of the body and soul, a sort of cellular immortality in which life survives chemically.

Proust, in his classic retreat from life, is the very symbol of the modern artist—the sick giant who locks himself up in a cork-lined

111

cell to take his brains apart. He is the incarnation of that last and fatal disease: *the disease of the mind*. In *Ulysses* Joyce gives us the complete identification of the artist with the tomb in which he buries himself. *Ulysses* has been spoken of as seeming like "a solid city". Not so much a solid city, it seems to me, as a dead world-city. Just as there is, beneath the hollow dynamism of the city, an appalling weariness, a monotony, a fatigue insuperable, so in the works of Proust and Joyce the same qualities manifest themselves. A perpetual stretching of time and space, an obedience to the law of inertia, as if to atone, or compensate, for the lack of a higher urge. Joyce takes Dublin with its worn-out types; Proust takes the microscopic world of the Faubourg St. Germain, symbol of a dead past. The one wears us out because he spreads himself over such an enormous artificial canvas; the other wears us out by magnifying his thumb-nail fossil beyond all sensory recognition. The one uses the city as a universe, the other as an atom. The curtain never falls. Meanwhile the world of living men and women is huddling in the wings clamoring for the stage.

In these epics everything is of equal prominence, equal value, whether spiritual or material, organic or inorganic, live or abstract. The array and content of these works suggest to the mind the interior of a junk-shop. The effort to parallel space, to devour it, to install oneself in the time process—the very nature of the task is foreboding. The mind runs wild. We have sterility, onanism, logomachy. *And*—the more colossal the scope of the work the more monstrous the failure!

Compared to these dead moons how comforting the little works which stick out like brilliant stars! Rimbaud, for example! His *Illuminations* outweighs a shelf of Proust, Joyce, Pound, Eliot, etc. Times there are, to be sure, when the colossal work compels admiration, when, as with Bach or Dante, it is ordered by an inner plan, by the organic mechanism of faith. Here the work of art assumes the form and dimensions of a cathedral, a veritable tree of life. But with our latter-day exponents of head-culture the great monuments are lying on their sides, they stretch away like huge petrified forests, and the landscape itself becomes *nature-morte*.

Though we do, as Edmund Wilson says, "possess Dublin seen, heard, smelt and felt, brooded over, imagined, remembered", it is, in a profound sense, no possession at all: it is possession through the dead ends of the brain. As a naturalistic canvas *Ulysses* makes its appeal to the sense of smell only: it gives off a sublime mortuary odor. It is not the reality of nature here, still less the reality of the five senses. *It is the sick reality of the mind.* And so, if we possess Dublin at all, it is only as a shade wandering through an excavated Troy or Knossus; the historical past juts out in geological strata.

In referring to *Work in Progress* Louis Gillet, an admirer of Joyce, says: "One sees how the themes are linked together in this strange symphony; men are, to-day, as at the beginning of the world, the playthings of nature; they translate their impressions into myths which comprise the fragments of experience, the shreds of reality which are held in the memory. And thus is made a legend, a sort of extra-temporal history, formed of the residue of all histories, which one might call (in using a title of Johann Sebastian Bach) a cantata for all time".

A noble ring to these words, but absolutely false. This is not how legends are made! The men who are capable of creating an "extra-temporal history" are not the men who create legends. The two are not co-eval in time and space. The legend is the soul emerging into form, a singing soul which not only carries hope, but which contains a promise and a fulfillment. In the "extra-temporal", on the other hand, we have a flat expanse, a muddy

113

residue, a sink without limits, without depths, without light and shadow—an abyss into which the soul is plunged and swallowed up. It marks the end of the great trajectory: the tapeworm of history devours itself. If this be legend, it is legend that will never survive, and most certainly never be sung. Already, almost coincidentally with their appearance, we have, as a result of *Ulysses* and *Work in Progress*, nothing but dry analyses, archaeological burrowings, geological surveys, laboratory tests of the Word. The commentators, to be sure, have only begun to chew into Joyce. The Germans will finish him! They will make Joyce palatable, understandable, clear as Shakespeare, better than Joyce, better than Shakespeare. Wait! The mystagogues are coming!

As Gillet has well said—*Work in Progress* represents "a picture of the flowing reminiscences, of the vain desires and confused wishes which wander in our sleepy, loosened soul, which comprises the crepuscular life of thought . . ." But who is interested in this language of night? *Ulysses* was obscure enough. But *Work in Progress* . . .? Of Proust at least we may say that his myopia served to render his work exciting, stimulating: it was like seeing the world through the eyes of a horse, or a fly. Joyce's deformity of vision, on the other hand, is depressing, crippling, dwarfing: it is a defect of the soul, and not an artistic, metaphysical device. Joyce is growing more blind every day—blind in the pineal eye. For passion he is substituting books; for men and women rivers and trees —or wraiths. Life to Joyce, as one of his admirers says, is a mere tautology. Precisely. We have here the clue to the whole symbolism of defeat. And, whether he is interested in history or not, Joyce *is* the history of our time, of this age which is sliding into darkness. Joyce is the blind Milton of our day. But whereas Milton glorified Satan, Joyce, because his sense of vision has atrophied, merely surrenders to the powers of darkness. Milton was a rebel, a demonic force, a voice that made itself heard. Milton blind, like Beethoven deaf, only grew in power and eloquence; the inner eye, the inner ear, became more attuned to the cosmic rhythm. Joyce, on the other hand, is a blind and deaf *soul*: his voice rings out over a waste land and the reverberations are nothing but the echoes of a lost soul. Joyce is the lost soul of this soulless world; his interest is not in life, in men and deeds, not in history, not in God, but in the dead dust of books. He is the high priest of the lifeless literature of to-day. He writes a hieratic script which not even his admirers and disciples can decipher. He is burying himself under an obelisk for whose script there will be no key.

It is interesting to observe in the works of Proust and Joyce, and of Lawrence as well, how the milieu from which they sprang determined the choice of the protagonist as well as the nature of the disease against which they fought. Joyce, springing from the priest class, makes Bloom, his "average" man or double, the supreme object of ridicule. Proust, springing from the cultured middle-class, though himself living only on the fringe of society, *tolerated*, as it were, makes Charlus, his king figure, a bitter object of ridicule. And Lawrence, springing from the common classes, makes the type Mellors, who appears in a variety of ideal roles, but usually as the man of the soil, his hope of the future—treating him, however, no less unsparingly. All three have idealized in the person of the hero those qualities which they felt themselves to lack supremely.

Joyce, deriving from the mediaeval scholar, with the blood of the priest in him, is consumed by his inability to participate in the ordinary, everyday life of human beings. He creates Bloom, the shadow of *Odysseus*, Bloom the eternal Jew, the symbol of the outcast Irish race whose tragic story is so close to the author's heart. Bloom is the projected wanderer of Joyce's inner restlessness, of his dissatisfaction with the world. He is the man who is misunderstood and despised by the world, rejected by the world because he himself rejected the world. It is not so strange as at first blush it may seem that, searching for a counterpart to Daedalus, Joyce chose a Jew; instinctively he selected a type which has always given proof of its ability to arouse the passions and prejudices of the world.

In giving us Dublin Joyce gave us the scholar-priest's picture of the world as is. Dirty Dublin! Worse even than London, or Paris. The worst of all possible worlds! In this dirty sink of the world-as-is we have Bloom, the fictive image of the man in the street, crass, sensual, inquisitive but unimaginative—the educated nincompoop hypnotized by the abracadabra of scientific jargon. Molly Bloom, the Dublin slut, is an even more successful image of the common run. Molly Bloom is an archetype of the eternal feminine. She is the rejected mother whom the scholar and priest in Joyce had to liquidate. She is the veridic whore of creation. By comparison, Bloom is a comic figure. Like the ordinary man, he is a medal without a reverse. And like the ordinary man, he is most ludicrous when he is being made cocu. It is the most persistent, the most fundamental image of himself which the "average" man retains in this woman's world of to-day where his importance is so negligible.

Charlus, on the other hand, is a colossal figure, and Proust has handled him in colossal fashion. As symbol of the dying world of caste, ideals, manners, etc., Charlus was selected, whether with thought or not, from the forefront of the enemy's ranks. Proust, we know, was outside that world which he has so minutely described. As a pushing little Jew, he fought or wormed his way inside—and with disastrous results. Always shy, timid, awkward, embarrassed. Always a bit ridiculous. A sort of cultivated Chaplin! And, characteristically, this world which he so ardently desired to join he ended by despising. It is a repetition of the Jew's eternal fight with an alien world. A perpetual effort to become part of this hostile world and then, because of inability to become assimilated, rejecting it or destroying it. But if it is typical of the mechanism of the Jew, it is no less typical of the artist. And, true artist that he was, thoroughly sincere, Proust chose the best example of that alien world for his hero, Charlus. Did he not, in part, become like that hero himself later on, in his unnatural effort to become assimilated? For Charlus, though he had his counterpart in reality, quite as famous as the fictive creation, Charlus is, nevertheless, the image of the later Proust. He is, indeed, the image of a whole world of aesthetes who have now incorporated under the banner of homosexualism.

The beautiful figure of the grandmother, and of the mother, the sane, touching, moral atmosphere of the household, so pure and integrated, so thoroughly Jewish, stands opposed to the glamorous, the romantic, alien world of the Gentile which attracts and corrodes. It stands out in sharp contrast to the milieu from which Joyce sprang. Where Joyce leaned on the Catholic Church and its traditional masters of exegesis, thoroughly vitiated by the arid intellectualism of his caste, we have in Proust the austere atmosphere of the Jewish home contaminated by a hostile culture, the most strongly rooted culture left in the Western world—French Hellenism. We have an uneasiness, a maladjustment, a war in the spiritual realm which, projected in the novel, continued throughout his life. Proust was touched only superficially by French culture. His art is eminently un-French. We have only to think of his devout admiration for Ruskin. Ruskin! of all men!

And so, in describing the decay of his little world, this microcosm which was for him the world, in depicting the disintegration of his hero, Charlus, Proust sets before us the collapse of the outer and the inner world. The battleground of love, which began normally enough with Gilberte, becomes transferred, as in the world

117

to-day, to that plane of depolarized love wherein the sexes fuse, the world where doubt and jealousy, thrown out of their normal axes, play diabolical roles. Where in Joyce's world a thoroughly normal obscenity slops over into a slimy, glaucous fluid in which life sticks, in Proust's world vice, perversion, loss of sex breaks out like a pox and corrodes everything.

In their analysis and portrayal of disintegration both Proust and Joyce are unequalled, excepting perhaps by Dostoievski and Petronius. They are both *objective* in their treatment—technically classic, though romantic at heart. They are naturalists who present the world as they find it, and say nothing about the causes, nor derive from their findings any conclusions. They are defeatists, men who escape from a cruel, hideous, loathsome reality into ART. After writing the last volume, with its memorable treatise on art, Proust goes back to his death-bed to revise the pages on Albertine. This episode is the core and climax of his great work. It forms the arch of that Inferno into which the mature Proust descended. For if, retiring ever deeper into the labyrinth, Proust had cast a glance back at that which he left behind, he must have seen there in the figure of woman that image of himself in which all life was mirrored. It was an image which tantalized him, an image which lied to him from every reflection, because he had penetrated to an underworld in which there were nothing but shadows and distortions. The world he had walked out on was the masculine world in process of dissolution. With Albertine as the clue, with this single thread in his hand which, despite all the anguish and sorrow of knowledge he refuses to let slip, he feels his way along the hollows of the nerves, through a vast, subterranean world of remembered sensations in which he hears the pumping of the heart but knows not whence it comes, or what it is.

It has been said that *Hamlet* is the incarnation of doubt, and

Othello the incarnation of jealousy, and so they may be, but—the episode of Albertine, reached after an interval of several centuries of deterioration, seems to me a dramaturgic study of doubt and jealousy so infinitely more vast and complex than either *Hamlet* or *Othello* that the Shakespearean dramas, by comparison, resemble the feeble sketches which later are to assume the dimensions of a great fresco. This tremendous convulsion of doubt and jealousy which dominates the book is the reflection of that supreme struggle with Fate which characterizes our entire European history. To-day we see about us Hamlets and Othellos by the thousands—such Hamlets, such Othellos, as Shakespeare never dreamed of, such as would make him sweat with pride could he turn over in his grave. This theme of doubt and jealousy, to seize upon its most salient aspects only, is in reality only the reverberation of a much greater theme, a theme more complex, more ramified, which has become heightened, or *muddied*, if you like, in the interval of time between Shakespeare and Proust. Jealousy is the little symbol of that struggle with Fate which is revealed through doubt. The poison of doubt, of introspection, of conscience, of idealism, overflowing into the arena of sex, develops the marvellous bacillus of jealousy which, to be sure, will ever exist, but which in the past, when life ran high, was held in place and served its proper role and function. Doubt and jealousy are those points of resistance on which the great whet their strength, from which they rear their towering structures, their *masculine* world. When doubt and jealousy run amok it is because the body has been defeated, because the spirit languishes and the soul becomes unloosed. Then it is that the germs work their havoc and men no longer know whether they are devils or angels, nor whether women are to be shunned or worshiped, nor whether homosexuality is a vice or a blessing. Alternating between the most ferocious display of cruelty and the most

119

supine acquiescence we have conflicts, revolutions, holocausts—over *trifles, over nothing*. The last war, for example. The loss of sex polarity is part and parcel of the larger disintegration, the reflex of the soul's death, and coincident with the disappearance of great men, great deeds, great causes, great wars, etc.

Herein lies the importance of Proust's epic work, for here in the Albertine episode we have the problem of love and jealousy depicted in Gargantuan fashion, the malady become all-inclusive, turning in on itself through the inversion of sex. The great Shakespearean dramas were but the announcement of a disease which had just begun to run its staggering course; in Shakespeare's time it had not yet eaten into every layer of life, it could still be made the subject of heroic drama. There was man and there was the disease, and the conflict was the material for drama. But now the toxin is in the blood. For such as us, who have been eaten away by the virus, the great dramatic themes of Shakespeare are but swashbuckling oratory and pasteboard sets. Their impression is nil. We have become inoculated. And it is in Proust that we can sense the deterioration of the heroic, the cessation of conflict, the surrender, the thing become itself.

I repeat that we have in our midst to-day greater Hamlets, greater Othellos, than Shakespeare ever dreamed of. We have now the ripe fruit of the seeds planted by the masters of old. Like some marvellous unicellular organism in endless process of exfoliation these types reveal to us all the varieties of body cells which formerly entered into the making of blood, bone, muscle, hair, teeth, nails, etc. We have now the monstrous flower whose roots were watered by the Christian myth. We are living amidst the ruins of a world in collapse, amidst the husks which must rot away to make new loam.

This formidable picture of the world-as-disease which Proust and

Joyce have given us is indeed less a picture than a microscopic study which, because we see it magnified, prevents us from recognizing it as the world of everyday in which we are swimming. Just as the art of psycho-analysis could not have arisen until society was sick enough to call for this peculiar form of therapy, so we could not have had a faithful image of our time until there arose in our midst monsters so ridden with the disease that their works resemble the disease itself.

Seizing upon the malodorous quality in Proust's work Edmund Wilson, the American critic, is moved to doubt the authenticity of the narrative. "When Albertine finally leaves him", he writes, "the emotional life of the book becomes progressively asphyxiated by the infernal fumes which Charlus has brought with him—until such a large percentage of the characters have tragically, gruesomely, irrevocably turned out to be homosexual that we begin for the first time to find the story a little incredible". Of course it is incredible—from a realistic point of view! It is incredible, as are all authentic revelations of life, because it is too true. We have modulated into a higher realm of reality. It is not the author whom we should take to task, but life. The Baron de Charlus, like Albertine again, is precisely the illuminating figure on which to rivet attention. Charlus is Proust's supreme creation, his "hero", if this work can be said to have a hero. To call the Baron's behavior, or that of his satellites and imitators, incredible, is to deny the validity of Proust's whole edifice. Into the character of Charlus (derived from many accurately studied prototypes), Proust poured all that he knew of the subject of perversion, and that subject dominates the entire work—justly. Do we not know that he originally contemplated labelling the whole work by the title given to the cornerstone of his work—Sodom and Gomorrah! Sodom and Gomorrah! Do I not detect here a little of the smell of Ruskin?

At any rate, it is indisputable that Charlus is his grand effort. Like Stavrogin for Dostoievski, Charlus was the supreme test. Like Stavrogin also, observe how the figure of Charlus permeates and dominates the atmosphere when off scene, how the poison of his being shoots its virus into the other characters, the other scenes, the other dramas, so that from the moment of his entry, or even before, the atmosphere is saturated with his noxious gases. In analyzing Charlus, in ridiculing and pillorying him Proust, like Dostoievski, was endeavoring to expose himself, to understand himself perhaps.

When, in *The Captive*, Marcel and Albertine are discussing Dostoievski, Marcel feebly endeavoring to give a satisfactory response to Albertine's questions, how little did Proust realize, I wonder, that in creating the Baron de Charlus he was giving her the answer which then he seemed incapable of. The discussion, it may be recalled, centered about Dostoievski's propensities for depicting the ugly, the sordid, particularly his prepossession for the subject of *crime*. Albertine had remarked that crime was an obsession with Dostoievski, and Marcel, after venturing some rather weak remarks about the multiple nature of genius, dismisses the subject with something to the effect that *that* side of Dostoievski really interested him but little, that in truth he found himself incapable of understanding it.

Nevertheless, when it came to the delineation of Charlus, Proust showed himself capable of performing a prodigious piece of creative imagination. Charlus seems so removed from Proust's actual experience of life that people often wonder where he gathered the elements for his creation. Where? In his own soul! Dostoievski was not a criminal, not a murderer, Dostoievski never *lived* the life of Stavrogin. But Dostoievski was obsessed with the *idea* of a Stavrogin. He *had* to create him in order to live out his *other* life, his life as a creator. Little matter that he may have known a Stavrogin in the course of his manifold experiences. Little matter that Proust had under his eye the *actual* figure of Charlus. The originals, if not discarded, were certainly radically recast, transformed, in the light of inner truth, inner vision. In both Dostoievski and Proust there existed a Stavrogin, a Charlus, far more real than the actual figures. For Dostoievski the character of Stavrogin was bound up with the search for God. Stavrogin was the ideal image of himself which Dostoievski jealously preserved. More than that—Stavrogin was the god in him, the fullest portrait of God which Dostoievski could give.

Between Stavrogin and Charlus, however, there is an enormous gulf. It is the difference between Dostoievski and Proust, or if you like, the difference between the man of God whose hero is himself and the modern man for whom not even God can be a hero. All of Dostoievski's work is pregnant with conflict, *heroic* conflict. In an essay on *Aristocracy* Lawrence writes—"Being alive constitutes an aristocracy which there is no getting beyond. He who is most alive, intrinsically, is King, whether men admit it or not . . . More life! More *vivid* life! Not more safe cabbages, or meaningless masses of people. All creation contributes, and must contribute to this: towards the achieving of a vaster, vivider, cycle of life. That is the goal of living. He who gets nearer the sun is leader, the aristocrat of aristocrats. Or he who, like Dostoievski, gets nearest the moon of our not-being".

Proust, early in life, relinquished this conflict. As did Joyce. Their art is based on submission, on surrender to the stagnant flux. The Absolute remains outside their works, dominates them, destroys them, just as in life idealism dominates and destroys the ordinary man. But Dostoievski, confronted by even greater powers of frustration, boldly set himself to grapple with the mystery; he crucified himself for this purpose. And so, wherever in his works there is chaos and confusion, it is a rich chaos, a meaningful confusion; it is positive, vital, soul-infected. It is the aura of the beyond, of the unattainable, that sheds its lustre over his scenes and characters—not a dead, dire obscurity. Needless to say, with Proust and Joyce there is an obscurity of another order. With the former we enter the twilight zone of the mind, a realm shot through with dazzling splendors, but always the pale lucidity, the insufferable, obsessional lucidity of the mind. With Joyce we have the night mind, a profusion even more incredible, more dazzling than with Proust, as though the last intervening barriers of the soul had been broken down. But again, a mind!

Whereas with Dostoievski, though the mind is always there, always effective and powerfully operative, it is nevertheless a mind constantly held in leash, subordinated to the demands of the soul. It works as mind should work—that is, as machinery, and not as generative power. With Proust and Joyce the mind seems to resemble a machine set in motion by a human hand and then abandoned. It runs on perpetually, or will, until another human hand stops it. Does anybody believe that for either of these men death could be anything but an accidental interruption? When did death occur for them? Technically one is still alive. But were they not both dead before they commenced to write?

It is in Joyce that one observes that peculiar failing of the modern artist—the inability to communicate with his audience. Not a wholly new phenomenon, admitted, but always a significant one. Endowed with a Rabelaisian ability for word invention, embittered by the domination of a church for which his intellect had no use, harassed by the lack of understanding on the part of family and friends, obsessed by the parental image against which he vainly rebels, Joyce has been seeking escape in the erection of a fortress composed of meaningless verbiage. His language is a ferocious masturbation carried on in fourteen tongues. It is a dervish executed on the periphery of meaning, an orgasm not of blood and semen, but of dead slag from the burnt out crater of the mind. The Revolution of the Word which his work seems to have inspired in his disciples is the logical outcome of this sterile dance of death.

Joyce's exploration of the night world, his obsession with myth, dream, legend, all the processes of the unconscious mind, his tearing apart of the very instrument itself and the creating of his own world of phantasy, is very much akin to Proust's dilemma. Ultra-civilized products, both, we find them rejecting all question of soul; we find them sceptical of science itself, though bearing witness through their works of an unadmitted allegiance to the principle of causality, which is the very cornerstone of science. Proust, imagining himself to be making of his life a book, of his suffering a poem, exhibits through his microscopic and caustic analysis of man and society the plight of the modern artist for whom there is no faith, no meaning, no life. His work is the most triumphant monument to disillusionment that has ever been erected.

At the root of it was his inability, confessed and repeatedly glorified, to cope with reality—the constant plaint of the modern man. As a matter of fact, his life was a living death, and it is for this reason that his case interests us. For, intensely aware of his predicament, he has given us a record of the age in which he found himself imprisoned. Proust has said that the idea of death kept him company as incessantly as the idea of his own identity. That idea relates, as we know, to that night when, as he says himself, "his parents first indulged him". That night which "dates the decline of the will" also dates his death. Thenceforth he is incapable of living in the world—of *accepting* the world. From that night on he is dead to the world, except for those brief intermittent flashes which not only illuminate the dense fog which is his work but which made his work possible. By a miracle, familiar enough now to the psychiatrist, he stepped beyond the threshold of death. His work like his life, was a biological continuum punctuated by the meaningless interruption of statistical death.

And so it is no surprise when, standing on the two uneven flagstones and re-experiencing to the ultimate degree those sensational truths which had assailed him several times during the course of his life, he proceeds with a clarity and subtlety unrivalled to develop those thoughts which contain his final and highest views of life and art—magnificent pages dedicated to a lost cause. Here, when he speaks of the artist's instincts, his necessity to obey the small, inner voice, to eschew realism and simply to "translate" what is there ever surging upward, ever struggling for expression, here we realize with devastating intensity that for him, Proust, life was not a living, but a feasting upon sunken treasures, a life of retrospect; we realize that for him what joy remained was nothing but the joy of the archeologist in rediscovering the relics and ruins of the past, of musing among these buried treasures and re-imagining the life that had once given form to these dead things. And yet, sad as it is to contemplate the grandeur and nobility of these pages, moving as it is to observe that a great work had been built up out of suffering and disease, it is also tonic to realize that in these same passages there had been dealt the death-blow to that school of realism which, pretending to be dead, had resuscitated itself under the guise of psychologism. After all Proust was concerned with a view of life; his work has meaning and content, his characters do live, however distorted they are made to seem by his laboratory method of dissection and analysis. Proust was pre-eminently a man of the 19th century, with all the tastes, the ideology, and the respect for the powers of the conscious mind which dominated the men of that epoch. His work now seems like the labor of a man who has revealed to us the absolute limits of such a mind.

The breakdown which, in the realm of painting, gave rise to the school of Impressionism is evident also in Proust's literary method. The process of examining the medium itself, of subjecting the external world to microscopic analysis, thereby creating a new perspective and hence the illusion of a new world, has its counterpart in Proust's technique. Weary of realism and naturalism, as were the painters, or rather finding the existent picture of reality unsatisfying, unreal, owing to the explorations of the physicists, Proust strove, through the elaborate diffraction of incident and character, to displace the psychologic realism of the day. His attitude is coincident with the emergence of the new analytical psychology. Throughout those veritably ecstatic passages in the last volume of his work—the passages on the function of art and the role of the artist—Proust finally achieves a clarity of vision which presages the finish of his own method and the birth of a wholly new kind of artist. Just as the physicists, in their exploration of the material nature of the universe, arrived at the brink of a new and mysterious realm, so Proust, pushing his powers of analysis to the utmost limits, arrived at that frontier between dream and reality which henceforth will be the domain of the truly creative artists.

It is when we come to Joyce, who succeeds Proust by a short interval, that we notice the change in the psychologic atmosphere. Joyce who in his early work gives us a romantic confessional account of the "I", suddenly moves over into a new domain. Though smaller in scope, the canvas which Joyce employs gives the illusion of being even more vast than Proust's; we lose ourselves in it, not as with Proust, in dream fashion, but as one loses himself in a strange city. Despite all the analysis, Proust's world is still a world

127

of nature, of monstrous yet live fauna and flora. With Joyce we enter the inorganic world—the kingdom of minerals, of fossil and ruin, of dead dodos. The difference in technique is more than remarkable—it is significant of a wholly new order of sensation. We are done now with the 19th century sensibility of Proust; it is no longer through the nerves that we receive our impressions, no longer a personal and sub-conscious memory ejecting its images. As we read *Ulysses* we have the impression that the mind has become a recording machine: we are aware of a double world as we move with the author through the great labyrinth of the city. It is a perpetual day dream in which the mind of the sick scholar runs amok.

And, just as Proust's animus was directed against that little society which had first snubbed him, so with Joyce the satire and the bitterness is directed towards the philistine world of which he remains the eternal enemy. Joyce is not a realist, nor even a psychologist; there is no attempt to build up character—there are caricatures of humanity only, types which enable him to vent his satire, his hatred, to lampoon, to vilify. For at bottom there is in Joyce a profound hatred for humanity—the scholar's hatred. One realizes that he has the neurotic's fear of entering the living world, the world of men and women in which he is powerless to function. He is in revolt not against institutions, but against mankind. Man to him is pitiable, ridiculous, grotesque. And even more so are man's ideas—not that he is without understanding of them, but that they have no validity for him; they are ideas which would connect him with a world from which he has divorced himself. His is a medieval mind born too late: he has the taste of the recluse, the morals of an anchorite, with all the masturbative machinery which such a life entrains. A Romantic who wished to embrace life realistically, an idealist whose ideals were bankrupt, he was faced with a dilemma which he was incapable of resolving. There was only one way out—to plunge into the collective realm of phantasy. As he spun out the fabric of his dreams he also unloaded the poison that had accumulated in his system. *Ulysses* is like a vomit spilled by a delicate child whose stomach has been overloaded with sweetmeats. "So rich was its delivery, its pent-up outpouring so vehement", says Wyndham Lewis, "that it will remain eternally a cathartic, a monument like a record diarrhoea". Despite the maze of facts, phenomena and incident detailed there is no grasp of life, no *picture* of life. There is neither an organic conception, nor a vital sense of life. We have the machinery of the mind turned loose upon a dead abstraction, *the city*, itself the product of abstractions.

It is in comparing this city-world, vague, diffuse, amorphous, with that narrower, but more integrated and still perfumed, if wholly decadent, world of Proust's that we realize the change which has come over the world in but a few years. The things men discussed in that artificial world of the Faubourg St. Germain no longer bear resemblance to that which passes for conversation in the streets and pubs and brothels of Dublin. That fragrance which emanates from the pages of Proust, what is it but the fragrance of a dying world, the last faint perfume of things running to seed?

When, via *Ulysses*, we penetrate Dublin and there detect the flora and fauna stratified in the memory of a highly civilized, highly sensitive being such as Joyce, we realize that the absence of fragrance, the deodorization, is the result of death. What seem to be alive and walking, loving, talking, drinking people are not people, but ghosts. The drama is one of liquefaction; it is not even static, as in Proust's case. Analysis is no longer possible because the organism is defunct. Instead of the examination of a dying, though still intact, organism, as with Proust, we find ourselves inspecting cell life, wasted organs, diseased membranes. A study in etiology, such as the Egyptologists give us in their post-mortems of post-mortems. A description of life via the mummy. The great Homeric figure of Ulysses, shrunk to the insignificant shadow now of Bloom, now of Daedalus, wanders through the dead and forsaken world of the big city; the anaemic, distorted and desiccated reflections of what were once epic events which Joyce is said to have plotted out in his famous ground-plan remain but simulacra, the shadow and tomb of ideas, events, people.

When one day the final interpretation of *Ulysses* is given us by the "anatomists of the soul" we shall have the most astounding revelations as to the significance of this work. Then indeed we shall know the full meaning of this "record diarrhoea". Perhaps then we shall see that not Homer but *defeat* forms the real ground-plan, the invisible pattern of his work.

In the famous chapter of question and answer is it wittingly or unwittingly that Joyce reveals the empty soul quality of the modern man, this wretch who is reduced to a bundle of tricks, this encyclopaedic ape who displays the most amazing technical facility? *Is Joyce this man who can imitate any style—even the text-book and the encyclopaedia?* This form of humor, in which Rabelais also indulged, is the specific remedy which the intellectual employs to defeat the moral man: it is the dissolvent with which he destroys a whole world of meaning. With the Dadaists and the Surrealists the powerful stress on humor was part of a conscious and deliberate attitude toward breaking down the old ideologies. We see the same phenomenon in Swift and Cervantes. But observe the difference between the humor of Rabelais, with whom the author of *Ulysses* is so frequently and unjustly compared, and Joyce. Mark the difference between that formidable Surrealist, Jonathan Swift, and the feeble iconoclasts who to-day call themselves Surrealists! Rabelais' humor was still healthy; it had a stomachic quality, it was inspired by the Holy Bottle. Whereas with our contemporaries it is all in the head, above the eyes—a vicious, envious, mean, malign, humorless mirth. To-day they are laughing out of desperation, out of despair. Humor? Hardly. A reflexive muscular twitch, rather—more gruesome than mirth-provoking. A sort of Onanistic laughter . . . In those marvellous passages where Joyce marries his rich excretory images to his sad mirth there is a poignant, wistful undercurrent which smells of reverence and idolatry. Reminiscent, too reminiscent, of those devout mediaeval louts who kneeled before the Pope to be anointed with dung.

In this same chapter of riddle and conundrum there is a profound despair, the despair of a man who is giving the works to the last myth—*Science*. That disintegration of the ego which was sounded in *Ulysses*, and is now being carried to the extreme limits in *Work in Progress*, does it not correspond faithfully to the outer, world disintegration? Do we not have here the finest example of that phenomenon touched on before—*schizophrenia?* The dissolution of the macrocosm goes hand in hand with the dissolution of the soul. With Joyce the Homeric figure goes over into its opposite; we see him splitting off into multitudes of characters, heroes, legendary figures, into trunks, arms, legs, into river, tree and rock and beast. Working down and down and down into the now stratified layers of the collective being, groping and groping for his lost soul, struggling like an heroic worm to re-enter the womb. What did he mean, Joyce, when on the eve of *Ulysses* he wrote that he wanted "to forge in the smithy of his soul the uncreated conscience of his race?" When he cried out—"No, mother, let me be; let me live!"—was that a cry of anguish from a soul imprisoned in the womb? That opening picture of the bright morning sea, the image of navel and scrotum, followed by the harrowing scene with the mother—everywhere and throughout the mother image. "I love everything that flows", he says to one of his admirers, and in his new book there are hundreds of rivers, including his own native Liffey. What a thirst! What a longing for the waters of life! If only he could be cast up again on a distant shore, in another clime, under different constellations! Sightless bard . . . lost soul . . . eternal wanderer. What longing, groping, seeking, searching for an all-merciful bosom, for the night in which to drown his restless, fruit-less spirit! Like the sun itself which, in the course of a day, rises from the sea and disappears again, so *Ulysses* takes its cosmic stance, rising with a curse and falling with a sigh. But like a sun that is up-to-date the split-hero of *Ulysses* wanders, not over the waters of life and death, but through the eternal, monotonous, mournful, empty, lugubrious streets of the big city—dirty Dublin, the sink of the world.

If the *Odyssey* was a remembrance of great deeds *Ulysses* is a forgetting. That black, restless, never-ending flow of words in which the twin-soul of Joyce is swept along like a clot of waste matter passing through the drains, this stupendous deluge of pus and ex-crement which washes through the book languidly seeking an out-let, at last gets choked and, rising like a tidal wave, blots out the whole shadowy world in which this shadowy epic was conceived. The chapter before the last, which is the work of a learned des-perado, is like the dynamiting of a dam. The dam, in the uncon-scious symbology of Joyce, is the last barrier of tradition and culture which must give way if man is to come into his own. Each idiotic question is a hole drilled by a madman and charged with dynamite; each idiotic answer is the detonation of a devastating explosion. Joyce, the mad baboon, herein gives the works to the patient ant-like industry of man which has accumulated about him like an iron ring of dead learning.

When the last vestige has been blown up comes the flood. The final chapter is a free fantasia such as has never been seen before in all literature. It is a transcription of the deluge—except that there is no ark. The stagnant cesspool of the cultural drama which comes again and again to nought in the world-city, this drama which was personified by the great whore of Babylon, is echoed in the timeless reverie of Molly Bloom whose ears are stuffed by the lapping of the black waters of death. The very image of Woman, Molly Bloom bulks large and enduring. Beside her the others are reduced to pygmies. Molly Bloom is water, tree, and earth. She is mystery, she is the devourer, the ocean of night in which the lost hero finally plunges, and with him the world.

There is something about Molly Bloom, as she lies a-dreaming on her dirty, crummy bed, which carries us back to primordial images. She is the quintessence of the great whore which is Woman, of Babylon the vessel of abominations. Floating, unresisting, eternal, all-contained, she is like the sea itself. Like the sea she is receptive, fecund, voracious, insatiable. She begets and she destroys; she nourishes and she devastates. With Molly Bloom, con anonyme, woman is restored to prime significance—as womb and matrix of life. She is the image of nature itself, as opposed to the illusory world which man, because of his insufficiency, vainly endeavors to displace.

And so, with a final, triumphant vengeance, with suicidal glee, all the threads which were dropped throughout the book are recapitulated; the pale, diminutive hero, reduced to an intestinal worm and carried like a tickling little phallus in the great body of the female, returns to the womb of nature, shorn of everything but the last symbol. In the long retrospective arc which is drawn we

133

have the whole trajectory of man's flight from unknown to unknown. The rainbow of history fades out. The great dissolution is accomplished. After that closing picture of Molly Bloom a-dreaming on her dirty bed we can say, as in Revelation—*And there shall be no more curse!* Henceforth no sin, no guilt, no fear, no repression, no longing, no pain of separation. The end is accomplished—man returns to the womb.

Jabberwhorl Cronstadt

HE LIVES IN THE BACK of a sunken garden, a sort of bosky glade shaded by whiffletrees and spinozas, by deodars and baobabs, a sort of queasy Buxtehude diapered with elytras and feluccas. You pass through a sentry box where the concierge twirls his mustache con furioso like in the last act of Ouida. They live on the third floor behind a mullioned belvedere filigreed with snaffled spaniels and sebaceous wens, with debentures and megrims hanging out to dry. Over the bell-push it says: JABBERWHORL CRONSTADT, poet, musician, herbologist, weather man, linguist, oceanographer, old clothes, colloids. Under this it reads: "Wipe your feet and blow your nose!" And under this is a rosette from a second-hand suit.

"There's something strange about all this," I said to my companion whose name is Dschilly Zilah Bey. "He must be having his period again."

After we had pushed the button we heard a baby crying, a squeaky, brassy wail like the end of a horse-knacker's dream.

Finally Katya comes to the door—Katya from Hesse-Cassel—and behind her, thin as a wafer and holding a bisque doll, stands little Pinochinni. And Pinochinni says: "You should go in the drawing-room, they aren't dressed yet." And when I asked would they be very long because we're famished she said, "Oh no! They've been dressing for hours. You are to look at the new poem father wrote to-day—it's on the mantelpiece."

And while Dschilly unwinds her serpentine scarf Pinochinni giggles and jiggles, saying oh, dear, what is the matter with the world anyway, everything is so behind-time and did you ever read about the lazy little girl who hid her toothpicks under the mattress? It's very strange, father read it to me out of a large iron book.

There is no poem on the mantelpiece, but there are other things —*The Anatomy of Melancholy*, an empty bottle of Pernod Fils, *The Opal Sea*, a slice of cut plug tobacco, hairpins, a street directory, an ocarina . . . and a machine to roll cigarettes. Under the machine are notes written on menus, calling cards, toilet paper, match boxes . . . "meet the Cuntess Cathcart at four" . . . "the opalescent mucus of Michelet" . . . "defluxions . . . cotyledons . . . phthisical" . . . "if Easter falls in Lady Day's lap, beware old England of the clap" . . . "from the ichor of which springs his successor" . . . "the reindeer, the otter, the marmink, the mink-frog".

The piano stands in a corner near the belvedere, a frail black box with silver candle-sticks; the black keys have been bitten off by the spaniels. There are albums marked Beethoven, Bach, Liszt,

Chopin, filled with bills, manicure sets, chess pieces, marbles and dice. When he is in good humor Cronstadt will open an album marked "Goya" and play something for you in the key of C. He can play operas, minuets, schottisches, rondos, sarabands, preludes, fugues, waltzes, military marches; he can play Czerny, Prokofief or Granados, he can even improvise and whistle a Provençal air at the same time. *But it must be in the key of C.*

So it doesn't matter how many black keys are missing or whether the spaniels breed or don't breed. If the bell gets out of order, if the toilet doesn't flush, if the poem isn't written, if the chandelier falls, if the rent isn't paid, if the water is shut off, if the maids are drunk, if the sink is stopped and the garbage rotting, if dandruff falls and the bed creaks, if the flowers are mildewed, if the milk turns, if the sink is greasy and the wall-paper fades, if the news is stale and calamities fail, if the breath is bad or the hands sticky, if the ice doesn't melt, if the pedals won't work, it's all one and come Christmas because everything can be played in the key of C if you get used to looking at the world that way.

Suddenly the door opens to admit an enormous epileptoid beast with fungoid whiskers. It is Jocatha the famished cat, a big, buggerish brute with a taupe fur and two black walnuts hidden under its kinkless tail. It runs about like a leopard, it lifts its hind leg like a dog, it micturates like an owl.

"I'm coming in a minute," says Jabberwhorl through the sash of the door. "I'm just putting on my pants."

Now Elsa comes in—Elsa from Bad Nauheim—and she places a tray with blood-red glasses on the mantelpiece. The beast is bounding and yowling and thrashing and caterwauling: he has a few grains of Cayenne pepper on the soft lily-pad of his nose, the butt of his nose soft as a dum-dum bullet. He thrashes about in large Siamese wrath and the bones in his tail are finer than the finest sardines. He claws the carpet and chews the wall-paper, he rolls into a spiral and unrolls like a corolla, he whisks the knots out of his tail, shakes the fungus out of his whiskers. He bites clean through the floor to the bone of the poem. He's in the key of C and mad clean through. He has magenta eyes, like old-fashioned vest buttons; he's mowsy and glaubrous, brown like arnica and then green as the Nile; he's quaky and qualmy and queasy and teasey; he chews chasubles and ripples rasubly.

Now Anna comes in—Anna from Hanover-Minden—and she brings cognac, red pepper, absinthe and a bottle of Worcestershire sauce. And with Anna come the little Temple cats—Lahore, Mysore and Cawnpore. They are all males, including the mother. They roll on the floor, with their shrunken skulls, and bugger each other mercilessly. And now the poet himself appears saying what time is it though time is a word he has stricken from his list, time sib to death. Death's the surd and time's the sib and now there is a little time between the acts, an oleo in which the straight man mixes a drink to get his stomach muscles twitching. Time, time, he says, shaking a little Cayenne pepper into his cognac. A time for everything, though I scarcely use the word any more, and so saying he examines the tail of Lahore which has a kink in it and scratching his own last coccyx he adds that the toilet has just been done in silver where you'll find a copy of *Humanité*.

"You're very beautiful," he says to Dschilly Zilah Bey and with that the door opens again and Jill comes forward in a chlamys of Nile green.

"Don't you think she's beautiful?" says Jab.

Everything has suddenly grown beautiful, even that big buggerish brute Jocatha with her walnuts brown as cinnamon and soft as lichee.

Blow the conch and tickle the clavicle! Jab's got a pain in the belly where his wife ought to have it. Once a month, regular as the moon, it comes over him and it lays him low, nor will inunctions do him any good. Nothing but cognac and Cayenne pepper—to start the stomach muscles twitching. "I'll give you three words," he says, "while the goose turns over in the pan: whimsical, dropsical, phthisical."

"Why don't you sit down?" says Jill. "He's got his period."

Cawnpore is lying on an album of 24 Preludes. "I'll play you a fast one," says Jab, and flinging back the cover of the little black box he goes plink, plank, plunk! "I'll do a tremolo," he says, and employing every finger of his right hand in quick succession he hits the white key C in the middle of the board and the chess pieces and the manicure sets and the unpaid bills rattle like drunken tiddledywinks. "That's technique!" he says, and his eyes are glaucous and rimed with hoar-frost. "There's only one thing travels as fast as light and that's angels. Only angels can travel as fast as light. It takes a thousand light years to get to the planet Uranus but nobody has ever been there and nobody is ever going to get there. Here's a Sunday newspaper from America. Did you ever notice how one reads the Sunday papers? First the rotagravure, then the funny sheet, then the sports column, then the magazine, then the theatre news, then the book reviews, then the headlines. Recapitulation. Ontogeny-phylogeny. Define your terms and you'll never use words like time, death, world, soul. In every statement there's a little error and the error grows bigger and bigger until the snake is scotched. The poem is the only flawless thing, provided you know what time it is. A poem is a web which the poet spins out of his own body according to a logarithmic calculus of his own divination. It's always right, because the poet starts from the center and works outward . . ."

The phone is ringing.

"Pythagoras was right . . . Newton was right . . . Einstein is right . . ."

"Answer the phone, will you!" says Jill.

"*Hello!* Oui, c'est le Monsieur Cronstadt. Et votre nom, s'il vous plaît? *Bimberg?* Listen, you speak English, don't you? So do I . . . *What?* Yes, I've got three apartments—to rent or to sell. *What?* Yes, there's a bath and a kitchen and a toilet too . . . No, a regular toilet. No, not in the hall—in the apartment. One you sit down on. Would you like it in silver or in gold leaf? *What?* No, the toilet! I've got a man here from Munich, he's a refugee. *Refugee! Hitler! Hitler! Compris?* Yeah, that's it. He's got a swastika on his chest, in blue . . . *What?* No, I'm serious. Are you serious? *What?* Listen, if you mean business it means cash . . . *Cash!* You've got to lay out *cash. What?* Well, that's the way things are done over here. The French don't believe in checks. I had a man last week, tried to do me out of 750 francs. Yeah, an American check. *What?* If you don't like that one I've got another one for you with a dumbwaiter. It's out of order now but it could be fixed. *What?* Oh, about a thousand francs. There's a billiard room on the top floor . . . *What?* No . . . no . . . no. Don't have such things over here. Listen, Mr. Bimberg, you've got to realize that you're in France now. Yeah, that's it . . . When in Rome . . . Listen, call me tomorrow morning, will you? I'm at dinner now. *Dinner.* I'm eating. *What?* Yeah, cash . . . 'bye!"

"You see," he says, hanging up, "that's how we do things in this house. Fast work, what? Real estate. You people are living in a fairyland. You think literature is everything. You eat literature. Now in this house we eat goose, for instance. Yeah, it's almost done now. *Anna! Wie geht es? Nicht fertig? Merde alors!* Three girls . . . refugees. I don't know where they come from. Somebody gave them our address. Fine girls. Hale, hearty, buxom, sound as a berry. No room for them in Germany. Einstein is busy writing poems about light. These girls want a job, a place to live. Do you know anybody who wants a maid? Fine girls. They're well educated. But it takes the three of them to make a meal. Katya, she's the best of the lot: she knows how to iron. That one, Anna—she borrowed my typewriter yesterday . . . said she wanted to write a poem. I'm not keeping you here to write poems, I said. In this house *I* write the poems—if there are any to write. You learn how to cook and darn the socks. She looked peeved. Listen, Anna, I said, you're living in an imaginary world. The world doesn't need any more poems. The world needs bread and butter. Can you produce more bread and butter? That's what the world wants. Learn French and you can help me with the real estate. Yeah, people have to have places to live in. Funny. But that's how the world is now. It was always like that, only people never believed it before. The world is made for the future . . . for the planet Uranus. Nobody will ever visit the planet Uranus, but that doesn't make any difference. People must live places and eat bread and butter. For the sake of the future. That's the way it was in the past. That's the way it will be in the future. *The present?* There's no such thing as the present. There's a word called Time, but nobody is able to define it. There's a past and there's a future, and Time runs through it like an electric current. The present is an imaginary condition, a dream state . . . *an oxymoron.* There's a word for you —I'll make you a present of it. Write a poem about it. I'm too busy . . . real estate presses. Must have goose and cranberry sauce . . . Listen, Jill, what was that word I was looking up yesterday?"

"Omoplate?" says Jill promptly.

"No, not that. Omo . . . omo . . ."

"Omphalos?"

"No, no. Omo . . . omo . . ."

"I've got it!" cries Jill. "*Omophagia!*"

"Omophagia, that's it! Do you like that word? Take it away with you! What's the matter? You're not drinking. Jill, where the hell's that cocktail shaker I found the other day in the dumb-waiter? Can you imagine it—a *cocktail shaker!* Anyway, you people seem to think that literature is something vitally necessary. It ain't. It's just literature. I could be making literature too—if I didn't have these refugees to feed. You want to know what the present is? Look at that window over there. No, not there . . . the one above. *There!* Every day they sit there at that table playing cards—just the two of them. She's always got on a red dress. And he's always shuffling the cards. *That's the present.* And if you add another word it becomes subjunctive . . ."

"Jesus, I'm going to see what those girls are doing," says Jill.

"No you don't! That's just what they're waiting for—for you to come and help them. They've got to learn that this is a *real* world. I want them to understand that. Afterwards I'll find them jobs. I've got lots of jobs on hand. First let them cook me a meal."

"Elsa says everything's ready. Come on, let's go inside."

"Anna, Anna, bring these bottles inside and put them on the table!"

Anna looks at Jabberwhorl helplessly.

"There you are! They haven't even learned to speak English yet. What am I going to do with them? Anna . . . *hier! 'Raus mit 'em! Versteht?* And pour yourself a drink, you blinking idiot!"

The dining room is softly lighted. There is a candelabra on the table and the service glitters. Just as we are sitting down the phone rings. Anna gathers up the long cord and brings the apparatus from the piano to the side-board just behind Cronstadt. "Hello!" he yells, and unslacking the long cord, "just like the intestines . . . *hello!* Oui! Oui, madame . . . je suis le Monsieur Cronstadt . . . et votre nom, s'il vous plaît? Oui, il y a un salon, un entresol, une cuisine, deux chambres à coucher, une salle de bain, un cabinet . . . oui, madame . . . Non, ce n'est pas cher, pas cher du tout . . . on peut s'arranger facilement . . . comme vous voulez, madame . . . A quelle heure? Oui . . . avec plaisir . . . *Comment?* Que dites-vous? Ah non! au contraire! Ça sera un plaisir . . . un *grand* plaisir . . . Au revoir, madame!" Slamming it up—Küss die Hand, madame! Would you like your back scratched, madame? Do you take milk with your coffee, madame? Will you . . . ?

"Listen," says Jill, "who the hell was that? You were pretty smooth with her. Oui, madame . . . non, madame! Did she promise to buy you a drink too?" Turning to us—"can you imagine it, he has an actress up here yesterday while I'm taking a bath . . . some trollop from the Casino de Paris . . . and she takes him out and gets him soused . . ."

"You don't tell that right, Jill. It's this way . . . I'm showing her a lovely apartment—with a dumbwaiter in it—and she says to me won't you show me your poetry—*poésie* . . . sounds better in French . . . and so I bring her up here and she says I'll have them printed for you in Belgian."

"Why Belgian, Jab?"

"Because that's what she was, a Belgian—or a Belgianess. Anyway, what difference does it make what language they're printed in? Somebody has to print them, otherwise nobody will read them."

"But what made her say that—so quick like?"

"Ask me! Because they're good, I suppose. Why else would people want to print poems?"

"Baloney!"

"See that! She doesn't believe me."

"Of course I don't! If I catch you bringing any prima donnas up here, or any toe dancers, or any trapeze artists, or anything that's French and wears skirts, there's going to be hell to pay. Especially if they offer to print your poems!"

"There you are," says Jabberwhorl, glaucous and glowbry. "That's why I'm in the real estate business . . . Go ahead and eat, you people . . . I'm watching."

He mixes another dose of cognac and pepper.

"I think you've had enough," says Jill. "Jesus, how many of them have you had to-day?"

"Funny," says Jabberwhorl, "I fixed her up all right a few moments ago—just before you came—but I can't fix myself up . . ."

"Jesus, where's that goose?" says Jill. "Excuse me, I'm going inside and see what the girls are doing."

"No you don't!" says Jab, pushing her back into her seat. "We're gonna sit right here and wait . . . wait and see what happens. Maybe the goose'll never come. We'll be sitting here waiting . . . waiting forever . . . just like this, with the candles and the empty soup plates and the curtains and . . . I can just imagine us sitting here like this and some one outside plastering a wall around us . . . We're sitting here waiting for Elsa to bring the goose and time passes and it gets dark and we sit here for days and days . . . See those candles? We'd eat 'em. And those flowers over there? Them too. We'd eat the chairs, we'd eat the side-board, we'd eat the alarm clock, we'd eat the cats, we'd eat the curtains, we'd eat the bills and the silverware and the wall-paper and the bugs underneath . . . we'd eat our own dung and that nice new fœtus Jill's got inside her . . . we'd eat each other . . ."

Just at this moment Pinochinni comes in to say good-night. She's hanging her head like and there's a quizzical look in her eye.

"What's the matter with you to-night?" says Jill. "You look worried."

144

"Oh, I don't know what it is," says the youngster. "There's something I want to ask you about . . . it's awfully complicated. I don't really know if I can say what I mean."

"What is it, snookums?" says Jab. "Say it right out in front of the lady and the gentleman. You know *him*, don't you? Come on, spit it out!"

The youngster is still holding her head down. Out of the corner of her eye she looks up at her father slyly and then suddenly she blurts out: "Oh, what's it all about? What are we here for anyway? Do we have to have a world? Is this the only world there is and why is it? That's what I want to know."

If Jabberwhorl Cronstadt was somewhat astonished he gave no sign of it. Picking up his cognac nonchalantly, and adding a little Cayenne pepper, he answered blithely: "Listen, kid, before I answer that question—if you *insist* on my answering that question —you'll have to first define your terms."

Just then there came a long shrill whistle from the garden.

"Mowgli!" says Cronstadt. "Tell him to come on up."

"Come up!" says Jill, stepping to the window.

No answer.

"He must have gone," says Jill. "I don't see him any more."

Now a woman's voice floats up. "*Il est saoul . . . complètement saoul.*"

"Take him home! Tell her to take him home!" yells Cronstadt.

"*Mon mari dit qu'il faut rentrer chez vous . . . oui, chez vous.*"

"*Y 'en a pas!*" floats up from the garden.

"Tell her not to lose my copy of Pound's *Cantos*," yells Cronstadt. "And don't ask them up again . . . we have no room here. Just enough space for German refugees."

"That's a shame," says Jill, coming back to the table.

"You're wrong again," says Jab. "It's very good for him."

"Oh, you're drunk," says Jill. "Where's that damned goose anyhow? Elsa! Elsa!"

"Never mind the goose, darling! This is a game. We're going to sit here and outlast 'em. The rule is, jam to-morrow and jam yesterday—but never jam to-day. Wouldn't it be wonderful if you people sat here just like you are and I began to grow smaller and smaller . . . until I got to be just a tiny, weeny little speck . . . so that you had to have a magnifying glass to see me? I'd be a little spot on the tablecloth and I'd be saying—Timoor . . . Ti-*moor!* And you'd say where is he? And I'd be saying—Timoor, logodaedaly, glycophosphates, Billancourt, Timoor . . . O timbus twaddle down the brawkish brake . . . and you'd say . . ."

"Jesus, Jab, you're drunk!" says Jill. And Jabberwhorl glausels with gleerious glitter, his awbrous orbs atwit and twitter.

"He'll be getting cold in a minute," says Jill, getting up to look for the Spanish cape.

"That's right," says Jab. "Whatever she says is right. You think I'm a very contrary person. You," he says, turning to me, "you with your Mongolian verbs, your transitives and intransitives, don't you see what an affable being I am? You're talking about China all the time . . . *this* is China, don't you see that? *This* . . . this what? Get me the cape, Jill, I'm cold. This is a terrible cold . . . subglacial cold. You people are warm, but I'm freezing. I can feel the ice caps coming down again. A fact. Everything is rolling along nicely, the dollar is falling, the apartments are rented, the refugees are all refuged, the piano is tuned, the bills are paid, the goose is cooked and what are we waiting for? *For the next Ice Age!* It's coming to-morrow morning. You'll go to the window and everything'll be frozen tight. No more problems, no more history, no more nothing. *Settled.* We'll be sitting here like this waiting for Anna to bring in the goose and suddenly the ice will roll over us.

146

I can feel the terrible cold already, the bread all icicled, the butter blenched, the goose gazzled, the walls wildish white. And that little angel, that bright new embryo that Jill's got under her belt, that'll be frozen in the womb, a glairy gawk with ice-cold wings and the lips of a snail. Jugger, jugger, and everything'll be still and quiet. Say something warm! My legs are frozen. Herodotus says that on the death of its father the phœnix embalms the body in an egg made of myrrh and once every five hundred years or so it conveys the little egg embalmed in myrrh from the desert of Arabia to the temple of the sun at Heliopolis. *Do you like that?* According to Pliny there is only one egg at a time and when the bird perceives that its end is near it builds a nest of cassia twigs and frankincense and dies upon it. From the body of the nest is born a little worm which becomes the phœnix. Hence *bennu*, symbol of the resurrection. *How's that?* I need something hotter. Here's another one . . . The fire-walkers in Bulgaria are called *Nistingares*. They dance in the fire on the 21st of May during the feast of Saint Helena and Saint Constantine. They dance on the red-hot embers until they're blue in the face, and then they utter prophecies."

"Don't like that at all," says Jill.

"Neither do I," says Jab. "I like the one about the little soul-worms that fly out of the nest for the resurrection. Jill's got one inside her too . . . it's sprouting and sprouting. Can't stop it. Yesterday it was a tad-pole, to-morrow it'll be a honeysuckle vine. Can't tell what it's going to be yet . . . not eventually. It dies in the nest every day and the next day it's born again. Put your ear to her belly . . . you can hear the whirring of its wings. Whirrrr . . . whirrrr. Without a motor. Wonderful! She's got millions of them inside her and they're all whirring around in there dying to get out. Whirrrr . . . whirrrr. And if you just put a needle inside and punctured the bag they'd all come whirring out . . . imagine it . . . a great cloud of soul-worms . . . millions of them . . . and so thick the swarm that we wouldn't be able to see each other . . . A fact! No need to write about China. Write about *that!* About what's inside of you . . . the great vertiginous vertebration . . . the zoospores and the leucocytes . . . the wamroths and the hohenlindens . . . every one's a poem. The jellyfish is a poem too—the finest kind of poem. You poke him here, you poke him there, he slithers and slathers, he's dithy and clabberous, he has a colon and intestines, he's vermiform and ubisquishous. And Mowgli in the garden whistling for the rent, he's a poem too, a poem with big ears, a wambly bretzular poem with logamundiddy of the goo-goo. He has round, auricular daedali, round robin-breasted ruches that open up like an open barouche. He wambles in the wambhorst whilst the whelkin winkles . . . he wabbles through the wendish wikes whirking his worstish wights . . . Mowgli . . . owgli . . . whist and wurst . . ."

"He's losing his mind," says Jill.

"Wrong again," says Jabber. "I've just found my mind, only it's a different sort of mind than you imagined. You think a poem must have covers around it. The moment you write a thing the poem ceases. The poem is the present which you can't define. You live it. Anything is a poem if it has time in it. You don't have to take a ferry-boat or go to China to write a poem. The finest poem I ever lived was a kitchen sink. Did I ever tell you about it? There were two faucets, one called Froid and the other Chaud. Froid lived a life *in extenso*, by means of a rubber hose attached to his schnausel. Chaud was bright and modest. Chaud dripped all the time, as if he had the clap. On Tuesdays and Fridays he went to the Mosque where there was a clinic for venereal faucets. Tuesdays and Fridays Froid had to do all the work. He was a bugger for work. It was his whole world. Chaud on the other hand had to be petted and coaxed. You had to say 'not so fast', or he'd scald the skin off you. Once in a while they worked in unison, Froid and Chaud, but that was seldom. Saturday nights, when I washed my feet at the sink, I'd get to thinking how perfect was the world over which these twain ruled. Never anything more than this iron sink with its two faucets. No beginnings and no ends. Chaud the alpha and Froid the omega. Perpetuity. The Gemini, ruling over life and death. Alpha-Chaud running out through all degrees of Fahrenheit and Reaumur, through magnetic filings and comets' tails, through the boiling cauldron of Mauna Loa into the dry light of the Tertiary moon; Omega-Froid running out through the Gulf Stream into the paludal bed of the Sargasso Sea, running through the marsupials and the foraminifera, through the mammal whales and the Polar fissures, running down through island universes, through dead cathodes, through dead bone and dry rot, through the follicles and tentacles of worlds unformed, worlds untouched, worlds unseen, worlds unborn and forever lost. Alpha-Chaud dripping, dripping; Omega-Froid working, working. Hands, feet, hair, face, dishes, vegetables, fish washed clean and away; despair, ennui, hatred, love, jealousy, crime . . . dripping, dripping. I, Jabberwhorl, and my wife Jill, and after us legions upon legions . . . all standing at the iron sink. Seeds falling down through the drain: young canteloupes, squash, caviar, macaroni, bile, spittle, phlegm, lettuce leaves, sardine bones, Worcestershire sauce, stale beer, urine, bloodclots, Kruschen salts, oatmeal, chew tobacco, pollen, dust, grease, wool, cotton threads, match sticks, live worms, shredded wheat, scalded milk, castor oil. Seeds of waste falling away forever and forever coming back in pure draughts of a miraculous chemical substance which refuses to be named, classified, labelled, analysed, or drawn and quartered. Coming back as Froid and Chaud perpetually, like a truth that can't be downed. You can take it hot or cold, or you can take it tepid. You can wash your feet or gargle your throat; you can rinse the soap out of your eyes or drive the grit out of the lettuce leaves; you can bathe the new-born babe or swab the rigid limbs of the dead; you can soak bread for fricadellas or dilute your wine. First and last things. Elixir. I, Jabberwhorl, tasting the elixir of life and death. I, Jabberwhorl, of waste and H^2O composed, of hot and cold and all the intermediate realms, of scum and rind, of finest, tiniest substance never lost, of great sutures and compact bone, of ice fissures and test tubes, of semen and ova fused, dissolved, dispersed, of rubber schnausel and brass spigot, of dead cathodes and squirming infusoria, of lettuce leaves and bottled sunlight . . . I, Jabberwhorl, sitting at the iron sink am perplexed and exalted, never less and never more than a poem, an iron stanza, a boiling follicle, a lost leucocyte. The iron sink where I spat out my heart, where I bathed my tender feet, where I held my first child, where I washed my sore gums, where I sang like a diamond-backed terrapin and I am singing now and will sing forever though the drains clog and the faucets rust, though time runs out and I be all there is of present, past and future. *Sing*, Froid, sing transitive! *Sing* Chaud, sing intransitive! Sing Alpha and Omega! Sing Hallelujah! Sing out, O sink! Sing while the world sinks . . ."

And singing loud and clear like a dead and stricken swan on the bed we laid him out.

An Open Letter to Surrealists Everywhere

BELOW THE BELT all men are brothers. Man has never known *solitude* except in the upper regions where one is either a poet or a madman—or a criminal. "To-day," writes Paul Eluard, "the solitude of poets is breaking down. They are now men among men, they have brothers." It is unfortunately too true, and that is why the poet is becoming more and more rare. I still prefer the anarchic life; unlike Paul Eluard I cannot say that the word "fraternisation" exalts me. Nor does it seem to me that this idea of brotherhood arises from a poetic conception of life. It is not at all what Lautréamont meant when he said that poetry must be made by all. The brotherhood of man is a permanent delusion common to idealists everywhere in all epochs: it is the reduction of the principle of individuation to the least common denominator of intelligibility. It is what leads the masses to identify themselves with movie stars and megalomaniacs like Hitler and Mussolini. It is what prevents them from reading and appreciating and being influenced by and creating in turn such poetry as Paul Eluard gives us. That Paul Eluard is desperately lonely, that he strives with might and main to establish communication with his fellow-man, I understand and subscribe to with all my heart. But when Paul Eluard goes down into the street and becomes a man he is not making himself understood and liked for what he is—*for the poet that he is,* I mean. On the contrary, he is establishing communication with his fellowmen by capitulation, by renunciation of his individuality, his high role. If he is accepted it is only because he is willing to surrender those qualities which differentiate him from his fellow-men and make him unsympathetic and unintelligible to them. It is not at all strange that madmen are put under lock and key and saviours crucified and prophets stoned. At any rate, one thing is certain: it is not in this way that poetry will be made by all.

(Query: And why should poetry be made by all? Why?)

In every age, just as in every life worthy of the name, there is the effort to re-establish that equilibrium which is disturbed by the power and tyranny which a few great individuals exercise over us. This struggle is fundamentally personal and religious. It has nothing to do with liberty and justice, which are idle words signifying nobody knows precisely what. It has to do with making poetry, or, if you will, with making life a poem. It has to do with the adoption of a creative attitude towards life. One of the most effective ways in which it expresses itself is in killing off the tyrannical influences wielded over us by those who are already dead. It consists not in denying these examplars, but in absorbing them, assimilating them, and eventually surpassing them. Each man has to do this for himself. There is no feasible scheme for universal liberation. The tragedy which surrounds the life of almost every great figure is forgotten in the admiration which we bestow on the man's work. It is forgotten that the glorious Greeks, whom we never cease admiring, treated their men of genius more shamefully, more cruelly perhaps than any other people we know of. It is forgotten that the mystery which attaches itself to Shakespeare's life is a mystery only because the English do not wish to admit that Shakespeare was driven mad by the stupidity, non-understanding and intolerance of his countrymen, that he finished his days in a mad-house.

Life is either a feast or a famine, as the old Chinese proverb goes. Right now it is pretty much of a famine. Without having recourse to the wisdom of such a sage as Freud, it is obvious that in times of famine men behave differently than when there is abundance. In times of famine one prowls the streets with a rapacious eye. One looks at his brother, sees in him a succulent morsel, and straightaway he waylays and devours him. This is done in the name of the revolution. The fact is that it doesn't matter much in what name it is done. When men get brotherly they also get slightly cannibalistic. In China, where famines are more frequent and more devastating, the people have become so hysterical (beneath the renowned Oriental mask) that when they see a man being executed they quite often forget themselves and laugh.

The famine which we are living through is a peculiar one in that it occurs in the midst of plenty. It is more of a *spiritual* famine, we might say, than a physical one. People are not fighting for bread this time, but for a *right* to their piece of bread, which is a distinction of some importance. Bread, figuratively speaking, is everywhere, but most of us are hungry. Shall I say—especially the poets? I ask because it is in the tradition of poets to starve. It is a little strange therefore to find them identifying their habitual physical hunger with the spiritual hunger of the masses. Or is it vice versa? Anyway, now we are all starving, except the rich, to be sure, and the smug bourgeoisie who have never known what it is to starve, either spiritually or physically.

Originally men killed one another in the direct pursuit of booty —food, weapons, implements, women, and so on. There was sense to it, even though there was no charity or sympathy. Now we have become sympathetic and charitable and brotherly, but we go on killing just the same, and we kill without the least hope of attaining our ends. We kill one another for the benefit of those to come, that they may enjoy a life more abundant. *(The hell we do!)*

There has been mention throughout this book on Surrealism *
of our great indebtedness to Freud et alia. But there is one thing which Freud and all his tribe have made painfully clear and which is singularly missing in this account of our supposed indebtedness. It is something like this . . . Every time we fail to strike or to kill the person who threatens to humiliate or degrade or enslave or enchain us we pay the penalty for it in collective suicide, which is war, or in fratricidal slaughter, which is revolution. Every day that we fail to live out the maximum of our potentialities we kill the Shakespeare, Dante, Homer, Christ which is in us. Every day that we live in harness with the woman whom we no longer love we destroy our power to love and to have the woman whom we merit. The age we live in is the age which suits us: it is we who make it, not God, not Capitalism, not this or that, call it by any name you like. The evil is in us—and the good too! But as the old bard said—"the good is oft interred with our bones."

The basic effectiveness of the psycho-analytic doctrine lies in the

* Surrealism, by Herbert Read (Faber and Faber Ltd.).

recognition of the creative aspect of responsibility. Neurosis is not a new phenomenon in the history of human maladies, nor is its most wonderful bloom, schizophrenia. This is not the first time that the cultural soil, and even the sub-soil, has become exhausted. This is a famine which goes to the roots, and it is not at all paradoxical, on the contrary, it is absolutely logical, that it should occur in the midst of plenty. In the midst of this rotting plenty it is altogether fitting and natural that we the living dead should sit like lepers with outstretched arms and beg a little charity. Or, get up and kill one another, which is a little more diverting, but which comes to the same thing in the end. That is, nullity.

When at last each man realizes that nothing is to be expected from God, or society, or friends, or benevolent tyrants, or democratic governments, or saints, or saviours, or even from the holiest of holies, *education*, when each man realizes that he must work with his own hands to save himself, and that he need expect no mercy, perhaps then . . . *Perhaps!* Even then, seeing what manner of men we are, I doubt. The point is that we are doomed. Maybe we are going to die to-morrow, maybe in the next five minutes. Let us take stock of ourselves. We can make the last five minutes worth while, entertaining, even gay, if you will, or dissipate them as we have the hours and the days and months and years and centuries. No god is coming to save us. No system of government, no belief will provide us with that liberty and justice which men whistle for with the death-rattle.

The renascence of wonder, which Mr. Read writes about, will be brought about, if it *is* brought about, by a few individuals for whom this phrase has vital significance, by those, in short, who are unable not to act in accordance with a truth perceived. What distinguishes the majority of men from the few is their inability to act according to their beliefs. The hero is he who raises himself above the crowd. He is not a hero because he lays down his life for his country, or for a cause or principle. Indeed, in making such a sacrifice he is often cowardly rather than heroic. To run with the herd, and die with the herd, is the natural animal instinct which man shares with other beasts. To be a pacifist is not necessarily heroic either. "For if a man," to quote from the devil himself, "is unprepared or unable to fight for his life, just Providence has already decreed his end." To fight for one's life, though Herr Hitler did not mean it this way, usually means to lose one's life. To get men to rally round a cause, a belief, an idea, is always easier than to persuade them to lead their own lives. We live in the swarm and our fine principles, our glorious ideas, are but blinders which we put over our eyes in order to make death palatable. We have not advanced a peg beyond the primitive man's idea of the fertility of death. Since the dawn of civilization we have been killing one another off—on *principle*. The fact is—I must repeat it again because the Surrealists are guilty of the same mistake as all other warring idealists—that human beings have an imperative need to kill. The distinguishing trait of the civilized man is that he kills *en masse*. Sadder than that, however, is the fact that *he lives the life of the masses*. His life is lived according to totem and taboo, as much now as in the past, even more, perhaps.

The role which the artist plays in society is to revive the primitive, anarchic instincts which have been sacrificed for the illusion of living in comfort. If the artist fails we will not necessarily have a return to an imaginary Eden filled with wonder and cruelty. I am afraid, on the contrary, that we are much more apt to have a condition of perpetual work, such as we see in the insect world. Myself I do not believe that the artist will fail. On the other hand, it doesn't matter a damn to me whether he fails or not. It is a problem beyond my scope. If I choose to remain an artist rather than go down in the street and shoulder a musket or sling a stick of dynamite it is because my life as an artist suits me down to the ground. It is not the most comfortable life in the world but I know that it is *life*, and I am not going to trade it for an anonymous life in the brotherhood of man—which is either sure death, or quasi-death, or at the very best cruel deception. I am fatuous enough to believe that in living my own life in my own way I am more apt to give life to others (though even that is not my chief concern) than I would if I simply followed somebody else's idea of how to live my life and thus become a man among men. It seems to me that this struggle for liberty and justice is a confession or admission on the part of all those engaging in such a struggle that they have failed to live their own lives. Let us not deceive ourselves about "humanitarian impulses" on the part of the great brotherhood. The fight is for life, to have it more abundantly, and the fact that millions are now ready to fight for something they have ignominiously surrendered for the greater part of their lives does not make it more *humanitarian*.

"I came not to bring peace, but a sword!" said the great humanitarian. That is not the utterance of a militarist, nor is it the utterance of a pacifist: it is the utterance of one of the greatest artists that ever lived. If his words mean anything they mean that the struggle for life, for more life, must be carried on day by day. It means that life itself is struggle, *perpetual struggle*. This sounds almost banal, and in fact it has become banal, thanks to the frog-like perspective of Darwin and such like. Banal because our struggle has become banal, because our struggle is for food and shelter—not even that, by God, but *for work*. Men are struggling for the right to work! It sounds almost incredible but that is precisely what it amounts to, the great goal of the civilized man. What an heroic struggle! Well, for my part, I will say that whatever else I may want, I know I don't want work.

To live as an artist I stopped work some ten or twelve years ago. I made it extremely uncomfortable for myself. I cannot even say that it was a matter of choice, my decision. I had to do it, or die of boredom. Naturally I was not paid to stop work and live as an artist. The time came quickly enough when I had to beg for a crust of bread. They said strange things to me, those whom I asked for food or shelter. Brother, said one man, why didn't you save your money for a rainy day? Said another: brother, open your heart to God that you may be saved. And another: join the union and we will find you a job so that you may eat and have a place to sleep. None of them gave me money, which is all I had asked for. I realized that I was ostracized and I understood quickly enough that this was just, because if one chooses to live his own life in his own way he must pay the penalty.

I cannot help seeing in men what I know them to be from my own experience of life. Their illusions and delusions are poignantly touching to me, but they do not convince me that I should offer my life for them. It seems to me that the men who would create a Fascist world are the same at heart as those who would create a Communist world. They are all looking for leaders who will provide them with enough work to give them food and shelter. I am looking for something more than that, something which no leader can give me. I am not against leaders per se. On the contrary, I know how necessary they are. They will be necessary so long as men are insufficient unto themselves. As for myself, I need no leader and no god. I am my own leader and my own god. I make my own bibles. *I believe in myself*—that is my whole credo.

An age such as ours is the most difficult one of all for an artist. There is no place for him. At least, that is what one hears on all sides. Nevertheless, some few artists of our time have made a place for themselves. Picasso made a place for himself. Joyce made a

158

place for himself. Matisse made a place for himself. Céline made a place for himself. Should I rattle off the whole list? Perhaps the greatest of them all has not yet made a place for himself. But who is he? Where is he? If he is the greatest of all he will make himself heard. He will not be able to conceal himself.

Those who are perpetually talking about the inability to communicate with the world—have they made every effort? Have they learned what it is to "compromise"? Have they learned how to be as wise and cunning as the serpent, as well as strong and obstinate as a bull? Or are they braying like donkeys, whining about some ideal condition in the ever-receding future when every man will be recognized and rewarded for his labors? Do they really expect such a day to dawn, these simple souls?

I feel that I have some right to speak about the difficulty of establishing communication with the world since my books are banned in the only countries where I can be read in my own tongue. I have enough faith in myself however to know that I eventually will make myself heard, if not understood. Everything I write is loaded with the dynamite which will one day destroy the barriers erected about me. If I fail it will be because I did not put enough dynamite into my words. And so, while I have the strength and the gusto I will load my words with dynamite. I know that the timid, crawling ones who are my real enemies are not going to meet me face to face in fair combat. *I know these birds!* I know that the only way to get at them is to reach up inside them, through the scrotum; one has to get up inside and twist their sacred entrails for them. That's what Rimbaud did. That's what Lautréamont did. Unfortunately, those who call themselves their successors have never learned this technique. They give us a lot of piffle about the revolution—first the revolution of the word, now the revolution in the street. How are they going to make themselves heard and understood if they are going to use a language which is emasculated? Are they writing their beautiful poems for the angels above? Is it communication with the dead which they are trying to establish?

You want to communicate. All right, communicate! Use any and every means. If you expect the world to fall for your lingo because it is the right lingo, or even the *left* lingo, you are going to be cruelly deceived. It's like the "pug" who goes into the ring expecting to get it over with quickly. Generally he gets flattened stiff as a board. He thinks he'll deliver an uppercut or a swift one to the solar plexus. He forgets to defend himself. He lays himself wide open. Everybody who's gone out to fight has had to first learn something about the strategy of the ring. The man who refuses to learn how to box becomes what is called, in the language of the ring, "a glutton for punishment." Speaking for myself, I'll say that I've taken all the punishment I could assimilate. From now on I use my head, my bean, as they say. I watch for an opening. I do a little fancy stepping. I duck. I feint. I spar a bit, I bide my time. When the moment comes I let go with all my might.

I am against revolutions because they always involve a return to *status quo*. I am against the *status quo* both *before* and *after* revolutions. I don't want to wear a black shirt or a red shirt. I want to wear the shirt that suits my taste. And I don't want to salute like an automaton either. I prefer to shake hands when I meet someone I like. The fact is, to put it simply, I am positively against all this crap which is carried on first in the name of this thing, then in the name of that. I believe only in what is active, immediate and personal.

I was writing Surrealistically in America before I had ever heard the word. Of course I got a good kick in the pants for it. I wrote for ten years in America without once having a manuscript accepted. I had to beg, borrow and steal in order to get by. Finally I got out of the country. As a foreigner in Paris, without friends, I went through an even worse ordeal, though in another sense it was a thousand times better than the American experience. I grew so desperate that finally I decided to explode—and I did explode. The naive English critics, in their polite, asinine way, talk about the "hero" of my book (*Tropic of Cancer*) as though he were a character I had invented. I made it as plain as could be that I was talking in that book about myself. I used my own name throughout. I didn't write a piece of fiction: I wrote an autobiographical document, a *human* book.

I mention this only because this book marks a turning point in my literary career—I should say, *in my life*. At a certain point in my life I decided that henceforth I would write about myself, my friends, my experiences, what I knew and what I had seen with my own eyes. Anything else, in my opinion, is literature, and *I am not interested in literature*. I realized also that I should have to learn to content myself with what was within my grasp, my scope, my personal ken. I learned not to be ashamed of myself, to talk freely about myself, to advertise myself, to elbow my way in here and there when necessary. The greatest man America ever produced was not ashamed to peddle his own book from door to door. He had faith in himself and he has given tremendous faith to others. Goethe too was not ashamed to beg a friend to put in a good word for him with the critics. Gide and Proust were not ashamed to publish their first books at their own expense. Joyce had the courage to search for years for the person who would publish his *Ulysses*. Was the world better then? Were people more kind, more intelligent, more sympathetic, more understanding? Did Milton get a reasonable price for his *Paradise Lost*? I could go on multiplying instance after instance. What's the use?

Justice you ask for! Well, every day life metes out an inexorable justice. It's not ideal, it may not even be intelligent—from the viewpoint of a Marxian dialectician. But it's justice. The English are particularly noted for shouting about liberty and justice. They make a great point always about "fair play", even in war. As though war were a game played according to rules. But in crucial matters the English have never indulged in "fair play". If they had they would not own the vast empire on which the sun never sets, as they so fatuously boast. No, the English may *talk* about fair play, but in practice they have always employed the most dastardly tactics.

I know little about history, politics, literature, art, science, philosophy, religion, etc. I know only what I have seized through experience. I put no trust in the men who explain life to us in terms of history, economics, art, etc. They are the fellows who bugger us up, juggling their abstract ideas. I think it is a piece of the most cruel deception to urge men to place their hopes of justice in some external order, some form of government, some social order, some system of ideal rights. I read every day somewhere or other about the Marxian dialectic, as though not to understand this lingo were a blot on the intelligence of man. Well, I must confess, and very willingly, that I have never read a line of Karl Marx. I have never felt *compelled* to read him. And the more I listen to his disciples the more I realize that I have lost nothing. Karl Marx, so they say, explains the structure of our capitalistic society. I don't need an explanation of our capitalistic society. Fuck your capitalistic society! Fuck your Communistic society and your Fascist society and all your other societies! Society is made up of individuals. It is the individual who interests me—not the society.

What strikes one as pathetic, lamentable, deplorable and ridiculous, in riffling the pages of this English book on Surrealism, is

162

the effort "to get together". It's like a courtship between the serpent and the eagle, this momentary truce between the English and the French. André Breton, the great fish out of water, solemnly pontificates as usual. Reviving the language of Dr. Johnson, distorting it through his Freudian French, he seems to be giving the English elementary instruction in the art of tapping the Unconscious. In Hugh Sykes Davies he has an able disciple; this lad, blown up out of all proportion by his learning, is on the point of bursting. He needs only another breathful from André Breton.

No, the Dadaists were more entertaining. They had humor, at least. The Surrealists are too conscious of what they are doing. It's fascinating to read about their intentions—but when are they going to pull it off? On the other hand, take this from the Dada Manifesto 1918:

"I am neither for nor against and I do not explain for I hate good sense."

"Dialectic is an amusing machine which carries us—in a stupid manner—to opinions which we would have had in any case."

"God can afford not to be successful: Dada also."

And now to quote again from the devil: "*The greatness of any active organization which is the embodiment of an idea lies in the spirit of religious fanaticism and intolerance with which it attacks all others, being fanatically convinced that it alone is right. If an idea is right in itself, and, being armed with such weapons, wages warfare on this earth, it is invincible and persecution only increases its internal strength.*"

One would like to ask where Hitler got this sound and crazy notion. From Jerome? From Augustine? From Luther? Anyway, humanity is always marching in the van triumphant. To get the right idea! What a beautiful, senseless dream of a clean solution!

But don't lose sight of the "religious fanaticism and intolerance!" That's important . . .

Last night I was glancing over that essay in indirect criticism called *The Laic Mystery*. It's a step in a direction which the English have never taken and never will, even though the whole nation becomes Surrealist. Here's a bit at random . . .

"Nothing is more touching than an animal trying to regain the secret of human speech which it has discovered and then lost."

"Without puns and puzzles there is no serious art. That is to say there is nothing but serious art."

This may be irrelevant, but it's Surrealistically true: Diamond Jim Brady was a capitalist who was on the level. He had a good heart. He was magnanimous. So-and-So, on the other hand, was a rapacious idiot even before he had grown senile. He would be a disgrace to any society in any time. If you follow the logic you get a free ride.

We are always talking about society as though it were made up of two classes, those who have and those who have not. In addition to class lines the men of civilized society are divided by intelligence (the lowest going far below the intelligence of the savage), temperament, race, language, occupation, belief, principles, a thousand and one things. Cut a slice anywhere any time and you have a history of the evolution of the human race from start to finish.

Coming back to Freud . . . From a letter I once wrote to a painter who had just been analyzed and wondered why he couldn't paint any more:

"As far as we know, man has never been free of disease. Health and disease have always co-existed. The interest of the medical man has been and still is in disease, *not in health*. No physician has ever proposed to give man health—only to eradicate disease. His whole attention centers upon disease. Health is kept in the background, like an ideal, but one moves realistically in a curve towards this ideal. One does not move towards the ideal of health directly, drastically, fanatically. Part of the great fear of disease which is in us has its origin in the unconscious desire of the physician to exploit disease.

"This much is indisputable, that disease is a constant and vital factor of life, that in stressing *health* we are stressing an untenable ideal, a delusion. Moreover, despite all our warfare against disease we have made no real progress; we have merely set up new configurations of health-disease. Also falsely, casuistically, we have minimized the importance, the *benefits*, of disease. In short, we have interpreted the history of the warfare between health and disease as we have interpreted all other histories—according to our intuitions, our prejudices. (I trust it is not necessary to specify the very genuine contributions to civilization made by the great plagues, or by such admittedly tainted individuals as Buddha, Jesus, St. Francis, Joan of Arc, Nietzsche, Dostoievski, Napoleon, Genghis Khan et alii.)

"Coming to the more immediate problem, the all-important conflict between the artist and the collectivity . . . the growing attitude among the public that the artist is a leper, the attitude of the analysts that art is merely the expression of a neurotic conflict, the intensification and objectification of a condition found in other strata of society, the confused attitude among artists themselves as to the nature and purpose of art, together with the very definite belief on the part of many artists that 'art is a cure' . . . The question, it seems to me, which each one must pose for himself is this: which reality is more vital, more life-giving, more valid, more durable—the reality of science or the reality of art? (I realize that the question itself is open to criticism. We enter immediately into the realm of metaphysics, from which there is no escape, except into life.) But, assuming a divergence between the scientific and the poetic attitudes towards life, is it not clear enough that to-day the schism has grown impassable? To-day with the mass of mankind completely under the hypnotic sway of the scientific-minded, art is fighting for its life, for its very right to exist.

"I want to discover if you consider the work of the analyst to be an effort to adjust man to reality, and if so, whether you consider such an adjustment more important than the recreation of reality, through art. Do you prefer a smooth levelling down, a smooth functioning on the part of the individual in society to a state of tension, eruption, fertility? Naturally you will say NO. The implication is, however, that the artist sows discord, strife. To try to eradicate the disturbing elements of life by 'adjustment' is tantamount to expropriating the artist. Fear, love, hate, all the varying, contradictory expressions or reactions of the personality, are what compose the very warp and woof of life. You can't pull one of them out without the whole edifice crumbling.

"Here, no doubt, you will answer me by saying—This is precisely what the analyst is trying to do, to get people to accept life as a struggle, a conflict, a game. But, immediately the analyst enters the field in the role of medicine man, the question *why* our life presents such a pattern interests him exceedingly less than *how to combat it*. I say that with the increasing sway of the analyst there will occur an increasing prevalence of neurosis. Neurosis will become universal. It will take its legitimate place in the hierarchy of our diseases, just as tuberculosis, cancer, etc., took their place in the pattern of our ancestors' diseases. A niche will be made for it, and the more we pretend to fight it the more strongly will it become entrenched.

"Why do we not rid ourselves of tuberculosis, syphilis, cancer, etc., when we know so well how to combat them? Why do we not *prevent* instead of *cure?* Because cancer, syphilis, tuberculosis, neurosis, are as definite and fixed a part of our life as the machine, the aeroplane, the skyscraper, etc. This is the psychic and substantial configuration that we want. The moment we want another one we shall have it—*just by wanting!* And the aim of the artist, as I see it, is to make people *want* another, a *different* picture. The sane, the wise, the adjusted souls are always ready to reply—'But this is the way life is . . . you can't alter it . . . you're mad!' And the artist always answers: 'You are right. I want only the impossible, only the marvellous. To-morrow you will see that what I proclaimed was not impossible. But then it will be too late, for to-morrow we will see again with different eyes and again you will cry *Impossible!* You live to-morrow and yesterday; I live only to-day. Therefore, I live eternally. I am timeless. And since this is obviously untrue, you are right and I continue to be wrong. It is out of my wrongness that your right is created. To be right is to be either late or ahead of time. The only span between us is time!'

"Art, as I see it, is the expression of this chasm, this desynchronization: it is the projection of the universal picture of individuation. Man against the universe. *Against*, please notice. The work of art, *the poem*, is the symbol of his latitude and longitude, of his temporal position in time and space.

"Will analysis, or revolution, or anything else dissolve this picture? Is understanding a goal in itself, or is understanding a by-product? Do we want a closer rapport between artist and collectivity, or do we want an increasing tension? Do we want art to become more communicative, or do we want it to be more fecundating? Do we want every man to become an artist and thus eliminate art? Unconsciously I think that every great artist is trying with might and main to destroy art. By that I mean that he is

167

desperately striving to break down this wall between himself and the rest of humanity. Not for the sake of the brotherhood of man, because at bottom he is tyrant (like Mohammed, Buddha, Christ, Tamerlane), but in the hope of debouching into some more quick and vivid realm of human experience. He is not struggling to isolate himself from his fellow-men, since it is his very isolation which drives him to create, but rather to emancipate himself from false relations with his fellow-men, from false relations with nature and with all the objects which surround him. Art is only one of the manifestations of the creative spirit. What every great artist is manifesting in his work is a desire to lead a richer life; his work itself is only a description, an intimation, as it were, of those possibilities. The worst sin that can be committed against the artist is to take him at his word, to see in his work a fulfillment instead of an horizon. Da Vinci, who troubles us more than any other artist, who left so much unfinished . . . fortunately! . . . has left us the symbol of this desire in that upraised index finger which speaks to us more laconically than the famous Mona Lisa smile. Da Vinci was the forerunner of those anatomists of the soul who are now moving into the foreground with megaphones and amplifiers.

"Freud's contribution to the cause of human enlightenment (as the stupid saying goes) is creative and anarchic, in keeping with his race and temperament; there is the same uncompromising spirit in him as in his forerunners, the same arid, monotonous, luminous quality of the desert, the geometric line, the theorem, the axiom—and naturally, *the golden hypothesis*. The Absolute is in his blood. An anal rectitude, a frigid punctilio, a gray sprightliness in which there is neither joy nor sensuality. Unable to reconcile himself to the world (to the philosophy of the day, that is), he turned the world upside down. He created a fiction which helped to pass the time away. Which helped, if you please, not to adjust him to the world but to adjust the world to his own imaginings. His theory of psycho-analysis is a piece of art, like any other piece of art, and it will lead a pure isolated existence. The truth of it is incommunicable. What will happen to-morrow in the name of the holy cause may have little or nothing to do with his creation. Even Hitler, so rumor has it, was willing to use it for his own ends, as he does with astrology. The significance of Freud's creation is purely aesthetic. As he draws quietly nearer to the grave he is not only honestly dubious about the future, but downright pessimistic. There is a sort of wistful questioning, a doubting, one might say, as to the efficacy of his penetrative researches into the mysteries of the human psyche. (Is there not something slightly humorous about this, as if perhaps the old bird had never given himself a chance to think it all out?) However, no panaceas! That much is clear. And if at the end the great Sigmund Freud happens to find himself enmeshed in his own creative lie is there any denying the fact that thousands of individuals, believing implicitly in the efficacy of his therapy, have found greater enjoyment of life? In turning the world upside down I sometimes think that Freud more than anyone else must have been astonished to find that it tended to remain upside down. The disciples of Freud, as is the way with disciples, are struggling to put the world back on its feet again. The role of the disciple is always to betray the master. The moral is that no matter how great the master the world will not remain permanently upside down.

"There have always been and always will be men in the world who are healers, just as there will always be an order of priests, an order of prophets, an order of warriors, an order of kings, an order of poets. In our day the interest in physical maladies is on the wane. (The importance of surgery is only one of the many proofs of the fact.) Our world is suffering from mental disorders—from

169

the insanities and neuroses of one form and another. Just as literature swings at times from the poetic to the prosodic, so nowadays we have the swing from the physical disorders to the mental, with the inevitable emergence of new types of genius cropping out among the mental healers. All that the creative personality demands is a new field for the exercise of its powers; out of the dark, inchoate forces, these personalities will, by the exercise of their creative faculties, impose upon the world a new ideology, a new and vital set of symbols. What the collective mass desires is the concrete, visible, tangible substance . . . which the theories of Freud, Jung, Rank, Stekel, et alii provide. This they can pore over, chew, masticate, tear to pieces or prostrate themselves before. Tyranny always works best under the guise of liberating ideas. The tyranny of ideas is merely another way of saying the tyranny of a few great personalities.

"There is a vast parallelism between the religious figures of the past and the psychologists of to-day. The underlying theme is *salvation*, whether it be called 'finding God' or 'adapting oneself to reality'. ('May not one succeed in systematizing confusion and so assist the total discrediting of the world of reality?' asks Dali.) When the symbols by which man relates himself to the universe are exhausted he must perforce find new ones, vital ones, which will reintegrate him to the universe. This process which is one of oscillation, is known as a macro-microcosmizing of the universe. According to whichever way the pendulum happens to swing, man tends either to become himself, God, or to become mere *dreck*. To-day the world has become so inflated that God has been completely squeezed out. The exploration of the Unconscious, which is now under way, is a confession of the bankruptcy of the spirit. When we almost reach the Absolute, when we can no longer work in it, or with it, we let in the air . . . and establish a relative balance again.

"Recently at a Surindépendent showing I had a terrific feeling of this desire on the part of modern man to explore this uncharted world of the Unconscious. I am speaking more particularly of the Surrealist section of the exhibit. It was a strange afternoon, dark, foggy, ominous, like one of those days in the early Middle Ages when signs and portents were so frequently observed in the heavens, the ominous ones always occurring in mid-day. I arrive at the big hall towards four o'clock. No lights have been lit to illuminate these marvels. They swim around me in a sort of oceanic twilight. Looking about me I can discover only three people in this vast hall. I wander from zone to zone, as if under the ocean, and gradually I discover that I am the only spectator left. The darkness gets more intense. I have to approach within a foot of the pictures in order to make them out. It seems suddenly very strange to me that there should be hundreds of pictures in this vast gallery and no audience. And then jokingly, also a little desperately, I add, half-aloud; 'You're the whole audience; the show is for you!' Immediately the thought formulates itself—it seems to me singularly right that it should be thus, that only I am there to voice an unheard appreciation. After a bit I observe that the guardians are prowling about in my wake, also examining the pictures . . . and with more than usual interest, it would seem. I observe them more attentively, and would you believe it, I notice that it is to the Surrealist paintings that they instinctively turn. Maybe then these robots, whose appreciation nobody gives a fuck about, maybe then these half-wits and myself are the only valid audience for a Surrealist show! Excellent! Anyway, I see it as strangely significant, symbolic if you like. Not only the absence of the crowd, but the frost and the fog . . . and the utter lack of illumination. One might very well imagine that a plague had swept the country and that only a few monkish souls, the guardians and myself included, were left to enjoy the benefits of a vanished civilization. A strange question then presented itself to my mind. Were these Surrealist specimens part of our vanished civilization and thus forgotten without ever being known, or were they already existing in a time which had not yet commenced and therefore invisible to the ordinary eye? I wondered how and if Dali would recover his remarkable etherized horse and whether, through handling or neglect, it would undergo a metamorphosis which would so astonish everybody as to produce something in the nature of a miracle. If, for example, the horse suddenly got detached from the frame and managed to hide away in the chandelier swinging high above. If they had discovered that it was a real horse, only somewhat abnormal, which the painter Dali had drugged in order to plaster him over his canvas. How would the damp and the mould affect him—the horse, I mean? All sorts of enigmas presented themselves to my mind in quick fashion.

"And what was it I witnessed in this festival of the Unconscious? What were the masters of this unexplored realm bringing up from the depths? For one thing, the organs of the human body, the parts we look at without shuddering only in the butcher's shop. I saw the insides coming out and smearing themselves in extrovert fashion over the feeble mass of skin and bones. I saw the hungry, gnawing innards of man so long hidden away, despised, ignored, denigrated, blasphemed, I saw them issuing forth in bold assertiveness, weaving a bloody and hysterical, but *marvellously* bloody and hysterical, legend on the frost-sweated walls of Versailles. Amongst these hysterical phantoms of the deep I feel absolutely at home. A thousand times more at home than in the butcher's shop or the funeral parlor. I float among them in

172

the deepening twilight in a genuine ecstasy. Dali's horse with the motorized sex organs is far more real than reality, which of course is in the nature of an oxymoron, if you happen to be the victim of pedantry. This horse with the female head, its motored sex borrowed from Darwin, Edison, Freud & Co., Inc., its mythological and atavistic remnants and fragments, the baited hook like a spur driven through the rectum, the color and odor of it, the nostalgia it evokes (Troy, Bucephalus, Man of War, The Dime Museum, Laotse, Meissonier, Heliogabolus, Montezuma, Infanticide, Lady of the Lake, to mention a few), the incongruous and anomalous parts, the absurd which is devastating, together with the sense of space which is absent and yet devours you, all of it, sex, nonsense, poison, nostalgia, Darwinian hypothesis, and electric light bulbs, not overlooking the penny arcades and the statues forgotten to be pulled down, make up a totality of reality so enticing that one feels like walking into the canvas, folding up and dying there. And if, cher ami, as you once remarked walking down the Rue de la Gaieté, it is impossible or futile to paint the Unconscious, then please accept in my name this replica of the Unconscious which will have to serve until detachments are brought up and the trenches consolidated. This perhaps is not even a representation of the Unconscious, but a necessity of the Unconscious. And, let me add, that whenever between Idea and Representation there occurs such an inviolable marriage we may without let or fear take one for the other or vice versa.

"As in olden times, when the Christian myth had man by the balls so that he was powerless to paint anything but madonnas, angels, demons and their like, so now it seems to me that in the paintings of the Surrealists we have the embryonic spawn of the coming angels, demons and madonnas, etc. I see some dim relationship between the bankruptcy of the conscious intellectual forces (the insanity of our present world) and the emergence of this great new empire of darkness (the insanity of the future) which, in its demand to be explored and charted, will revive the sensory powers of man so that he may look upon the world about him with renewed exaltation and more vivid consciousness. I see it as a desire to deflate the abstract, materialistic universe of the scientific-minded man, a desire to fill in the chinks of his hole-and-theory conception of Nature so that we may live, if necessary, even in a space no bigger than a padded cell and feel at one with the universe. The artist is now giving a first coat of paint to that tautly stretched canvas which the scientist has been so busy stretching that he has forgotten the use he intended to put it to. The whole world has almost forgotten what the canvas was meant for. The artists too had almost forgotten, most of them at any rate. A few of them, however, have started in to lay down a nice thick coat of unconscious; they have covered up a few of the gaping holes already.

"I come back again to the path-finders, the great pioneers, such as Father Freud, Jung the Mystic, et alii, and I say that what they are striving for is not to create a technique of psychoanalysis, nor even a philosophic-scientific theory. Nothing of the kind. What they are doing is to offer themselves to us as examples of the potentialities which reside in each and all of us. They are trying to eliminate themselves as doctors, scientists, philosophers, theoreticians, trying to reveal to us the miraculous nature of man, the vast possibilities which stretch before him. They do not want disciples and expounders, they do not want to be imitated—they want merely to point the way. We ought, I say, to turn our backs on their theories, we ought to smash their theories. We ought to make all these theories unnecessary. Let each one turn his gaze inward and regard himself with awe and wonder, with mystery and

174

reverence; let each one promulgate his own laws, his own theories; let each one work his own influence, his own havoc, his own miracles. Let each one as an individual, assume the roles of artist, healer, prophet, priest, king, warrior, saint. No division of labor. Let us recombine the dispersed elements of our individuality. Let us reintegrate.

"The religious leader, like the analyst, awakens men to a consciousness of the Id, the great unknown reservoir and fundament of humanity. In making men conscious of this identity of substratum, this brotherhood below the belt, this lurking humanity, so to speak, he sets in motion an oppositional force, divinity. If you make a psychological graph of the human mind you have something like an iceberg, with one-third visible and two-thirds invisible, below the surface of the sea, below the threshold of consciousness. What distinguishes the great icebergs from the little ones is height and profundity—the measure of the one is the measure of the other. The same force which thrusts one iceberg higher up also thrusts it deeper down than the others. Isolation is the index of profundity. Of what use then for the analysts to stress adaptation to reality? What reality? Whose reality? The reality of iceberg Prime or icebergs X, Y, Z? We are all swimming in the ocean depths and flying in the stratosphere. Some dive a little lower, some climb a little higher—but it's always air and water, always reality, even if it's a completely crazy reality. The analyst stresses the lower depths reality, the religious leader the stratospheric spiritual reality. Neither of them is adequate. Both are distorting the picture of reality in the passionate pursuit of truth. The artist is not interested in truth or beauty per se. The artist puts the picture into whack *because he is thoroughly disinterested*. His vision goes round the obstacle; it refuses to exhaust itself in straight line attacks. His work, which is simply the expres-

175

sion of his struggle to adapt himself to a reality of his own making, sums up all other approaches to reality and gives them significance.

"Experience alone is valueless, and idea alone is valueless. To give either validity one must employ them together plastically. In short, we are never going to be cured of our diseases (physical or mental), we are never going to reach a heaven (either real or imaginary) and we are never going to eliminate our evil, thwarting instincts (whatever these may be). In the realm of ideas the best we shall ever have will be a philosophy of life (not a science of life, which is a contradiction in terms); in the realm of experience we shall never have a better expression than the living out of our animal nature (not our cultural patterns). The highest aim of man, as thinker, is to achieve a pattern, a synthesis, to grasp life poetically; the chief and highest aim of man as animal is to live out his instincts, obey his instincts, take him where they will. So long as he cannot operate as a savage or less than savage, and think as a god, or better than a god, he will suffer, he will propose to himself remedies, governments, religions, therapies. Back of all his behaviour is fear—fear of death. Could he overcome this he might live as god and beast. The fear of death has created a whole cosmogony of lesser fears which plague us in a thousand different ways. We are forever tinkering with the little fears, the minor aches. That is what gives life its melodic minors, as we know. The bigger the personality the greater the simplification, the greater the diapason, the tension, the polarity, the juice, the vitality. One can take fear, isolate it, and against it counterpoint a grand symphony of life. Or one can refuse to acknowledge it, fight a million trivial battles every day of his life, and achieve that stale hash which the majority of men serve up to themselves in lieu of solid nutriment."

Perhaps we are only charged with the liquidation of some spiritual inheritance which it is in every one's interest to repudiate, and that is all. (André Breton)

Surrealism starts out innocently enough as a revolt against the insanity of every-day life. It is expressed marvellously in one of Breton's early pronunciamentoes: "I am resolved to render powerless that *hatred of the marvellous* which is so rampant among certain people." Naturally he is not referring to concierges alone. He means everybody (who is not living as a poet), from the President of France on down to the chimney-sweep. It is a big order. It is a defi to the whole world practically. But there is no confusion behind the idea. It is clear as a bell.

"The marvellous is always beautiful. Anything that is marvellous is beautiful. Indeed nothing but the marvellous is beautiful."

If one takes a sweeping glance at the paraphernalia which distinguishes our civilization from those of the past—I mean our battleships, factories, railways, torpedoes, gas-masks, etc.—one realizes that this *is* our civilization and not something else which we imagine civilization to be. Civilization is drugs, alcohol, engines of war, prostitution, machines and machine slaves, low wages, bad food, bad taste, prisons, reformatories, lunatic asylums, divorce, perversion, brutal sports, suicides, infanticide, cinema, quackery, demagogy, strikes, lockouts, revolutions, putsches, colonization, electric chairs, guillotines, sabotage, floods, famine, disease, gangsters, money barons, horse racing, fashion shows, poodle dogs, chow dogs, Siamese cats, condoms, pessaries, syphilis, gonorrhea, insanity, neuroses, etc., etc.

When Dali talks of systematizing confusion does he mean this, this confusion which is truly marvellous, though perhaps not so beautiful? All this marvellous confusion is systematized. If one

177

added another drop of confusion to it the bubble would burst. Surrealism is an expression of this universal confusion. Christianity was also the expression of a universal confusion.

But the point is that the early Christians were not mad. No more than the Surrealists are to-day. They were simply unhappy, unfit for the struggle which life demanded of them. The Christians invented a life hereafter where they would have pie in the sky, as we say. The Surrealists are almost as other worldly. "Is a man ready to risk everything so that at the very bottom of the crucible into which we propose throwing our poor abilities . . . he may have the joy of getting a glimpse of the light which will cease to flicker?"

There is no doubt about it, Surrealism is the secret language of our time, the only spiritual counterpart to the materialistic activities of the socialist forces which are now driving us to the wall. The seeming discrepancies between the language of Breton and Lenin, or Marx, are only superficial. Surrealism will give a new, deeper, truer, more immediate spiritual doctrine to the economic, social and political revolutionists. The Church has not been defeated after all. Christianity is *not* dead. It is about to triumph . . . after 2,000 years of futile struggle. The world *is* going to be turned upside down—and this time it may stay upside down. Unless "doubt's duck with the vermouth lips" comes along and upsets all calculations . . .

Before me, as I write this, lies the latest issue of the *Minotaure*, that most valuable index of the times. The cover design is by Dali, and as best I make out, represents a modern conception of the Minotaur. In the margin is a series of pen points all of different design. The most striking feature of Dali's Minotaur is the hollow thorax in which he has lodged a vicious looking lobster. Striking because the vitals have been entirely hollowed out! In the cusp of each thigh is an object, the right leg containing a glass cup and spoon, the left one a dark bottle with a cork in it. The left leg seems also to button and unbutton. The right one holds a key and just above the ankle a manacle bites through the tendons and flesh. But the chief feature, as I said, is the missing vitals— with the lobster still muscling in.

Riffling the pages of this magazine, I see that it deals entirely with disintegration—with nerve ends, necrophilism, sadism, eschatology, fetichism, embryology. *Ici on charcute l'embryon.* It is a perfect picture of our time, a pretty little fireside picture which corroborates the impression I had upon reading Céline's speech in honor of Emile Zola. This speech of Céline's is entirely about the death instincts in man, about his hallucinating desire for self-destruction. There are no young men to-day, he says. They are born old. We are in the grip of a sadist-masochist obsession and there will be no liberation until we are all wiped out. Hitler is nothing to the monsters who are to come. He adds that the worst ones will probably be bred here in France. With all of which I thoroughly agree.

By the year 2000 A.D. we will be completely under the sway of Uranus and Pluto. The word Communism will be an obsolete expression known only to philologists and etymologists. We shall be breaking ground for the new anarchy which will come in with the advent of the new zodiacal sign, Aquarius. Circa 2160 A.D. There won't be any A.D. any more, as the symbol will cease to mean anything. We shall have a wholly new calendar before we definitely enter the sign of Aquarius. I predict it now.

A man lives with dead suns inside him or he goes out like a flame and lives the life of the moon. Or he disintegrates entirely and throws a flaming comet across the horizon. But all the while, everywhere in the world, the lobster is muscling in and gnawing out the vitals. The Minotaur is we ourselves standing on the threshold of a new era. We must be devoured whilst devouring. The bottle, the key, the little coffee cup and spoon, these are the last relics hidden in the flesh. When they unbutton the leg of our once sacred body in the years to come, they will find these little treasures and prize them. The ethnologists, what I mean. These birds, ditto the archaeologists, we shall have with us always. Things will go on this way, ruins and relics, new battleships, new skyscrapers, peace treaties, holy wars, repartitions, alignments, discoveries, inventions, more ruins, more relics, progress everywhere all the time amidst famine, floods, pestilence, on and on like that for thousands of years until we have passed through every sign of the zodiac. Then one fine day we shall burst the belt and be out in the wide world of space in a bright new realm, the a-historical realm in which art will have disappeared completely—because life itself will have become an art. All things point steadily towards this miracle, believe it or not. The miracle is MAN, man full blown and travelling with his mother the earth in a new field of constellations. Now he is busy weighing the stars and measuring the distance between them; *then* he will be of the stars and there will be no need to record, neither with instruments, nor with paper and ink, nor with signs and symbols. The meaning of destiny is to throw away the truss which the zodiacal belt represents and to live it out *ad hoc* and *post rem*. That is what Breton means when he says with apocalyptic precision: "We should carry ourselves as though we were really *in the world!*"

———

Madness is tonic and invigorating. It makes the sane more sane. The only ones who are unable to profit by it are the insane. Very often the Surrealists give us the impression that they are insane in

180

a very sane way—that it is "ice-box madness", as my friend Lawrence Durrell puts it, and not real madness.

When we look at the Surrealistic products of such men as Hieronymus Bosch or Grunewald or Giotto we notice two elements which are lacking in the works of the Surrealists to-day; *guts and significance*. Without vital guts there can be no true madness; without a healthy scepticism there can be no real significance in a work of art, or in life, for that matter. Breton says somewhere that "it had to be with lunatics that Columbus set out to discover America." That is a sad joke. Columbus set out with a bunch of desperate, hopeless men. Far from being dreamers, far from being fanatical believers, his men were ignorant, superstitious and filled with greed. The voyage may have been risky, but the idea was not. It wasn't even a gamble. And in the last analysis, Columbus never set out to discover America: he set out to discover a short route to India.

And another thing . . . it is a mistake to speak about Surrealism. There is no such thing: there are only Surrealists. They have existed in the past and they will exist in the future. The desire to posit an ism, to isolate the germ and cultivate it, is a bad sign. It means impotency. It is on a par with that impotency which makes of a man a Christian, a Buddhist, or a Mohammedan. A man who is full of God is outside the faith.

It seems to me that it is a very simple error which the Surrealists are guilty of; they are trying to establish an Absolute. They are trying with all the powers of consciousness to usher in the glory of the Unconscious. They believe in the Devil but not in God. They worship the night but refuse to acknowledge the day. They talk of magic, but they practise voodooism. They await the miracle, but they do nothing to assist it, to bring about an accouchement. They talk of ushering in a general confusion, but

181

they live like the bourgeoisie. A few of them have committed suicide, but not one of them has as yet assassinated a tyrant. They believe in the revolution but there is no real revolt in them.

It is true, they have dug up some interesting old post-cards; it is true they have pulled off some interesting seances; it is true they have staged some amusing riots; it is true they have managed to edit one of the most de luxe reviews to be found anywhere in the world; it is true that from time to time there have been included in their group some of the best artists in the world. But, as *Surrealists* have they given us the greatest masterpieces, either in music, literature, or painting? Have they been able to retain among their numbers *one* great figure in the world of art?

They say they are against the current order, but have their lives been endangered by their actions . . . as was the case with Villon, Rabelais, Sade, Voltaire, to mention but a few? Why are they allowed to shoot their mouths off without fear of arrest? Because the authorities know they are harmless, and they are harmless because they lack guts, and lacking guts they are unable to convince those to whom they address their appeals. The failure to "communicate" is entirely their own. Jesus managed to communicate; so did Gautama the Buddha; so did Mohammed; so did St. Francis; so did a host of lesser men. There is no great mystery behind the lives of these men. In each case the simple fact is that the man acted upon his belief, *regardless of the consequences*. Each one had a revelation to make and he made it. Society was no more favorable then to the ideas which they brought forward than society is to-day to the Surrealist doctrine. Paul Eluard says somewhere: "Mind can only triumph in its most perilous activities. *No daring is fatal.*" In his poetry Paul Eluard proves the truth of this. But there is something beyond mind, and that is *the whole being of man*, which he expresses in action. What is disastrous is

182

the divorce between mind and action. The ultimate can only be expressed in conduct. Example moves the world more than doctrine. The great exemplars are the poets of action, and it makes little difference whether they be forces for good or forces for evil. There is one thing which the surrealists stress repeatedly, and that is the necessity for poetry in life. Despite what anybody says, poetry *is* communicable—because it is of the nature of the marvellous and man is precisely the one creature on earth which can be moved by the marvellous. His religions prove it; his art proves it; history proves it. Everything of value that has been accomplished by man has been accomplished in spite of reason, in spite of logic, in spite of honor, justice and all other shibboleths. The marvellous, and only the marvellous, is what hypnotizes man. That is what makes him a gullible fool, an idiot, a criminal, a martyr, a saint, a hero, a death-eater. In his moments of genius he is mad; if he is not mad enough he goes insane, and then he is unable to distinguish between what is marvellous and what is not marvellous. The Surrealists are the last of all people to go insane. They have too great a need, too great a thirst, for the marvellous. When Lautréamont, in a moment of high lucidity, said, "Nothing is incomprehensible", he was saying something marvellous. But only a poet has a right to say this. The ignorance of the poet is not a negative thing; it is a crucible in which all knowledge is refunded. In this state of true and humble ignorance everything is clear and knowledge is therefore superfluous. Knowledge is a sifting, a categorizing, a comparing, an analyzing. Knowledge was never essential to the poet. The poet comprehends because he feels; his passion is to embrace the world, not with his mind, but with his heart. The world is always in a wrong condition for the man who knows too much; as one becomes more ignorant one accepts more graciously. Knowledge makes everything finally incomprehensible. One only begins to comprehend when one begins to stop trying to know.

The Surrealists are trying to open a magic chamber of man's being through knowledge. That is where the fatal mistake lies. They are looking backwards instead of forwards. To discredit the world of reality, as they suggest, is an act of will, not of fate. What is really discredited is done silently, unostentatiously, and alone. People band together to proclaim an ideal, or a principle, to establish a movement, to organize a cult. But if they believed, each and every one wholeheartedly, they would have no need of numbers, nor of creeds, nor of principles, etc. The fear of standing alone is the evidence that the faith is weak. Man is happier when he is in a crowd; he feels safe and justified in what he is doing. But crowds have never accomplished anything, except destruction. The man who wants to organize a movement is invoking aid to help tear down something which he is powerless to combat single-handed. When a man is truly creative he works single-handed and he wants no help. A man acting alone, on faith, can accomplish what trained armies are incapable of accomplishing. To believe in one's self, in one's own powers, is apparently the most difficult thing in the world. Unfortunately there is nothing, absolutely nothing, more efficacious than believing in one's self. When a movement dies there is left only the memory of the man who originated the movement, the man who believed in what he was saying, what he was doing. The others are without name; they contributed only their faith in an idea. And that is never enough.

And just as I get this off my chest, someone walks in and hands me another book edited by Herbert Read, called *Unit 1. Unit 1* is the name of a group of eleven English artists who have banded together to stand by each other and defend their beliefs. "Unit One", says Paul Nash, "may be said to stand for the expression of a truly contemporary spirit, for that which is recognized as peculiarly of to-day in painting, sculpture and architecture."

Mr. Read, who writes the Introduction, goes on to say that "the modern artist is essentially an individualist; his general desire is not to conform to any pattern, to follow any lead, to take any instructions—but to be as original as possible, to be himself and to express himself in his art." If what Mr. Read says is so then this group is not composed of modern artists nor of individuals, but of rank imitators, men without originality who have banded together in self-defense. Looking at the reproductions one sees the ghosts of Brancusi, Picasso, Braque, Chirico, Max Ernst et alii. *Unit One* is not a group of "New" artists, we are informed. No, they are British artists of established reputation. Which is tantamount to saying there is no British art!

The most revelatory feature of this little book is the statements of the artists themselves, made in answer to a questionnaire submitted to them. There is something about the British mentality which baffles me. You ask a pertinent question and the man begins to talk about the wax in his ear, or about the rainfall in Uganda last summer. In the main questionnaires are idiotic, and this one is no exception to the rule. Nevertheless the questionnaire gives the artist an opportunity to talk about art, not about apple sauce. The British artist, like the British general, is muddle-headed. Perhaps it's the perpetual fog in which he is obliged to work. Perhaps it's the British diet. God knows what is responsible, but the fact remains that these eleven individuals talk like grammar-school students. It is difficult to get a clear idea of what they are driving at because none of them has a clear idea in his head.

Take this, for example, from John Armstrong, a painter: "It began to seem clear that my painting could not stand on its own legs, much less climb on them, that perhaps no painting ever had, that art had always to have a shove from behind from religion or politics, and a lift by the scruff of the neck from architecture in order to achieve anything."

Or this from Douglas Cooper who answers for Edward Burra: "Hieronymus Bosch was a moralist; he was trying to educate the people of his time: he was not merely dreaming, he was giving plastic expression to what were in his era undeniable truths: so, too, is Burra. Both are phantasists, but whereas Bosch throughout his whole life was concerned with educating his public (for Flemish art in the fifteenth century was primarily literary) Burra freed by 'the march of progress' from any such necessity, relied entirely on his imagination, and has been carried into the realms of the surreal." (The fact that both names begin with B seems to serve as the liaison. Why no mention was made of Burra's obvious master, Chirico, is a mystery to me. Perhaps Mr. Cooper was being "delicate".)

Or the profundity of Edward Wadsworth: "We change with age, but without change we are dead." . . . "Art evolves with the human race." . . . "The artists of this country have added—from time to time—their contribution to the ideography of Occidental painting, and they will continue to do so if they combine their craftsmanship with a more universal point of view of what they want to say."

It seems to me that there is a sort of cultivated feeble-mindedness here. To any one who has had the privilege of conversing with British people this comes as no shock. As my friend Lawrence Durrell says: "They have confused the inner struggle with the outer one. They want to bread poultice a primary chancre." As a matter of fact, they don't even have to go that far: they want to pretend there is no chancre. The reason why there is no British painter, poet, musician or sculptor worthy of the name is because

186

ever since the Elizabethan Age the British have been walking around with blinders over their eyes. They have created an unreality which is the exact opposite of the "surreal", as one of these artists puts it. It may be too that the effort expended in producing a Shakespeare—which seems to be the crowning achievement of British genius—was so tremendous that not a crumb of originality was left for the men who came after. And even Shakespeare, greatest of the lot, was not exactly a model of originality.

The suave, self-patronizing way in which Paul Nash takes cognizance of this lack of originality also seems typically British to me. "The kind of art practised by the individuals of *Unit One*", says he blithely, "is no doubt traceable to origins; its counterpart is to be found in many countries to-day; that, however, is no reason for underestimating its value". If that is not a reason, the only reason, for underestimating its value, then I should like to know what is the reason. A statement like this might have been made by a British diplomat who, as we all know, has a genius for saying nothing. I find the same sort of wool-gathering in Herbert Read's Introduction to the book *Surrealism*. Obliged to make some mention of Wyndham Lewis, here is how he drags him in: "English plastic arts had to wait for the inspiration of Picasso to show any real revival. In the last twenty years we have produced potentially great artists—Wyndham Lewis is the typical example—but they have suffered from a disastrous form of individualism. The English sin has always been eccentricity (sic!); by which I do not mean a lack of social coherence." What the last phrase means I haven't the slightest idea. But I do know what he means by "potentially great artists": artists who were nipped in the bud! On the other hand, why the English plastic arts had to wait for the inspiration of Picasso is not at all clear to me. Why? Because they did? At any rate, by means of this scurrilous and wishy-washy sort of legerdemain Wyndham Lewis, who is the only English artist of importance, outside of D. H. Lawrence, whom the English produced in the last couple of generations, is flippantly pushed into the background. It is obvious that Wyndham Lewis is not in the swing, that he chooses to remain, as always, the Enemy. That alone speaks well of him, in my opinion. For whenever an English artist of any value has arisen he has been marked as Public Enemy No. 1. Including the great Shakespeare! It may be comforting for the pygmies who are banding together to-day to believe that a proper understanding of the Marxian dialectic, together with a dash of Freud, may solve this time old difficulty, but I am afraid they are doomed to bitter disappointment. In order for England to have art, the English will have to undergo a radical transformation. They may even have to change the climate! Or else wait another five hundred years or so for a real inspiration. The question is, where did Picasso get his inspiration from?

———

Scarcely anything has been as stimulating to me as the theories and the products of the Surrealists. I say scarcely anything because I feel impelled to make mention of a few other things equally stimulating: China, for instance, everything associated with the name; the work of Otto Rank and Minkowski, the poet of schizophrenia; Keyserling, yes Count Herman Keyserling; the language and the ideas of Elie Faure; and, of course, D. H. Lawrence, and Nietzsche, and Dostoievski. Even Emerson and Rimbaud; even Goethe. And not least of all, Lewis Carroll.

If, as Goethe says somewhere—"only that which is fecund is true"—then in all these men whom I have cited, and in the whole idea of China, there must be truth. But truth is everywhere, in everything. It is useless to search for truth, as it is useless to search for beauty or for power. As it is useless also to search for God. Beauty, truth, power, God, all these come without searching, without effort. The struggle is not for these; the struggle is deeper than that. The struggle is to synchronize the potential being with the actual being, to make a fruitful liaison between the man of yesterday and the man of to-morrow. It is the process of growth which is painful, but unavoidable. We either grow or we die, and to die while alive is a thousand times worse than to "shuffle off this mortal coil". In a thousand different languages, in a thousand different ways, men everywhere are trying to express the same idea: that one must fight to keep vitally alive. Fight in order to realize one's potential self. Guilt, sin, conscience—there is no eradicating these factors of human consciousness. They are part and parcel of consciousness itself. The stress on the Unconscious forces of man does not necessarily imply the elimination of consciousness. On the contrary it implies the expansion of consciousness. There can be no return to an instinctive life, and in fact, even among primitive men I see no evidence of a purely instinctive life. The strict taboos, which belong to the order of consciousness, permit a greater release of the instinctive life. Civilized man has his taboos also, but the penalty, instead of being quick death, is a slow and poisonous one. By contrast with primitive people, civilized people seem dead, quite dead. They are not really more dead, to be sure, but they give the semblance of death because the tension, the polarity, is breaking down. Through this breakdown the stress shifts from the collective life to the individual life. The life of the primitive man is a collective life par excellence; but the life of the civilized man is not wholly individualistic. The goal is unmistakable, but the powers are lacking. Paradoxically enough, the more man approaches self-mastery the more fear he develops. As his sphere of influence widens his sense of isolation, of aloneness, increases. For thousands of years man has run with the herd; for thousands of years he has been—and still is—a predatory animal, killing with the pack. Civilization has not eliminated the instinct to kill, nor will it ever. But civilization has done another thing, almost unwittingly: it has encouraged the development of man's ego, of his individuality. I say civilization, but in reality I mean a *few men*, a few great, extraordinary individuals whose spiritual development has so far outstripped that of the ordinary man that they remain unique and exert over the great majority of men a tyranny which is to all intents and purposes obsessive. The cold, sterile crystallization of the truths which they perceived and acted upon forms the framework of what is called civilization. Just as with primitive man, so with the civilized man it is fear again which operates most powerfully, which dominates his consciousness. In the neurotic individual this fear comes to supreme expression; the paralyzed neurotic is the symbol of the thwarting power of civilization. He it is who is the victim of so-called "progress". He stands out in our midst as a warning, a sort of flesh-and-blood totem representing the powers of evil.

It is just here that a phrase of André Breton's—"the crisis of consciousness"—comes to my mind with significant force. Neurosis, is, in a way, precisely this—*the crisis of consciousness*. The neurotic is the victim of a new way of life which we must take or perish. For the neurotic is the victim of a soul struggle which takes place in the amphitheatre of the mind. It is a Narcissistic struggle with the self, and whichever way the issue turns it is he himself who is the victim. It is a sacrificial struggle waged by our highest types, and we the spectators are either going to eliminate these sufferers from our midst, in creating a more equilibrated individual, or we are going to imitate them and perish as they are perishing.

Analysis is not going to bring about a cure of neurosis. Analysis is merely a technique, a metaphysic, if you wish, to illustrate and explain to us the nature of a malady which is universal among civilized beings. Analysis brings no curative powers in its train; it merely makes us conscious of the existence of an evil, which, oddly enough, is consciousness.

This may sound confusing, but actually it is very clear and very simple. Everything that lives, that has being, whether it be a star, a plant, an animal, or a human being—even God Almighty—has direction. This idea might be explained equally well mathematically or by physics or psychologically. Or finally, religiously. Along the road which each of us is travelling there is no turning back. It is forward or dead stop, which is living death. This forward movement, or direction, is nothing but consciousness. It is movement along a gamut which makes itself known to us in the form of opposites, by duality, in other words. Everything is a question of degree, as we say. It is all one, and yet it is not one. It is two. The mystic, who is more dual than other men, arrives momentarily at a solution of the enigma by achieving a state of ecstasy in which he is at one with the universe. Needless to say, in such moments he has no need of God, or anything beyond him. He is beyond himself, so to speak, in the sense that his consciousness has so far expanded as to embrace the two opposite poles of his being. Struggle is unthinkable. He knows the meaning, in this trance-like state, of the ineffable. Everything is clear and acceptable; he is one with destiny. He is, in such moments, direction itself. That is, consciousness.

The condition of ecstasy is, as we know, not a permanent state of being. It is an experience which permits us to undergo a radical transformation, a fruitful metamorphosis, a renewal. The man who is with God, who sees God and talks to him, returns to the world of reality profoundly altered. By means of his experience he in turn alters reality itself. He puts a little more of God into it, so to speak. So that the vital problems which yesterday plagued us no longer exist. More difficult problems now confront us. Always problems, however. Every Utopia confers upon us a new hell. The chasm widens and deepens. The isolation becomes more intense.

The example which the lives of the mystics afford us is that progress and direction are two totally different things. Back of the idea of progress, which is the false idea underlying all civilizations —and the reason why they perish—is the notion of conquering over Nature. Neither offers a way out. There is no way out, as a matter of fact. We must accept the dilemma, if we are to accept life itself.

Herbert Read, in the closing paragraph of his Introduction to *Surrealism* speaks of "the renascence of wonder". It is a phrase which I should like to put beside that of Paul Eluard—"no daring is fatal". Wonder and daring! Dionysian concepts which are restored to us as we journey towards the night of the *Unconscious*. The day face of the world is unbearable, it is perhaps true. But this mask which we wear, through which we look at the world of reality, who has clapped it on us? Have we not grown it ourselves? The mask is inevitable: we cannot meet the world with naked skins. We move within grooves, formerly taboos, now conventions. Are we to throw away the mask, the lying day face of the world? *Could we*, even if we chose? It seems to me that only the lunatic is capable of making such a gesture—and at what a price! Instead of the conventional but flexible groove, which irks more or less, he adopts the obsessional mould which clamps and imprisons. He has completely lost contact with reality, we say of the insane man. But has he liberated himself? Which is the prison—reality or anarchy? Who is the gaoler?

"We make for ourselves", writes Amiel, "in truth, our own spiritual world monsters, chimeras, angels; we make objective what ferments in us. All is marvellous for the poet, all is divine for the saint; all is great for the hero; all is wretched, miserable, ugly and bad for the base and sordid soul. The bad man creates around him a pandemonium, the artist an Olympus, the elect soul a paradise, which each of them sees for himself alone. *We are all visionaries, and what we see is our soul in things . . .*"

All is marvellous for the poet! Yes, the more one is a poet the more marvellous everything becomes. Everything! That is to say, not just the life to come, not merely what is unknown and dimly apprehended, not the ideal, not truth, beauty, madness, but what is here and now, the flux of life, the dead as well as the alive, the common, the sordid, the worthless, the ugly, the boring, all, all, because the transforming vision alters the aspect of the world. The Surrealists themselves have demonstrated the possibilities of the marvellous which lie concealed in the commonplace. They have done it by juxtaposition. But the effect of these strange transpositions and juxtapositions of the most unlike things has been to freshen the vision. Nothing more. For the man who is vitally alive it would be unnecessary to rearrange the objects and conditions of this world. The vision precedes the arrangement, or rearrangement. The world doesn't grow stale. Every great artist by his work reaffirms this fact. The artist is the opposite of the politically-minded individual, the opposite of the reformer, the opposite of the idealist. The artist does not tinker with the universe: he recreates it out of his own experience and understanding of life. He knows that the transformation must proceed from within outward, not vice versa. The world problem becomes the problem of the Self. The world problem is the projection of the inner problem. It is a process of expropriating the world, of becoming God. The striving toward this limit, the expansion of the Self, in other words, is what truly brings about the condition of the marvellous. Knowledge is not involved, nor power. But vision.

It is but natural that the tremendous emphasis on the marvellous which the Surrealists have given to the movement should be the reaction against the crippling, dwarfing harmony imposed by French culture. In the fake Hellenism of French culture the sense of the marvellous, the sense of magic, of wonder, awe, mystery, was doomed to perish. In France "the lying cultural mask" which Nietzsche speaks of has become real; it is no longer a mask. Employing a ritual and ceremonial less rigid, less elaborate than the Chinese, the French nevertheless have come to resemble them in spirit more closely than any European nation. French life has become stylized. It is not a life rhythm but a death rhythm. The culture is no longer vital . . . it is decayed. And the French, securely imprisoned within this cultural wall, are rotting away. That is why, so it seems to me, the individual Frenchman appears to possess more vitality than his surrounding neighbors. In each and every Frenchman it is the cultural mould which manifests itself. Before you can kill off the individual Frenchman you have to kill off the culture which produced him. Nowhere else in Europe is this true. With the others the mould has already broken and what we smell in them is an amorphous, anonymous culture which is extinct. To be a good European now means to become a polyglot and nomadic cultural nobody. (Goethe was the last good European.)

If it serves to destroy this death grip Surrealism will serve a valuable function. But it rather seems to me that Surrealism is merely the reflection of the death process. It is one of the manifestations of a life becoming extinct, a virus which quickens the inevitable end. Even so it is a movement in the right direction. Europe must die, and France with it. Sooner or later a new life must begin, a life from the roots.

"As yet", writes Keyserling, "only the few are conscious of the extent to which the course of the historic process is a phenomenon resembling that of counterpoint in music. Just because the masses have triumphed to an unheard of degree for the time being, we are approaching a decidedly aristocratic epoch. Just because quantity alone is the decisive factor to-day, the qualitative will soon mean more than ever before. Just because the mass appears to be everything, all great decisions will soon be taken within the smallest circle. They, and they alone, as the Ark during the Flood, are the safeguards of the future.

"For this reason we who are spiritual should consciously assume the counterpoint attitude to everything which is going on to-day. Let the culture of making-all-things-easy overspread the earth like a flood. An age whose day is past is being drowned in the deluge. We will not even try to stem the tide. Let us recognize the fact that for a long time to come everything within view, and in the first instance the state, will have to serve the process of liquidation. But at the same time let us remain proudly conscious of this other fact: that to-day everything depends on those who keep aloof, who are officially inconspicuous and not in view of the many. All the future is theirs."

There remain the death-eaters, those who are coming more and more into control as the bright future opens up. Destined to hasten the collapse of a world already defunct they are galvanizing the dead youth of the world into a temporary enthusiasm. Everywhere youth is being called to the colors; as in every epoch the young are being groomed for the ritual slaughter. The cause! The sacred cause! For the sake of "the cause" the demons will soon be unleashed and we shall all be commanded to fly at each other's throats. It is as clear as can be. Under the sign of DEATH all sides, all forces, are secretly making common cause. *Death:* that is the real motive, the real urge. Whoever doubts that we are going to escape this death-feast is an imbecile. In this stupid infatuation for death the Surrealists are no different from the others. We are all going down together—red shirts, black shirts, pacifists, militarists, dadaists, Surrealists, nonconformists, all kinds of ists and isms together. Down into the bottomless pit.

Now, my dear fellows, my dear Belgian, Swedish, Japanese, Dutch, British, French, American, Rhodesian, Arthurian, Cro-Magnon, Neanderthalian Surrealists, now is the time to grab hold of that most wonderful prehensile tail which has been dragging in the mud for countless centuries. Get hold of it, if you can, and swing for your lives! It's one chance out of a million, and I wish you luck, you poor bleeding bastards.

Via Dieppe-Newhaven

THE THING WAS that I wanted to be among English-speaking people again, for a little while at least. I had nothing against the French; on the contrary, I had at last made a bit of a home for myself in Clichy and everything would have been swell if it hadn't been for the fact that I had just gone through a crisis with my wife. She was living in Montparnasse and I was living with my friend Fred, who had taken an apartment, in Clichy just outside the Porte. We had agreed to separate; she was going back to America as soon as the money arrived for the boat fare.

So far so good. I had said good-bye to her and I thought every-

thing was finished. Then one day when I walked into the grocer's
the old woman informed me that my wife had just been in with a
young man and that they had taken away a good supply of groceries
which they had charged up to my account. The old woman seemed
a bit perplexed and a little worried too. I told her it was O. K.
And it was O. K. too, because I knew my wife didn't have any
money, and after all a wife has to eat just like any other person.
About the young man, that was O. K. too: he was just a fairy who
felt sorry for her and I supposed he had put her up for the time
being in his apartment. In fact, everything was O. K. except that
she was still in Paris, and when in Christ's name was she going to
beat it, that's what I was wondering about.

A few more days passed and then she dropped in one late after-
noon to have dinner with us. Why not? We could always scrape
up a bit of food whereas in Montparnasse among the riff-raff she
was obliged to hang out where food was almost unobtainable. After
the dinner she got hysterical: she said she was suffering from dys-
entery ever since she had left me and that it was my fault, that I
had tried to poison her. I walked her to the Metro station at the
Porte without saying a word. I was sore as hell, so god-damned
sore that I couldn't talk. She was sore too, sore because I refused
to argue the matter with her. I thought to myself, walking back,
well this is the last straw, she surely won't come back again. I
poisoned her. Good, if she wants to think that way let her! That
ought to settle the issue.

A few days later I had a letter from her asking for a little cash
with which to meet the rent. Seems she wasn't living with the fairy
at all, but in a cheap hotel back of the Gare Montparnasse. I
couldn't give her the money immediately as I didn't have any my-
self so I let a few days intervene before going to her hotel and
settling the bill. While I was trotting round to her hotel a pneu-

matique had come for me saying that she simply must have the money or she'd be kicked out. If I had had a little money I wouldn't have put her to all these humiliations, but the point is I didn't have any. However, she didn't believe me. And even if it were true, she said, I could at least have borrowed it for her. Which was also true. But I was never good on borrowing large sums; all my life I had been used to asking for hand-outs, for chicken feed, and feeling damned grateful when I got that. She seemed to have forgotten that. It was natural enough that she should because she was bitter and her pride had been wounded. And to do her justice I must add that had the situation been reversed the money would have been forthcoming; she always knew how to raise money for me but never for herself. That I've got to admit.

I was getting pretty wrought up about the whole thing. I felt like a louse. And the worse I felt the less I was able to do. I even suggested that she come back and stay with us until the money which she was expecting for the boat trip should come. But this she wouldn't hear of, naturally. Or was it natural? I was so damned perplexed and humiliated and confused that I didn't know any more what was natural and what wasn't. Money. Money. All my life it had been a question of money. I would never be able to solve the problem and I didn't hope to.

After turning round and round like a rat in a trap I got the brilliant idea of beating it myself. Just walk out on the problem, that's always the easiest way. I don't know how the idea came to me but suddenly I had decided that I would go to London. If you had offered me a chateau in Touraine I would have said no. For some reason or other I had made up my mind that it must be London and no other place. The reason I gave myself was that she'd never think of looking for me in London. She knew I hated the place. But the real reason, as I soon discovered, was that I wanted to be among English-speaking people; I wanted to hear English spoken twenty-four hours of the day, and nothing but English. In my weak condition that was like falling back on the bosom of the Lord. Talking and listening to English meant just that less strain. God knows, when you're in a jam to talk a foreign language, or even just to listen to it—because you can't shut your ears even if you try to—is a subtle form of torture. I had absolutely nothing against the French, nor against the language they spoke. Up until she arrived on the scene I had been living in a sort of Paradise. Suddenly everything had gone sour. I found myself muttering things against the French, and against the language particularly, which I would never have dreamed of thinking in my sober senses. I knew it was my own fault, but that only made it worse. Well, London then. A little vacation and perhaps by the time I returned she would have left. That's all there was to it.

I rustled up the dough for a visa and a return trip ticket. I bought a visa for a year thinking that if by any chance I should change my mind about the English I might go back a second or a third time to England. It was getting on towards Christmas and I began to think what a jolly old place London might be during the holidays. Perhaps I would find a different sort of London than the one I knew, a Dickensian London such as tourists always dream of. I had the visa and the ticket in my pocket and just about enough dough to last me for ten days. I was feeling almost jubilant about the trip.

When I got back to Clichy it was almost dinner time. I walked into the kitchen and there was my wife helping Fred with the dinner. They were laughing and joking as I walked in. I knew that Fred wouldn't say anything to her about my going to London and so I sat down to the table and laughed and joked a bit myself. It was a jolly meal, I must say, and everything would have gone off splendidly if Fred hadn't been obliged to go to the newspaper office after dinner. I had been canned a few weeks ago but he was still working, though expecting the same fate any day. The reason I was canned was that, even though I was an American, I had no right to be working on an American newspaper as a proof-reader. According to French theory the job could just as well have been held by a Frenchman who knew English. That griped me a bit and no doubt contributed to my feeling sour towards the French the last few weeks. Anyway, that was over and done with and I was a free man again and I would soon be in London talking English all day long and far into the night if I wanted to. Besides, my book was coming out very soon and that might change everything. All in all things weren't half as black as they had seemed a few days back. Thinking how nicely I was going to duck the whole thing I got a bit careless and ran out, in a moment of exuberation, to buy a bottle of Chartreuse which I knew she liked better than anything. That was a fatal mistake. The Chartreuse made her mellow and then hysterical and then reproving. We sat there at the table, the two of us, and I guess we rehearsed a lot of things that should have been forgotten. Finally I got to such a point of guilt and tenderness that I blurted out the whole thing—about the trip to London, the money I had borrowed, and so on and so forth. I forked the whole thing out and laid it on the table. There it was, I don't know how many pounds and shillings, all in bright new English money. I told her I was sorry and to hell with the trip and to-morrow I would try to get a refund on the tickets and give that to her too.

And here again I must render her justice. She really didn't want to take the money. It made her wince, I could see that, but finally she accepted it reluctantly and stuffed it away in her bag. As she was leaving she forgot the bag and I was obliged to run down the stairs after her and hand it to her. As she took the bag she said good-bye again and this time I felt that it was the last good-bye. She said good-bye and she stood there on the stairs looking up at me with a strange sorrowful smile. If I had made the least gesture I know she would have thrown the money out of the window and rushed back into my arms and stayed with me forever. I took a long look at her, walked slowly back to the door, and closed it. I went back to the kitchen table, sat there a few minutes looking at the empty glasses, and then I broke down and sobbed like a child.

It was about three in the morning when Fred came back from work. He saw right away that something had gone wrong. I told him what had happened and then we sat down and ate, and after we had eaten we drank some good Algerian wine and then some Chartreuse and after that a little cognac. It was a damned shame, in Fred's opinion, and I was a fool to have forked up all the money. I agreed, but I felt good about it just the same.

"And what about London? Do you mean to tell me you're not going to London?" he says.

"No," I said, "I've given up the idea. Besides, I couldn't go now even if I wanted to. Where's the dough to come from?"

Fred didn't seem to think the lack of dough was any grave obstacle. He thought he could borrow a couple of hundred francs at the office and on pay-day, which was only a few days off, he would wire me more. We sat there discussing the thing until dawn, and of course drinking a bit too. When I hit the hay I could hear the Westminster chimes—and a few rusty sleigh bells too. I saw a beautiful blanket of snow lying over dirty London and everybody greeting me with a hearty "Merry Christmas!"—in *English*, to be sure.

I made the Channel crossing at night. It was a miserable night and we stayed indoors shivering with the cold. I had a hundred franc note and some change—that was all. The idea was that as soon as I found a hotel I was to cable and Fred would cable back some more dough. I sat at the long table in the salon listening to the conversation going on around me. The thought uppermost in my mind was how to make the hundred francs stretch as far as possible, because the more I thought about it the less sure I was that Fred would raise the dough immediately. The scraps of conversation I picked up also had to do with money. Money. Money. The same thing everywhere and all the time. It seems that England had just that day paid her debt to America, much against her will. She had kept her word, as they were saying all about me. England always kept her word. And more of that and more, until I felt like strangling them for their bloody honesty.

I hadn't intended to break the hundred franc note until absolutely necessary, but with this silly conversation going on about England keeping her word and knowing that they had spotted me as an American I finally got so jumpy that I ordered a beer and a ham sandwich. That brought me directly into contact with the steward. He wanted to know what I thought about the situation. I could see that he thought it was a bloody crime what we had done to England. I felt sore that he should make me responsible for the situation just because I happened to be born an American. So I told him I didn't know anything about the situation, that it was none of my affair, and furthermore that it was a matter of absolute indifference to me whether England paid her debts or didn't pay her debts. He didn't relish this very much. A man ought to have an interest in the affairs of his country, even if his country is in the wrong, that's what he thought. I told him I didn't give a damn about America or Americans. I told him I didn't have an ounce of patriotism in me. At that moment a man who had been pacing up and down beside the table stopped to listen to me. I had a feeling that he was a spy or a detective. I piped down almost at once and turned to the young man beside me who had also called for a beer and a sandwich.

Apparently he had been listening to me with some interest. He wanted to know where I came from and what I was going to do in England. I told him I was taking a little vacation, and then, impulsively, I asked him if he could recommend a very cheap hotel. He said he had been away from England quite a long while and that he didn't know London very well anyhow. Said he had been living in Australia the last few years. Just then the steward happened along and the young man interrupted himself to ask the steward if he knew of any good cheap little hotel in London. The steward called the waiter over and asked him the same question, and just as he put the question to the waiter the man who looked like a spy came along and paused a moment to listen in. From the serious way in which the subject was discussed I could see at once that I had made a mistake. One shouldn't ask questions like that of a steward or a waiter. I felt that they were looking me over suspiciously, that they were giving my pocket-book the X-ray. I tossed off the beer at one gulp and, as though to prove that money was the least of my worries I called for another and then, turning to the young man at my elbow, I asked him if he wouldn't let me buy him a drink too. When the steward came back with the drinks we were deep in the wilds of Australia. He started to say something about a hotel but I old him immediately to forget about it. It was just an idle question, I added. That seemed to stump him. He stood there a few moments not knowing what to do, then suddenly, moved by some friendly impulse, he blurted out that he would be glad to put me up in his own home at Newhaven if I cared to spend the night there. I thanked him warmly and told him not to worry about it any more, that I would go on to London just the same. It really isn't important, I added. And the moment I said it I knew that that too was a mistake, because somehow, despite myself, I had made the thing seem quite important to everybody.

There was still a bit of time to kill and so I listened to the young Englishman who had had a strange time of it in Australia. He was telling me of his life as a sheep herder, how they castrated I don't know how many thousands of sheep in a day. One had to work fast. So fast, in fact, that the most expedient thing to do was to grab the testicles with your teeth and then a quick slit with the knife and spit them out. He was trying to estimate how many thousand pair of testicles he had bitten off in this hand to mouth operation during his sojourn in Australia. And as he was going through his mental calculations he wiped his mouth with the back of his hand.

"You must have had a strange taste in your mouth," I said, instinctively wiping my own mouth.

"It wasn't as bad as you might imagine," he answered calmly. "You get used to everything—in time. No, it wasn't a bad taste at all . . . the idea is worse than the actual thing. Just the same, I never thought when I left my comfortable home in England that I would be spitting out those things for a living. A man can get used to doing most anything when he's really up against it."

I was thinking the same thing. I was thinking of the time I burned brush in an orange grove in Chula Vista. Ten hours a day in the broiling sun running from one fire to another and the flies biting like mad. And for what? To prove to myself that I was a man, I suppose, that I could take it on the chin. And another time working as a gravedigger: to show that I wasn't afraid of tackling anything. The gravedigger! With a volume of Nietzsche under his arm, and trying to memorize the last part of Faust to and from work. Well, as the steward says, "*the English never twist you!*" The boat is coming to a stop. Another swig of beer to drown the taste of sheep's nuts and a handsome little tip for the waiter just to prove that Americans pay their debts too sometimes. In the excitement I find myself quite alone, standing behind a bulky Englishman with a checkered cap and a big ulster. Landing in any other country the checkered cap would look ridiculous, but as it's his own country he can do as he pleases, and what's more I almost admire him for it, it makes him seem so big and independent. I'm beginning to think that they're not such a bad race after all.

On deck it's dark and drizzly. The last time I pulled into England, that was coming up the Thames, it was also dark and drizzly and the faces were ashen gray and the uniforms were black and the houses were grim and grimy. And up High Holborn Street every morning I remember there passed me the most respectable, lamentable, dilapidated paupers God ever made. Gray, watery paupers with bowlers and cutaways and that absurd air of respectability which only the English can muster in adversity. And now the language is coming to me a little stronger and I must say I don't like it at all: it sounds oily, slimy, servile, unctuous. I feel the class line cutting through the accents. The man with the checkered cap and the ulster has suddenly become a pompous ass; he seems to be talking Choctaw to the porters. I hear Sir all the time. Can I do this, *Sir?* Which way, *Sir?* Yes, *Sir.* No, *Sir.* Bugger me if it doesn't make me a bit creepy, all this yes sir and no sir. *Sir* my ass, I say under my breath.

At the Immigration Office. Waiting my turn on the line. The rich bastards go first, as usual. We move up inch by inch. Those who've passed through are having their baggage inspected on the quay. The porters are bustling about loaded down like donkeys. Only two people ahead of me now. I have my passport in my hand

and my train ticket and my baggage checks. Now I'm standing square in front of him, offering him my passport. He looks at the big white sheet beside him, finds my name and checks it off.

"How long do you intend to stay in England, Mr. Miller?" he says, holding the passport in his hand as though ready to give it back to me.

"A week or two," I answer.

"You're going to London, are you?"

"Yes."

"What hotel are you stopping at, Mr. Miller?"

I have to smile at this. "Why, I don't know," I respond, still smiling. "Perhaps you can recommend me a hotel."

"Have you any friends in London, Mr. Miller?"

"No."

"Just what are you going to do in London, if I may ask?"

"Why, I'm going to take a little vacation." Still smiling.

"I suppose you have enough money for your stay in England?"

"I think so," says I, still nonchalant, still smiling. And thinking to myself what a cinch it is to bluff it through with questions like that.

"Do you mind showing me your money, Mr. Miller?"

"Of course not," and reaching into my jeans I haul out the remains of the hundred franc note. The people next to me are laughing. I try to laugh too, but I'm not very successful. As for my inquisitor, he gives a feeble little chuckle and looking me square in the eye he says with all the sarcasm he can put into it: "You didn't expect to stay very long in London on that, did you, Mr. Miller?"

Always this *Mr. Miller* tacked on to every phrase! I'm beginning to dislike the son-of-a-bitch. What's more it's beginning to get uncomfortable.

"Look here," I say, still amiable and still outwardly nonchalant, "I don't intend to have a vacation on that. As soon as I get a hotel I expect to wire for money. I left Paris in a great hurry and . . ."

He cuts me short. Can I give him the name of my bank in Paris, he wants to know.

"I haven't got a bank account," I'm obliged to answer. That makes a very bad impression I realize at once. I can feel the hostility growing up all about me. People who were holding their bags are putting them down now, as though they knew they were in for a long siege. The passport which he had been holding in his hands like a little testament he puts on the counter before him and holds it there, like a damaging piece of evidence, with outstretched finger-tips.

"Where were you going to get the money from, Mr. Miller?" he asks more blandly than ever.

"Why, from a friend of mine, the man who lives with me in Paris."

"Has he a bank account?"

"No, but he's got a job. He works on the Chicago Tribune."

"And you think he will send you the money for your vacation?"

"I don't think so, I *know* so," I answered tartly. "I'm not trying to give you a cock and bull story. I told you I left in a hurry. I left with the understanding that he'd send me the money as soon as I arrived in London. Besides, it's my money, not his."

"You left your money with him rather than put it in a bank, is that it, Mr. Miller?"

"Well," I said, beginning to lose my temper, "it isn't a hell of a lot of money and besides, I don't see the point of all this. If you don't believe me I'll stay right here and you can send a cable and find out for yourself."

"Just a minute, Mr. Miller. You say the two of you live together . . . do you live in a hotel or in an apartment?"

"An apartment."

"And the apartment is in your name?"

"No, in his. That is, it belongs to the both of us, but it's in his name because he's a Frenchman and it makes it easier."

"And he keeps your money for you?"

"No, not usually. You see, I left under rather unusual circumstances. I . . ."

"Just a minute, Mr. Miller," and he motions to me to step back from the ranks a bit. At the same time he calls one of his assistants over and hands him my passport. The latter takes the passport and goes behind a screen some distance off. I stand there watching the others go through.

"You might go and have your baggage inspected meanwhile," I hear him say as if in a trance. I move off to the shed and open my luggage. The train is waiting for us. It looks like a team of Eskimo dogs straining at the leash. The locomotive is puffing and steaming. Finally I walk back and take my stand in front of my interlocutor. The last few passengers are being hustled through the examination.

Now the tall thin man from behind the screen comes forward with the passport in his hand. He seems determined in advance that I'm a malefactor.

"You're an American citizen, Mr. Miller?"

"Obviously," I answer. With this guy I know there's going to be no mercy. He hasn't a speck of humor in him.

"How long have you been in France?"

"Two or three years, I guess. You can see the date there for yourself . . . Why? What's that got to do with it?"

"You were thinking of spending several months in England, were you?"

"No, I wasn't. I was thinking of spending a week or ten days there, that's all. But now . . ."

"So you bought a visa for a year, thinking to spend a week."

"I bought a return trip ticket too, if that interests you."

"One could always throw the return ticket away," he says with a malicious twist of the mouth.

"One could if he were an idiot. I don't get the point. And anyway, look here, I'm tired of all this nonsense. I'm going to stay in Newhaven overnight and take the next boat back. I don't have to spend my vacation in England."

"Not so fast, Mr. Miller. I think we ought to look into this a little more closely."

As he said this I heard the whistle blow. The passengers were all aboard and the train was just starting. I thought of my trunk which I had checked through to London. Nearly all my manuscripts were in it, and my typewriter too. A nice mess, I thought to myself. All because of that chicken feed I slapped down on the counter.

The little fat fellow with the bland imperturbable mask now joined us. He seemed to be expecting a treat.

Hearing the train roll out of the station I resigned myself to the inquisition. Thinks I to myself, now that they've fucked me, let's see how far they can prolong the agony. First of all, however, I demanded my passport back. If they wanted to grill me a little more O. K. There was nothing to do at that hour of the night and before turning in at Newhaven I thought I'd go through with the song and dance.

To my amazement the tall thin fellow refused to return my passport. That made me furious. I demanded to know if there was an American Consul on hand. "Listen," I said, "you may think what you like, but that passport belongs to me and I want it back."

"There's no need to get excited, Mr. Miller. You'll have your passport before you leave. But first there are a few questions I'd like to put to you . . . I see that you are a married man. Is your wife living with you—and your friend? Or is she in America?"

"I don't see that that's any of your business," I said. "But since you brought the subject up I'm going to tell you something now. The reason I came away with so little money is because I gave the money for my trip to my wife before leaving. We're separating and she's going back to America in a few days. I gave her the money because she was broke."

"How much money did you give her, if I may ask?"

"You're asking so damned many questions that you have no right to ask I don't see why you shouldn't ask that too. If you want to know, I gave her about 60 pounds. Let's see. I may still have the exchange slip in my wallet . . ." And I made a gesture as if to reach for my wallet and look for the slip.

"Wasn't that rather foolish to give your wife all that money and come to England penniless, or almost so?"

I gave him a sour smile. "My dear man, I've tried to explain to you that I'm not coming to England as a pauper. If you had let me go to London and wire for the money everything would have been all right. I suppose it's a waste of time to say a thing like this to you but try to understand me, will you? *I'm a writer.* I do things impulsively. I don't have bank accounts and I don't plan things years in advance. When I want to do something I do it. For some reason or other you seem to think that I want to come to England to . . . frankly, I don't know what the hell's in your mind. I just wanted to come to England to hear English, if you can believe it—and partly too to escape my wife. Does that make sense to you?"

"I should say it does," says the tall thin fellow. "You want to run away from your wife and let her become a public charge. How do you know she won't follow you to England? And how will you take care of her in England—without money?"

I felt as though I were talking to a stone wall. What was the use of rehearsing the whole thing again? "Listen," I said, "as far as I'm concerned I don't care what happens to her. If she becomes a public charge that's her affair, not mine."

"You're working for the Chicago Tribune, you say?"

"I never said anything of the kind. I said my friend, the man who was to send me the money, he's working on the Chicago Tribune."

"You never worked for the newspaper then?"

"Yes, I used to work for them, but I don't now. They fired me a few weeks ago."

He snapped me up immediately. "Oh, then you *did* work for the newspaper in Paris?"

"Didn't I just say so? Why? Why do you ask?"

"Mr. Miller, could I see your carte d'identité . . . I suppose you *have* a carte d'identité, living in Paris, as you say."

I fished it out for him. The two of them looked it over together.

"You have a non-worker's card—yet you worked for the Chicago Tribune as a proof-reader. How do you explain that, Mr. Miller?"

"No, I suppose I can't explain that to you. I suppose it's useless to explain to you that I'm an American citizen and that the Chicago Tribune is an American newspaper and that therefore . . ."

"Excuse me, but why were you dismissed from the newspaper?"

"That's just what I was coming to. You see, the French officials, those who have to do with the red tape, seem to take the same attitude as you do. Perhaps I could have remained on the Tribune if

I hadn't also been a bad proof-reader. That's the real reason why I was fired, if you want to know."

"You seem rather proud of the fact."

"I am. I think it's a mark of intelligence."

"And so, not having a job on the Tribune any more you thought you'd come to England for a little vacation. And you provided yourself with a visa for a year and a return trip ticket."

"Also to hear English and to escape my wife," I added.

Here the little round-faced fellow spoke up. The tall fellow seemed ready to relinquish the tussle.

"You're a writer, Mr. Miller?"

"Yes."

"You mean you write books and stories?"

"Yes."

"Do you write for the magazines in America?"

"Yes."

"Which ones . . . can you name a few?"

"Certainly. The American Mercury, Harper's, Atlantic Monthly, Scribner's, the Virginia Quarterly, The Yale Review . . ."

"Just a minute." He walked back to the counter and bending down he pulled out a big fat directory. "American Mercury . . . American Mercury . . ." he kept mumbling as he thumbed the pages. "Henry V. Miller, isn't it? Henry V. Miller . . . Henry V. Miller . . . Was it this year or last year, Mr. Miller?"

"It may be three years ago—for the Mercury," I said blandly.

Apparently he had no book on hand that went back that far. Couldn't I give him the name of a magazine I had written for in the last year or two? I said no, I had been too busy writing a book the last year or so.

Had the book been published? What was the name of the American publisher?

213

I said it had been published by an Englishman.

What was the name of the publisher?

"The Obelisk Press."

He scratched his head. "An *English* publisher?" He couldn't seem to remember any English house by that name. He called his side-kick who had disappeared behind the screen with my passport. "Ever hear of the Obelisk Press?" he yelled.

At this point I thought it timely to tell him that my English publisher published from Paris. That seemed to make him hopping mad. An English publisher in Paris! It was a violation of the rules of nature. Well, anyway, what were the names of the books?

"There's only one," I said. "It's called *Tropic of Cancer*."

At this I thought he would throw a fit. I didn't know what had come over him for the moment. Finally he seemed to bring himself under partial control and, in the suavest, the most sarcastic voice imaginable, he said: "Come, Mr. Miller, you don't mean to tell me that you write *medical* books too?"

It was my turn to be flabbergasted. The two of them were standing there boring me through with their mean gimlet-like eyes.

"The *Tropic of Cancer*", I said slowly and solemnly, "is *not* a medical book."

"Well, what is it then?" they asked simultaneously.

"The title," I answered, "is a symbolic title. The Tropic of Cancer is a name given in text-books to a temperate zone lying above the Equator. Below the Equator you have the Tropic of Capricorn, which is the south temperate zone. The book, of course, has nothing to do with climatic conditions either, unless it be a sort of mental climate. Cancer is a name which has always intrigued me: you'll find it in zodiacal lore too. Etymologically it comes from chancre, meaning crab. In Chinese symbolism it is a sign of great importance. The crab is the only living creature which can walk

214

backwards and forwards and sideways with equal facility. Of course my book doesn't treat of all this explicitly. It's a novel, or rather an autobiographical document. If my trunk were here I might have shown you a copy. I think you'd be interested in it. By the way, the reason it was published in Paris is because it's too obscene for England or America. Too much cancer in it, if you know what I mean . . ."

This brought the discussion to a close. The tall slim fellow packed his brief case, put on his hat and coat and waited impatiently for the little fellow to get ready. I asked for my passport again. The tall slim fellow went behind the screen and got it for me. I opened it and I saw that he had drawn a big black X through my visa. That infuriated me. It was like a black mark against my good name. "Where's a place to put up for the night in this burg?" I asked, putting as much snot and venom in it as I could muster.

"The constable here will take care of that," says the big fellow, giving me a wry smile and turning on his heel. And with that I see a very tall man dressed in black with a big helmet and a cadaverous face coming towards me out of the gloom of the far corner.

"What do you mean?" I yelled. "Do you mean that I'm under arrest?"

"No, I wouldn't say *that*, Mr. Miller. The constable will put you up for the night and in the morning he'll put you on the boat for Dieppe." And he started to walk away again.

"O. K." I said. "But you're going to see me back here, maybe next week."

By this time the constable was at my side and had me by the arm. I was white with rage, but that firm grasp of the arm told me it was useless to say anything more. It was like the hand of death itself.

As we walked towards the door I explained very calmly to the constable that my trunk had gone on to London and that it contained all my manuscripts as well as other things.

"We can take care of that, Mr. Miller," he says in a quiet, low, steady voice. "Just step this way with me," and he made for the telegraph office. I gave him the necessary dope and he assured me in his quiet, easy voice that I'd have my things in the morning, the first thing in the morning. I knew from the way he spoke that he was a man of his word. Somehow I had an instant respect for him. I did wish, however, that he'd let go my arm. Shit, I wasn't a criminal, and even if I did want to make a break for it where would I go? I couldn't jump in the sea, could I? However, it was no use starting things with him. He was a man who obeyed orders and it was enough just to take one look at him to know that he had been trained like a dog. He escorted me gently and firmly to the hoosegow. We had to pass through a number of vacant, dim-lit rooms or halls to get to the joint. Each time we opened a door he paused and, taking out a bunch of keys, locked the door behind us. It was impressive. I began to get a bit of a thrill out of it. It was ridiculous and awesome at the same time. Christ knows what he would have done if I had been a really dangerous criminal. I suppose he'd have manacled me first. Anyway, finally we got to the hoosegow, which was a sort of big gloomy waiting room very dimly lit. There wasn't a soul in the place, nothing but a few long empty benches, as far as I could make out.

"Here's where we spend the night," said the constable in the same quiet, steady voice. Really a gentle voice it was. I was beginning to take a liking to him. "There's a wash room in there," he added, pointing to a door just in back of me.

"I don't need to wash up," I said. "What I'd really like to do is to take a crap.'

"You'll find the place in there," he answered, and opening the door he turned on the light for me.

I went in, took my coats off and sat down. Suddenly, as I was sitting there I looked up and to my amazement there was the constable sitting by the doorway on a little stool. I wouldn't say he was watching me, but certainly he had one eye on me, as they say. At once my bowels were paralyzed. *That*, I thought to myself, that beats everything! And then and there I made a mental note to write about the incident.

As I was buttoning up I expressed a little of my amazement. He took what I said in good part, replying very simply that it was part of his duty. "I've got to keep you under observation until I hand you over to the captain in the morning," he said. "Those are the orders."

"Do people try to run away sometimes?" I asked.

"Not very often," he said. "But things are very bad now, you know, and lots of people are trying to get into England who don't belong here. People who are looking for work, you know."

"Yes, I know," I said. "Things are in a mess."

I was pacing slowly up and down in the big waiting room. Suddenly I felt rather chilly. I went over to the big bench where my overcoat was lying and flung it around my shoulders.

"Would you like me to build you a fire, sir?" the constable suddenly asked.

I thought it was damned considerate of him to ask a question like that and so I said "Why, I don't know. How about you? Do you want a fire too?"

"It isn't that, sir," he said. "You see the law entitles you to a fire, if you wish it."

"The hell with that!" I said. "The question is, would it be a bother to make one? Perhaps I can help you."

"No, it's my duty to make you a fire if you wish it. I have nothing to do but look after you."

"Well, if that's the case, let's have a fire," I said. I sat down on the bench and watched him getting it started. Pretty decent, I thought to myself. So the law entitles you to a fire. Well, I'll be God-damned!

When the fire was made the constable suggested that I stretch out on the bench and make myself comfortable. He dug up a cushion from somewhere and a blanket. I lay there looking at the fire and thinking what a strange world it is after all. I mean how on the one hand they manhandle you and on the other hand they nurse you like a baby. All written down in the same book, like debit and credit columns in a ledger. The government is the invisible bookkeeper who makes the entries, and the constable is just a sort of human blotter who dries the ink. If you happen to get a kick in the ass or a couple of teeth pushed down your throat that's gratis and no record is made of it.

The constable was sitting on the little stool by the fireside reading the evening paper. He said he would just sit there and read a bit until I fell asleep. He said it in a neighborly way, without the slightest malice or sarcasm. A different species entirely from the other two bastards whom I had just left.

I watched him reading the paper for a while and then I started to talk to him, in a human way, what I mean, not like he was the constable and me the prisoner. He was not an unintelligent man, nor did he lack sensibility. He struck me, in fact, very much like a fine greyhound, something anyway with blood and breeding. Whereas those other two farts, who were also doing their duty by the government, impressed me as a couple of sadistic jakes, as mean, low, cringing bastards who enjoyed doing their dirty work for the government. I'm sure if the constable were to kill a man in the line of duty you could forgive him for it. But those other pimps! Bah! I spat into the fire with disgust.

I was curious to know if the constable ever did any serious reading. To my surprise he told me that he had read Shaw and Belloc and Chesterton— and some of Somerset Maugham's work. *Of Human Bondage* was a great book, he thought. I thought so too and I scored another strike for the constable on my mental blackboard.

"And you're a writer too?" he said, very gently, almost timidly, I thought.

"A bit of a one," I said diffidently. And then impulsively, falteringly, stutteringly, I launched into an account of *Tropic of Cancer*. I told him about the streets and the cafes. I told him how I had tried to put it all in the book and whether I had succeeded or not I didn't know. "But it's a *human* book," I said, getting up from the bench and moving very close to him. "And I tell you one thing, constable, you impress me as being very human too. I've enjoyed this evening with you and I want you to know that I have a respect and admiration for you. And if you don't think it's immodest of me why I'd like to send you a copy of my book when I get back to Paris."

He wrote his name and address in my notebook and told me he would read the book with great pleasure. "You're a very interesting man," he said, "and I'm sorry we had to meet under such painful circumstances."

"Well, let's not talk about that," I said. "What do you say we do a wink of sleep now? Eh?"

"Why yes," he said, "you can make yourself comfortable on the bench there. I'll just sit here and doze a bit. By the way," he added, "would you like me to order breakfast for you in the morning?"

I thought to myself well that's a pretty swell guy, about as decent as they make 'em. And with that I closed my eyes and dozed off.

In the morning the constable took me aboard the boat and handed me over to the captain. There were no passengers aboard yet. I waved good-bye to the constable and then I stood at the prow of the boat and took a good look at England. It was one of those quiet, peaceful mornings with a clear sky overhead and the gulls flying. Always, looking at England from the sea, I am impressed by the gentle, peaceful, somnolent quality of the landscape. England comes so gently down to the sea, it's almost touching. Everything seems so still, so civilized. I stood there looking at Newhaven with tears in my eyes. I wondered where the steward lived and whether he was up and eating his breakfast or pottering around the garden. In England every man ought to own a garden: it's meant to be that way, you feel it immediately. As I say, it couldn't have been a better day and England couldn't have looked lovelier, more inviting, than she looked at this moment. I thought of the constable again and how he fitted into the landscape. I want him to know, if he ever reads this, how much I regret the fact, seeing how gentle and sensitive he was, that I had to take a crap in front of him. If I had ever dreamed that he was going to sit there and keep an eye on me I would have held it in until we got to sea. I want him to know that. As for the other two bastards, I want to warn them here and now that if ever I encounter them again in this life I am going to spit in their eye. And may the curse of Job be on them for the rest of their lives. May they die in agony in a foreign land!

One of the most beautiful mornings I have ever known. The little village of Newhaven nestling in the white chalk cliffs. The end of the land, where civilization slips quietly into the sea. I stood there in a reverie for a long while, and a profound peace came over me. In such moments it seems that everything that happens to you happens for the best. Standing there quiet and peaceful like that I got to thinking of our own New Haven (Connecticut), where I had gone once to visit a man in jail. He was a man who had worked for me as a messenger and we had become friends. And then one day in a fit of jealousy he had shot his wife and then himself. Fortunately both of them recovered. After they had transferred him from the hospital to the prison I went to see him one day; we had a long talk through a steel mesh. When I left the prison I suddenly remarked how beautiful it was outdoors and, acting on the impulse, I went to a beach nearby and took a dip. It was one of the strangest days I ever spent at the ocean. When I dove off the springboard I had a feeling that I was taking leave of the earth forever. I didn't try to drown myself, but I didn't care a hoot if I were to drown. It felt marvellous to dive off the earth, to leave behind me all that man-made muck which we glorify with the word civilization. Anyway, as I came up and swam around I seemed to be looking at the world with new eyes. Nothing was like it had been before. People looked curiously separate and detached; they were sitting around like seals drying themselves in the sun. What I'm trying to say is that they seemed absolutely devoid of significance. They were just part of the landscape, like the rocks and the trees and the cows in the meadows. How they had ever assumed such a colossal importance on this earth was a mystery to me. I saw them plainly and distinctly as natural objects, as animals or plants. I felt that day that I could commit the most dastardly crime with a clear conscience. A crime without reason. Yes, it was that that I felt strongly: to kill some innocent person without reason.

As soon as the boat turned its nose towards Dieppe my thoughts began to take a different turn. I had never been out of France before and here I was returning in disgrace with that black mark against my visa. What would the French think? Perhaps they would begin to cross-examine me too. What was I doing in France? How did I make my living? Was I taking bread out of the mouths of French workers? Was I apt to become a public charge?

Suddenly I got into a panic. Supposing they refused to let me return to Paris? Supposing they transferred me to another boat and shipped me back to America? I got into a terrible funk. America! To be shipped back to New York and dumped there like a load of rotten apples! No, if they were going to try that stunt I'd jump overboard. I couldn't bear the thought of returning to America. It was Paris I wanted to see again. Never again would I grumble over my lot. It wouldn't matter if I had to live the rest of my life in Paris as a beggar. Better a beggar in Paris than a millionaire in New York!

I rehearsed a marvellous speech, in French, which I intended to make to the officials. It was such an elaborate, melodramatic speech that the crossing of the Channel passed like a dream. I was trying to conjugate a verb in the subjunctive when suddenly I saw the land popping up and the passengers flocking to the rail. Now it's coming, I thought. Brace up, me bucko, and unloose the subjunctives!

I stood apart from the others instinctively, as though not to contaminate them. I didn't know just what the procedure would be in stepping off—whether there'd be an agent to meet me or whether somebody would just pounce on me with the grappling hooks as I hit the gangplank. It was all much more simple than my anxiety led me to anticipate. As the boat pulled into the wharf the captain came forward and, grasping me by the arm just as the constable had done, he led me to the rail where I was in plain view of the men ashore. When he had caught the eye of the man on the quay whom he was seeking he raised his left hand aloft with the index finger pointing heavenward and then motioned to me. It was like saying *One!* One head of cabbage to-day! One head of cattle! I was more amazed than ashamed. It was so direct and logical, too, that you could hardly quarrel about it. After all, I was on a boat and the boat was pulling in and I was the man they were looking for and why send a cablegram or telephone when all you need to do is raise your arm and point like that? What could be simpler, less expensive?

When I observed the man whom I was being delivered to my heart sank. He was a big brute of a fellow with black handlebars for moustache and an enormous derby which half crushed his big appetizing ears. Even at long range his hands looked like big hams. And he too was dressed all in black. Clearly things were against me.

Walking down the gangplank I was struggling desperately to recall fragments of the speech which I had rehearsed only a few moments ago. I couldn't remember a blooming phrase. All I kept saying to myself was—"Oui, monsieur, je suis un Américain—mais je ne suis pas un mendiant. Je vous jure, monsieur, je ne suis pas un mendiant."

"Votre passeport, s'il vous plaît!"

"Oui, monsieur!"

I knew I was destined to say "Oui, monsieur" over and over again. Each time it came out of me I cursed myself for saying it. But what are you going to do? That's the first thing that's drummed into you when you come to France. *Oui, monsieur! Non, monsieur!* You feel like a cockroach at first. And then you get used to it and you say it unconsciously, and if the other fellow doesn't say it you notice it and you hold it against him. And when you're in trouble that's the first thing that pops out of your mouth. "*Oui, monsieur!*" You say it like an old billy-goat.

Anyway, I had only said it once or twice, because like the constable this chap was also a silent man. His duty consisted, as I happily discovered, in nothing more than escorting me to the office of another official who again demanded my passport and my carte d'identité. Here I was politely asked to sit down. I did so with a great feeling of relief and at the same time, taking a last look at the big brute who had dismissed me, I asked myself—where have I seen that man before?

After the grilling of the night before one great difference made itself felt immediately: *Respect for one's individuality!* I think now that even if he had put me on a boat for America I would have accepted my fate tranquilly. There was an inner order to the language, for one thing. He said nothing capricious, nothing insolent, nothing mean or foul or vindictive. He was talking the language of his people and there was form in it, an inner form which had come out of a deep experience of life. It was all the more striking, this clarity, in comparison with the external chaos in which he moved. In fact, it was almost ridiculous, this disorder which enveloped him. It was not altogether ridiculous because what inspired it was human, human foibles, human fallibilities. It was a disorder in which you feel at home, which is a purely French disorder. He had, after a few entirely perfunctory questions, left me undisturbed. I still had no idea what my fate was to be, but I knew definitely that whatever his verdict it would not be capricious or malevolent. I sat there in silence observing the way he went about his work. Nothing seemed to work just right, neither the pen, nor the blotter, nor the ink, nor the ruler. It was as though he had just opened the office and I was his first client. But he had had other offices before, thousands of them, and so he was not greatly perturbed if things didn't go smoothly all at once. The important thing, as he had learned, was to get it all down correctly in the

224

proper books. And to have the necessary stamps and seals which were to give the case its legal, orthodox aspect. Who was I? What had I done? Ca ne me regarde. pas! I could almost hear him saying it to himself. All he had asked me was—where were you born? where do you live in Paris? when did you come to France? With those three facts in his hand he was constructing a beautiful little dossier in my name to which he would finally sign his name with the proper flourish and then affix the stamps with the proper seal. That was his job and he understood it thoroughly.

It took him quite a little while to go about this task, I must admit. But time now was all in my favor. I would have sat there until the next morning quietly watching him if it had been necessary. I felt that he was working in my interest and in the interest of the French people and that our interests were one because clearly we were both intelligent and reasonable and why would either of us want to cause any one any trouble? I suppose he was a man whom the French would call a quelconque, which is not quite the same as a nobody in English, because Mr. Anybody or Everybody in France is quite another species from Mr. Nobody in America or England. A quelconque is not a nobody in France. He is a man like any other man, but he has a history and a tradition and a race behind him which often makes him more than the so-called Somebodies in other countries. Like this patient little man working on my dossier these men are often shabbily dressed: they look ragged about the edges and sometimes, be it said, they are not very clean either. But they know how to mind their own business, which is a very great deal.

As I say, it took him a little while to transcribe this data from one record to another. There were carbons to be adjusted, receipts to be detached, little labels to be pasted on, and so forth. Meanwhile the pencil had to be sharpened, a new stub had to be inserted in the penholder, the scissors had to be found, and they were found finally in the waste basket, the ink had to be changed, a new blotter dug up . . . there were lots of things to be done. And to complicate matters he discovered at the last minute that my French visa had expired. Perhaps it was out of delicacy that he merely *suggested* that it would be a good thing if I were to renew my visa—in case I intended to travel out of France again, he said. I was only too delighted to fall in line with the suggestion, feeling at the same time however that it would be a long time before I would ever think of leaving France again. I gave my consent more out of politeness and consideration for his valiant efforts on my behalf.

When everything had been put in order and my passport and carte d'identité were safely in my pocket again I very respectfully suggested that we have a little drink together at the bar across the way. He very graciously accepted the invitation and together we sauntered leisurely out to the *bistrot* opposite the station. He asked me if I liked living in Paris. A little more exciting than this hole, eh? he added. We didn't have time for much of a conversation as the train was due to leave in a few minutes. I thought perhaps at the end he would say—"how did you ever come to get into such a mess?"—but no, not the slightest allusion to the subject.

We walked back to the quay and as the whistle blew we shook hands cordially and he wished me a bon voyage. As I took my seat he was still standing there. He waved his hand and again he said: "Au revoir, Monsieur Miller, et bon voyage!" This time the *Monsieur Miller* sounded good to my ears, and perfectly natural. In fact it sounded so good and natural that it brought tears to my eyes. Yes, as the train rolled out of the station I distinctly remember two big tears rolling down my cheeks and falling on to my hands. I felt safe again and among human beings. The "bon voyage" was ringing in my ears. *Bon voyage! Bon voyage!*

A light drizzle was falling over Picardy. It made the thatched roofs look invitingly black and the grass a little greener. Now and then a patch of ocean veered into sight, to be swallowed up immediately by rolling sand dunes, then farms and meadows and brooks. A silent, peaceful countryside where each man minds his own business.

Suddenly I felt so god-damned happy I wanted to stand up and shout or sing. But all I could think of was "*bon voyage!*" What a phrase that! All our lives we're knocking about here and there mumbling that phrase which the French have given us, but do we ever take the *bon voyage*? Do we realize that even when we walk to the bistrot, or to the corner grocer, that it's a voyage from which we may never return? If we keenly felt that, that each time we sailed out of the house we were embarking on a voyage, would it make our lives a little different? While we make the little trip to the corner, or to Dieppe, or to Newhaven, or wherever it may be, the earth too is making her little trip, where nobody knows, not even the astronomers. But all of us, whether we move from here to the corner or from here to China, are making a voyage with our mother the earth, and the earth is moving with the sun and with the sun the other planets too are moving . . . Mars, Mercury, Venus, Neptune, Jupiter, Saturn, Uranus. The whole firmament is moving and with it, if you listen closely, you will hear "*Bon Voyage!*" "*Bon Voyage!*" And if you get still as a needle and don't ask a lot of foolish questions you will realize that to make a voyage is only an idea, that there is nothing in life but voyage, voyage within voyage, and that death is not the last voyage but the beginning of a new voyage and nobody knows why or whither, but *bon voyage* just the same! I wanted to stand up and sing that in the key of Ut-Mineur. I saw the whole universe like a network of tracks, some deep and invisible like the planetary grooves, and in this vast misty slithering to and fro, in the ghost-like passage from one realm to another, I saw all things animate and inanimate waving to one another, the cockroaches to the cockroaches, the stars to the stars, man to man, and God to God. All aboard for the big trek to nowhere, but *Bon Voyage* just the same! From osmosis to cataclysm, all a vast, silent, and perpetual movement. To stand still within the big crazy mòvement, to move with the earth however she wobbles, to join up with the cockroaches and the stars and the gods and men, that's voyaging! And out there in space where we are moving, where we leave our invisible tracks, out there is it possible that I hear a faint, sarcastic echo, a slimy, anaemic little English voice asking incredulously—"Come, Mr. Miller, you don't mean to say that you write *medical* books too?" Yes, by Jesus, now I can say it with a clean conscience. Yes, Mr. Nobody from Newhaven, I *do* write medical books too, marvellous medical books which cure all the ills of time and space. In fact, I am writing now, this very minute, the one great purgative of the human consciousness: *the sense of voyage!*

And just as I imagined I saw the idiot from Newhaven cocking his ear to hear me better a big shadow loomed in front of him and blotted him out. Just as I was about to say to myself—"Where have I seen this face before?"—it dawned on me like a flash. The man with the moustache at Dieppe, that face I had seen somewhere before, I recognized it now: it was the face of Mack Swain! He was The Big Bad Wolf and Charlie was Samson Agonistes. That's all. I just wanted to straighten it out in my mind. *Et bon voyage. Bon voyage à tout le monde!*

Hamlet: A Letter

Dear F.   Nov. 8, 1935.

It's very good of you to give me such explicit answers. Only, my feeling is that you are trying to muddle me. You seem to take for granted that I have the utmost confidence in your "erudition", that I will take what you say about Hamlet on faith. You are mistaken here, in two ways. First, I distrust *all* erudition, yours included. Secondly, your letter contains no erudition. If I ask you a few simple and direct questions it's in order to know what you think, and not what you have learned that others think about Hamlet. The real erudite in our midst, as you will discover sooner or later, is little Alf. If you ask him a question he will spend the rest of his life in the library to bring you back the answer. No, I did not want the low-down on Hamlet, as you pretend to give it to me, but a simple statement of your own reactions. But perhaps this is your Hamlet-like way of answering questions. I suspect you of padding the book . . .

Just the same, your answers provoke me into giving you a little clearer picture of my impression of Hamlet, for, as I explained to you previously, the original Hamlet (meaning in this instance Shakespeare's *Hamlet*) is now swallowed up in the universal Hamlet. Whatever Shakespeare had to say is now irrelevant and thoroughly unimportant, except as a basis of departure. However weak may have been Prince Alfred's thesis about "objectivity", nevertheless the same criticism of Shakespeare registers itself in my mind —that he was a puppet-master. And in my case I make bold to add recklessness to ignorance by stating that it was only because of this puppet-show quality in Shakespeare that his works have had such a universal appeal. This universal appeal, like the Bible's, I must add parenthetically, is based on faith and non-investigation. People simply do not read Shakespeare any more, nor the Bible either. They read about Shakespeare. The critical literature built up about his name and works is vastly more fruitful and stimulating than Shakespeare himself, about whom nobody seems to know very much, his very identity being a mystery. This, I want to point out to you, is not true about other writers of the past, notably Petronius, Boccaccio, Rabelais, Dante, Villon, etc. It *is* true of Homer, Virgil, Torquato Tasso, Spinoza, etc. Hugo, the great French God, is read only by adolescents to-day, and *ought* only to be read by them. Shakespeare, the English god, is also read to-day mostly by adolescents—compulsory reading. When you pick him up later in life you find it almost impossible to overcome the prejudice established against him by the schoolmasters, by their

230

way of presenting him. Shakespeare was just the pompous, flatulent sort of giant whom the English *would* convert into a sacred bull. Lacking depth they gave him girth and girth that ill conceals the stuffed pillows.

But as I say, I want to give you a little more of my own recollection of *Hamlet*, rather confused, it is true, but honest. I don't doubt that if a questionnaire were sent around the English speaking world there would be still more confusion about the subject. To begin with, I dismiss the first reading, which was compulsory and, *par consequent*, absolutely nil in results. (Except for a detestation of the subject which over a period of years has gradually changed into an archaeological curiosity, so to speak.) I mean by this that to-day I am much more interested in hearing what Mr. X (Mister Nobody) has to say about *Hamlet*—or Othello, or Lear, or Macbeth—than in knowing what the Shakespearean scholar has to say. From the latter I can learn absolutely nothing—it is all sawdust. But from the nobodies, among whom I include myself, I have everything to learn.

Anyway, it was after I had been out of school some time that, through the tenacity and insatiable curiosity of a Scotch friend of mine—Bill Dyker was his name—my curiosity in *Hamlet* was awakened. We agreed one night, after a long discussion about Shakespeare and his supposed value to the world, that it would be a good thing to read him again. We also discussed at length that night the question of which play we would tackle first. It's almost inevitable that, when this question comes up, as you've probably noticed, Hamlet shall be *the* play. (This, too, is extremely fascinating to me—this obsessive recurrence of the one play, as though to say, if you *would* know Shakespeare then by all means read Hamlet. Hamlet! Hamlet! Why *Hamlet* always?)

And so we read the play. We had agreed beforehand to get

together at a certain date and discuss the play in the light of our individual reactions. Well, the night came, and we met. It so happened, however, that my friend Bill Dyker had also made a date that night to meet a woman uptown. She was an unusual woman, too, it seems, and perhaps there was some excuse for postponing the discussion of *Hamlet*. She was a literary woman who was unable to enjoy ordinary intercourse because "she was built too small." That's how my friend Dyker put it to me, at least. I remember how we started walking uptown in the rain that evening, along Broadway. Somewhere in the Forties we ran across a whore. (It was before the war and the whores were still walking the streets, both by day and night. The saloons were going full blast too.) The strange thing about this meeting was—a coincidence, you will see—that this whore was also a "literary" woman. She had been a writer for the pulps and she had gone under. Before that she had been a dance hall jane in Butte, Montana. Anyway, it was most natural to start in with "literature" and work up. It also happened that that night I had under my arm a book called *Esoteric Buddhism* which at that period I pronounced e-*sot*-eric *bud*-ism. Naturally I hadn't the faintest idea of what it was all about. It was probably one of those books which Brisbane used to recommend to his readers. (At that time I was intent upon reading only the "best" books, those that broadened the mind.) It wasn't long, of course, before the whore herself assumed first importance. She was of Irish stock, weak and lovable, and possessed with the usual gift of gab. In addition she was dogmatic. We were dogmatic too. In those days everybody was dogmatic. You could afford to be. When, by a natural process, we finally got to the point the whore of course was disgusted to think that we were going to keep a date with a woman whose predicament was such as I described to you. Furthermore, she didn't believe the story.

232

She said it was incredible. She said, which was the truth, as we discovered later, that the woman was probably a nymphomaniac. It was a delicate situation. *A time to act!* But action was precisely what we were incapable of, even in those days. This was more particularly true of my Scotch friend than of myself. He had what is called a "judicial mind"—he could see all around a subject and never scotch it.

The only thing to do, since we couldn't come to a decision was to keep on drinking. We left the saloon we were in and went to a French bar in the Thirties somewhere. They were shooting dice at the bar when we blew in, and my friend Dyker had a passion for dice. There were also a few whores at the bar and, despite the girl at our elbow, they began making overtures to us. The situation kept growing steadily worse, the whore intent on making us and thinking, since we seemed impervious to her physical charms, that it must be her intellect which appealed to us. And so, gradually, we came back to *Hamlet*, very much involved now with the subject of going to bed or not going to bed, the dangers of disease (which went on in asides), the money problem, the question of honor, of keeping our word with the other woman, etc., etc. From this strange bog in which Hamlet became mired I have never been able to extricate him. As for Ophelia, she is inseparable in my mind from a tow-haired girl who was sitting in the back room and whom I had to pass on my way to the toilet every now and then. I remember the pathetic, stupefied look on this girl's face; when later I saw somewhere an illustration of Ophelia floating face up, the hair braided and tangled in the pond lilies, I thought of the girl in the back room of the bar, her eyes glazed, her hair strawlike, as Ophelia's. As for Hamlet himself, my friend Dyker with his "judicial mind" was the quintessence of all the Hamlets I have ever met. He was incapable of making even the decision to empty his bowels. A fact! He used to have a note hanging on the wall of his den reading: "Don't forget to go to the toilet!" His friends, seeing the note, would have to remind him of it. Otherwise he'd have died of constipation. A little later, when he fell in love with a girl and began to think about marrying her, the problem which plagued him was what to do about the sister. The two sisters were practically inseparable. It was like him, of course, to fall in love with both of them. Sometimes the three of them would go to bed together, pretending to take a nap. And while the one sister slept he would make merry with the other. It was quite immaterial to him *which* sister. I remember his painful endeavors to explain all this to me. We used to go over it night after night, seeking a solution ...

My close friendship with Bill Dyker, you can readily see, got the upper hand of *Hamlet*. Here was a Hamlet in life, one whom I could study at leisure without pain of research. Now that I think of it, how characteristic that from that night when we were going to "discuss" *Hamlet* the latter died, never to be mentioned by either of us again. Nor do I think that from that day on Bill Dyker ever read another book. Not even *my* book, which I handed him on arriving in New York and of which he said to me, when leaving —"I'll try to get round to reading it sometime, Henry." As though I had imposed a heavy duty on him which, out of long-standing friendship, he would do his best to discharge. No, I don't think he has ever opened my book, or ever will. And I am his best and oldest friend. A rum bird, this Bill Dyker, what!

I have gotten a little afield in talking of Bill Dyker. I meant to tell you my impressions of *Hamlet* as they seeped through during years of wandering, years of idle talk, years of browsing through this and that. How, in the course of time, *Hamlet* got mixed up with all the other books I have read and forgotten, so that to-day

234

Hamlet is absolutely amorphous, absolutely polyglot—in a word, universal, like the elements themselves. In the first place, whenever I utter the name there registers immediately an image of Hamlet, an image of a darkened stage on which a pale, thin man with a poetic mop of hair stands in hose and doublet orating to a skull which is held in his extended right hand. (Bear in mind, please, that I have never seen *Hamlet* acted!) In the back of the stage is an open grave about which the earth is heaped up. A lantern reposes on the mound of dirt. Hamlet is talking—talking the utmost gibberish, as far as I can make out. He has been standing there like that, talking, for centuries. The curtain never falls. The speech is never terminated. What should happen after this scene I have always imagined in some such fashion as this, though of course it never really happens. In the midst of the skull talk a courier arrives —probably one of the Guildenstern-Rosenkranz boys. The courier whispers something in Hamlet's ear which Hamlet, being a dreamer, naturally ignores. Suddenly three men in black capes appear and draw their swords. Avaunt! they cry, and with that Hamlet, ridiculously lightning like and unexpected, draws his sword and the fight's on. The men are killed, of course, in short order. Killed with the lightning like rapidity of a dream, leaving Hamlet to stare at his bloody sword as a few moments previous he was staring at the skull. Only now—*speechless!*

That's what I see, as I say, when Hamlet's name is mentioned. Always the same scene, always the same characters, same lantern, same gestures, same words. And always, at the end, *speechless.* That, I think, from my scanty reading of Freud, is decidedly a wish fulfillment. And I am grateful to Freud for learning so.

So far so good—as to images. When I *talk* about *Hamlet* another mechanism gets into operation. This is what I call the "free fantasia", and it is made up not only of *Hamlet*, but of *Werther*,

Jerusalem Delivered, Iphigenia in Tauris, Parsifal, Faust, the
Odyssey, the *Inferno* (a comedy!), *Midsummer Night's Dream,*
Gulliver's Travels, The Holy Grail, Ayesha, Ouida (just Ouida, no
particular book), *Rasselas, The Count of Monte Cristo, Evange-*
line, The Gospel According to Luke, The Birth of Tragedy, Ecce
Homo, The Idiot, Lincoln's *Gettysburg Address, The Decline and*
Fall of the Roman Empire, Lecky's *History of European Morals,*
The Evolution of the Idea of a God, The Ego and His Own, In-
stead of a Book by a Man too busy to Write One, and so on and so
forth, including *Through the Looking Glass*—not the least impor-
tant! When this stew gets rattling around in my brain I do my best
thinking about *Hamlet. Hamlet* is in the dead center, with a rapier in
his hand. I see the Ghost—not of Hamlet, but of Macbeth—stalking
the stage. Hamlet addresses it. The ghost vanishes and the play be-
gins. That is, the play around Hamlet. Hamlet does nothing—he
does not even kill the swift couriers at the end, as I imagine when
just the bare name is pronounced. No, Hamlet is standing there in
the center of the stage and people are poking and prodding him, as
though he were a dead jelly-fish cast up on the ocean shore. This goes
on for maybe twelve acts, during which time a great many people are
killed, or else kill themselves. *All to talk,* understand. The best
speeches are always made the moment before death. But none of
these speeches advance us anywhere. It's like Lewis Carroll's check-
erboard. First you're standing outside a castle and it's raining—an
English rain which is good for the swede and turnip crop and for
the making of fine woolens. Then there is thunder and lightning,
and maybe the ghost reappears. Hamlet talks to the ghost fa-
miliarly, easily—because talk is his *métier.* Between times messen-
gers come and go. They whisper now in Hamlet's ear, now in the
Queen's ear, now in Polonius' ear. A buzz buzz that goes on
throughout the whole twelve acts. Polonius comes out now and

then in a dunce cap. He has his son Laertes in hand and he brushes the dandruff affectionately from Laertes' coat collar. He does this to throw dust in Hamlet's eye. Hamlet is sullen, and now and then taciturn. He puts his hand on the hilt of his rapier. His eyes flash. Then Ophelia comes out, with her long flaxen hair hanging in braids down her shoulder. She walks with hands clasped over her stomach, mumbling the rosary and looking coy, demure, a little silly withal. She pretends not to notice Hamlet who is standing right in her path. She picks a buttercup by the way and holds it to her nostrils. Hamlet, convinced that she is not all there, makes advances to her—by way of passing the time. This precipitates a drama. It means that Hamlet and his best friend, Laertes, must fight a duel to the death. Hamlet, always loth to act, nevertheless kills his friend Laertes in quick fashion, sighing as he plunges the rapier through his beloved friend's body. Hamlet sighs constantly throughout the play. It's a way of informing the audience that he is not in a cataleptic trance. And after each murder he scrupulously cleans his sword—cleans it with the kerchief that Ophelia dropped on her way out. There is something about Hamlet's gestures which reminds one instinctively of the English gentleman. That is why I asked you before if the play occurs in England. For me it's England and nobody can convince me to the contrary. It's the very heart of England, too, I should say somewhere in the neighborhood of Sherwood Forest. The Queen Mother is a virago. She has false teeth, as had all the English queens from time immemorial. She has also a high stomach which in the end invites Hamlet's sword. Somehow I can't detach her from the image of the red Queen in the *Alice* tale. She seems to be talking about butter all the time, how to make it creamy and palatable. Whereas Hamlet is concerned only with Death. The conversation between these two of necessity takes on a strange hue. Surrealistic, we would call it to-day. And yet it's very much to the point. Hamlet suspects his mother of concealing a foul crime. He suspects that he was fouled in the nest. He accuses his mother openly, but she, being given to tergiversation, always manages to turn the conversation back to butter. In fact, in her sly English way, she almost makes Hamlet believe that he himself is guilty of some monstrous crime, just what is never revealed. Hamlet cordially detests his mother. He would strangle her with his bare hands, if he could. But the Queen mother is too slippery for him. She gets his uncle to put on a play in which Hamlet is made to seem foolish. Hamlet stalks out of the hall before the play is finished. In the vestibule he meets Guildenstern and Rosenkranz. They whisper something in his ear. He says he will go away, on a voyage. They persuade him not to go. He goes out into the garden, by the moat, and in the midst of his reverie he suddenly espies the dead Ophelia floating down the stream, her hair neatly braided, her hands clasped demurely over her stomach. She seems to be smiling in her sleep. Nobody knows how many days she has been in the water or why the body looks so natural when by all the laws of nature it should now be bloated with gas. Anyway, Hamlet decides to make a speech. He starts in with that famous one—"to be or not to be . . ." Ophelia is floating gently down-stream, her ears stopped, but still smiling sweetly as is expected of the English upper classes, even in death. It is this sickly sweet smile of a water-logged corpse which enrages Hamlet. He doesn't mind Ophelia's death—it's the smile which drives him mad. Again he draws the rapier, and with blood in his eyes, he makes for the banquet hall. Suddenly we are in Denmark, at the castle of Elsinore. Hamlet is a complete stranger, a ghost come to life. He rushes in, intending to murder them all in cold blood. But he is met by his uncle, the erstwhile king. The uncle, full of blandishments, escorts Hamlet to the head of the table. Hamlet refuses to eat. He is fed up with the whole show. He demands to know outright who killed his father, a fact which had completely escaped his attention throughout but of which he is suddenly reminded now that it is time to eat. There is a clatter of dishes and a general hubbub. Polonius, thinking to smooth matters over, tries to make a pretty speech about the weather. Hamlet stabs him behind the arras. The king, feigning not to notice the occurrence, raises the goblet to his lips and bids Hamlet make a toast. Hamlet quaffs the poison goblet, but does not die immediately. Instead the king himself falls dead at Hamlet's feet. Hamlet runs him through, like a piece of cold pork, with his sword. Then, turning to the queen mother, he runs her through the stomach—gives her the high enema for once and all. At this moment Guildenstern and Rosenkranz appear. They draw their swords. Hamlet is growing weak. He sinks to a chair. The gravediggers appear with the lantern and spades. They hand Hamlet a skull. Hamlet takes the skull in his right hand and holding it away from him addresses it in eloquent language. Hamlet is now dying. He knows that he is dying. So he begins his last and best speech which, unfortunately, is never terminated. Rosenkranz and Guildenstern sneak out by the back door. Hamlet is left alone at the banquet table, the floor strewn with corpses. He is talking a blue streak. The curtain slowly falls . . .

Into the Night Life

OVER THE FOOT of the bed is the shadow of the cross. There are chains binding me to the bed. The chains are clanking loudly, the anchor is being lowered. Suddenly I feel a hand on my shoulder. Some one is shaking me vigorously. I look up and it is an old hag in a dirty wrapper. She goes to the dresser and opening a drawer she puts a revolver away.

There are three rooms, one after the other, like a railroad flat. I am lying in the middle room in which there is a walnut book-case and a dressing-table. The old hag removes her wrapper and stands before the mirror in her chemise. She has a little powder puff in her hand and with this little puff she swabs her arm-pits, her bosom, her thighs. All the while she weeps like an idiot. Finally she comes over to me with an atomizer and she squirts a fine spray over me. I notice that her hair is full of rats.

I watch the old hag moving about. She seems to be in a trance. Standing at the dresser she opens and closes the drawers, one after the other, mechanically. She seems to have forgotten what she remembered to go there for. Again she picks up the powder puff and with the powder puff she daubs a little powder under her arm-pits. On the dressing-table is a little silver watch attached to a long piece of black tape. Pulling off her chemise she slings the watch around her neck; it reaches just to the pubic triangle. There comes a faint tick and then the silver turns black.

In the next room, which is the parlor, all the relatives are assembled. They sit in a semi-circle, waiting for me to enter. They sit stiff and rigid, upholstered like the chairs. Instead of warts and wens there is horsehair sprouting from their chins.

I spring out of bed in my night-shirt and I commence to dance the dance of King Kotschei. In my night-shirt I dance, with a parasol over my head. They watch me without a smile, without so much as a crease in their jowls. I walk on my hands for them, I turn somersaults, I put my fingers between my teeth and whistle like a blackbird. Not the faintest murmur of approval or disapproval. They sit there solemn and imperturbable. Finally I begin to snort like a bull, then I prance like a fairy, then I strut like a peacock, and then realizing that I have no tail I quit. The only thing left to do is to read the Koran through at lightning speed, after which the weather reports, the *Rime of the Ancient Mariner* and the Book of Numbers.

Suddenly the old hag comes dancing in stark naked, her hands aflame. Immediately she knocks over the umbrella stand the place

241

is in an uproar. From the upturned umbrella stand there issues a steady stream of writhing cobras traveling at lightning speed. They knot themselves around the legs of the tables, they carry away the soup tureens, they scramble into the dresser and jam the drawers, they wriggle through the pictures on the wall, through the curtain rings, through the mattresses, they coil up inside the women's hats, all the while hissing like steam boilers.

Winding a pair of cobras about my arms I go for the old hag with murder in my eyes. From her mouth, her eyes, her hair, from her vagina even, the cobras are streaming forth, always with that frightful steaming hiss as if they had been ejected fresh from a boiling crater. In the middle of the room where we are locked an immense forest opens up. We stand in a nest of cobras and our bodies come undone.

I am in a strange, narrow little room, lying on a high bed. There is an enormous hole in my side, a clean hole without a drop of blood showing. I can't tell any more who I am or where I came from or how I got here. The room is very small and my bed is close to the door. I have a feeling that some one is standing on the doorsill watching me. I am petrified with fright.

When I raise my eyes I see a man standing at the doorsill. He wears a gray derby cocked on the side of his head; he has a flowing mustache and is dressed in a checkerboard suit. He asks my name, my address, my profession, what I am doing and where I am going and so on and so forth. He asks endless prying questions to which I am unable to respond, first because I have lost my tongue, and second because I cannot remember any longer what language I speak. "Why don't you speak?" he says, bending over me jeeringly, and taking his light rattan stick he jabs a hole in my side. My anguish is so great that it seems I must speak even if I have no tongue, even if I know not who I am or where I came from. With my two hands I try to wrench my jaws apart, but the teeth are locked. My chin crumbles away like dry clay, leaving the jaw-bone exposed. "Speak!" he says, with that cruel, jeering smile, and taking his stick once again he jabs another hole through my side.

I lie awake in the cold dark room. The bed almost touches the ceiling now. I hear the rumbling of trains, the regular, rhythmic bouncing of the trains over the frozen trestle, the short, throttled puffs of the locomotive, as if the air were splintered with frost. In my hand are the pieces of dry clay which crumbled from my chin. My teeth are locked tighter than ever; I breathe through the holes in my side. From the window of the little room in which I lie I can see the Montreal bridge. Through the girders of the bridge, driven downward by the blinding blizzard, the sparks are flying. The trains are racing over the frozen river in wreaths of fire. I can see the shops along the bridgeway gleaming with pies and hamburger sandwiches. Suddenly I do remember something. I remember that just as I was about to cross the border they asked me what I had to declare and, like an idiot, I answered: "I want to declare that I am a traitor to the human race." I remember distinctly now that this occurred just as I was walking up a tread-mill behind a woman with balloon skirts. There were mirrors all around us and above the mirrors a balustrade of slats, series after series of slats, one on top of another, tilted, toppling, crazy as a nightmare. In the distance I could see the Montreal bridge and below the bridge the ice-floes over which the trains raced. I remember now that when the woman looked around at me she had a skull on her shoulders, and written into the fleshless brow was the word sex stony as a lizard. I saw the lids drop down over her eyes and then the sightless cavern without bottom. As I fled from her I tried to read what was written on the body of a car racing beside me, but I could catch only the tail end and it made no sense.

At the Brooklyn Bridge I stand as usual waiting for the trolley to swing round. In the heat of the late afternoon the city rises up like a huge polar bear shaking off its rhododendrons. The forms waver, the gas chokes the girders, the smoke and the dust wave like amulets. Out of the welter of buildings there pours a jellywash of hot bodies glued together with pants and skirts. The tide washes up in front of the curved tracks and splits like glass combs. Under the wet headlines are the diaphanous legs of the amœbas scrambling on to the running boards, the fine, sturdy tennis legs wrapped in cellophane, their white veins showing through the golden calves and muscles of ivory. The city is panting with a five o'clock sweat. From the tops of the skyscrapers plumes of smoke soft as Cleopatra's feathers. The air beats thick, the bats are flapping, the cement softens, the iron rails flatten under the broad flanges of the trolley wheels. Life is written down in headlines twelve feet high with periods, commas and semi-colons. The bridge sways over the gasoline lakes below. Melons rolling in from Imperial Valley, garbage going down past Hell Gate, the decks clear, the stanchions gleaming, the hawsers tight, the slips grunting, the moss splitting and spelching in the ferry slips. A warm sultry haze lying over the city like a cup of fat, the sweat trickling down between the bare legs, around the slim ankles. A mucous mass of arms and legs, of half-moons and weather-vanes, of cock-robins and round-robins, of shuttle-cocks and bright bananas with the light lemon pulp lying in the bell of the peel. Five o'clock strikes through the grime and sweat of the afternoon, a strip of bright shadow left by the iron girders. The trolleys wheel round with iron mandibles, crunching the papier-maché of the crowd, spooling it down like punched transfers.

As I take my seat I see a man I know standing on the rear platform with a newspaper in his hand. His straw hat is tilted on the

244

back of his head, his arm rests on the motorman's brass brake. Back of his ears the cable web spreads out like the guts of a piano. His straw hat is just on a level with Chambers Street; it rests like a sliced egg on the green spinach of the bay. I hear the cogs slipping against the thick stub of the motorman's toe. The wires are humming, the bridge is groaning with joy. Two little rubber knobs on the seat in front of me, like two black keys on a piano. About the size of an eraser, not round like the end of a cane. Two gummy thingamajigs to deaden the shock. The dull thud of a rubber hammer falling on a rubber skull.

The countryside is desolate. No warmth, no snugness, no closeness, no density, no opacity, no numerator, no denominator. It's like the evening newspaper read to a deaf mute standing on a hat rack with a palmetto leaf in his hand. In all this parched land no sign of human hand, of human eye, of human voice. Only headlines written in chalk which the rain washes away. Only a short ride on the trolley and I am in a desert filled with thorns and cactus.

In the middle of the desert is a bath-house and in the bath-house is a wooden horse with a log-saw lying athwart it. By the zinc-covered table, looking out through the cobwebbed window, stands a woman I used to know. She stands in the middle of the desert like a rock made of camphor. Her body has the strong white aroma of sorrow. She stands like a statue saying good-bye. Head and shoulders above me she stands, her buttocks swoopingly grand and out of all proportion. Everything is out of proportion—hands, feet, thighs, ankles. She's an equestrian statue without the horse, a fountain of flesh worn away to a mammoth egg. Out of the ball-room of flesh her body sings like iron. Girl of my dreams, what a splendid cage you make! Only where is the little perch for your three-pointed toes? The little perch that swung backward and forward between the brass bars? You stand by the window, dead as a canary, your toes stiff, your beak blue. You have the profile of a line drawing done with a meat-axe. Your mouth is a crater stuffed with lettuce leaves. Did I ever dream that you could be so enormously warm and lopsided? Let me look at your lovely jackal paws; let me hear the croaking, dingy chortle of your dry breath.

Through the cobwebs I watch the nimble crickets, the long, leafy spines of the cactus oozing milk and chalk, the riders with their empty saddle-bags, the pommels humped like camels. The dry desert of my native land, her men gray and gaunt, their spines twisted, their feet shod with rowel and spur. Above the cactus bloom the city hangs upside down, her gaunt, gray men scratching the skies with their spurred boots. I clasp her bulging contours, her rocky angles, the strong dolmen breasts, the cloven hoofs, the plumed tail. I hold her close in the choked spume of the canyons under the locked watersheds twisted with golden sands while the hour runs out. In the blinding surge of grief the sand slowly fills my bones.

A pair of blunt, rusty scissors lies on the zinc-covered table beside us. The arm which she raises is webbed to her side. The hoary inflexible movement of her arm is like the dull raucous screech of day closing and the cord which binds us is wired with grit. The sweat stands out on my temples, clots there and ticks like a clock. The clock is running down with nervous wiry sweat. The scissors move between on slow rusty hinges. My nerves race along the teeth of the comb, my spurs bristle, the veins glow. Is all pain dull and bearable like this? Along the scissors' dull edge I feel the rusty blunt anguish of day closing, the slow webbed movement of hunger satisfied, of clean space and starry sky in the arms of an automaton.

I stand in the midst of the desert waiting for the train. In my heart there is a little glass bell and under the bell there is an edelweiss. All my cares have dropped away. Even under the ice I sense the bloom which the earth prepares in the night.

Reclining in the luxurious leather seat I have a vague feeling that it is a German line on which I am travelling. I sit by the window reading a book; I am aware that some one is reading over my shoulder. It is my own book and there is a passage in it which baffles me. The words are incomprehensible. At Darmstadt we descend a moment while the engines are being changed. The glass shed rises to a nave supported by lacy black girders. The severity of the glass shed has a good deal the appearance of my book—when it lay open on my lap and the ribs showed through. In my heart I can feel the edelweiss blooming.

At night in Germany, when you pace up and down the platform, there is always some one to explain things to you. The round heads and the long heads get together in a cloud of vapor and all the wheels are taken apart and put together again. The sound of the language seems more penetrating than other tongues, as if it were food for the brain, substantial, nourishing, appetizing. Glutinous particles detach themselves and they dissipate slowly, months after the voyage, like a smoker exhaling a fine stream of smoke through his nostrils after he has taken a drink of water. The word *gut* is the longest lasting word of all. "*Es war gut!*" says some one, and his *gut* rumbles in my bowels like a rich pheasant. Surely nothing is better than to take a train at night when all the inhabitants are asleep and to drain from their open mouths the rich succulent morsels of their unspoken tongue. When every one sleeps the mind is crowded with events; the mind travels in a swarm, like summer flies that are sucked along by the train.

Suddenly I am at the seashore and no recollection of the train stopping. No remembrance of it departing even. Just swept up on the shore of the ocean like a comet.

Everything is sordid, shoddy, thin as pasteboard. A Coney Island of the mind. The amusement shacks are running full blast, the shelves full of chinaware and dolls stuffed with straw and alarm clocks and spittoons. Every shop has three balls over it and every game is a ball game. The Jews are walking around in mackintoshes, the Japs are smiling, the air is full of chopped onions and sizzling hamburgers. Jabber, jabber, and over it all in a muffled roar comes the steady hiss and boom of the breakers, a long, uninterrupted adenoidal wheeze that spreads a clammy catarrh over the dirty she-bang. Behind the pasteboard street-front the breakers are plough-ing up the night with luminous argent teeth; the clams are lying on their backs squirting ozone from their anal orifices. In the oceanic night Steeplechase looks like a wintry beard. Everything is sliding and crumbling, everything glitters, totters, teeters, titters.

Where is the warm summer's day when first I saw the green-carpeted earth revolving and men and women moving like pan-thers? Where is the soft gurgling music which I heard welling up from the sappy roots of the earth? Where am I to go if everywhere there are trap-doors and grinning skeletons, a world turned inside out and all the flesh peeled off? Where am I to lay my head if there is nothing but beards and mackintoshes and peanut whistles and broken slats? Am I to walk forever along this endless paste-board street, this pasteboard which I can punch a hole in, which I can blow down with my breath, which I can set fire to with a match? The world has become a mystic maze erected by a gang of carpenters during the night. Everything is a lie, a fake. Pasteboard.

I walk along the ocean front. The sand is strewn with human clams waiting for some one to pry their shells apart. In the roar and hubbub their pissing anguish goes unnoticed. The breakers club them, the lights deafen them, the tide drowns them. They lie behind the pasteboard street in the onyx-colored night and they listen to the hamburgers sizzling. Jabber, jabber, a sneezing and a wheezing, balls rolling down the long smooth troughs into tiny little holes filled with bric-à-brac, with chinaware and spittoons and flower-pots and stuffed dolls. Greasy Japs wiping the rubber-plants with wet rags, Armenians chopping onions into microcosmic particles, Macedonians throwing the lasso with molasses arms. Every man, woman and child in a mackintosh has adenoids, spreads catarrh, diabetes, whooping cough, meningitis. Everything that stands upright, that slides, rolls, tumbles, spins, shoots, teeters, sways and crumbles is made of nuts and bolts. The monarch of the mind is a monkey-wrench. Sovereign pasteboard power.

The clams have fallen asleep, the stars are dying out. Everything that is made of water snoozes now in the flap-pocket of a hyaena. Morning comes like a glass roof over the world. The glassy ocean sways in its depths, a still, transparent sleep.

It is neither night nor day. It is the dawn travelling in short waves with the flir of an albatross's wings. The sounds that reach me are cushioned, gonged, muffled, as if man's labors were being performed under water. I feel the tide ebbing without fear of being sucked in; I hear the waves splashing without fear of drowning. I walk amidst the wrack and debris of the world, but my feet are not bruised. There is no finitude of sky, no division of land and sea. I move through sluice and orifice with gliding slippery feet. I smell nothing, I hear nothing, I see nothing, I feel nothing. Whether on my back or on my belly, whether sidewise like the crab or spiral like a bird, all is bliss downy and undifferentiated.

The white chalk breath of Plymouth stirs the geologic spine; the tip of her dragon's tail clasps the broken continent. Unspeakably brown earth and men with green hair, the old image recreated in soft, milky whiteness. A last wag of the tail in non-human tranquillity; an indifference to hope or despair or melancholy. The brown earth and the oxide green are not of air or sky or sight or touch. The peace and solemnity, the far-off, intangible tranquillity of the chalk cliffs distils a poison, a noxious, croaking breath of evil that hangs over the land like the tip of a dragon's tail. I feel the invisible claws that grip the rocks. The heavy, sunken green of the earth is not the green of grass or hope but of slime, of foul, invincible courage. I feel the brown hoods of the martyrs, their matted hair, their sharp talons hidden in scrabrous vestments, the brown wool of their hatred, their ennui, their emptiness. I have a tremendous longing for this land that lies at the end of the earth, this irregular spread of earth like an alligator basking. From the heavy, sexless lid of her batted eye there emanates a deceptive, poisonous calm. Her yawning mouth is open like a vision. It is as if the sea and all who had been drowned in it, their bones, their hopes, their dreamy edifices, had made the white amalgam which is England.

My mind searches vainly for some remembrance which is older than any remembrance, for the myth engraved on a tablet of stone which lies buried under a mountain. Under the elevated structure, the windows full of pies and hamburgers, the rails swiftly turning, the old sensations, the old memories invade me again. All that belongs with docks and wharves, with funnels, cranes, pistons, wheels, ties, bridges, all the paraphernalia of travel and hunger repeats itself like a blind mechanism. As I come to the crossroads the living street spreads out like a map studded with awnings and wine shops. The noonday heat cracks the glazed surface of the map. The streets buckle and snap.

Where a rusty star marks the boundary of the past there rises up a clutter of sharp, triangular buildings with black mouths and broken teeth. There is the smell of iodoform and ether, of formaldehyde and ammonia, of fresh tin and wet iron moulds. The buildings are sagging, the roofs are crushed and battered. So heavy is the air, so acrid and choking, that the buildings can no longer hold themselves erect. The entrance ways have sunk to below the level of the street. There is something croaking and frog-like about the atmosphere. A dank, poisonous vapor envelops the neighborhood, as if a marsh-bog underlay the very foundations.

When I reach my father's home I find him standing at the window shaving, or rather not shaving, but stropping his razor. Never before has he failed me, but now in my need he is deaf. I notice now the rusty blade he is using. Mornings with my coffee there was always the bright flash of his blade, the bright German steel laid against the smooth dull hide of the strop, the splash of lather like cream in my coffee, the snow banked on the window ledge, putting a felt around his words. Now the blade is tarnished and the snow turned to slush; the diamond frost of the window panes trickles in a thin grease that stinks of toads and marsh gas. "Bring me huge worms," he begs, "and we will plough the minnows." Poor, desperate father that I have. I clutch with empty hands across a broken table.

A night of bitter cold. Walking along with head down a whore sidles up to me and putting her arm in mine leads me to a hotel with a blue enamel sign over the door. Upstairs in the room I take a good look at her. She is young and athletic, and best of all, she is ignorant. She doesn't know the name of a single king. She doesn't even speak her own language. Whatever I relate to her she licks up like hot fat. She lards herself with it. The whole process is one of getting warm, of putting on a coat of grease for the winter, as she explains to me in her simple way. When she has extracted all the grease from my marrow bones she pulls back the coverlet and with the most astounding sprightliness she commences her trapezoid

251

flights. The room is like a humming bird's nest. Nude as a berry she rolls herself into a ball, her head tucked between her breasts, her arms pinned to her crotch. She looks like a green berry out of which a pea is about to burst.

Suddenly, in that silly American way, I hear her say: "Look, I can do *this*, but I can't do *that!*" Whereupon she does it. Does what? Why, she commences to flap the lips of her vagina, just like a humming bird. She has a furry little head with frank dog-like eyes. Like a picture of the devil when the Palatinate was in flower. The incongruity of it sledges me. I sit down under a trip-hammer: every time I glance at her face I see an iron slit and behind it a man in an iron mask winking at me. A terrifying drollery because he winks with a blind eye, a blind, teary eye that threatens to turn into a cataract.

If it weren't that her arms and legs were all entangled, if she weren't a slippery, coiling snake strangled by a mask, I could swear that it was my wife Alberta, or if not my wife Alberta then another wife, though I think it's Alberta. I thought I'd always know Alberta's crack, but twisted into a knot with a mask between her legs one crack is as good as another and over every sewer there's a grating, in every pod there's a pea, behind every slit there's a man with an iron mask.

Sitting in the chair by the iron bedstead, with my suspenders down and a trip-hammer pounding the dome of my skull, I begin to dream of the women I have known. Women who deliberately cracked their pelvis in order to have a doctor stick a rubber finger inside them and swab the crannies of their epiglottis. Women with such thin diaphragms that the scratch of a needle sounded like Niagara Falls in their fallen bladders. Women who could sit by the hour turning their womb inside out in order to prick it with a darning needle. Queer dog-like women with furry heads and always an alarm clock or a jig-saw puzzle hidden in the wrong place; just at the wrong moment the alarm goes off; just when the sky is blazing with Roman candles and out of the wet sparks crabs and star fish, just then always and without fail a broken saw, a wire snapping, a nail through the finger, a corset rotting with perspiration. Queer dog-faced women in stiff collars, the lips drooping, the eyes twitching. Devil dancers from the Palatinate with fat behinds and the door always on a crack and a spittoon where the umbrella stand should be. Celluloid athletes who burst like ping-pong balls when they shoot through the gaslight. Strange women—and I'm always sitting in a chair beside an iron bedstead. Such skilful fingers they have that the hammer always falls in the dead center of my skull and cracks the glue of the joints. The brain-pan is like a hamburger steak in a steaming window.

Passing through the lobby of the hotel I see a crowd gathered around the bar. I walk in and suddenly I hear a child howling with pain. The child is standing on a table in the midst of the crowd. It's a girl and she has a slit in the side of her head, just at the temple. The blood is bubbling from her temple. It just bubbles—it doesn't run down the side of her face. Every time the slit in her temple opens I see something stirring inside. It looks like a chick in there. I watch closely. This time I catch a good glimpse of it. It's a cuckoo! People are laughing. Meanwhile the child is howling with pain.

In the anteroom I hear the patients coughing and scraping their feet; I hear the pages of a magazine closing and the rumble of a milk wagon on the cobblestones outside. My wife is sitting on a white stool, the child's head is against my breast. The wound in her temple is throbbing, throbbing as if it were a pulse laid against my heart. The surgeon is dressed in white; he walks up and down, up and down, puffing at his cigarette. Now and then he stops at the windows to see how the weather looks. Finally he washes his hands and puts on the rubber gloves. With the sterilized gloves on his hands he lights a flame under the instruments; then he looks at his watch absent-mindedly and fingers the bills lying on the desk. The child is groaning now; her whole body is twitching with pain. I've got her arms and legs pinned. I'm waiting for the instruments to boil.

At last the surgeon is ready. Seating himself on a little white stool he selects a long, delicate instrument with a red-hot point and without a word of warning he plunges it into the open wound. The child lets out such a blood-curdling scream that my wife collapses on the floor. "Don't pay any attention to *her!*" says the cool, collected surgeon, shoving her body aside with his foot. "Hold tight now!" And dipping his cruelest instrument into a boiling antiseptic he plunges the blade into the temple and holds it there until the wound bursts into flames. Then, with the same diabolical swiftness, he suddenly withdraws the instrument to which there is attached, by an eyelet, a long white cord which changes gradually into red flannel and then into chewing gum and then into popcorn and finally into sawdust. As the last flake of sawdust spills out the wound closes up clean and solid, leaving not even the suggestion of a scar. The child looks up at me with a peaceful smile and, sidling off my lap, walks steadily to the corner of the room where she sits down to play.

"That was excellent!" says the surgeon. "Really quite excellent!"

"Oh, it was, eh?" I scream. And jumping up like a maniac I knock him off the stool and with my knees firmly planted in his chest I grab the nearest instrument and commence to gouge him with it. I work on him like a demon. I gouge out his eyes, I burst his ear-drums, I slit his tongue, I break his wind-pipe, I flatten his nose. Ripping the clothes off him I burn his chest until it smokes, and while the flesh is still raw and quivering from the hot iron I roll back the outer layers and I pour nitric acid inside—until I hear the heart and lungs sizzling. Until the fumes almost keel me over.

The child meanwhile is clapping her hands with glee. As I get up to look for a mallet I notice my wife sitting in the other corner. She seems too paralyzed with fright to get up. All she can do is to whisper—"Fiend! Fiend!" I run downstairs to look for the mallet.

In the darkness I seem to distinguish a form standing beside the little ebony piano. The lamp is guttering but there is just sufficient light to throw a halo about the man's head. The man is reading aloud in a monotonous voice from a huge iron book. He reads like a rabbi chanting his prayers. His head is thrown back in ecstasy, as if it were permanently dislocated. He looks like a broken street lamp gleaming in a wet fog.

As the darkness increases his chanting becomes more and more monotonous. Finally I see nothing but the halo around his head. Then that vanishes also and I realize that I have grown blind. It is like a drowning in which my whole past rises up. Not only my personal past, but the past of the whole human race which I am traversing on the back of a huge tortoise. We travel with the earth at a snail-like pace; we reach the limits of her orbit and then with a curious lop-sided gait we stagger swiftly back through all the empty houses of the zodiac. We see the strange phantasmal figures of the animal world, the lost races which had climbed to the top of the ladder only to fall to the ocean floor. Particularly the soft red bird whose plumes are all aflame. The red bird speeding like an arrow, always to the north. Winging her way north over the bodies of the dead there follows in her wake a host of angle-worms, a blinding swarm that hides the light of the sun.

Slowly, like veils being drawn, the darkness lifts and I discern the silhouette of a man standing by the piano with the big iron book in his hands, his head thrown back and the weary monotonous voice chanting the litany of the dead. In a moment he commences pacing back and forth in a brisk, mechanical way, as if he were absent-mindedly taking exercise. His movements obey a jerky, automatic rhythm which is exasperating to witness. He behaves like a laboratory animal from which part of the brain has been removed. Each time he comes to the piano he strikes a few chords at random—plink, plank, plunk! And with this he mumbles something under his breath. Moving briskly towards the east wall he mumbles—"theory of ventilation"; moving briskly towards the west wall he mumbles—"theory of opposites"; tacking north-north-west he mumbles—"fresh air theory all wet." And so on and so forth. He moves like an old four-masted schooner bucking a gale, his arms hanging loosely, his head drooping slightly to one side. A brisk indefatigable motion like a shuttle passing over a loom. Suddenly heading due north he mumbles—"Z for zebra . . . zeb, zut, Zachariah . . . no sign of b for bretzels . . ."

Flicking the pages of the iron book I see that it is a collection of poems from the Middle Ages dealing with mummies; each poem contains a prescription for the treatment of skin diseases. It is the Day Book of the great plague written by a Jewish monk. A sort of elaborate chronicle of skin diseases sung by the troubadours. The writing is in the form of musical notes representing all the beasts of evil omen or of creeping habits, such as the mole, the toad, the basilisk, the eel, the beetle, the bat, the turtle, the white mouse. Each poem contains a formula for ridding the body of the possessed of the demons which infest the under-layers of the skin.

My eye wanders from the musical page to the wolf hunt which is going on outside the gates. The ground is covered with snow and in the oval field beside the castle walls two knights armed with long spears are worrying the wolf to death. With miraculous grace and dexterity the wolf is gradually brought into position for the death stroke. A voluptuous feeling comes over me watching the long drawn out death deal. Just as the spear is about to be hurled the horse and rider are gathered up in an agonizing elasticity: in one simultaneous movement the wolf, the horse and the rider revolve about the pivot of death. As the spear wings through the body of the wolf the ground moves gently upward, the horizon slightly tilted, the sky blue as a knife.

Walking through the colonnade I come to the sunken streets which lead to the town. The houses are surrounded by tall black chimneys from which a sulphurous smoke belches forth. Finally I come to the box factory from a window of which I catch a view of the cripples standing in line in the court-yard. None of the cripples have feet, few have arms; their faces are covered with soot. All of them have medals on their chest.

To my horror and amazement I slowly perceive that from the long chute attached to the wall of the factory a steady stream of coffins is being emptied into the yard. As they tumble down the chute a man steps forward on his mutilated stumps and pausing a moment to adjust the burden to his back slowly trudges off with his coffin. This goes on ceaselessly, without the slightest interruption, without the slightest sound. My face is streaming with perspiration. I want to run but my feet are rooted to the spot. Perhaps I have no feet. I am so frightened that I fear to look down. I grip the window sash and without daring to look down I cautiously and fearfully raise my foot until I am able to touch the heel of my shoe with my hand. I repeat the experiment with the other foot. Then, in a panic, I look about me swiftly for the exit. The room in which I am standing is littered with empty packing boxes; there are nails and hammers lying about. I thread my way among the empty boxes searching for the door. Just as I find the door my foot stumbles against an empty box. I look down into the empty box and behold, it is not empty! Hastily I cast a glance at the other boxes. None of them are empty! In each box there is a skeleton packed in excelsior. I run for the door in a sweat. I run from one corridor to another searching frantically for the staircase. Flying through the halls I catch the stench of embalming fluid issuing from the open doors. Finally I reach the staircase and as I bound down the stairs I see a white enamel hand on the landing below pointing to—The Morgue.

It is night and I am on my way home. My path lies through a wild park such as I had often stumbled through in the dark when my eyes were closed and I heard only the breathing of the walls. I have the sensation of being on an island surrounded by rocky coves and inlets. There are the same little bridges with their paper lanterns, the rustic benches strewn along the graveled paths, the pagodas in which confections were sold, the brilliant skups, the sun-shades, the rocky crags above the cove, the flimsy Chinese wrappers in which the firecrackers were hidden. Everything is exactly as it used to be, even to the noise of the carrousel and the kites fluttering in the tangled boughs of the trees. *Except that now it is winter.* Mid-winter and all the roads covered with snow, a deep snow which has made the roads almost impassable.

At the summit of one of the curved Japanese bridges I stand a moment, leaning over the hand-rail, to gather my thoughts. All the roads are clearly spread out before me. They run in parallel lines. In this wooded park which I know so well I feel the utmost security. Here on the bridge I could stand forever, sure of my destination. It hardly seems necessary to go the rest of the way for now I am on the threshold, as it were, of my kingdom and the imminence of it stills me. How well I know this little bridge, the

258

wooded clump, the stream that flows beneath! Here I could stand forever, lost in a boundless security, lulled and forever rapt by the lapping murmur of the stream. Over the mossy stones the stream swirls endlessly. A stream of melting snow, sluggish above and swift below. Icy clear under the bridge. So clear that I can measure the depth of it with my eye. Icy clear to the neck.

And now, out of the dark-clustered wood, amidst the cypresses and evergreens, there comes a phantom couple arm in arm, their movements slow and languid. A phantom couple in evening dress —the woman's low-necked gown, the man's gleaming shirt-studs. Through the snow they move with airy steps, the woman's feet so soft and dry, her arms bare. No crunch of snow, no howling wind. A brilliant diamond light and rivulets of snow dissolving in the night. Rivulets of powdered snow sliding beneath the evergreens. No crunch of jaw, no moan of wolf. Rivulets and rivulets in the icy light of the moon, the rushing sound of white water and petals lapping the bridge, the island floating away in ceaseless drift, her rocks tangled with hair, her glens and coves bright black in the silver gleam of the stars.

Onward they move in the phantasmal flux, onward towards the knees of the glen and the white-whiskered waters. Into the clear icy depths of the stream they walk, her bare back, his gleaming shirt-studs, and from afar comes the plaintive tinkle of glass curtains brushing the metal teeth of the carrousel. The water rushes down in a thin sheet of glass between the soft white mounds of the banks; it rushes below the knees, carrying the amputated feet forward like broken pedestals before an avalanche. Forward on their icy stumps they glide, their bat-wings spread, their garments glued to their limbs. And always the water mounting, higher, higher, and the air growing colder, the snow sparkling like powdered diamonds. From the cypresses above a dull metallic green seeps down, sweeps

259

like a green shadow over the banks and stains the clear icy depths of the stream. The woman is seated like an angel on a river of ice, her wings spread, her hair flown back in stiff glassy waves.

Suddenly, like spun-glass under a blue flame, the stream quickens into tongues of fire. Along a street flaming with color there moves a dense equinoctial throng. It is the street of early sorrows where the flats string out like railroad cars and all the houses flanked with iron spikes. A street that slopes gently towards the sun and then forward like an arrow to lose itself in space. Where formerly it curved with a bleak, grinding noise, with stiff, pompous roofs and blank dead walls, now like an open switch the gutter wheels into place, the houses fall into line, the trees bloom. Time nor goal bothers me now. I move in a golden hum through a syrup of warm lazy bodies.

Like a prodigal son I walk in golden leisure down the street of my youth. I am neither bewildered nor disappointed. From the perimeter of the six extremes I have wandered back by devious routes to the hub where all is change and transformation, a white lamb continually shedding its skin. When along the mountain ridges I howled with pain, when in the sweltering white valleys I was choked with alkali, when fording the sluggish streams my feet were splintered by rock and shell, when I licked the salty sweat of the lemon fields or lay in the burning kilns to be baked, *when was all this that I never forgot what is now no more?*

When down this cold funereal street they drove the hearse which I hailed with joy had I already shed my skin? I was the lamb and they drove me out. I was the lamb and they made of me a striped tiger. In an open thicket I was born with a mantle of soft white wool. Only a little while did I graze in peace, and then a paw was laid upon me. In the sultry flame of closing day I heard a breathing behind the shutters; past all the houses I wandered slowly, listening to the thick flapping of the blood. And then one night I awoke on a hard bench in the frozen garden of the South. Heard the mournful whistle of the train, saw the white sandy roads gleaming like skull tracks.

If I walk up and down the world without joy or pain it's because in Tallahassee they took my guts away. In a corner against a broken fence they reached inside me with dirty paws and with a rusty jack-knife they cut away everything that was mine, everything that was sacred, private, taboo. In Tallahassee they cut my guts out; they drove me round the town and striped me like the tiger. Once I whistled in my own right. Once I wandered through the streets listening to the blood beating through the filtered light of the shutters. Now there's a roar inside me like a carnival in full blast. My sides are bursting with a million barrel-organ tunes. I walk down the street of early sorrows with the carnival going full blast. I rub my way along spilling the tunes I have learned. A glad, lazy depravity swinging from curb to curb. A skein of human flesh that swings like a heavy rope.

By the spiral-hung gardens of the casino where the cocoons are bursting a woman slowly mounting the flowerpath pauses a moment to train the full weight of her sex on me. My head swings automatically from side to side, a foolish bell stuck in a belfry. As she moves away the sense of her words begins to make itself manifest. *The cemetery, she said. Have you seen what they did to the cemetery?* Moseying along in the warm wine-press, the blinds all thrown open, the stoops swarming with children, I keep thinking of her words. Moseying along with light niggerish fancy, bare-necked, splay-footed, toes spread, scrotum tight. A warm southern fragrance envelops me, a good-natured ease, the blood thick as molasses and flapping with condors' wings.

What they have done for the street is what Joseph did for Egypt.

What *they* have done? No *you* and no *they* any more. A land of ripe golden corn, of red Indians and black bucks. Who *they* are or were I know not. I know only that they have taken the land and made it smile, that they have taken the cemetery and made of it a fertile, groaning field. Every stone has been removed, every wreath and cross has vanished. Hard by my home now there lies a huge sunken checkerboard groaning with provender; the loam is rich and black, the sturdy, patient mules sink their slender hoofs into the wet loam which the plough cuts through like soft cheese. The whole cemetery is singing with its rich fat produce. Singing through the blades of wheat, the corn, the oats, the rye, the barley. The cemetery is bursting with things to eat, the mules are switching their tails, the big black bucks are humming and chanting and the sweat rolls down their shanks.

The whole street is living now off the cemetery grounds. Plenty for everybody. More than enough. The excess provender goes off in steam, in song and dance, in depravity and recklessness. Who would have dreamed that the poor dead flat-chested buggers rotting under the stone slabs contained such fertilizing wisdom? Who would have thought that these bony Lutherans, these spindle-shanked Presbyterians, had such good fat meat left on their bones, that they could make such a marvellous harvest of corruption, such nestfuls of worms? Even the dry epitaphs which the stone-cutters chiseled out have worked their fecundating power. Quietly there under the cool sod these lecherous, fornicating ghouls are working their power and glory. Nowhere in the whole wide world have I seen a cemetery blossom like this. Nowhere in the whole wide world such rich, steaming manure. Street of early sorrows, I embrace you! No more pale white faces, no Beethoven skulls, no cross-bones, no spindle-shanks. I see nothing but corn and maize, and golden-rods and lilacs; I see the common hoe, the mule in his traces, flat broad feet with toes spread and rich silky loam of earth sloshing between the toes. I see red handkerchiefs and faded blue shirts and broad sombreros glistening with sweat. I hear flies droning and the drone of lazy voices. The air hums with careless, reckless joy; the air hums with insects and their powdered wings spread pollen and depravity. I hear no bells, no whistles, no gongs, no brakes grinding; I hear the clink of the hoe, the drip of water dripping, the buzz and quiet pandemonium of toil. I hear the guitar and the harmonica, a soft tam-tam, a patter of slippered feet; I hear the blinds being lowered and the braying of a jackass deep in his oats.

No pale white faces, thanks be to Christ! I see the coolie, the black buck, the squaw. I see chocolate and cinnamon shades, I see a Mediterranean olive, a tawny Hawaiian gold; I see every pure and every cross shade, but no white. The skull and cross-bones have disappeared with the tomb-stones; the white bones of a white race have yielded their harvest. I see that everything pertaining to their name and memory has faded away, and that, that makes me wild with joy. In the buzz of the open field, where once the earth was humped into crazy little sods, I mosey along down the sunken wet furrows with thirsty tinkling toes; right and left I spatter the juicy cabbage loam, the mud pressed by the wheel, the broad green leaves, the crushed berries, the tart juice of the olive. Over the fat worms of the dead, squashing them back into the sod, I walk in benediction. Like the drunken sailor man I reel from side to side, my feet wet, my hands dry. I look through the wheat towards the puffs of cloud; my eye travels along the river, her low-laden dhows, her slow drift of sail and mast. I see the sun shooting down its broad rays, sucking gently at the river's breast. On the farther shore the pointed poles of wigwams, the lazy curl of smoke. I see the tomahawk sailing through the air to the sound of familiar blood-curdling yells. I see painted faces, bright beads, the soft moccasin dance, the long flat teats and the braided papoose.

Delaware and Lackawanna, Monongahela, the Mohawk, the Shenandoah, Narragansett, Tuskegee, Oskaloosa, Kalamazoo, Seminole and Pawnee, Cherokee, the great Manitou, the Blackfeet, the Navajo range: like a huge red cloud, like a pillar of fire, a vision of the outlawed magnificence of our earth passes before my eyes. I see no Letts, Croats, Finns, Danes, Swedes, no micks, no wops, no chinks, no polaks, no frogs, no heinies, no kikes. I see the Jews sitting in their crows' nests, their parched faces dry as leather, their skulls shrivelled and boneless.

Once more the tomahawk gleams, scalps fly, and out of the river-bed there rolls a bright billowy cloud of blood. From the mountain sides, from the great caves, from the swamps and Everglades pour a flood of blood-flecked men. From the Sierras to the Appalachians the land smokes with the blood of the slain. My scalp is cut away, the gray meat hangs over my ears in shreds; my feet are burned away, my sides pierced with arrows. In a pen against a broken fence I lie with my bowels beside me; all mangled and gory the beautiful white temple that was stretched with skin and muscle. The wind roars through my broken rectum, howls like sixty white lepers. A white flame, a jet of blue ice, a torch-spray spins in my hollow guts. My arms are yanked from their sockets. My body is a sepulchre which the ghouls are rifling. I am full of raw gems that bleed with icy brilliance. Like a thousand pointed lances the sun pierces my wounds, the gems flame, the gizzards shriek. Night or day I know not which; the tent of the world collapses like a gas-bag. In a flame of blood I feel the cold touch of a tong: through the river gorge they drag me, blind and helpless, choking, gasping, shrieking with impotence. Far away I hear the rush of icy water, the moan of jackals 'neath the evergreens;

through the dark green forest a stain of light spreads, a vernal, prussic light that stains the snow and the icy depths of the stream. A pleasant, choking gurgle, a quiet pandemonium as when the angel with her wings outstretched floated legless under the bridge.

The gutters are choked with snow. It is winter and the sun glares down with the low bright glint of noon. Going down the street past the flats. For an hour or two, while the sun lasts, everything turns to water, everything flows, trickles, gurgles. Between the curbs and the snow-banks a freshet of clear blue water rises. Within me a freshet that chokes the narrow gorge of my veins. A clear, blue stream inside me that circulates from my toes to the roots of my hair. I am completely thawed out, choking with an ice-blue gaiety.

Going down the street past the flats, an ice-blue gaiety in my narrow, choking veins. The winter's snow is melting, the gutters are swimming over. Sorrow gone and joy with it, melted, trickling away, pouring into the sewer. Suddenly the bells begin to toll, wild funereal bells with obscene tongues, with wild iron clappers that smash the glass haemorrhoids of the veins. Through the melting snow a carnage reigns: low Chinese horses hung with scalps, long finely-jointed insects with green mandibles. In front of each house an iron railing spiked with blue flowers.

Down the street of early sorrows comes the witch mother stalking the wind, her wide sails unfurled, her dress bulging with skulls. Terrified we flee the night, perusing the green album, its high decor of frontal legs, the bulging brow. From all the rotting stoops the hiss of snakes squirming in the bag, the cord tied, the bowels knotted. Blue flowers spotted like leopards, squashed, blood-sucked, the earth a vernal stain, gold, marrow, bright bone dust, three wings aloft and the march of the white horse, the ammonia eyes.

The melting snow melts deeper, the iron rusts, the leaves flower. On the corner, under the elevated, stands a man with a plug hat, in blue serge and linen spats, his white mustache chopped fine. The switch opens and out rolls all the tobacco juice, the golden lemons, the elephant tusks, the candelabras. Moishe Pippik, the lemon dealer, fowled with pigeons, breeding purple eggs in his vest pocket and purple ties and watermelons and spinach with short stems, stringy, marred with tar. The whistle of the acorns loudly stirring, flurry of floozies bandaged in lysol, ammonia and camphor patches, little mica huts, peanut shells triangled and corrugated, all marching triumphantly with the morning breeze. The morning light comes in creases, the window panes are streaked, the covers are torn, the oil cloth is faded. Walks a man with hair on end, not running, not breathing, a man with a weathervane that turns the corners sharply and then bolts. A man who thinks not how or why but just to walk in lustreless night with all stars to port and loaded whiskers trimmed. Gow-selling in the grummels he wakes the plaintive night with pitfalls tuning left to right, high noon on the wintry ocean, high noon all sides aboard and aloft to starboard. The weathervane again with deep oars coming through the portholes and all sounds muffled. Noiseless the night on all fours, like the hurricane. Noiseless with loaded caramels and nickel dice. Sister Monica playing the guitar with shirt open and laces down, broad flanges in either ear. Sister Monica streaked with lime, gum wash, her eyes mildewed, craped, crapped, crenellated.

The street of early sorrows widens, the blue lips blubber, the albatross wings ahead her gory neck unhinged, her teeth agibber. The man with the bowler hat creaks his left leg, two notches further down to the right, under the gunwales, the Cuban flag spliced with noodles and mock oranges, with wild magnolias and young palmetto shoots chaffed with chalk and green slaver. Under the silver bed the white geranium bowl, two stripes for the morning, three for the night. The castors crooning for blood. The blood comes in white gulps, white choking gulps of clay filled with broken teeth, with mucilage and wasted bones. The floor is slippery with the coming and going, with the bright scissors, the long knives, the hot and cold tongs.

In the melting snow outside the menagerie breaks loose, first the zebras with gorgeous white flanks, then the fowling birds and rooks, then the acacias and the diamond backs. The greenery yawns with open toes, the red bird wheels and dives below, the scrum-tuft breaks a beak, the lizard micturates, the jackal purrs, the hyaenas belch and laugh and belch again. The whole wide cemetery safely sprinkled cracks its joints in the night. The automatons crack too with mighty suits of armor encumbered and hinges rusted and bolts unlocked, abandoned by the tin trust. The butter blossoms out in huge fan wreaths, fat, oleandrous butter marked with crows' feet and twice spliced by the hangman John the Crapper. The butter yowsels in the mortuary, pale shafts of moonbeam trickling through, the estuaries clogged, the freights ashudder, the sidings locked. Brown beagled bantams trimmed with red craw and otter's fur browse the bottom lands. The larkspur does a hemorrhage. The magnesia wells ignite, the eagle soars aloft with a cleaver through the ankle.

Bloody and wild the night with all hawks' feet slashed and trimmed. Bloody and wild the night with all the belfries screeching and all the slats torn and all the gas mains bursting. Bloody and wild the night with every muscle twisted, the toes crossed, the hair on end, the teeth red, the spine cracked. All the world wide awake, twittering like the dawn, and a low red fire crawling over the gums. All through the night the combs break, the ribs sing. Twice the dawn breaks, then steals away again. In the trickling

267

snow the oxide fumes. All through the street the hearses pass up and down, up and down, the drivers munching their long whips, their white crapes, their cotton gloves.

North towards the white pole, south towards the red heron, the pulse beats wild and straight. One by one, with bright glass teeth, they cut away the cords. The duck comes with his broad bill and then the low-bellied weasel. One after another they come, summoned from the fungus, their tails afeather, their feet webbed. They come in waves, bent like trolley poles, and pass under the bed. Mud on the floor and strange signs, the windows blazing, nothing but teeth, then hands, then carrots, then great nomadic onions with emerald eyes, comets that come and go, come and go.

East towards the Mongols, west towards the redwoods, the pulse swings back and forth. Onions marching, eggs chattering, the menagerie spinning like a top. Miles high on the beaches lie the red caviar beds. The breakers foam, snap their long whips. The tide roars beneath the green glaciers. Faster, faster, spins the earth.

Out of black chaos whorls of light with port-holes jammed. Out of the static null and void a ceaseless equilibrium. Out of whale-bone and gunnysack this mad thing called sleep that runs like an eight-day clock.

Un Etre Etoilique

As I WRITE these lines Anaïs Nin has begun the fiftieth volume of her diary, the record of a twenty year struggle towards self-realization. Still a young woman she has produced on the side, in the midst of an intensely active life, a monumental confession which when given to the world will take its place beside the revelations of St. Augustine, Petronius, Abélard, Rousseau, Proust, and others.

Of the twenty years recorded half the time was spent in America, half in Europe. The diary is full of voyages; in fact, like life itself it might be regarded as nothing but voyage. The epic quality of it, however, is eclipsed by the metaphysical. The diary is not a journey towards the heart of darkness, in the stern Conradian sense of destiny, not a *voyage au bout de la nuit*, as with Céline, nor even a voyage to the moon in the psychological sense of escape. It is much more like a mythological voyage towards the source and fountain head of life—I might say an *astrologic* voyage of metamorphosis.

The importance of such a work for our time hardly needs to be stressed. More and more, as our era draws to a close, are we made aware of the tremendous significance of the human document. Our literature, unable any longer to express itself through dying forms, has become almost exclusively biographical. The artist is retreating behind the dead forms to rediscover in himself the eternal source of creation. Our age, intensely productive, yet thoroughly un-vital, un-creative, is obsessed with a lust for investigating the mysteries of the personality. We turn instinctively towards those documents—fragments, notes, autobiographies, diaries—which appease our hunger for more life because, avoiding the circuitous expression of art, they seem to put us directly in contact with that which we are seeking. I say they "seem to", because there are no short cuts such as we imagine, because the most direct expression, the most permanent and the most effective is always that of art. Even in the most naked confessions there exists the same ellipsis of art. The diary is an art form just as much as the novel or the play. The diary simply requires a greater canvas; it is a chronological tapestry which, in its ensemble, or at whatever point it is abandoned, reveals a form and language as exacting as other literary forms. A work like *Faust*, indeed, reveals more discrepancies, irrelevancies and enigmatic stumbling blocks than a diary such as Amiel's, for example. The former represents an artificial mode of synchronization; the latter has an organic integration which even the interruption of death does not disturb.

The chief concern of the diarist is not with truth, though it may seem to be, any more than the chief concern of the conscious artist is with beauty. Beauty and truth are the by-products in a quest for something beyond either of these. But just as we are impressed by the beauty of a work of art, so we are impressed by the truth and sincerity of a diary. We have the illusion, in reading the pages of an intimate journal, that we are face to face with the soul of its author. This is the illusory quality of the diary, its art quality, so to speak, just as beauty is the illusory element in the accepted work of art. The diary has to be read differently from the novel, but the goal is the same: self-realization. The diary, by its very nature, is quotidian and organic, whereas the novel is timeless and conventional. We know more, or seem to know more, immediately about the author of a diary than we do about the author of a novel. But as to what we *really* know of either it is hard to say. For the diary is not a transcript of life itself any more than the novel is. It is a medium of expression in which truth rather than art predominates. But it is not *truth*. It is not for the simple reason that the very problem, the obsession, so to say, is truth. We should look to the diary, therefore, not for the truth about things but as an expression of this struggle to be free of the obsession for truth.

It is this factor, so important to grasp, which explains the tortuous, repetitive quality of every diary. Each day the battle is begun afresh; as we read we seem to be treading a mystic maze in which the author becomes more and more deeply lost. The mirror of the author's own experiences becomes the well of truth in which ofttimes he is drowned. In every diary we assist at the birth of Narcissus, and sometimes the death too. This death, when it occurs, is of two kinds, as in life. In the one case it may lead to dissolution, in the other to rebirth. In the last volume of Proust's great work the nature of this rebirth is magnificently elaborated in the author's disquisitions on the metaphysical nature of art. For it is in *Le Temps Retrouvé* that the great fresco wheels into another dimension and thus acquires its true symbolic significance. The analysis which had been going on throughout the preceding volumes reaches its climax finally in a vision of the whole; it is almost like the sewing up of a wound. It emphasizes what Nietzsche pointed out long ago as "the healing quality of art". The purely personal, Narcissistic element is resolved into the universal; the seemingly interminable confession restores the narrator to the stream of human activity through the realization that life itself is an art. This realization is brought about, as Proust so well points out, through obeying the still small voice within. It is the very opposite of the Socratic method, the absurdity of which Nietzsche exposed so witheringly. The mania for analysis leads finally to its opposite, and the sufferer passes on beyond his problems into a new realm of reality. The therapeutic aspect of art is then, in this higher state of consciousness, seen to be the religious or metaphysical element. The work which was begun as a refuge and escape from the terrors of reality leads the author back into life, not adapted to the reality about, but superior to it, as one capable of recreating it in accordance with his own needs. He sees that it was not life but himself from which he had been fleeing, and that the life which had heretofore been insupportable was merely the projection of his own phantasies. It is true that the new life is also a projection of the individual's own phantasies but they are invested now with the sense of real power; they spring not from dissociation but from integration. The whole past life resumes its place in the balance and creates a vital, stable equilibrium which would never have resulted without the pain and the suffering. It is in this sense that the endless turning about in a cage which characterized the author's thinking, the endless fresco which seems never to be brought to a conclusion, the ceaseless fragmentation and analysis which goes on night and day, is like a gyration which through sheer centrifugal force lifts the sufferer out of his obsessions and frees him for the rhythm and movement of life by joining him to the great universal stream in which all of us have our being.

A book is a part of life, a manifestation of life, just as much as a tree or a horse or a star. It obeys its own rhythms, its own laws, whether it be a novel, a play, or a diary. The deep, hidden rhythm of life is always there—that of the pulse, the heart beat. Even in the seemingly stagnant waters of the journal this flux and reflux is evident. It is there in the whole of the work as much as in each fragment. Looked at in its entirety, especially for example in such a work as that of Anaïs Nin's, this cosmic pulsation corresponds to the death and rebirth of the individual. Life assumes the aspect of a labyrinth into which the seeker is plunged. She goes in unconsciously to slay her old self. One might say, as in this case, that the disintegration of the self had come about through a shock. It would not matter much what had produced the disintegration; the important thing is that at a given moment she passed into a state of two-ness. The old self, which had been attached to the father who abandoned her and the loss of whom created an insoluble conflict in her, found itself confronted with a nascent other self which seems to lead her further and further into darkness and confusion. The diary, which is the story of her retreat from the world into the chaos of regeneration, pictures the labyrinthine struggle waged by these conflicting selves. Sinking into the obscure regions of her soul she seems to draw the world down over her head and with it the people she meets and the relationships engendered by her meetings. The illusion of submergence, of darkness and stagna-

273

tion, is brought about by the ceaseless observation and analysis which goes on in the pages of the diary. The hatches are down, the sky shut out. Everything—nature, human beings, events, relationships—is brought below to be dissected and digested. It is a devouring process in which the ego becomes a stupendous red maw. The language itself is clear, painfully clear. It is the scorching light of the intellect locked away in a cave. Nothing which this mind comes in contact with is allowed to go undigested. The result is harrowing and hallucinating. We move with the author through her labyrinthine world like a knife making an incision into the flesh. It is a surgical operation upon a world of flesh and blood, a Caesarian operation performed by the embryo with its own private scissors and cleaver.

Let me make a parenthetical remark here. *This diary is written absolutely without malice.* The psychologist may remark of this that the pain inflicted upon her by the loss of her father was so great as to render her incapable of causing pain to others. In a sense this is true, but it is a limited view of the matter. My own feeling is rather that we have in this diary the direct, naked thrust which is of the essence of the great tragic dramas of the Greeks. Racine, Corneille, Molière may indulge in malice—not the Greek dramatists. The difference lies in the attitude towards Fate. The warfare is not with men but with the gods. Similarly, in the case of Anaïs Nin's journal: the war is with herself, with God as the sole witness. The diary was written not for the eyes of others, but for the eye of God. She has no malice any more than she has the desire to cheat or to lie. To lie in a diary is the height of absurdity. One would have to be really insane to do that. Her concern is not with others, except as they may reveal to her something about herself. Though the way is tortuous the direction is always the same, always inward, further inward, towards the heart of the self. Every encounter is a preparation for the final encounter, the confrontation with the real Self. To indulge in malice would be to swerve from the ordained path, to waste a precious moment in the pursuit of her ideal. She moves onward inexorably, as the gods move in the Greek dramas, on towards the realization of her destiny.

There is a very significant fact attached to the origin of this diary and that is that it was begun in artistic fashion. By that I do not mean that it was done with the skill of an artist, with the conscious use of a technique; no, but it was begun as something to be read by some one else, as something to influence some one else. In that sense as an artist. Begun during the voyage to a foreign land, the diary is a silent communion with the father who has deserted her, a gift which she intends to send him from their new home, a gift of love which she hopes will reunite them. Two days later the war breaks out. By what seems almost like a conspiracy of fate the father and child are kept apart for many years. In the legends which treat of this theme it happens, as in this case, that the meeting takes place when the daughter has come of age.

And so, in the very beginning of her diary, the child behaves precisely like the artist who, through the medium of his expression, sets about to conquer the world which has denied him. Thinking originally to woo and enchant the father by the testimony of her grief, thwarted in all her attempts to recover him, she begins little by little to regard the separation as a punishment for her own inadequacy. The difference which had marked her out as a child, and which had already brought down upon her the father's ire, becomes more accentuated. The diary becomes the confession of her inability to make herself worthy of this lost father who has become for her the very paragon of perfection.

In the very earliest pages of the diary this conflict between the old, inadequate self which was attached to the father and the bud-ding, unknown self which she was creating manifests itself. It is a struggle between the real and the ideal, the annihilating struggle which for most people is carried on fruitlessly to the end of their lives and the significance of which they never learn. Scarcely two years after the diary is begun comes the following passage:

"Quand aucun bruit ne se fait entendre, quand la nuit a recouvert de son sombre paletot la grande ville dont elle me cache l'éclat trompeur, alors il me semble entendre une voix mystérieuse qui me parle; je suppose qu'elle vient de moi-même car elle pense comme moi . . . Il me semble que je cherche quelque chose, je ne sais pas quoi, mais quand mon esprit libre dégage des griffes puissantes de ce mortel ennemi, le Monde, il me semble que je trouve ce que je voulais. Serait-ce l'oubli? le silence? Je ne sais, mais cette même voix, quand je crois être seule, me parle. Je ne puis comprendre ce qu'elle dit mais je me dis que l'on ne peut jamais être seule et oubliée dans le monde. Car je nomme cette voix: Mon Génie: mauvais ou bon, je ne puis savoir . . ."

Even more striking is a passage in the same volume which begins: "Dans ma vie terrestre rien n'est changé . . ." After recounting the petty incidents which go to make up her earthly life, she adds, but:

"Dans la vie que je mène dans l'infini cela est différent. Là, tout est bonheur et douceur, car c'est un rêve. Là, il n'y a pas d'école aux sombres classes, mais il y a Dieu. Là, il n'y a pas de chaise vide dans la famille, qui est toujours au complet. Là, il n'y a pas de bruit, mais de la solitude qui donne la paix. La, il n'y a pas d'inquiétude pour l'avenir, car c'est un autre rêve. Là, il n'y a pas de larmes, car c'est un sourire. Voilà l'infini où je vis, car *je vis deux fois.* Quand je mourrai sur la terre, il arrivera, comme il arrive a **deux lumières** allumées à la fois, quand l'une s'éteint l'autre se rallume, et celà avec plus de force. Je m'éteindrai sur la terre, mais je me rallumerai dans l'infini . . ."

She speaks of herself mockingly at times as "une étoilique"—a word which she has invented, and why not, since as she says, we have the word lunatique. Why not "étoilique"? "To-day", she writes, "I described very poorly le pays des merveilles où mon esprit était. Je volais dans ce pays lointain où rien n'est impossible. Hier je suis revenue, à la réalité, à la tristesse. Il me semble que je tombais d'une grande splendeur à une triste misère."

One thinks inevitably of the manifestoes of the Surrealists, of their unquenchable thirst for the marvellous, and that phrase of Breton's, so significant of the dreamer, the visionary: "we should conduct ourselves as though we were really in the world!" It may seem absurd to couple the utterances of the Surrealists with the writings of a child of thirteen, but there is a great deal which they have in common and there is also a point of departure which is even more important. The pursuit of the marvellous is at bottom nothing but the sure instinct of the poet speaking and it manifests itself everywhere in all epochs, in all conditions of life, in all forms of expression. But this marvellous pursuit of the marvellous, if not understood, can also act as a thwarting force, can become a thing of evil, crushing the individual in the toils of the Absolute. It can become as negative and destructive a force as the yearning for God. When I said a while back that the child had begun her great work in the spirit of an artist I was trying to emphasize the fact that, like the artist, the problem which beset her was to conquer the world. In the process of making herself fit to meet her father again (because to her the world was personified in the Father) she was unwittingly making herself an artist, that is, a self-dependent creature for whom a father would no longer be necessary. When she does encounter him again, after a lapse of almost twenty years, she is a full-fledged being, a creature fashioned after her own image. The meeting serves to make her realize that she has emancipated herself; more indeed, for to her amazement and dismay she also realizes that she has no more need of the one she was seeking. The significance of her heroic struggle with herself now reveals itself symbolically. That which was beyond her, which had dominated and tortured her, which *possessed* her, one might say, no longer exists. She is de-possessed and free at last to live her own life.

Throughout the diary the amazing thing is this intuitive awareness of the symbolic nature of her role. It is this which illuminates the most trivial remarks, the most trivial incidents she records. In reality there is nothing trivial throughout the whole record; everything is saturated with a purpose and significance which gradually becomes clear as the confession progresses. Similarly there is nothing chaotic about the work, although at first glance it may give that impression. The fifty volumes are crammed with human figures, incidents, voyages, books read and commented upon, reveries, metaphysical speculations, the dramas in which she is enveloped, her daily work, her preoccupation with the welfare of others, in short with a thousand and one things which go to make up her life. It is a great pageant of the times patiently and humbly delineated by one who considered herself as nothing, by one who had almost completely effaced herself in the effort to arrive at a true understanding of life. It is in this sense again that the human document rivals the work of art, or in times such as ours, *replaces* the work of art. For, in a profound sense, this *is* the work of art which never gets written—because the artist whose task it is to create it never gets born. We have here, instead of the consciously or technically finished work (which to-day seems to us more than ever empty and illusory), the unfinished symphony which achieves consummation because each line is pregnant with a soul struggle. The conflict with the world takes place within. It matters little, for the artist's purpose, whether the world be the size of a pinhead or an incommensurable universe. *But there must be a world!* And this world, whether real or imaginary, can only be created out of despair and anguish. For the artist there is no other world. Even if it be unrecognizable, this world which is created out of sorrow and deprivation is true and vital, and eventually it expropriates the "other" world in which the ordinary mortal lives and dies. It is the world in which the artist has his being, and it is in the revelation of his undying self that art takes its stance. Once this is apprehended there can be no question of monotony or fatigue, of chaos or irrelevance. We move amidst boundless horizons in a perpetual state of awe and humility. We enter, with the author, into unknown worlds and we share with the latter all the pain, beauty, terror and illumination which exploration entails.

Of the truly great authors no one has ever complained that they over-elaborated. On the contrary, we usually bemoan the fact that there is nothing further left us to read. And so we turn back to what we have and we re-read, and as we re-read we discover marvels which previously we had ignored. We go back to them again and again, as to inexhaustible wells of wisdom and delight. Almost invariably, it is curious to note, these authors of whom I speak are observed to be precisely those who have given us more than the others. They claim us precisely because we sense in them an unquenchable flame. Nothing they wrote seems to us insignificant—not even their notes, their jottings, not even the designs which they scribbled unconsciously in the margins of their copy books. Whereas with the meagre spirits everything seems superfluous, themselves as well as the works they have given us.

At the bottom of this relentless spirit of elaboration is care—

Sorgen. The diarist in particular is obsessed with the notion that everything must be preserved. And this again is born out of a sense of destiny. Not only, as with the ordinary artist, is there the tyrannical desire to immortalize one's self, but there is also the idea of immortalizing the world in which the diarist lives and has his being. Everything must be recorded because everything must be preserved. In the diary of Anaïs Nin there is a kind of desperation, almost like that of a shipwrecked sailor thrown up on a desert island. From the flotsam and jetsam of her wrecked life the author struggles to create anew. It is a heart-breaking effort to recover a lost world. It is not, as some might imagine, a deliberate retreat from the world; it is an involuntary separation from the world! Every one experiences this feeling in more or less degree. Every one, whether consciously or unconsciously, is trying to recover the luxurious, effortless sense of security which he knew in the womb. Those who are able to realize themselves do actually achieve this state; not by a blind, unconscious yearning for the uterine condition, but by transforming the world in which they live into a veritable womb. It is this which seems to have terrified Aldous Huxley, for example, when standing before El Greco's painting, "The Dream of Philip 2nd". Mr. Huxley was terrified by the prospect of a world converted into a fish-gut. But El Greco must have been supremely happy inside his fish-gut world, and the proof of his contentment, his ease, his satisfaction, is the world-feeling which his pictures create in the mind of the spectator. Standing before his paintings one realizes that *this is a world!* One realizes also that it is a world dominated by vision. It is no longer a man looking *at* the world, but a man inside his own world ceaselessly reconstructing it in terms of the light within. That it is a world englobed, that El Greco seems to Aldous Huxley, for example, much like a Jonah in the belly of the whale, is precisely the comforting thing about

El Greco's vision. The lack of a boundless infinity, which seems so to disturb Mr. Huxley, is on the contrary, a most beneficent state of affairs. Every one who has assisted at the creation of a world, any one who has made a world of his own, realizes that it is precisely the fact that his world has definite limits which is what is good about it. One has to first lose himself to discover the world of his own, the world which, because it is rigidly limited, permits the only true condition of freedom.

Which brings us back to the labyrinth and the descent into the womb, into the night of primordial chaos in which "knowledge is refunded into ignorance". This laborious descent into the infernal regions is really the initiation for the final descent into the eternal darknesss of death. He who goes down into the labyrinth must first strip himself of all possessions, as well as of prejudices, notions, ideals, ideas, and so on. He must return into the womb naked as the day he was born, with only the core of his future self, as it were. No one, of course, offers himself up to this experience unless he is harried by vision. The vision is first and foremost, always. And this vision is like the voice of conscience itself. It is a double vision, as we well know. One sees forwards and backwards with equal clarity. But one does not see what is directly under the nose; one does not see the world which is immediately about. This blindness to the everyday, to the normal or abnormal circumstances of life, is the distinguishing feature of the restless visionary. The eyes, which are unusually endowed, have to be trained to see with normal vision. Superficially this sort of individual seems to be concerned only with what is going on about him; the daily communion with the diary seems at first blush to be nothing more than a transcription of this normal, trivial, everyday life. And yet nothing can be further from the truth. The fact is that this extraordinary cataloguing of events, objects, impressions, ideas, etc. is only a keyboard exercise, as it were, to attain the faculty of seeing what is so glibly recorded. Actually, of course, few people in this world see what is going on about them. Nobody really sees until he understands, until he can create a pattern into which the helter-skelter of passing events fits and makes a significance. And for this sort of vision a personal death is required. One has to be able to see first with the eyes of a Martian, or a Neptunian. One has to have this extraordinary vision, this clairvoyance, to be able to take in the multiplicity of things with ordinary eyes. Nobody sees with his eyes alone; we see with our souls. And this problem of putting the soul into the eye is the whole problem of a diarist such as Anaïs Nin. The whole vast diary, regarded from this angle, assumes the nature of the record of a second birth. It is the story of death and transfiguration.

Or one might put it still more figuratively and say it was the story of an egg which was splitting in two, that this egg went down into the darkness to become a single new egg made of the ingredients of the old. The diary then resembles a museum in which the world that made up the old split egg goes to pieces. Superficially it would seem as though every crumbling bit had been preserved in the pages of the diary. Actually not a crumb remains; everything that made up the former world not only goes to pieces but is devoured again, re-digested and assimilated in the growth of a new entity, the new egg which is one and indivisible. This egg is indestructible and forms a vital component element of that world which is constantly in the making. It belongs not to a personal world but to the cosmic world. In itself it has very definite limits, as has the atom or the molecule. But taken in relation with other similar identities it forms, or helps to form, a universe which is truly limitless. It has a spontaneous life of its own which knows a true freedom because its life is lived in accordance with the most rigid laws. The whole process does indeed seem to be that union with nature of which the poets speak. But this union is achieved parabolically, through a spiritual death. It is the same sort of transfiguration which the myths relate of; it is what makes intelligible to us such a phrase as "the spirit which animates a place". Spirit in taking possession of a place, so identifies itself with it that the natural and the divine coalesce.

It is in this same way that human spirits take possession of the earth. It is only in the understanding of this, which by some is considered miraculous, that we can look without the least anguish upon the deaths of millions of fellow men. For we do distinguish not only between the loss of a near one and a stranger, but also, and how much more, between the loss of a near one and the loss of a great personality, a Christ, a Buddha, or a Mahomet. We speak of them, quite naturally, as though they never had died, as though they were still with us, in fact. What we mean is that they have so taken possession of the world that not even death can dislodge them. Their spirit does truly pass into the world and animate it. And it is only the animation of such spirits which gives to our life on earth significance. But all these figures had to die first in the spirit. All of them renounced the world first. That is the cardinal fact about them.

In the later volumes of the diary we note the appearance of titles. For instance, and I give them in chronological order, the following: "The Definite Disappearance of the Demon"; "Death and Disintegration"; "The Triumph of White Magic"; "The Birth of Humor in the Whale"; "Playing at Being God"; "Fire"; "Audace"; "Vive la dynamite"; "A God who Laughs". The use of titles to indicate the nature of a volume is an indication of the gradual emergence from the labyrinth. It means that the diary itself has undergone a radical transformation. No longer a fleeting panorama of impressions, but a consolidation of experience into little bundles of fibre and muscle which go to make up the new body. The new being is definitely born and travelling upward towards the light of the every-day world. In the previous volumes we had the record of the struggle to penetrate to the very sanctum of the self; it is a description of a shadowy world in which the outline of people, things and events becomes more and more blurred by the involutional inquisition. The further we penetrate into the darkness and confusion below, however, the greater becomes the illumination. The whole personality seems to become a devouring eye turned pitilessly on the self. Finally there comes the moment when this individual who has been constantly gazing into a mirror sees with such blinding clarity that the mirror fades away and the image rejoins the body from which it had been separated. It is at this point that normal vision is restored and that the one who had died is restored to the living world. It is at this moment that the prophecy which had been written twenty years earlier comes true— "Un de ces jours je pourrais dire: mon journal, je suis arrivée au fond!"

Whereas in the earlier volumes the accent was one of sadness, of disillusionment, of being de trop, now the accent becomes one of joy and fulfillment. Fire, audacity, dynamite, laughter—the very choice of words is sufficient to indicate the changed condition. The world spreads out before her like a banquet table: something to enjoy. But the appetite, seemingly insatiable, is controlled. The old obsessional desire to devour everything in sight in order that it be preserved in her own private tomb is gone. She eats now only what nourishes her. The once ubiquitous digestive tract, the great whale into which she had made herself, is replaced by other organs with other functions. The exaggerated sympathy for others which had dogged her every step diminishes. The birth of a sense of humor denotes the achievement of an objectivity which alone the one who has realized himself attains. It is not indifference, but toleration. The totality of vision brings about a new kind of sympathy, a free, non-compulsive sort. The very pace of the diary changes. There are now long lapses, intervals of complete silence in which the great digestive apparatus, once all, slows up to permit the development of complementary organs. The eye too seems to close, content to let the body *feel* the presence of the world about, rather than pierce it with a devastating vision. It is no longer a world of black and white, of good and evil, or harmony and dissonance; no, now the world has at last become an orchestra in which there are innumerable instruments capable of rendering every tone and color, an orchestra in which even the most shattering dissonances are resolved into meaningful expression. It is the ultimate poetic world of *As Is*. The inquisition is over, the trial and torture finished. A state of absolution is reached. This is the true catholic world of which the Catholics know nothing. This is the eternally abiding world which those in search of it never find. For with most of us we stand before the world as before a mirror; we never see our true selves because we can never come before the mirror unawares. We see ourselves as actors, but the spectacle for which we are rehearsing is never put on. To see the true spectacle, to finally participate in it, one must die before the mirror in a blinding light of realization. We must lose not only the mask and the costume but the flesh and bone which conceals the secret self. This we can only do by illumination, by voluntarily going down into death. For when this moment is attained we who imagined that we were sitting in the belly of the whale and doomed to nothingness suddenly discover that the whale was a projection of our own insufficiency. The whale remains, but the whale becomes the whole wide world, with stars and seasons, with banquets and festivals, with everything that is wonderful to see and touch, and being that it is no longer a whale but something nameless because something that is inside as well as outside us. We may, if we like, devour the whale too— piecemeal, throughout eternity. No matter how much is ingested there will always remain more whale than man; because what man appropriates of the whale returns to the whale again in one form or another. The whale is constantly being transformed as man himself becomes transformed. There is nothing but man and whale, and the man is *in* the whale and possesses the whale. Thus, too, whatever waters the whale inhabits man inhabits also, but always as the inner inhabitant of the whale. Seasons come and go, whale-like seasons, in which the whole organism of the whale is affected. Man, too, is affected, as that inner inhabitant of the whale. But the whale never dies, nor does man inside him, because that which they have established together is undying—their relationship. And it is in this that they live, through and by which they live: not the waters, nor the seasons, nor that which is swallowed nor that which passes away. In this passing beyond the mirror, as it were, there is an infinity which no infinity of images can give the least idea of. One lives within the spirit of transformation and not in the act. The legend of the whale thus becomes the celebrated book of transformations destined to cure the ills of the world. Each man who climbs into the body of the whale and works therein his own resurrection is bringing about the miraculous transfiguration of the world which, because it is human, is none the less limitless. The whole process is a marvellous piece of dramatic symbolism whereby he who sat facing his doom suddenly awakes and lives, and through the mere act of declaration—the act of declaring his livingness— causes the whole world to become alive and endlessly alter its visage. He who gets up from his stool in the body of the whale automatically switches on an orchestral music which causes each living member of the universe to dance and sing, to pass the end-less time in endless recreation.

And here I must return once again to El Greco's "Dream of Philip the 2nd" which Mr. Huxley so well describes in his little essay. For in a way this diary of Anaïs Nin's is also a curious dream of something or other, a dream which takes place fathoms deep below the surface of the sea. One might think that in this retreat from the daylight world we are about to be ushered into an her-metically sealed laboratory in which only the ego flourishes. Not at all. The ego indeed seems to completely disappear amidst the furniture and trappings of this subterranean world which she has created about her. A thousand figures stalk the pages, caught in their most intimate poses and revealing themselves as they never reveal themselves to the mirror. The most dramatic pages are those perhaps in which the gullible psychoanalysts, thinking to unravel the complexities of her nature, are themselves unravelled and left dangling in a thousand shreds. Every one who comes under her glance is lured, as it were, into a spider web, stripped bare, dis-sected, dismembered, devoured and digested. All without malice! Done automatically, as a part of life's processes. The person who is doing this is really an innocent little creature tucked away in the lining of the belly of the whale. In nullifying herself she really be-comes this great leviathan which swims the deep and devours everything in sight. It is a strange *dédoublement* of the personality in which the crime is related back to the whale by a sort of self-induced amnesia. There, tucked away in a pocket of the great intes-tinal tract of the whale, she dreams away throughout whole vol-umes of something which is not the whale, of something greater, something beyond which is nameless and unseizable. She has a little pocket mirror which she tacks up on the wall of the whale's intestinal gut and into which she gazes for hours on end. The whole drama of her life is played out before the mirror. If she is sad the mirror reflects her sadness; if she is gay the mirror reflects her gayety. But everything the mirror reflects is false, because the moment she realizes that her image is sad or gay she is no longer sad or gay. Always there is another self which is hidden from the mirror and which enables her to look at herself in the mirror. This other self tells her that it is only her image which is sad, only her image which is gay. By looking at herself steadily in the mirror she really accomplishes the miracle of not looking at herself. The mirror enables her to fall into a trance in which the image is completely lost. The eyes close and she falls backward into the deep. The whale too falls backward and is lost into the deep. This is the dream which El Greco dreamed that Philip the 2nd dreamed. It is the dream of a dream, just as a double mirror would reflect the image of an image. It can as well be the dream of a dream of a dream, or the image of an image of an image. It can go back like that endlessly, from one little Japanese box into another and another and another without ever reaching the last box. Each lapse backward brings about a greater clairvoyance; as the darkness increases the inner eye develops in magnitude. The world is boxed off and with it the dreams that shape the world. There are endless trap-doors, but no exits. She falls from one level to another, but there is never a final ocean floor. The result is often a sensation of brilliant crystalline clarity, the sort of frozen wonder which the metamorphosis of a snow-flake awakens. It is something like what a molecule would experience in decomposing into its basic elements, if it had the ability to express its awareness of the transformation going on. It is the nearest thing to ultimate sensation without completely losing identity. In the ordinary reader it is apt to produce a sensation of horror. He will find himself suddenly slipping into a world of monstrous crimes committed by an angel who is innocent of the knowledge of crime. He will be terrified by the mineralogical aspect of these crimes in which no blood is spilt, no wounds left unhealed. He will miss the normally attendant elements of violence and so be utterly confounded, utterly hallucinated.

There are some volumes, in which attention is focussed almost entirely on one or two individuals, which are like the raw pith of some post-Dostoievskian novel; they bring to the surface a lunar plasm which is the logical fruit of that drive towards the dead slag of the ego which Dostoievski heralded and which D. H. Lawrence was the first to have pointed out in precise language. There are three successive volumes, of this sort, which are made of nothing but this raw material of a drama which takes place entirely within the confines of the female world. It is the first female writing I have ever seen: it rearranges the world in terms of female honesty. The result is a language which is ultra-modern and yet which bears no resemblance to any of the masculine experimental processes with which we are familiar. It is precise, abstract, cloudy and unseizable. There are larval thoughts not yet divorced from their dream content, thoughts which seem to slowly crystallize before your eyes, always precise but never tangible, never once arrested so as to be grasped by the mind. It is the opium world of woman's physiological being, a sort of cinematic show put on inside the genito-urinary tract. There is not an ounce of man-made culture in it; everything related to the head is cut off. Time passes, but it is not clock time; nor is it poetic time such as men create in their passion. It is more like that aeonic time required for the creation of gems and precious metals; an embowelled sidereal time in which the female knows that she is superior to the male and will eventually swallow him up again. The effect is that of starlight carried over into day-time.

The contrast between this language and that of man's is forcible; the whole of man's art begins to appear like a frozen edelweiss under a glass bell reposing on a mantelpiece in the deserted home of a lunatic. In this extraordinary unicellular language of the female we have a blinding, gem-like consciousness which disperses the ego like star-dust. The great female corpus rises up from its sleepy marine depths in a naked push towards the sun. The sun is at zenith—permanently at zenith. Space broadens out like a cold Norwegian lake choked with ice-floes. The sun and moon are fixed, the one at zenith, the other at nadir. The tension is perfect, the polarity absolute. The voices of the earth mingle in an eternal resonance which issues from the delta of the fecundating river of death. It is the voice of creation which is constantly being drowned in the daylight frenzy of a man-made world. It comes like the light breeze which sets the ocean swaying; it comes with a calm, quiet force which is irresistible, like the movement of the great Will gathered up by the instincts and rippling out in long silky flashes of enigmatic dynamism. Then a lull in which the mysterious centralized forces roll back to the matrix, gather up again in a sublime all-sufficiency. Nothing lost, nothing used up, nothing relinquished. The great mystery of conservation in which creation and destruction are but the antipodal symbols of a single constant energy which is inscrutable.

It is at this point in the still unfinished symphony of the diary that the whole pattern wheels miraculously into another dimension; at this point that it takes its cosmic stance. Adopting the universal language, the human being in her speaks straight out from under the skin to Hindu, Chinaman, Jap, Abyssinian, Malay, Turk, Arab, Tibetan, Eskimo, Pawnee, Hottentot, Bushman, Kaffir, Persian, Assyrian. The fixed polar language known to all races: a serpentine, sybilline, sibilant susurrus that comes up out of the astral marshes: a sort of cold, tinkling, lunar laughter which comes from under the soles of the feet: a laughter made of alluvial deposit, of mythological excrement and the sweat of epileptics. This is the language which seeps through the frontiers of race, color, religion, sex; a language which soaks through the litmus paper of the mind and saturates the quintessential human spores. The language of bells without clappers, heard incessantly throughout the nine months in which every one is identical and yet mysteriously different. In this first tinkling melody of immortality lapping against the snug and cosy walls of the womb we have the music of the still-born sons of men opening their lovely dead eyes one upon another.

The Tailor Shop

THE DAY USED TO START LIKE THIS: "ask so-and-so for a little something on account, *but don't insult him!*" They were ticklish bastards, all these old farts we catered to. It was enough to drive any man to drink. There we were, just opposite the Olcott, Fifth Avenue tailors even though we weren't on the Avenue. A joint corporation of father and son, with mother holding the boodle.

Mornings, eight A.M. or thereabouts, a brisk intellectual walk from Delancey Street and the Bowery to just below the Waldorf. No matter how fast I walked old man Berger was sure to be there ahead of me, raising hell with the cutter because neither of the bosses was on the job. How was it we could never get there ahead of that old buzzard Berger? He had nothing to do, Berger, but run from the tailor to the shirt-maker and from the shirt-maker to the jeweler's; his rings were either too loose or too tight, his watch was either twenty-five seconds slow or thirty-three seconds fast. He raised hell with everybody, including the family doctor, because the latter couldn't keep his kidneys clear of gravel. If we made him a sack coat in August by October it was too large for him, or too small. When he could find nothing to complain about he would dress on the right side so as to have the pleasure of bawling the pants maker out because he was strangling his, H. W. Berger's, balls. A difficult guy. Touchy, whimsical, mean, crotchety, miserly, capricious, malevolent. When I look back on it all now, see the old man sitting down to table with his boozy breath and saying *shit why don't some one smile, why do you all look so glum*, I feel sorry for him and for all merchant tailors who have to kiss rich people's asses. If it hadn't been for the Olcott bar across the way and the sots he picked up there God knows what would have become of the old man. He certainly got no sympathy at home. My mother hadn't the least idea what it meant to be kissing rich people's backsides. All she knew how to do was to groan and lament all day, and with her groaning and lamenting she brought on the boozy breath and the potato dumplings grown cold. She got us so damned jumpy with her anxiety that we would choke on our own spittle, my brother and I. My brother was a half-wit and he got on the old man's nerves even more than H. W. Berger with his "Pastor So-and-so's going to Europe . . . Pastor So-and-so's going to open a bowling alley", etc. "Pastor So-and-so's an ass," the old man would say, "and why aren't the dumplings hot?"

There were three Bergers—H. W., the grumpy one, A. F., whom the old man referred to in the ledger as Albert, and R. N., who never visited the shop because his legs were cut off, a circumstance, however, which did not prevent him from wearing out his trousers in due season. R. N. I never saw in the flesh. He was an item in the ledger which Bunchek the cutter spoke of glowingly because there was always a little schnapps about when it came time to try on the new trousers. The three brothers were eternal enemies; they never referred to one another in our presence. If Albert, who was a little cracked and had a penchant for dotted vests, happened to see a cutaway hanging on the rack with the words H. W. Berger written in green ink on the try-on notice, he would give a feeble little grunt and say—"feels like spring to-day, eh?" There was not supposed to be a man by the name of H. W. Berger in existence, though it was obvious to all and sundry that we were not making clothes for ghosts.

Of the three brothers I liked Albert the best. He had arrived at that ripe age when the bones become as brittle as glass. His spine had the natural curvature of old age, as though he were preparing to fold up and return to the womb. You could always tell when Albert was arriving because of the commotion in the elevator— a great cussing and whining followed by a handsome tip which accompanied the process of bringing the floor of the elevator to a dead level with the floor of our tailor shop. If it could not be brought to within a quarter of an inch exactitude there was no tip and Albert with his brittle bones and his bent spine would have a devil of a time choosing the right buttons to go with his dotted vest, his *latest* dotted vest. (When Albert died I inherited all his vests—they lasted me right through the war.) If it happened, as was sometimes the case, that the old man was across the street taking a little nip when Albert arrived, then somehow the whole day became disorganized. I remember periods when Albert grew so vexed with the old man that sometimes we did not see him for three days; meanwhile the vest buttons were lying around on little cards and there was talk of nothing but vest buttons, vest buttons, as if the vest itself didn't matter, only the buttons. Later, when Albert had grown accustomed to the old man's careless ways—they had been growing accustomed to each other for twenty-seven years —he would give us a ring to notify us that he was on the way. And just before hanging up he would add: "I suppose it's all right my coming in at eleven o'clock . . . it won't inconvenience you?" The purport of this little query was twofold. It meant—"I suppose you'll have the decency to be on hand when I arrive and not make me fiddle around for a half hour while you swill it down with your cronies across the street." And, it also meant—"At eleven o'clock I suppose there is little danger of bumping into a certain individual bearing the initials H. W.?" In the twenty-seven years during which we made perhaps 1,578 garments for the three Berger brothers it so happened that they never met, not in our presence at least. When Albert died R. N. and H. W. both had mourning bands put on their sleeves, on all the left sleeves of their sack coats and overcoats —that is, those which were not black coats—but nothing was said of the deceased, nor even who he was. R. N., of course, had a good excuse for not going to the funeral—his legs were gone. H. W. was too mean and too proud to even bother offering an excuse.

About ten o'clock was the time the old man usually chose to go down for his first nip. I used to stand at the window facing the hotel and watch George Sandusky hoisting the big trunks on to the taxis. When there were no trunks to be hoisted George used to stand there with his hands clasped behind his back and bow and scrape to the clients as they swung in and out of the revolving doors. George Sandusky had been scraping and bowing and hoisting and opening doors for about twelve years when I first came to the tailor shop and took up my post at the front window. He was a charming, soft-spoken man with beautiful white hair, and strong as an ox. He had raised this ass-kissing business to an art. I was amazed one day when he came up the elevator and ordered a suit from us. In his off hours he was a gentleman, George Sandusky. He had quiet tastes—always a blue serge or an Oxford gray. A man who knew how to conduct himself at a funeral or a wedding.

After we got to know each other he gave me to understand that he had found Jesus. With the smooth tongue he had, and the brawn, and the active help of said Jesus he had managed to lay aside a nest-egg, a little something to ward off the horrors of old age. He was the only man I ever met in that period who had not taken out life insurance. He maintained that God would look after those who were left behind just as He had looked after him, George Sandusky. He had no fear of the world collapsing upon his decease. God had taken care of everybody and everything up to date—no reason to suppose He would fall down on the job after George Sandusky's death. When one day George retired it was difficult to find a man to replace him. There was no one oily or unctuous enough to fill the bill. No one who could bow and scrape like George. The old man always had a great affection for George. He used to try to persuade him to take a drink now and then, but George always refused with that habitual and stubborn politeness which had endeared him to the Olcott guests.

The old man often had moods when he would ask anybody to take a drink with him, even such as George Sandusky. Usually late in the afternoon on a day when things were going wrong, when nothing but bills were coming in. Sometimes a week would pass without a customer showing up, or if one did show up it was only to complain, to ask for an alteration, to bawl the piss out of the coat maker, or to demand a reduction in the price. Things like this would make the old man so blue that all he could do was to put on his hat and go for a drink. Instead of going across the street as usual he would wander off base a bit, duck into the Breslin or the Broztell, sometimes getting as far off the path as the Ansonia where his idol, Julian Legree, kept a suite of rooms.

Julian, who was then a matinée idol, wore nothing but gray suits, every shade of gray imaginable, but only grays. He had that depressingly cheerful demeanor of the beefy-faced English actor who lounges about here and there swapping stories with woolen salesmen, liquor dealers and others of no account. His accent alone was enough to make men swarm about him; it was English in the traditional stage sense, warm, soapy, glutinous English which gives to even the most insignificant thought an appearance of importance. Julian never said anything that was worth recording but that voice of his worked magic on his admirers. Now and then, when he and the old man were doing the rounds, they would pick up a derelict such as Corse Payton who belonged across the river in the ten-twenty-thirties. Corse Payton was the idol of Brooklyn! Corse Payton was to art what Pat McCarren was to politics.

What the old man had to say during these discussions was always a source of mystery to me. The old man had never read a book in his life, nor had he ever been to a play since the days when the Bowery gave way to Broadway. I can see him standing there at the free lunch counter—Julian was very fond of the caviar and the sturgeon that was served at the Olcott—sponging it up like a thirsty dog. The two matinée idols discussing Shakespeare—whether *Hamlet* or *Lear* was the greatest play ever written. Or else arguing the merits of Bob Ingersoll.

Behind the bar at that time were three doughty Irishmen, three low-down micks such as made the bars of that day the congenial haunts they were. They were so highly thought of, these three, that it was considered a privilege to have such as Patsy O'Dowd, for example, call you a god-damned degenerate cock-sucking son of a bitch who hadn't sense enough to button up his fly. And if, in return for the compliment, you asked him if he wouldn't have a little something himself said Patsy O'Dowd would coldly and sneeringly reply that only such as yourself were fit to pour such rot-gut down your throat, and so saying he would scornfully lift your glass by the stem and wipe the mahogany because that was part of his job and he was paid to do it but be damned to you if you thought you could entice such as him to poison his intestines with the vile stuff. The more vicious his insults the more he was esteemed; financiers who were accustomed to having their asses wiped with silk handkerchiefs would drive all the way uptown, after the ticker closed down, in order to have this foul-mouthed bastard of an Irish mick call them god-damned degenerate cock-sucking sons of bitches. It was the end of a perfect day for them.

The boss of this jaunty emporium was a portly little man with aristocratic shanks and the head of a lion. He always marched with his stomach thrown forward, a little wine cask hidden under his vest. He usually gave a stiff, supercilious nod to the sots at the bar, unless they happened to be guests of the hotel, in which case he would pause a moment, extend three fat little fingers with blue veins and then, with a swirl of his mustache and a gingerly, creaky pirouette, he would whisk away. He was the only enemy the old man had. The old man simply couldn't stomach him. He had a feeling that Tom Moffatt looked down upon him. And so when Tom Moffatt came round to order his clothes the old man would tack on ten or fifteen per cent to cover the rents in his pride. But Tom Moffatt was a genuine aristocrat: he never questioned the price and he never paid his bills. If we dunned him he would get his accountant to find a discrepancy in our statements. And when it came time to order another pair of flannel trousers, or a cutaway, or a dinner jacket, he would sail in with his usual portly dignity, his stomach well forward, his mustache waxed, his shoes brightly polished and squeaky as always, and with an air of weary indifference, of aloof disdain, he would greet the old man as follows: "Well, have you straightened out that error yet?" Upon which the old man would fly into a rage and palm off a remnant or a piece of American goods on his enemy Tom Moffatt. A long correspondence ensued over the "little error" in our statements. The old man was beside himself. He hired an expert accountant who drew up statements three feet long—but to no avail. Finally the old man hit upon an idea.

Towards noon one day, after he had had his usual portion, after he had stood treat to all the woolen salesmen and the trimmings salesmen who were gathered at the bar, he quietly picked up the bar stubs and taking a little silver pencil which was attached to his watch chain he signed his name to the checks and sliding them across to Patsy O'Dowd he said: "Tell Moffatt to charge them up to my account." Then he quietly moved off and, inviting a few of his select cronies, he took a table in the dining room and commanded a spread. And when Adrian the frog presented the bill he calmly said: "Give me a pencil. There . . . them's my demi-quivers. Charge it up to my account." Since it was more pleasant to eat in the company of others he would always invite his cronies to lunch with him, saying to all and sundry—"if that bastard Moffatt won't pay for his clothes then we'll eat them." And so saying he would commandeer a juicy squab, or a lobster à la Newburg, and wash it down with a fine Moselle or any other vintage that Adrian the frog might happen to recommend.

To all this Moffatt, surprisingly enough, pretended to pay no heed. He continued to order his usual allotment of clothes for winter, spring, fall and summer, and he also continued to squabble about the bill which had become easier to do now since it was complicated with bar checks, telephone calls, squabs, lobsters, champagne, fresh strawberries, Benedictines, etc., etc. In fact, the old man was eating into that bill so fast that spindle-shanks Moffatt couldn't wear his clothes out quickly enough. If he came in to order a pair of flannel trousers the old man had already eaten it the next day.

Finally Moffatt evinced an earnest desire to have the account straightened out. The correspondence ceased. Patting me on the back one day as I happened to be standing in the lobby he put on his most cordial manner and invited me upstairs to his private office. He said he had always regarded me as a very sensible young man and that we could probably straighten the matter out between ourselves, without bothering the old man. I looked over the accounts and I saw that the old man had eaten way into the minus side. I had probably eaten up a few raglans and shooting jackets myself. There was only one thing to do if we were to keep Tom Moffatt's despised patronage and that was to find an error in the account. I took a bundle of bills under my arm and promised the old geezer that I would look into the matter thoroughly.

The old man was delighted when he saw how things stood. We kept looking into the matter for years. Whenever Tom Moffatt came round to order a suit the old man would greet him cheerily and say: "Have you straightened out that little error yet? Now here's a fine Barathea weave that I laid aside for you . . ." And Moffatt would frown and grimace and strut back and forth like a turkey cock, his comb bristling, his thin little legs blue with malice. A half hour later the old man would be standing at the bar swilling it down. "Just sold Moffatt another dinner jacket," he would say. "By the way, Julian, what would you like to order for lunch to-day?"

It was towards noon, as I say, that the old man usually went down for an appetizer; lunch lasted anywhere from noon till four or five in the afternoon. It was marvelous the companionship the old man enjoyed in those days. After lunch the troupe would stagger out of the elevator, spitting and guffawing, their cheeks aflame, and lodge themselves in the big leather chairs beside the cuspidors. There was Ferd Pattee who sold silk linings and trimmings such as skeins of thread, buttons, chest padding, canvas, etc. A great hulk of a man, like a liner that's been battered by a typhoon, and always walking about in a somnambulistic state; so tired he was that he could scarcely move his lips, yet that slight movement of the lips kept everybody about him in stitches. Always muttering to himself—about cheeses particularly. He was passionate about cheese, about schmierkäse and limburger especially—the mouldier the better. In between the cheeses he told stories about Heine and Schubert, or he would ask for a match just as he was about to break wind and hold it under his seat so that we could tell him the color of the flame. He never said good-bye or see you tomorrow; he commenced talking where he had left off the day before, as though there had been no interruption of time. No matter whether it was nine in the morning or six in the evening he walked with the same exasperating slow shambling gait, muttering in his vici-kids, his head down, his linings and trimmings under his arm, his breath foul, his nose purple and translucent. Into the thickest traffic he would walk with head down, schmierkäse in one pocket and limburger in the other. Stepping out of the elevator he would say in that weary monotonous voice of his that he had some new linings and the cheese was fine last night were you thinking of returning the book he had loaned you and better pay up soon if you want more goods or like to see some dirty pictures please scratch my back there a little higher that's it excuse me I'm going to fart now have you the time I can't waste all day here better tell the old man to put on his hat it's time to go for a drink. Still mumbling and grumbling he turns on his big scows and presses the elevator button while the old man with a straw hat on the back of his head is making a slide for the home plate from the back of the store, his face lit up with love and gratitude and saying: "Well, Ferd, how are you this morning? It's good to see you." And Ferd's big heavy mask of a face relaxes for a moment into a broad amiable grin. Just a second he holds it and then, lifting his voice he bellows at the top of his lungs—so that even Tom Moffatt across the way can hear it—"BETTER PAY UP SOON WHAT THE HELL DO YOU THINK I'M SELLING THESE THINGS FOR?"

And as soon as the elevator has started down out comes little Rubin from the busheling room and with a wild look in his eye he says to me: "Would you like me to sing for you?" He knows damned well that I would. So, going back to the bench, he picks up the coat that he's stitching and with a wild Cossack shout he lets loose.

If you were to pass him in the street, little Rubin, you would say "dirty little kike", and perhaps he was a dirty little kike but he knew how to sing and when you were broke he knew how to put his hand in his pocket and when you were sad he was sadder still and if you tried to step on him he spat on your shoe and if you were repentant he wiped it off and he brushed you down and put a crease in your trousers like Jesus H. Christ himself couldn't do.

They were all midgets in the busheling room—Rubin, Rapp and Chaimowitz. At noon they brought out big round loaves of Jewish bread which they smeared with sweet butter and slivers of lax. While the old man was ordering squabs and Rhine wine Bunchek the cutter and the three little bushelmen sat on the big bench among the goose irons and the legs and sleeves and talked earnestly

302

and solemnly about things like the rent or the ulcers that Mrs. Chaimowitz had in her womb. Bunchek was an ardent member of the Zionist party. He believed that the Jews had a happy future ahead of them. But despite it all he could never properly pronounce a word like "screw". He always said: "He *scruled* her." Besides his passion for Zionism Bunchek had another obsession and that was to make a coat one day that would hug the neck. Nearly all the customers were round-shouldered and pot-bellied, especially the old bastards who had nothing to do all day but run from the shirt-maker to the tailor and from the tailor to the jeweler's and from the jeweler's to the dentist and from the dentist to the druggist. There were so many alterations to be made that by the time the clothes were ready to be worn the season had passed and they had to be put away until next year, and by next year the old bastards had either gained twenty pounds or lost twenty pounds and what with sugar in their urine and water in the blood it was hell to please them even when the clothes did fit.

Then there was Paul Dexter, a $10,000 a year man but always out of work. Once he almost had a job, but it was at $9,000 a year and his pride wouldn't permit him to accept it. And since it was important to be well groomed, in the pursuit of this mythical job, Paul felt it incumbent upon him to patronize a good tailor such as the old man. Once he landed the job everything would be settled in full. There was never any question about that in Paul's mind. He was thoroughly honest. But he was a dreamer. He came from Indiana. And like all dreamers from Indiana he had such a lovable disposition, such a smooth, mellow, honeyed way that if he had committed incest the world would have forgiven him. When he had on the right tie, when he had chosen the proper cane and gloves, when the lapels were softly rolled and the shoes didn't squeak, when he had a quart of rye under his belt and the weather wasn't too damp or dismal then there flowed from his personality such a warm current of love and understanding that even the trimmings salesmen, hardened as they were to soft language, melted in their boots. Paul, when all circumstances were favorably conjoined, could walk up to a man, any man on God's green earth and, taking him by the lapel of his coat, drown him in love. Never did I see a man with such powers of persuasion, such magnetism. When the flood began to rise in him he was invincible.

Paul used to say: "Start with Marcus Aurelius, or Epictetus, and the rest will follow." He didn't recommend studying Chinese or learning Provençal: he began with the fall of the Roman Empire. It was my great ambition in those days to win Paul's approbation, but Paul was difficult to please. He frowned when I showed him *Thus Spake Zarathustra*. He frowned when he saw me sitting on the bench with the midgets trying to expound the meaning of *Creative Evolution*. Above all, he loathed the Jews. When Bunchek the cutter appeared, with a piece of chalk and a tape measure slung around his neck, Paul became excessively polite and condescending. He knew that Bunchek despised him, but because Bunchek was the old man's right hand man he rubbed him down with oil, he larded him with compliments. So that eventually even Bunchek had to admit that there was something to Paul, some strange mark of personality which, despite his shortcomings, endeared him to every one.

Outwardly Paul was all cheerfulness. But at bottom he was morose. Every now and then Cora, his wife, would sail in with eyes brimming with tears and implore the old man to take Paul in hand. They used to stand at the round table near the window conversing in a low voice. She was a beautiful woman, his wife, tall, statuesque, with a deep contralto voice that seemed to quiver with anguish whenever she mentioned Paul's name. I could see the old man putting his hand on her shoulder, soothing her, and promising her all sorts of things no doubt. She liked the old man, I could see that. She used to stand very close to him and look into his eyes in a way that was irresistible. Sometimes the old man would put his hat on and the two of them would go down the elevator together, arm in arm, as if they were going to a funeral. Off looking for Paul again. Nobody knew where to find him when he had a drinking fever on. For days on end he would disappear from sight. And then one day he would turn up, crestfallen, repentant, humiliated, and beg everybody's forgiveness. At the same time he would hand in his suit to be dry cleaned, to have the vomit stains removed, and a bit of expert repairing done at the knees.

It was after a bout that Paul talked most eloquently. He used to sit back in one of the deep leather chairs, the gloves in one hand, the cane between his legs, and discourse about Marcus Aurelius. He talked even better when he came back from the hospital, after he had had the fistula repaired. The way he lowered himself into the big leather chair made me think then that he came expressly to the tailor shop because nowhere else could he find such a comfortable seat. It was a painful operation either to sit down or to get up. But once accomplished Paul seemed to be in bliss and the words rolled off his tongue like liquid velvet. The old man could listen to Paul all day long. He used to say that Paul had the gift of gab, but that was only his inarticulate way of saying that Paul was the most lovable creature on God's earth and that he had a fire in his bowels. And when Paul was too conscience-stricken to order another suit the old man would coax him into it, saying to Paul all the while, "nothing's too good for you, Paul . . . nothing!"

Paul must have recognized something of a kindred nature in the old man too. Never have I seen two men look at each other with

305

such a warm glow of admiration. Sometimes they would stand there looking into each other's eyes adoringly until the tears came. In fact, neither of them was ashamed of showing his tears, something which seems to have gone out of the world now. I can see Paul's homely freckled face and his rather thick, blubbery lips twitching as the old man told him for the thousandth time what a great guy he was. Paul never spoke to the old man about things he wouldn't understand. But into the simple, everyday things which he discoursed about so earnestly he put such a wealth of tenderness that the old man's soul seemed to leave his body and when Paul was gone he was like a man bereaved. He would go then into the little cubby-hole of an office and he would sit there quietly all by himself staring ecstatically at the row of pigeon coops which were filled with letters unanswered and bills unpaid. It used to affect me so, to see him in one of these moods, that I would sneak quietly down the stairs and start to walk home, down the Avenue to the Bowery and along the Bowery to the Brooklyn Bridge, and then over the bridge past the string of cheap flops that extended from City Hall to Fulton Ferry. And if it were a summer's evening, and the entrance ways crowded with loungers, I would look among these wasted figures searchingly, wondering how many Pauls there were among them and what it is about life that makes these obvious failures so endearing to men. The others, the successful ones, I had seen with their pants off; I had seen their crooked spines, their brittle bones, their varicose veins, their tumors, their sunken chests, their big bread-baskets which had grown shapeless with years of swilling it. Yes, all the silk-lined duffers I knew well—we had the best families in America on our roster. And what a pus and filth when they opened their dirty traps! It seemed as though when they had undressed before their tailor they felt compelled to unload the garbage which had accumulated in the plugged up sinks which they had made of their minds. All the beautiful diseases of boredom and riches. Talked about themselves *ad nauseam*. Always "I", "I". I and my kidneys. I and my gout. I and my liverworts. When I think of Paul's dreadful hemorrhoids, of the marvelous fistula they repaired, of all the love and learning that issued from his grievous wounds, then I think that Paul was not of this age at all but sib brother to Moses Maimonides, he who under the Moors gave us those astounding learned treatises on "hemorrhoids, warts, carbuncles," etc.

In the case of all these men whom the old man so cherished death came quickly and unexpectedly. In Paul's case it happened while he was at the seashore. He was drowned in a foot of water. Heart failure, they said. And so, one fine day Cora came up the elevator, clad in her beautiful mourning garb, and wept all over the place. Never had she looked more beautiful to me, more svelte, more statuesque. Her ass particularly—I remember how caressingly the velvet clung to her figure. Again they stood near the round table at the front window, and this time she wept copiously. And again the old man put on his hat and down the elevator they went, arm in arm.

A short time later the old man, moved by some strange whim, urged me to call on Paul's wife and offer my condolences. When I rang the bell at her apartment I was trembling. I almost expected her to come out stark naked, with perhaps a mourning band around her breasts. I was infatuated with her beauty, with her years, with that somnolent, plant-like quality she had brought from Indiana and the perfume which she bathed in. She greeted me in a low-cut mourning gown, a beautiful clinging gown of black velvet. It was the first time I had ever had a tête-à-tête with a woman bereft, a woman whose breasts seemed to sob out loud. I didn't know what to say to her, especially about Paul. I stammered

307

and blushed, and when she asked me to sit beside her on the couch I almost fell over in my embarrassment.

Sitting there on the low sofa, the place flooded with soft lights, her big, heaving loins rubbing against me, the Malaga pounding my temples and all this crazy talk about Paul and how good he was, I finally bent over and without saying a word I raised her dress and slipped it into her. And as I got it into her and began to work it around she took to moaning like, a sort of delirious sorrowful guilt punctuated with gasps and little shrieks of joy and anguish, saying over and over again—"I never thought you would do this . . . I never thought you would do this!" And when it was all over she ripped off the velvet dress, the beautiful low-cut mourning gown, and she put my head down on her and she told me . . . . and with her two strong arms she squeezed me almost in half and moaned and sobbed. And then she got up and she walked around the room naked for a while. And then finally she got down on her knees beside the sofa where I was stretched out and she said in a low tearful voice—"You promise me you'll love me always, won't you? You promise me?" And I said Yes with one hand working around in her crotch. Yes I said and I thought to myself what a sap you've been to wait so long. She was so wet and juicy down there, and so child-like, so trustful, why anybody could have come along and had what's what. She was a push-over.

Always merry and bright! Regularly, every season, there were a few deaths. Sometimes it was a good egg like Paul, or Julian Legree, sometimes a bartender who had picked his nose with a rusty nail—hail and hearty one day, dead the next—but regularly, like the movements of the seasons themselves, the old buzzards dropped off, one by one. *Alors*, nothing to do but draw a red line slantwise down the right-hand side of the ledger and mark "dead".

Each death brought a little business—a new black suit or else mourning bands on the left sleeve of every coat. Those who ordered mourning bands were cheap-skates, according to the old man. And so they were.

As the old 'uns died off they were replaced by young blood. *Young blood!* That was the war-cry all along the Avenue, wherever there were silk-lined suits for sale. A fine bloody crew they were, the young bloods. Gamblers, race-track touts, stock-brokers, ham actors, prize fighters, etc. Rich one day, poor the next. No honor, no loyalty, no sense of responsibility. A fine bunch of gangrened syphilitics they were, most of 'em. Came back from Paris or Monte Carlo with dirty postcards and a string of big blue rocks in their groin. Some of them with balls as big as a lamb's fry.

One of them was the Baron Carola von Eschenbach. He had earned a little money in Hollywood posing as the Crown Prince. It was the period when it was considered riotously funny to see the Crown Prince plastered with rotten eggs. It must be said for the Baron that he was a good double for the Crown Prince. A death's head with arrogant nose, a waspish stride, a corseted waist, lean and ravished as Martin Luther, dour, glum, fanatical, with that brassy, fatuous glare of the Junker class. Before going to Hollywood he was just a nobody, the son of a German brewer in Frankfort. He wasn't even a baron. But afterwards, when he had been knocked about like a medicine ball, when his front teeth had been pushed down his throat and the neck of a broken bottle had traced a deep scar down his left cheek, afterwards when he had been taught to flaunt a red neck-tie, twirl a cane, clip his mustache short, like Chaplin, then he became somebody. Then he stuck a monocle in his eye and named himself Baron Carola von Eschenbach. And all might have gone beautifully for him had he not fallen for a red-haired walk-on who was rotting away with syphilis. That finished him.

Up the elevator he came one day in a cutaway and spats, a bright red rose in his buttonhole and the monocle stuck in his eye. Blithe and dapper he looked, and the card he took out of his wallet was handsomely engraved. It bore a coat of arms which had been in the family, so he said, for nine hundred years. "The family skeleton," he called it. The old man was highly pleased to have a baron among his clients, especially if he paid cash, as this one promised to do. And then too it was exhilarating to see the baron come sailing in with a pair of soubrettes on his arm—each time a different pair. Even more exhilarating when he invited them into the dressing room and asked them to help him off with his trousers. It was a European custom, he explained.

Gradually he got acquainted with all the old cronies who hung out in the front of the shop. He showed them how the Crown Prince walked, how he sat down, how he smiled. One day he brought a flute with him and he played the Lorelei on it. Another day he came in with a finger of his pig-skin glove sticking out of his fly. Each day he had a new trick up his sleeve. He was gay, witty, amusing. He knew a thousand jokes, some ʰhat had never been told before. He was a riot.

And then one day he took me aside and asked me if I could lend him a dime—for carfare. He said he couldn't pay for the clothes he had ordered but he expected a job soon in a little movie house on Ninth Avenue, playing the piano. And then, before I knew it, he began to weep. We were standing in the dressing room and the curtains were drawn fortunately. I had to lend him a handkerchief to wipe his eyes. He said he was tired of playing the clown, that he dropped in to our place every day because it was warm there and because we had comfortable seats. He asked me if I couldn't take him to lunch—he had had nothing but coffee and buns for the last three days.

I took him to a little German restaurant on Third Avenue, a bakery and restaurant combined. The atmosphere of the place broke him down completely. He could talk of nothing but the old days, the old days, the days before the war. He had intended to be a painter, and then the war came. I listened attentively and when he got through I proposed that he come to my home for dinner that evening—perhaps I could put him up with us. He was overwhelmed with gratitude. Sure, he would come—at seven o'clock *punkt*. Fine!

At the dinner table my wife was amused by his stories. I hadn't said anything about his being broke. Just that he was a baron—the Baron von Eschenbach, a friend of Charlie Chaplin's. My wife—one of my first ones—was highly flattered to sit at the same table with a baron. And Puritanical bastard that she was, she never so much as blushed when he told a few of his risqué stories. She thought they were delightful—*so European*. Finally, however, it came time to spill the beans. I tried to break the news gently, but how can you be gentle about a subject like syphilis? I didn't call it syphilis at first—I said "venereal disease". *Maladie intime, quoi!* But just that little word "venereal" sent a shudder through my wife. She looked at the cup he was holding to his lips and then she looked at me imploringly, as though to say—"how could you ask a man like that to sit at the same table with us?" I saw that it was necessary to bring the matter to a head at once. "The baron here is going to stay with us for a while," I said quietly. "He's broke and he needs a place to flop." My word, I never saw a woman's expression change so quickly. "*You!*" she said, "you ask *me* to do that? And what about the baby? You want us all to have syphilis, is that it? It's not enough that *he* has it—you want the baby to have it too!"

The baron of course was frightfully embarrassed by this outburst. He wanted to leave at once. But I told him to keep his shirt on. I was used to these scenes. Anyway, he got so wrought up that he began to choke over his coffee. I thumped him on the back until he was blue in the face. The rose fell out of his button-hole on to the plate. It looked strange there, as though he had coughed it up out of his own blood. It made me feel so god-damned ashamed of my wife that I could have strangled her on the spot. He was still choking and sputtering as I led him to the bath-room. I told him to wash his face in cold water. My wife followed us in and watched in murderous silence as he performed his ablutions. When he had wiped his face she snatched the towel from his hands and, flinging the bath-room window open, flung it out. That made me furious. I told her to get the hell out of the bath-room and mind her own business. But the baron stepped between us and flung himself at my wife supplicatingly. "You'll see, my good woman, and you, Henry, you won't have to worry about a thing. I'll bring all my syringes and ointments and I'll put them in a little valise— there, under the sink. You mustn't turn me away, I have nowhere to go. I'm a desperate man. I'm alone in the world. You were so good to me before—why must you be cruel now? Is it my fault that I have the syph? Anybody can get the syph. It's human. You'll see, I'll pay you back a thousand times. I'll do anything for you. I'll make the beds, I'll wash the dishes . . . I'll cook for you . . ." He went on and on like that, never stopping to take a breath for fear that she would say No. And after he had gotten all through with his promises, after he had begged her forgiveness a hundred times, after he had knelt down and tried to kiss her hand which she drew away abruptly, he sat down on the toilet seat, in his cutaway and spats, and he began to sob, to sob like a child. It was ghastly, the sterile, white-enamelled bath-room and the splintering light as if a thousand mirrors had been shattered under a magnifying glass, and then this wreck of a baron in his cutaway and spats, his spine filled with mercury, his sobs coming like the short puffs of a locomotive getting under way. I didn't know what the hell to do. A man sitting on the toilet like that and sobbing— it got under my skin. Later I became inured to it. I got hard-boiled. I feel quite certain now that had it not been for the 250 bed patients whom he was obliged to visit twice a day at the hospital in Lyons Rabelais would never have been so boisterously gay. I'm sure of it.

Anyhow, apropos the sobs . . . A little later, when another kid was on the way and no means of getting rid of it, though still hoping, still hoping that something would happen, a miracle perhaps, and her stomach blown up like a ripe watermelon, about the sixth or seventh month, as I say, she used to succumb to fits of melancholy and, lying on the bed with that watermelon staring her in the eye, she would commence to sob fit to break your heart. Maybe I'd be in the other room, stretched out on the couch, with a big, fat book in my hands, and those sobs of hers would make me think of the Baron Carola von Eschenbach, of his gray spats and the cutaway with braided lapels, and the deep red rose in his buttonhole. Her sobs were like music to my ears. Sobbing away for a little sympathy she was, and not a drop of sympathy in the house. It was pathetic. The more hysterical she grew the more deaf I became. It was like listening to the boom and sizzle of surf along the beach on a summer's night: the buzz of a mosquito can drown out the ocean's roar. Anyway, after she had worked herself up to a state of collapse, when the neighbors couldn't stand it any longer and there were knocks on the door, then her aged mother would

come crawling out of the bed-room and with tears in her eyes would beg me to go in there and quiet her a bit. "Oh, leave her be," I'd say, "she'll get over it." Whereupon, ceasing her sobs for a moment, the wife would spring out of bed, wild, blind with rage, her hair all down and tangled up, her eyes swollen and bleary, and still hiccoughing and sobbing she would commence to pound me with her fists, to lambast me until I became hysterical with laughter. And when she saw me rocking to and fro like a crazy man, when her arms were tired and her fists sore, she would yell like a drunken whore—"Fiend! Demon!"—and then slink off like a weary dog. Afterwards, when I had quieted her down a bit, when I realized that she really needed a kind word or two, I would tumble her on the bed again and throw a good fuck into her. Blast me if she wasn't the finest piece of tail imaginable after those scenes of grief and anguish! I never heard a woman moan and gibber like she could. "Do *anything* to me!" she used to say. "Do what you want!" I could stand her on her head and ....,
.. .., I could drag her past the parson's house, as they say, any god-damn thing at all—she was simply delirious with joy. Uterine hysteria, that's what it was! *And I hope God take me,* as the good master used to say, *if I am lying in a single word I say.*

(God, mentioned above, being defined by St. Augustine, as follows: "An infinite sphere, the centre of which is everywhere, the circumference nowhere.")

However, *always merry and bright!* If it was before the war and the thermometer down to zero or below, if it happened to be Thanksgiving Day, or New Year's, or a birthday, or just any old excuse to get together, then off we'd trot, the whole family, to join the other freaks who made up the living family tree. It always

seemed astounding to me how jolly they were in our family despite
the calamities that were always threatening. Jolly in spite of every-
thing. There was cancer, dropsy, cirrhosis of the liver, insanity,
thievery, mendacity, buggery, incest, paralysis, tape-worms, abor-
tions, triplets, idiots, drunkards, ne'er-do-wells, fanatics, sailors,
tailors, watch-makers, scarlet fever, whooping cough, meningitis,
running ears, chorea, stutterers, jail-birds, dreamers, story-tellers,
bartenders—and finally there was Uncle George and Tante Melia.
The morgue and the insane asylum. A merry crew and the table
loaded with good things;—with red cabbage and green spinach,
with roast pork and turkey and sauerkraut, with kartoffeln-klösze
and sour black gravy, with radishes and celery, with stuffed goose
and peas and carrots, with beautiful white cauliflower, with apple
sauce and figs from Smyrna, with bananas big as a black-jack, with
cinnamon cake and Streussel Kuchen, with chocolate layer cake
and nuts, all kinds of nuts, walnuts, butternuts, almonds, pecans,
hickory nuts, with lager beer and bottled beer, with white wines
and red, with champagne, kümmel, malaga, port, with schnapps,
with fiery cheeses, with dull, innocent store cheese, with flat Hol-
land cheeses, with limburger and schmierkäse, with home made
wines, elderberry wine, with cider, hard and sweet, with rice pud-
ding and tapioca, with roast chestnuts, mandarines, olives, pickles,
with red caviar and black, with smoked sturgeon, with lemon
meringue pie, with lady fingers and chocolate eclairs, with maca-
roons and cream puffs, with black cigars and long thin stogies, with
Bull Durham and Long Tom and meerschaums, with corn-cobs
and tooth-picks, wooden tooth-picks which gave you gum-boils the
day after, and napkins a yard wide with your initials stitched in the
corner, and a blazing coal fire and the windows steaming, every-
thing in the world before your eyes except a fingerbowl.

Zero weather and crazy George, with one arm bitten off by a

315

horse, dressed in dead men's remnants. Zero weather and Tante Melia looking for the birds she left in her hat. Zero, zero, and the tugs snorting below in the harbor, the ice floes bobbing up and down, and long thin streams of smoke curling fore and aft. The wind blowing down at seventy miles an hour; tons and tons of snow all chopped up into tiny flakes and each one carrying a dagger. The icicles hanging like cork-screws outside the window, the wind roaring, the panes rattling. Uncle Henry is singing "Hurrah for the German Fifth!" His vest is open, his suspenders are down, the veins stand out on his temples. *Hurrah for the German Fifth!*

Up in the loft the creaking table is spread; down below is the warm stable, the horses whinnying in the stalls, whinnying and champing and pawing and stomping, and the fine aromatic smell of manure and horse piss, of hay and oats, of steaming blankets and dry cruds, the smell of malt and old wood, of leather harness and tan-bark floats up and rests like incense over our heads.

The table is standing on horses and the horses are standing in warm piss and every now and then they get frisky and whisk their tails and they fart and whinny. The stove is glowing like a ruby, the air is blue with smoke. The bottles are under the table, on the dresser, in the sink. Crazy George is trying to scratch his neck with an empty sleeve. Ned Martini, the ne'er-do-well, is fiddling with the phonograph; his wife Carrie is guzzling it from the tin growler. The brats are downstairs in the stable, playing stink-finger in the dark. In the street, where the shanties begin, the kids are making a sliding-pond. It's blue everywhere, with cold and smoke and snow. Tante Melia is sitting in a corner fingering a rosary. Uncle Ned is repairing a harness. The three grandfathers and the two great-grandfathers are huddled near the stove talking about the Franco-Prussian war. Crazy George is lapping up the dregs. The women are getting closer together, their voices low, their tongues clacking. Everything fits together like a jig-saw puzzle—faces, voices, gestures, bodies. Each one gravitates within his own orbit. The phonograph is working again, the voices get louder and shriller. The phonograph stops suddenly. I oughtn't to have been there when they blurted it out, but I was there and I heard it. I heard that big Maggie, the one who kept a saloon out in Flushing, well that Maggie had slept with her own brother and that's why George was crazy. She slept with everybody—except her own husband. And then I heard that she used to beat George with a leather belt, used to beat him until he foamed at the mouth. That's what brought on the fits. And then Mele sitting there in the corner—she was another case. She was queer even as a child. So was the mother, for that matter. It was too bad that Paul had died. Paul was Mele's husband. Yes, everything would have been all right if that woman from Hamburg hadn't shown up and corrupted Paul. What could Mele do against a clever woman like that—against a shrewd strumpet! Something would have to be done about Mele. It was getting dangerous to have her around. Just the other day they caught her sitting on the stove. Fortunately the fire was low. But supposing she took it into her head to set fire to the house—when they were all asleep? It was a pity that she couldn't hold a job any more. The last place they had found for her was such a nice berth, such a kind woman. Mele was getting lazy. She had had it too easy with Paul.

The air was clear and frosty when we stepped outdoors. The stars were crisp and sparkly and everywhere, lying over the bannisters and steps and window-ledges and gratings, was the pure white snow, the driven snow, the white mantle that covers the dirty, sinful earth. Clear and frosty the air, pure, like deep draughts of ammonia, and the skin smooth as chamois. Blue stars, beds and beds of them, drifting with the antelopes. Such a beautiful, deep,

317

silent night, as if under the snow there lay hearts of gold, as if this warm German blood was running away in the gutter to stop the mouths of hungry babes, to wash the crime and ugliness of the world away. Deep night and the river choked with ice, the stars dancing, swirling, spinning like tops. Along the broken street we straggled, the whole family. Walking along the pure white crust of the earth, leaving tracks, foot-stains. The old German family sweeping the snow with a Christmas tree. The whole family there, uncles, cousins, brothers, sisters, fathers, grandfathers. The whole family is warm and winey and no one thinks of the other, of the sun that will come in the morning, of the errands to run, of the doctor's verdict, of all the cruel, ghastly duties that foul the day and make this night holy, this holy night of blue stars and deep drifts, of arnica blossoms and ammonia, of asphodels and carborundum.

No one knew that Tante Melia was going completely off her nut, that when we reached the corner she would leap forward like a reindeer and bite a piece out of the moon. At the corner she leapt forward like a reindeer and she shrieked. "The moon, the moon!" she cried, and with that her soul broke loose, jumped clean out of her body. Eighty-six million miles a minute it travelled. Out, out, to the moon, and nobody could think quick enough to stop it. Just like that it happened. In the twinkle of a star.

And now I'm going to tell you what those bastards said to me . . .

They said—*Henry, you take her to the asylum to-morrow. And don't tell them that we can afford to pay for her.*

Fine! *Always merry and bright!* The next morning we boarded the trolley together and we rode out into the country. If Mele asked where we were going I was to say—"to visit Aunt Monica."

But Mele didn't ask any questions. She sat quietly beside me and pointed to the cows now and then. She saw blue cows and green ones. She knew their names. She asked what happened to the moon in the day-time. And did I have a piece of liverwurst by any chance?

During the journey I wept—I couldn't help it. When people are too good in this world they have to be put under lock and key. There's something wrong with people who are too good. It's true Mele was lazy. She was born lazy. It's true that Mele was a poor housekeeper. It's true Mele didn't know how to hold on to a husband when they found her one. When Paul ran off with the woman from Hamburg Mele sat in a corner and wept. The others wanted her to do something—put a bullet in him, raise a rumpus, sue for alimony. Mele sat quiet. Mele wept. Mele hung her head. What little intelligence she had deserted her. She was like a pair of torn socks that are kicked around here, there, everywhere. Always turning up at the wrong moment.

Then one day Paul took a rope and hanged himself. Mele must have understood what had happened because now she went completely crazy. The day before they found her eating her own dung. The day before that they found her sitting on the stove.

And now she's very tranquil and she calls the cows by their first name. The moon fascinates her. She has no fear because I'm with her and she always trusted me. I was her favorite. Even though she was a half-wit she was good to me. The others were more intelligent, but their hearts were bad.

When brother Adolphe used to take her for a carriage ride the others used to say—"Mele's got her eye on him!" But I think that Mele must have talked just as innocently then as she's talking to me now. I think that Mele, when she was performing her marriage duties, must have been dreaming innocently of the beautiful gifts

319

she would give to everybody. I don't think that Mele had any knowledge of sin or of guilt or remorse. I think that Mele was born a half-witted angel. I think Mele was a saint.

Sometimes when she was fired from a job they used to send me to fetch her. Mele never knew her way home. And I remember how happy she was whenever she saw me coming. She would say innocently that she wanted to stay with us. Why couldn't she stay with us? I used to ask myself that over and over. Why couldn't they make a place for her by the fire, let her sit there and dream, if that's what she wanted to do? Why must everybody work—even the saints and the angels? Why must half-wits set a good example?

I'm thinking now that after all it may be good for Mele where I'm taking her. No more work. Just the same, I'd rather they had made a corner for her somewhere.

Walking down the gravel path towards the big gates Mele becomes uneasy. Even a puppy knows when it is being carried to a pond to be drowned. Mele is trembling now. At the gate they are waiting for us. The gate yawns. Mele is on the inside, I am on the outside. They are trying to coax her along. They are gentle with her now. They speak to her so gently. But Mele is terror-stricken. She turns and runs towards the gate. I am still standing there. She puts her arms through the bars and clutches my neck. I kiss her tenderly on the forehead. Gently I unlock her arms. The others are going to take her again. I can't bear seeing that. I must go. I must run. For a full minute, however, I stand and look at her. Her eyes seem to have grown enormous. Two great round eyes, full and black as the night, staring at me uncomprehendingly. No maniac can look that way. No idiot can look that way. Only an angel or a saint.

Mele wasn't a good housekeeper I said, but she knew how to make fricadellas. Here is the recipe, while I think of it: a distem-

320

per composed of a humus of wet bread (from a nice urinal) plus horse meat (the fetlocks only) chopped very fine and mixed with a little sausage meat. Roll in palm of hands. The saloon that she ran with Paul, before the Hamburg woman came along, was just near the bend in the Second Avenue L, not far from the Chinese pagoda used by the Salvation Army.

When I ran away from the gate I stopped beside a high wall and burying my head in my arms, my arms against the wall, I sobbed as I had never sobbed since I was a child. Meanwhile they were giving Mele a bath and putting her into regulation dress; they parted her hair in the middle, brushed it down flat and tied it into a knot at the nape of the neck. Thus no one looks exceptional. All have the same crazy look, whether they are half crazy or three-quarters crazy, or just slightly cracked. When you say "may I have pen and ink to write a letter" they say "yes" and they hand you a broom to sweep the floor. If you pee on the floor absent-mindedly you have to wipe it up. You can sob all you like but you mustn't violate the rules of the house. A bug-house has to be run in orderly fashion just as any other house.

Once a week Mele would be allowed to receive. For thirty years the sisters had been visiting the bug-house. They were fed up with it. When they were tiny tots they used to visit their mother on Blackwell's Island. The mother always said to be careful of Mele, to watch over her. When Mele stood at the gate with eyes so round and bright her mind must have travelled back like an express train. Everything must have leaped to her mind at once. Her eyes were so big and bright, as if they saw more than they could comprehend. Bright with terror, and beneath the terror a limitless confusion. That's what made them so beautifully bright. You have to be crazy to see things so lucidly, so all at once. If you're great you can stay that way and people will believe in you, swear by you, turn the world upside down for you. But if you're only partly great, or just a nobody, then what happens to you is lost.

Mornings a brisk intellectual walk under the screaming elevated line, walking north from Delancey Street towards the Waldorf where the evening before the old man had been lounging around in Peacock Alley with Julian Legree. Each morning I write a new book, walking from the Delancey Street station north towards the Waldorf. On the fly-leaf of each book is written in vitriol: *The Island of Incest.* Every morning it starts with the drunken vomit of the night before; it makes a huge gardenia which I wear in the buttonhole of my lapel, the lapel of my double-breasted suit which is lined with silk throughout. I arrive at the tailor shop with the black breath of melancholy, perhaps to find Tom Jordan in the busheling room waiting to have the spots removed from his fly. After having written 369 pages on the trot the futility of saying Good Morning prevents me from being ordinarily polite. I have just this morning finished the 23rd volume of the ancestral book, of which not even a comma is visible since it was all written extemporaneously without even a fountain pen. I, the tailor's son, am now about to say Good Morning to Endicott Mumford's crack woolen salesman who stands before the mirror in his underwear examining the pouches under his eyes. Every limb and leaf of the family tree dangles before my eyes: out of the crazy black fog of the Elbe there floats this changing island of incest which produces the marvellous gardenia that I wear in my buttonhole each morning. I am just about to say Good Morning to Tom Jordan. It trembles there on my lips. I see a huge tree rising out of the black fog and in the hollow of the trunk there sits the woman from Hamburg, her ass squeezed tightly through the back of the chair. The door is on the latch and through the chink I see her green face, the lips set tight, the nostrils distended. Crazy George is going from door to door with picture post-cards, the arm that was bitten off by a horse lost and buried, the empty sleeve flapping in the wind. When all the pages have been torn from the calendar except the last six Crazy George will ring the doorbell and, with icicles in his mustache, he will stand on the threshold, cap in hand, and shout—"Merry Christmas!" This is the craziest tree that ever rose out of the Elbe, with every limb blasted and every leaf withered. This is the tree that shouts regularly once a year—"Merry Christmas!" Despite the calamities, despite the flow of cancer, dropsy, thievery, mendacity, buggery, paralysis, tape-worms, running ears, chorea, meningitis, epilepsy, liverworts, et cetera.

I am just about to say Good Morning. It trembles there on my lips. The 23 volumes of the Domesday Book are written with incestuous fidelity, the covers bound in finest morocco and a lock and key for each volume. Tom Jordan's blood-shot eyes are pasted on the mirror; they shudder like a horse shaking off a fly. Tom Jordan is always either taking off his pants or putting on his pants. Always buttoning or unbuttoning his fly. Always having the stains removed and a fresh crease put in. Tante Melia is sitting in the cooler, under the shade of the family tree. Mother is washing the vomit stains out of last week's dirty wash. The old man is stropping his razor. The Jews are moving up from under the shadow of the bridge, the days are getting shorter, the tugs are snorting or croaking like bull-frogs, the harbor is jammed with ice cakes. Every chapter of the book which is written in the air thickens the blood; the music of it deafens the wild anxiety of the outer air. Night drops like a boom of thunder, deposits me on the floor of the pedestrian highway leading nowhere eventually, but brightly ringed with gleaming spokes along which there is no turning back nor standing still.

From the shadow of the bridges the mob moves up, closer and closer, like a ring-worm, leaving a huge festering sore that runs from river to river along 14th Street. This line of pus, which runs invisibly from ocean to ocean, and age to age, neatly divides the Gentile world that I knew from the ledger from the Jewish world that I am about to know from life. Between these two worlds, in the middle of the pus line that runs from river to river, stands a little flower pot filled with gardenias. This is as far as the mastodons roam, where the buffaloes can graze no more; here the cunning, abstract world rises like a cliff in the midst of which are buried the fires of the revolution. Each morning I cross the line, with a gardenia in my button-hole and a fresh volume written in the air. Each morning I wade through a trench filled with vomit to reach the beautiful island of incest; each day the cliff rises up more toweringly, the window-lines straight as a railroad track and the gleam of them even more dazzling than the gleam of polished skulls. Each morning the trench yawns more menacingly.

I should be saying Good Morning now to Tom Jordan, but it hangs there on my lips tremblingly. What morning is this that I should waste in salutation? Is it good, this morning of mornings? I am losing the power to distinguish morning from morning. In the ledger is the world of the fast disappearing buffalo; next door the riveters are sewing up the ribs of the coming skyscrapers. Cunning Oriental men with leaden shoes and glass craniums are plotting the paper world of tomorrow, a world made entirely of merchandise which rises box on box like a paper box factory, f. o. b. Canarsie. To-day there is still time to attend the funeral of the recent dead; to-morrow there will be no time, for the dead will be left on the spot and woe to him who sheds a tear. This is a good morning for a revolution if only there were machine guns instead of fire-crackers. This morning would be a splendid morning if yesterday's morning had not been an utter fiasco. The past is galloping away, the trench widens. To-morrow is further off than it was yesterday because yesterday's horse has run wild and the men with leaden shoes cannot catch up with him. Between the good of the morning and the morning itself there is a line of pus which blows a stench over yesterday and poisons the morrow. This is a morning so confused that if it were only an old umbrella the slightest sneeze would blow it inside out.

My whole life is stretching out in an unbroken morning. I write from scratch each day. Each day a new world is created, separate and complete, and there I am among the constellations, a god so crazy about himself that he does nothing but sing and fashion new worlds. Meanwhile the old universe is going to pieces. The old universe resembles a busheling room in which pants are pressed and stains removed and buttons sewn on. The old universe smells like a wet seam receiving the kiss of a red hot iron. Endless alterations and repairs, a sleeve lengthened, a collar lowered, a button moved closer, a new seat put in. But never a new suit of clothes, never a creation. There is the morning world, which starts from scratch each day, and the busheling room in which things are endlessly altered and repaired. And thus it is with my life through which there runs the sewer of night. All through the night I hear the goose irons hissing as they kiss the wet seams; the rinds of the old universe fall on the floor and the stench of them is sour as vinegar.

The men my father loved were weak and lovable. They went out, each and every one of them, like brilliant stars before the sun. They went out quietly and catastrophically. No shred of them remained—nothing but the memory of their blaze and glory. They flow now inside me like a vast river choked with falling stars. They form the black flowing river which keeps the axis of my world in constant revolution. Out of this black, endless, ever-expanding girdle of night springs the continuous morning which is wasted in creation. Each morning the river overflows its banks, leaving the sleeves and buttonholes and all the rinds of a dead universe strewn along the beach where I stand contemplating the ocean of the morning of creation.

Standing there on the ocean's shore I see crazy George leaning against the wall of the undertaker's shop. He has on a funny little cap, a celluloid collar and no tie; he sits on the bench beside the coffin, neither sad nor smiling. He sits there quietly, like an angel that has stepped outside of a Jewish painting. The man in the coffin, whose body is still fresh, is decked out in a modest pepper and salt suit just George's size. He has a collar and tie on and a watch in his vest pocket. George takes him out, undresses him and, while he changes his clothes, lays him on the ice. Not wishing to steal the watch he lays the watch on the ice beside the body. The man is lying on the ice with a celluloid collar around his neck. It is getting dark as George steps out of the undertaker's shop. He has a tie now and a good suit of clothes. At the corner drug store he stops off to buy a joke book which he saw in the window; he memorizes a few jokes standing in the subway. They are Joe Miller's jokes.

At precisely the same hour Tante Melia is sending a Valentine greeting to the relatives. She has a gray uniform on and her hair is parted in the middle. She writes that she is very happy with her new-found friends and that the food is good. She would like them to remember however that she asked for some *Fastnacht Kuchen* the last time—could they send some by mail, by parcel post? She says that there are some lovely petunias growing up around the garbage can outside the big kitchen. She says that she took a long walk on Sunday last and saw lots of reindeer and rabbits and ostriches. She says that her spelling is very poor, but that she was

326

never a good hand at writing anyway. Everybody is very kind and there is lots of work to do. She would like some *Fastnacht Kuchen* as soon as possible, by air-mail if possible. She asked the director to make her some for her birthday but they forgot. She says to send some newspapers because she likes to look at the advertisements. There was a hat she saw once, from Bloomingdale's, she thought, and it was marked down. Maybe they could send the hat along with the *Fastnacht Kuchen?* She thanks them all for the lovely cards they sent her last Christmas—she still remembers them, especially the one with the silver stars on it. Everybody thought it was lovely. She says that she will soon be going to bed and that she will pray for all of them because they were always so good to her.

It's growing dusky, always about the same hour, and I'm standing there gazing at the ocean's mirror. Ice-cold time, neither fast nor slow, but a stiff lying on the ice with a celluloid collar—and if only he had an erection it would be marvelous . . . too marvelous! In the dark hall-way below Tom Jordan is waiting for the old man to descend. He has two blowsers with him and one of them is fixing her garter; Tom Jordan is helping her to fix her garter. Same hour, toward dusk, as I say, Mrs. Lawson is walking through the cemetery to look once again at her darling son's grave. Her dear boy Jack, she says, though he was thirty-two when he kicked off seven years ago. They said it was rheumatism of the heart, but the fact is the darling boy had knocked up so many venereal virgins that when they drained the pus from his body he stank like a shit-pump. Mrs. Lawson doesn't seem to remember that at all. It's her darling boy Jack and the grave is always tidy; she carries a little piece of chamois in her hand-bag in order to polish the tomb-stone every evening.

Same dusky time, the stiff lying there on the ice, and the old man is standing in a telephone booth with the receiver in one hand and something warm and wet with hair on it in the other. He's calling up to say not to hold the dinner, that he's got to take a customer out and he'll be home late, not to worry. Crazy George is turning the leaves of Joe Miller's Joke Book. Down further, towards Mobile, they're practising the St. Louis Blues without a note in front of 'em and people are getting ready to go crazy when they hear it yesterday, to-day, to-morrow. Everybody's getting ready to get raped, drugged, violated, soused with the new music that seeps out of the sweat of the asphalt. Soon it'll be the same hour everywhere, just by turning a dial or hanging suspended over the earth in a balloon. It's the hour of the kaffee-klatchers sitting around the family table, each one operated on for a different thing, the one with the whiskers and the heavy rings on her fingers having had a harder time than any one else because she could afford it.

It's staggeringly beautiful at this hour when every one seems to be going his own private way. Love and murder, they're still a few hours apart. Love and murder, I feel it coming with the dusk: new babies coming out of the womb, soft, pink flesh to get tangled up in barbed wire and scream all night long and rot like dead bone a thousand miles from nowhere. Crazy virgins with ice-cold jazz in their veins egging men on to erect new buildings and men with dog collars around their necks wading through the muck up to the eyes so that the czar of electricity will rule the waves. What's in the seed scares the living piss out of me: a brand new world is coming out of the egg and no matter how fast I write the old world doesn't die fast enough. I hear the new machine guns and the millions of bones splintered at once; I see dogs running mad and pigeons dropping with letters tied to their ankles.

Always merry and bright, whether north from Delancey Street or south towards the pus line! My two soft hands in the body of the

328

world, ploughing up the warm entrails, arranging and disarranging, cutting them up, sewing them together again. The warm body feeling which the surgeon knows, together with oysters, warts, ulcers, hernias, cancer sprouts, the young kohlrabies, the clips and the forceps, the scissors and tropical growths, the poisons and gases all locked up inside and carefully covered with skin. Out of the leaking mains love gushing like sewer gas: furious love with black gloves and bright bits of garter, love that champs and snorts, love hidden in a barrel and blowing the bung-hole night after night. The men who passed through my father's shop reeked with love: they were warm and winey, weak and indolent, fast yachts trimmed with sex, and when they sailed by me in the night they fumigated my dreams. Standing in the center of New York I could hear the tinkle of the cow-bells, or, by a turn of the head, I could hear the sweet sweet music of the death-rattle, a red line down the page and on every sleeve a mourning band. By twisting my neck just a little I could stand high above the tallest skyscraper and look down on the ruts left by the huge wheels of modern progress. Nothing was too difficult for me if only it had a little grief and anguish in it. *Chez nous* there were all the organic diseases—and a few of the inorganic. Like rock crystal we spread, from one crime to another. A merry whirl, and in the center of it my twenty-first year already covered with verdigris.

And when I can remember no more I shall always remember the night I was getting a dose of clap and the old man so stinking drunk he took his friend Tom Jordan to bed with him. Beautiful and touching this—to be out getting a dose of clap when the family honor was at stake, when it was at *par*, you might say. Not to be there for the shindig, with mother and father wrestling on the floor and the broomstick flying. Not to be there in the cold morning light when Tom Jordan is on his knees and begging to be forgiven

329

but not being forgiven even on his knees because the inflexible heart of a Lutheran doesn't know the meaning of forgiveness. Touching and beautiful to read in the paper next morning that about the same hour the night before the pastor who had put in the bowling alley was caught in a dark room with a naked boy on his lap! But what makes it excruciatingly touching and beautiful is this, that not knowing these things, I came home next day to ask permission to marry a woman old enough to be my mother. And when I said "get married" the old lady picks up the bread knife and goes for me. I remember, as I left the house, that I stopped by the book-case to grab a book. And the name of the book was—*The Birth of Tragedy*. Droll that, what with the broomstick the night before, the bread knife, the dose of clap, the pastor caught red-handed, the dumplings growing cold, the cancer sprouts, et cetera . . . I used to think then that all the tragic events of life were written down in books and that what went on outside was just diluted crap. I though that a beautiful book was a diseased portion of the brain. I never realized that a whole world could be diseased!

Walking up and down with a package under my arm. A fine bright morning, let's say, and the spittoons all washed and polished. Mumbling to myself, as I step into the Woolworth Building—"Good morning, Mr. Thorndike, fine morning this morning, Mr. Thorndike. Are you interested in clothes, Mr. Thorndike?" Mr. Thorndike is not interested in clothes this morning; he thanks me for calling and throws the card in the waste basket. Nothing daunted I try the American Express Building. "Good morning, Mr. Hathaway, fine morning this morning!" Mr. Hathaway doesn't need a good tailor—he's had one for thirty-five years now. Mr. Hathaway is a little peeved and damned right he is thinks I to myself stumbling down the stairs. A fine, bright morning, no denying that, and so to take the bad taste out of my mouth and also have a view of the harbor I take the trolley over the bridge and call on a cheap skate by the name of Dyker. Dyker is a busy man. The sort of man who has his lunch sent up and his shoes polished while he eats. Dyker is suffering from a nervous complaint brought on by ... . He says we can make him a pepper and salt suit if we stop dunning him every month. The girl was only sixteen and he didn't want to knock her up. Yes, patch pockets, please! Besides, he has a wife and three children. Besides, he will be running for judge soon—judge of the Surrogate Court.

Getting towards matinee time. Hop back to New York and drop off at the Burlesk where the usher knows me. The first three rows always filled with judges and politicians. The house is dark and Margie Pennetti is standing on the runway in a pair of dirty white tights. She has the most wonderful ass of any woman on the stage and everybody knows it, herself included. After the show I walk around aimlessly, looking at the movie houses and the Jewish delicatessen stores. Stand awhile in a penny arcade listening to the siren voices coming through the megaphone. Life is just a continuous honeymoon filled with chocolate layer cake and cranberry pie. Put a penny in the slot and see a woman undressing on the grass. Put a penny in the slot and win a set of false teeth. The world is made of new parts every afternoon: the soiled parts are sent to the dry cleaner, the used parts are scrapped and sold for junk.

Walk uptown past the pus line and stroll through the lobbies of the big hotels. If I like I can sit down and watch other people walking through the lobby. Everybody's on the watch. Things are happening all about. The strain of waiting for something to happen is delirious. The elevated rushing by, the taxis honking, the ambulance clanging, the riveters riveting. Bell hops dressed in gorgeous livery looking for people who don't answer to their names. In the golden toilet below men standing in line waiting to take a

331

leak; everything made of plush and marble, the odors refined and pleasant, the flush flushing beautifully. On the sidewalk a stack of newspapers, the headlines still wet with murder, rape, arson, strikes, forgeries, revolution. People stepping over one another to crash the subway. Over in Brooklyn a woman's waiting for me. Old enough to be my mother and she's waiting for me to marry her. The son's got T. B. so bad he can't crawl out of bed any more. Tough titty going up there to her garret to make love while the son's in the next room coughing his lungs out. Besides, she's just getting over an abortion and I don't want to knock her up again—not right away anyhow.

The rush hour! and the subway a free for all Paradise. Pressed up against a woman so tight I can feel the hair on her twat. So tightly glued together my knuckles are making a dent in her groin. She's looking straight ahead, at a microscopic spot just under my right eye. By Canal Street I manage to get my penis where my knuckles were before. The thing's jumping like mad and no matter which way the train jerks she's always in the same position vis-à-vis my dickie. Even when the crowd thins out she stands there with her pelvis thrust forward and her eyes fixed on the microscopic spot just under my right eye. At Borough Hall she gets out, without once giving me the eye. I follow her up to the street thinking she might turn round and say hello at least, or let me buy her a frosted chocolate, assuming I could buy one. But no, she's off like an arrow, without turning her head the eighth of an inch. How they do it I don't know. Millions and millions of them every day standing up without underwear and getting a dry fuck. What's the conclusion—a shower? a rub down? Ten to one they fling themselves on the bed and finish the job with their fingers.

Anyway, it's going on towards evening and me walking up and

down with an erection fit to burst my fly. The crowd gets thicker and thicker. Everybody's got a newspaper now. The sky's choked with illuminated merchandise every single article of which is guaranteed to be pleasant, healthful, durable, tasty, noiseless, rainproof, imperishable, the *ne plus ultra* without which life would be unbearable were it not for the fact that life is already unbearable because there is no life. Just about the hour when old Henschke is quitting the tailor shop to go to the card club uptown. An agreeable little job on the side which keeps him occupied until two in the morning. Nothing much to do—just take the gentlemen's hats and coats, serve drinks on a little tray, empty the ash trays and keep the match boxes filled. Really a very pleasant job, everything considered. Towards midnight prepare a little snack for the gentlemen, should they so desire it. There are the spittoons, of course, and the toilet bowl. All such gentlemen, however, that there's really nothing to it. And then there's always a little cheese and crackers to nibble on, and sometimes a thimbleful of Port. Now and then a cold veal sandwich for the morrow. Real gentlemen! No gainsaying it. Smoke the best cigars. Even the butts taste good. Really, a very, very pleasant job!

Getting towards dinner time. Most of the tailors have closed shop for the day. A few of them, those who have nothing but brittle old geezers on the books, are waiting to make a try-on. They walk up and down with their hands behind their backs. Everybody has gone except the boss tailor himself, and perhaps the cutter or the bushelman. The boss tailor is wondering if he has to put new chalk marks on again and if the check will arrive in time to meet the rent. The cutter is saying to himself—"why yes, Mr. So-and-So, why to be sure . . . yes, I think it should be just a little higher there . . . yes, you're quite right . . . it *is* a little off on the left side . . . yes, we'll have that ready for you in a few days . . . yes,

Mr. So-and-So . . ., yes, yes, yes, yes, yes . . ." The finished clothes and the unfinished clothes are hanging on the rack; the bolts are neatly stacked on the tables; only the light in the busheling room is on. Suddenly the telephone rings. Mr. So-and-So is on the wire and he can't make it this evening but he would like his tuxedo sent up right away, the one with the new buttons which he selected last week, and he hopes to Christ it doesn't jump off his neck any more. The cutter puts on his hat and coat and runs quickly down the stairs to attend a Zionist meeting in the Bronx. The boss tailor is left to close the shop and switch out all the lights if any were left on by mistake. The boy that he's sending up with the tuxedo right away is himself and it doesn't matter much because he will duck round by the trade entrance and nobody will be the wiser. Nobody looks more like a millionaire than a boss tailor delivering a tuxedo to Mr. So-and-So. Spry and spruce, shoes shined, hat cleaned, gloves washed, mustache waxed. They start to look worried only when they sit down for the evening meal. No appetite. No orders to-day. No checks. They get so despondent that they fall asleep at ten o'clock and when it's time to go to bed they can't sleep any more.

Walking over the Brooklyn Bridge . . . Is this the world, this walking up and down, these buildings that are lit up, the men and women passing me? I watch their lips moving, the lips of the men and women passing me. What are they talking about—some of them so earnestly? I hate seeing people so deadly serious when I myself am suffering worse than any of them. One life! and there are millions and millions of lives to be lived. So far I haven't had a thing to say about my own life. Not a thing. Must be I haven't got the guts. Ought to go back to the subway, grab a Jane and rape her in the street. Ought to go back to Mr. Thorndike in the morning and spit in his face. Ought to stand on Times Square with my pecker in my hand and piss in the gutter. Ought to grab a revolver and fire point-blank into the crowd. The old man's leading the life of Reilly. He and his bosom pals. And I'm walking up and down, turning green with hate and envy. And when I turn in the old woman'll be sobbing fit to break her heart. Can't sleep nights listening to her. I hate her too for sobbing that way. The one robs me, the other punishes me. How can I go into her and comfort her when what I most want to do is to break her heart?

Walking along the Bowery . . . and a beautiful snot-green pasture it is at this hour. Pimps, crooks, cokies, panhandlers, beggars, touts, gunmen, chinks, wops, drunken micks. All gaga for a bit of food and a place to flop. *Walking and walking and walking.* Twenty-one I am, white, born and bred in New York, muscular physique, sound intelligence, good breeder, no bad habits, etc. etc. Chalk it up on the board. Selling out at par. Committed no crime, except to be born here.

In the past every member of our family did something with his hands. I'm the first idle son of a bitch with a glib tongue and a bad heart.

Swimming in the crowd, a digit with the rest. Tailored and re-tailored. The lights are twinkling—on and off, on and off. Sometimes it's a rubber tire, sometimes it's a piece of chewing gum. The tragedy of it is that nobody sees the look of desperation on my face. Thousands and thousands of us, and we're passing one another without a look of recognition. The lights jigging like electric needles. The atoms going crazy wtih light and heat. A conflagration going on behind the glass and nothing burns away. Men breaking their backs, men bursting their brains, to invent a machine which a child will manipulate. If I could only find the hypothetical child who's to run this machine I'd put a hammer in its hands and say: Smash it! Smash it!

Smash it! Smash it! That's all I can say. The old man's riding around in an open barouche. I envy the bastard his peace of mind. A bosom pal by his side and a quart of rye under his belt. My toes are blistering with malice. Twenty years ahead of me and this thing growing worse by the hour. It's throttling me. In twenty years there won't be any soft, lovable men waiting to greet me. Every bosom pal that goes now is a buffalo lost and gone forever. Steel and concrete hedging me in. The pavement getting harder and harder. The new world eating into me, expropriating me. Soon I won't even need a name.

Once I thought there were marvelous things in store for me. Thought I could build a world in the air, a castle of pure white spit that would raise me above the tallest building, between the tangible and the intangible, put me in a space like music where everything collapses and perishes but where I would be immune, great, god-like, holiest of the holies. It was *I* imagined this, *I* the tailor's son! I who was born from a little acorn on an immense and stalwart tree. In the hollow of the acorn even the faintest tremor of the earth reached me: I was part of the great tree, part of the past, with crest and lineage, with pride, *pride*. And when I fell to earth and was buried there I remembered *who* I was, *where* I came from. Now I am lost, *lost*, do you hear? You don't hear? I'm yowling and screaming—don't you hear me? Switch the lights off! Smash the bulbs! Can you hear me now? *Louder!* you say. *Louder!* Christ, are you making sport of me? Are you deaf, dumb and blind? Must I yank my clothes off? Must I dance on my head?

All right, then! I'm going to dance for you! A merry whirl, brothers, and let her whirl and whirl and whirl! Throw in an extra pair of flannel trousers while you're at it. And don't forget, boys, I dress on the right side. You hear me? Let 'er go! *Always merry and bright!*

Glittering Pie

It's WONDERFUL to come back to America as a foreigner. Better still if one had never heard or read a thing about America. You get it at one crack, just walking down the street. The newspapers may lie, the magazines may gloss it over, the politicians may falsify, but the streets howl with truth. I walk the streets and I see men and women talking, but there is no talk. I see wine and beer advertised everywhere, but there is no wine or beer anywhere. On every table I see the same glass of ice water, in every window the same glittering baubles, in every face the same empty story. The sameness of everything is appalling. It's like the proliferation of a cancer

337

germ. The disease spreads, it eats and eats away until there is nothing left but the thing itself—*cancer*.

Every day, every hour, every minute America becomes more American. It's as though the influx of immigrants, the great tidal waves of alien blood which bathed the great American organism, had proved ineffective against the disease. Now there is no new blood coming; the heart has stopped pumping. It's a race between the quick and the dead. Now the germs have a clear field of it: the disease must run its course. And the disease *is* running its course. The whole world is rapidly becoming inoculated with the virus of it. It's impossible to escape, no matter where you go. Even the Chinese are infected. The whole world must be infected before there can be a let-up—if ever there will be a let-up.

It's no use dreaming about economic salvation: the fight is not between the inherited and the disinherited, but between America and the rest of the world. The question is—will America destroy the world or will America itself be destroyed? That a cure is found for cancer, for instance, does not imply that cancer will be eradicated. On the contrary, it may flourish more luxuriantly than ever. We may lose our fear of it, that's all. And whether we live in fear of cancer or not, what produces cancer remains.

I thought, as we pulled into the harbor, that the sight of the skyline would have its effect upon me. After all, I was born here, right close to the river, and I grew up with this changing skyline. I had a right to expect some little thrill, some pull, some vestige of lost emotions. But no, I saw them just as I have always seen them in the past—with a sinking heart, with a feeling of foreboding. Everything seemed very familiar to me and very grim and very ugly —like coming out of a dream. *This*, I thought to myself, is the sensation people usually get when they talk about "reality". If going to Europe is a form of evasion, a running away from one's self, from

338

reality, then I knew that I was back again and *that this was reality*. Or it should have been, and might have been, had I not tasted a deeper reality in my absence from my native land.

Suddenly I was back where I had started from—the same faces, the same voices, the same blatant stupidity. I remembered that that's how it always was, and that's why I ran away. Nothing had changed, fundamentally, except that what was was more so now. And it was worse because I myself had changed. Whereas before I knew nothing very different, and could therefore condone or ignore, now I *knew* and the only thing to do was to try to understand. The truth is, I had almost forgotten what my countrymen were like. This may sound incredible, since even in Paris there are Americans. But a stray American abroad, or even a flock of Americans abroad, is quite another matter from a solid population of Americans in America. It's one thing to drink with a fellow-American on the terrasse of a cafe, and it's another thing to walk among them on their own grounds, to see millions and millions of them and nothing but them all the time. Milling around in herds their true qualities assert themselves. You can't be mistaken about them when every man does the same thing, talks the same way, wears the same clothes, has the same ailments. You can't doubt *who* they are or *what* they are when between the cop on the beat and the director of a big corporation there is no difference except the uniform.

Every familiar spot I pass, every object I recognize gives me a fresh start, a stab of pain. At every corner comes the recollection of an old misery, of despair, starvation, failure, desperation. I see my old self walking these streets ten, fifteen, twenty years ago, always raging and cursing. I'm talking now of a time that antedates the crisis. What I see happening to men and women now I myself tasted long before the bubble had collapsed. I realize that had

339

I never gone to Europe it would be the same for me now as it was then. I would be walking here unknown, unwanted, another piece of live junk for the scrap heap. Nothing here has value or durability, not even the skyscrapers. Sooner or later everything gets scrapped.

After the first shock of exposure to the American scene I am convinced that what I walked out on was, and still remains, a nightmare. Riding the subway it seems as if I were in the morgue; the bodies are labelled and ticketed, the destination clearly marked. Walking between the stiff, cold walls past the glitter of shops I see men and women walking, conversing, laughing sometimes or muttering to themselves, but they walk and talk and laugh and curse like ghosts. The day is full of activity, the night full of nightmares. On the surface things function smoothly—everything oiled and polished. But when it comes time to dream King Kong crashes through the windows; he pushes the skyscrapers down with one hand. "Skyscraper souls!" That was the last message from America that I caught walking down the Champs Elysees the eve of my departure. Now I walk through the marvelous tunnels with the rest of the sewer rats and I read: "*It's good to change the laxative*". Everything is better, cheaper, tastier, saner, healthier, lovelier than ever—if you believe in the advertisements. Everything has become more stupendous, more colossal, more this, more that. And yet everything is the same. It's marvelous. We've gotten beyond the superlative—we're in the higher mathematic row.

Walking through the waiting room of the Pennsylvania Station I get the feeling of unreality, of what it means to live between two worlds. Somewhere between the waiting room of the Pennsylvania Station and the phantom world of the advertising gentry lies reality. The train is standing on the siding, the freight is wheeling through the asteroids. The passengers sit in the vestibule waiting for the resurrection. They wait like the piano I saw this morning in the toilet room of a cafeteria. To invent something *different* from this situation would demand an act of creation—and this is impossible. We have left a few surprises, of a violent nature, *but no creation*. It is possible that the glittering pie which Celine cut into when he visited the Automat may metamorphose into a flaming flamingo. In fact, the whole city may rise up on wings and drown itself in the Dead Sea where, I understand, there are now beautiful casinos and gambling halls.

The City of New York is like an enormous citadel, a modern Carcassonne. Walking between the magnificent skyscrapers one feels the presence on the fringe of a howling, raging mob, a mob with empty bellies, a mob unshaven and in rags. The fighting goes on day and night, without let. The results are nil. The enemy is always at the gates, the bugles are always blowing. If one day a tiny little man should escape from the citadel, should get outside the gates and stand before the walls so that everybody could see him, if once everybody saw him plainly, saw that it was a man, a very little man, perhaps even a Jew, that little man, with just one breath of his lungs, could blow down the walls of the great citadel. Everything would crumble at a breath. Just the presence of a man outside the gates would kill off everything. Stop. *Full Stop.* The whole works would lie on the floor like the toys which a child drops when it falls asleep.

The faces I see! No anguish, no torment, no suffering registered in them. I feel as though I am walking through a lost world. What I saw years ago on the magazine covers I see now in actuality. The women's faces more particularly. That sweet, vapid, virginal look of the American woman! So putridly sweet and virginal! Even the whores have these vapid, virginal faces. They correspond exactly to the titles of the books and magazines for sale. It's a victory for the

341

editors and publishers, for the cheap illustrators and the inventive advertising gentry. No more sales resistance. It's a push-over. Palm Olive, Father John, Ex-Lax, Peruna, Lydia Pinkham—these have conquered!

The face of the American woman is the index of the life of the American male. Sex either from the neck up or from the neck down. No American phallus ever reaches the vital center. And so we get the gorgeous burlesk queen with the divinely beautiful body of a goddess and the mentality of an eight year old child, or less. On every burlesk stage a bevy of gorgeous nymphomaniacs, sexing and desexing at will; they writhe and squirm before an audience of mental masturbators. In all the world there are no bodies like these, nothing which for sheer physical beauty and perfection can compare with them. But if only they were decapitated! The addition of the head, of the sweet, virginal face, is heart-breaking. Their faces are like new coins which have never been put into circulation. Each day a fresh batch from the mint. They pile up, they choke the treasury vaults. While outside the treasury stands a hungry mob, an insatiable mob. The whole world has been ransacked, every available piece of gold melted down to make these gleaming new coins—but nobody knows how to put them into circulation. There she is, the American woman, buried in the treasury vaults. The men have created her in their image. She's worth her weight in gold—but nobody can get at her, lay a hand on her. She lies in the mint with gleaming face and her pure gold substance goes to waste.

I wander over to the cigar store to buy a cigarette which is not extensively advertised and which, therefore, I am reasonably sure must be more to my taste than the others. I see book racks stacked with the world's best literature: volumes of Goethe, Rabelais, Ovid, Petronius, etc. One might imagine that Americans had suddenly developed an astounding taste for the classics, that overnight, as it were, they had become a cultured people. Yes, one might—if his ears were stopped or his eyes sealed. One could imagine that this flatulent array of imposing literature indicated an awakening. But one would have to be a dreamer and never go to a movie and never read a newspaper.

Of nothing are you allowed to get the real odor or the real savour. Everything is sterilized and wrapped in cellophane. The only odor which is recognized and admitted as an odor is halitosis, and of this all Americans live in mortal dread. Dandruff may be a myth, but halitosis is real. It is the genuine odor of spiritual decomposition. The American body, when dead, can be washed and fumigated; some corpses even achieve a distinct beauty. But the live American body in which the soul is rotting away smells bad and every American knows it and that is why he would rather be a hundred percent American, alone and gregarious at the same time, than live breast to breast with the tribe.

It's almost impossible to escape the radio, the telephone, the fat newspapers, the glass of ice water. In the hotel where I'm stopping I have no need of an alarm clock because at seven-thirty sharp every morning my breakfast is thrown on the floor with a bang. It comes like a letter through the post, only it makes a loud noise. A "continental" breakfast—with the coffee in a vacuum bottle, the butter wrapped in cardboard, the sugar in paper, the cream in a sealed bottle, the jam in a little jar and the rolls wrapped in cellophane. It's a continental breakfast such as was never seen on the Continent. There's one thing about it which distinguishes it from any breakfast served anywhere on the Continent—*it's inhuman!* And though I've lived in the lousiest hotels that Paris boasts, I've never eaten my breakfast from a shoe-box under electric light with the radio going full blast.

If I strike a match I read "Ex-lax is non-habit forming", or some equally ridiculous piece of nonsense which provides hard-working imbeciles with a living wage. Walking down the hall a woman who resembles Carrie Nation says to the chamber maid: "Put an extra roll of toilet paper in my bath room, please". Just like that. In a drug store the title of a book reads: "Jews Without Money". The elevator runners look smart, immaculate and intelligent—more intelligent, more immaculate than the manager of the hotel. To get a clean towel you just push a button and pull. If you want something, no matter what—a piano, a valise, a fireman—you have only to lift the receiver and ask for it. Nobody thinks of asking why you want this or that. All day long I walk the streets, but I see no place to sit down—no place, I mean, that looks inviting. On my wall is the photograph of a chair in the Tuileries Gardens, a chair photographed by my friend Brassai. To me it's a poem. I no longer see a wire chair with holes in the seat but an empty throne. If I had my way I would have this chair, this vacant seat, stamped on every silver dollar. We need to sit down somewhere, to rest, to contemplate, to know that we have a body—and a soul.

People who don't know how to eat or drink, people who live vicariously through the newspapers and the movies, people who walk around like ghosts and automatons, people who make work a fetich because they have no other way to occupy their minds, people who vote Republican or Democrat whether the dinner-pail is full or half-empty or rusty or full of holes, people who never sit down except to guzzle a little swill—well, what difference does it make what the new line-up is? The money-grubbers pretend to be worried about the impending revolution. As far as I can see, the revolution is already a fact. The stage is set, the machinery is in full operation, the mentality ripe for the coming Utopia. All that is required is to give it a name. The era of the collectivity is already inaugurated. America *is* communized, from top to bottom. She needs only a Lenin, or a Mussolini, or a Hitler.

I repeat, it doesn't matter what the new line-up is called. Once the corpse is dressed everything will be lovely. And if you want to know what it will be like when everybody is washed, starched, fumigated, sterilized, castrated and securely clapped in harness just read the great American novel—there's a new one every week. From the standpoint of Utopia it may seem like looking through the wrong end of the telescope, but all you need to do to correct this is to turn the telescope around.

Until this colossal, senseless machine which we have made of America is smashed and scrapped there can be no hope. The boss is a pimp, the worker is a whore. An economic revolution will accomplish nothing. A political revolution will accomplish nothing. Even if all the parts are replaced and a new model installed nothing of any value will happen. The malady is at the roots. The whole body of American life is affected.

If you are an artist you have one consolation which is denied the others: you can play the role of undertaker. It is an old and honorable profession and demands only a bare working knowledge of the human anatomy. It offers the satisfaction of walking and working with death in dignity while being very much alive and joyous oneself.

The Brooklyn Bridge

ALL MY LIFE I have felt a great kinship with the madman and the criminal. Practically all my life I have dwelt in big cities; I am unhappy, uneasy, unless I am in a big city. My feeling for Nature is limited to water, mountain and desert. These three form a trine which is more imperative, for me, than any spiritual alimentation. But in the city I am aware of another element which is beyond all these in power of fascination: the labyrinth. To be lost in a strange city is the greatest joy I know; to become oriented is to lose everything. To me the city is crime personified, insanity personified. I feel at home. When, in the movies, for example, I see a great Chinese city, when I imagine myself in the midst of that anarchy and confusion, the tears come to my eyes. It is like a haven for me. No matter what the language I can get along with the man of a big city. We are brothers, we understand each other. Are we not travelling towards a common reality, a reality which had its genesis in crime?

To make the slightest advance one has to go back almost to the very beginning. Every man, when he has earned the rightful death which precedes maturity, returns to his childhood for inspiration and nourishment. It is then that his slumber is disturbed by prophetic, troubling dreams; he resorts to sleep in order to become more vividly awake. Thus he begins to habituate himself, unconsciously no doubt, to the state of annihilation which is earned through fulfilment. He begins to live in full consciousness, in order to enjoy the long, uninterrupted final death, the death which only a very few have experienced. The memory takes on a new character, one almost identical with the waking life. The memory ceases to be an interminable freight train. One consciousness—the same for dream, for memory, for waking life. All motion becomes circular, welling up from an inexhaustible source.

In the violent dreams and visions which accompanied the writing of Black Spring one image seems to have recurred with greater splendour and illumination than any other: the Brooklyn Bridge. For me the Brooklyn Bridge served very much as the rainbow did for Lawrence. Only whereas Lawrence was seeking the bright future which the rainbow seemed to promise, I was seeking a link which would bind me to the past. The bridge was for me a means of reinstating myself in the universal stream; it was far more stable and enduring than the rainbow, and it was at the same time destructive of hope and of longing. It enabled me to link the two ancestral streams which were circulating between the poles of death

347

and lunacy. Henceforth I could plant one foot firmly in China and the other in Mexico. I could walk tranquilly between the madman and the criminal. I was securely situated in my time, and yet above it and beyond it.

As far back as I can imagine, my ancestors were straining at the leash. The freaks and monsters which are still to be seen dangling from the family tree are the evidences of a continued violent effort to create new shoots. They were all wanderers, pioneers, explorers, navigators, homesteaders, even the poets and the musicians, even the ridiculous little tailors. On the female side they were Mongols, on the male side they were of Patagonian stock, so it is said. The two streams diverged, leaving traces in every nook and corner of the earth. Finally they commingled and formed the mysterious island of incest described in my book. This island of George Insel was peopled entirely by hippopotamic men, of whom the Atlanteans are one branch. Their peculiarity was to wear nothing but dead men's clothes.

In George Insel the tree and the skeleton became one. The event, which had been hatching for over 25,000 years, took place in a suburban saloon. Suddenly, the exogamists and the endogamists in the family came together—that is, the men who had come down through the Bering Straits as Chinamen encountered in this suburban saloon their brothers from Atlantis, who had walked across the ocean floor during a hippopotamic trance. George Insel came up from the depths like a crater in mid-Pacific. His origins he left behind him. He was straight as a totem pole and clean daft from stem to stern. No sooner had he taken a job as undertaker's assistant than he pounded on a juicy cadaver, evacuated the guts, and appropriated the cerements. When at Christmas-time he peddled postcards, his beard grew very white and sparkled like mica.

Walking back and forth over the Brooklyn Bridge everything became crystal clear to me. Once I cleared the tower and felt myself definitely poised above the river the whole past would click. It held as long as I remained over the water, as long as I looked down into the inky swirl and saw all things upside down. It was only in moments of extreme anguish that I took to the bridge, when, as we say, it seemed that all was lost. Time and again all was lost, irrevocably so. The bridge was the harp of death, the strange winged creature without an eye which held me suspended between the two shores.

I dreamt very violently on the bridge, often so violently that when I awoke I would find myself in Nevada or Mexico or some forgotten place like Imperial City. The feeling I experienced once in the last-named place surpasses description. A sense of desolation truly unprcedented, the more so since it was without cause. I found myself of a sudden in the body of a man bearing my name in this God-forsaken spot on the Pacific Coast, and as I walked aimlessly from one end of the city to the other I had the very distinct sensation of not belonging to this body which I had been made to inhabit. It was decidedly not my body. It had been loaned to me, perhaps, out of mercy, but it was not me. It was not terror so much as desolation that I knew. I who was suffering—where was I in this world at that moment? There I was conveniently incarcerated in a body which was walking through a strange city for reasons I knew not. This lasted a whole afternoon. It was perhaps the brief period when, according to the astrologers, insanity menaced me. There was no struggle, no great anguish; I was simply stricken desolate. In fact "I" was absent during the time. The "I" was simply a dim, approximate awareness of an ego, a consciousness temporarily held in leash during a crucial planetary conjunction in which my proper destiny was being worked out for me. It was the skeleton of an ego, the congealed cloud spirit of the self.

349

Not long after that I awoke one night, got dressed automatically, went down to the telegraph office and sent myself a telegram to come home. The next day I was on the train bound for New York, and when I arrived home the telegram was waiting for me.

Back in my own skin again I realized without the least disturbance that I should have to do a long penance. One does not escape so miraculously without paying a price for it. A salvation which is earned ahead of time is meaningless. Often on the bridge I had committed suicide. But as often I was back again, wrestling with the same enigmas. It does not matter much, in the long calculation, whether one actually dies or not. One must come back eventually to live, to live it out to the full, to the last meaningful dregs. This I came to understand finally when the bridge ceased to be a thing of stone and steel and became incorporated in my consciousness as a symbol.

During the process of inner transformation, the great current which had animated the family tree for 25,000 years or more became polarized. The terrors and obsessions which had eaten it hollow became fixed, death like a leaven at the base of the tree and lunacy like the air itself enshrouding the foliage. The strange, withered island of incest which was George Insel began to bloom like a magnolia. George Insel began to dream as a plant dreams in a stagnant night. Putting the corpse on the ice, he would lay himself down in the padded coffin of the undertaker's establishment and slowly, drowsily, deliberately dream.

What George Insel dreamed the men of Mexico dreamed before him. It is a dream which the North Americans are trying to shake off, but which they will never succeed in doing, for the whole continent is doomed. For a time, when the Mongols poured in from the north-west and rented out the uninhabited bodies of the Mexicans, it almost seemed as if the dream were a myth. But to-day, in the angelic countenance of the American assassin, one can see the hippopotamic sleep-walkers who deserted the valley of the Mediterranean in the blind quest for peace. It is in the bland, peaceful smile of the thug, the North American thug, that one can detect the germ of the artist type which was snuffed out at the time of the Flood. What is called history is merely the seismographic chart of the explosions and implosions produced by the aborting of a new and salutary type of man at some definite period in the dim past. This past, as well as the future which will dissolve it, impinges upon the consciousness of the man of to-day relentlessly. The man of to-day is being carried along on the face of his own flood; his most wakeful moments are no different in quality or texture from the stuff of dreams. His life is the foaming crest of a long tidal wave which is about to smash on the shores of an unknown continent. He has swept his own debris before him; he will break clean in one steady accumulated wave.

That is why, in studying the air-conditioned quality of the American nightmare, I am enchanted by the prospect of re-arranging the debris which has accumulated on the shores of that isolated island of incest called George Insel. I see among countless other things a faded flower from Death Valley, a piece of quartz from the Bad Lands, a Navajo bead, a rusty meat-axe from the slaughterhouse, a drop of serum from the Cancer Institute, a louse from a Jew's beard, a street called Myrtle Avenue, a city made entirely of celluloid, another of cellophane, a cereal like dried brains called Grape Nuts, and so on. In the dead center of the debris, thoroughly renovated and thoroughly ventilated, stands the Brooklyn Bridge. On one tower sits Tante Melia braiding her hair, on the other George Insel armed with an undertaker's syringe. The day breaks bright, and from the yardarms below in the Navy Yard the dead are swinging stiff and cheerily. Tante Melia is so conveniently situated now that if she desires the moon, as she sometimes does, she has only to reach for it with her mitt. Everything is in the best of taste, everything preconceived, predisposed, predigested, premeditated. The Aurora Borealis is in full swing and the sky is just one tremendously antiseptic omelette sprinkled with parsley and caraway seeds. It has been a fine day for everybody, including God. No sign of rain, no hint of blood or pestilence. The weather, like the sky, will continue this way ad infinitum. Below the river bed some miserable few thousand men are patiently bursting their lungs with riveting machines. Otherwise it's quite grand. I walk back and forth over the bridge with the peaceful smile of the North American thug. My anguish is trussed up by a permanent elastic suspensory; should I need to cough up blood there's a handy little cup attached to my rosary which I bought at the five and ten cent store once. The battleships are lining up for target practice; they must be getting into action soon, or they will be thrown on the dump heap. The rear-admirals are taking the azimuth; they too are going into action, like all the other heroes. Everybody will die with the utmost heroism, including the Grand Dali Lama of Thibet. Salvador Dali is cleaning his brushes; he feels a bit antedated. But his day is coming: the air will soon be thick with placentas, with winged marigolds and spittoons studded with human eyes. In Yucatan the chicleros are running amok. Driven to desperation, the Wrigley Brothers are chewing their own gum. On the shores of the Great Salt Lake the murdered buffaloes rise up like phantoms and charge the slaughter-house. And yet the sky is as bright as an omelette, with every sprig of parsley stoutly held in place. A wonderful day for everybody, including God.

The North Americans fear two things: death and insanity. In the root type these fears have been banished, seemingly. The killer is a man without nerves and without guilt. He goes about his work in a trance. In the electric chair he displays the same nonchalance as in the barbor shop, more in fact, because at the barber's death is apt to come accidentally, whereas the electric chair is a guaranteed paid investment. The man who is sound asleep can be killed over and over again—no pain or terror is involved. But that part of the man which is awake and which at certain periods is denied access to a body creates in time an unseen host which saturates the atmosphere with anguish. Thus the whole continent moves like an icefloe towards some tropical stream in which the tension is to be dissolved.

When I was in it and part of it I had the feeling that the rest of the world was gaga. When a whole continent is drifting there does seem to be direction. But when you stand at the tail end and you suddenly perceive that there is no rudder you get a very different feeling. And if you stand like that for very long you invariably go off the deep end. That is precisely what happened to me. I went off the deep end in a diving suit and cut the hawser. At the very bottom I felt at last that I was standing on solid ground. Looking through the marine depths with aqueous eyes I perceived the soles and heels of those above me who were skating on thin ice. It was exactly as if they were in heaven already, except that angels carry no gatling guns. But they all seemed to wear that blissful expression of those who have passed beyond. They were merely waiting for the scythe to mow them down.

In the act of making the long hippopotamic voyage I discovered a few things which my ancestors had tried without success to din into me. I discovered that one has to breathe very lightly, almost not at all. I discovered that one has to give way, to make painful detours, to swim with the current; I discovered that one must waste a lot of time floating on one's back, that one must cultivate the good graces of the most savage-looking creatures, that one must be absolutely supple and unathletic, a spineless, will-less wisp of the void—if one is to reach the other shore.

The other shore! Above all, one has to learn to forget that there is another shore. For the shore is always there, when it is necessary. Just as in the dream the way to avoid extinction is by coming awake, so in the under-water journey the shore is always conveniently there once you decide to lift yourself by the boot-straps. Insanity occurs only when you doubt that you can lift yourself by the boot-straps.

The death which awaits us all is the amnesia which inevitably comes to the dreamer who refuses to wake up at the crucial moment. Whole races of men have died off that way, in their sleep, so that death has become pretty much of a habit. And so too it has happened with those who have embarked on the great voyage—those, I mean, who have set out to arrive at the frontier of another reality—that when part of the way across they suddenly lost faith, and with it a foothold in even the flimsiest sort of reality.

The buffaloes which enjoy the longest life are those which are yoked and harnessed. The men who have stopped dying are those who have accepted their fate. The great female principle of surrender produces an equilibrium which keeps the cosmos perpetually cosmogonic and cosmologic. No brick and mortar, no steel girders are required to keep the universe in place, because everything which is is in its place.

No man who is in a state of grace, which is to say in a state of perfect equilibrium, would want to be a whit different than he is. Behind him, sustaining him like an arch, are the ancestors; before him, receding ever mysteriously into the inferno, are the mothers. He must breathe ever so lightly lest he break through the ancestral membrane which keeps him suspended above the void. He must believe in the miraculous power of his own breath if he would avoid being caught up again in the mill of birth and re-birth. The mothers labour ceaselessly, their loins ever heavy with sordid hopes and doubts. Nothing can arrest the pain of birth unless it be the acceptance of the miraculous nature of one's own being. As long as men deny their own powers the mothers will remain in the service of death.

There are fish which talk and plants which can swallow alive human beings; there are diamonds which are born in the night during a violent storm. So too there are stars which have not yet moved into our ken and which will announce themselves in good time, without the slightest aid of scientific instruments. When one looks at the thickly studded sky on a clear frosty night one can think two ways, either of which is right, according to one's inner position. One can think *how remote! how unseizable!* And one can also think *how near! how warm! how perfectly comprehensible!* Tante Melia had an obsession for the moon; she was perpetually reaching for it with her two hands. I remember the first time she reached for it, the night she went daft. Never did the moon seem so remote to me. And yet not hopelessly remote! Eternally out of reach, but only so by a hair's breadth, as it were. Some twenty years later I was to see Jupiter one night through a field glass. Jupiter, according to the astrologic lingo, is my benevolent planetary deity. What a remarkable face Jupiter bears! Never have I seen anything so radiant, so bursting with light, so fiery and so cold at the same time. Coming away from my friend's roof that night suddenly all the stars had moved in closer to me. And they have remained thus, some astronomical light leagues closer—and warmer, more radiant, more benevolent. When I look up at the stars now I am aware that they are all inhabited, every one of them, including the so-called dead planets such as our earth. The light which blazes forth from them is the eternal light, the fire of creation. This fire is cold and distant only to those who are looking away from their own warm bowels with crazy instruments of precision.

The book which I speak of was a sort of musical notation in alphabetical language of a new realm of consciousness which I am only now beginning to explore. Since then I have crossed the Equator and made my peace with the Neptunian forces. The whole southern hemisphere lies exposed, waiting to be charted. Here entirely new configurations obtain. The past, though invisible, is not dead. The past trembles like a huge drop of water clinging to the rim of a cold goblet. I stand in the closest proximity to myself in the midst of an open field of light. I describe now only what is known to all men before me and after me standing in similar relationship to themselves. It is impossible for me to say one thing which has not been lived, one thing which is beyond the tips of my hair.

My Mexican incarnation is over, my North American life is past. The thug in me is dead, and the fanatic and the lunatic also.

The Cosmological Eye

My FRIEND Reichel is just a pretext to enable me to talk about the world, the world of art and the world of men, and the confusion and eternal misunderstanding between the two. When I talk about Reichel I mean any good artist who finds himself alone, ignored, unappreciated. The Reichels of this world are being killed off like flies. It will always be so; the penalty for being different, for being an artist, is a cruel one.

Nothing will change this state of affairs. If you read carefully the history of our great and glorious civilization, if you read the biographies of the great, you will see that it has always been so;

and if you read still more closely you will see that these exceptional men have themselves explained why it must be so, though often complaining bitterly of their lot.

Every artist is a human being as well as painter, writer or musician; and never more so than when he is trying to justify himself as artist. As a human being Reichel almost brings tears to my eyes. Not merely because he is unrecognized (while thousands of lesser men are wallowing in fame), but first of all because when you enter his room, which is in a cheap hotel where he does his work, the sanctity of the place breaks you down. It is not quite a hovel, his little den, but it is perilously close to being one. You cast your eye about the room and you see that the walls are covered with his paintings. The paintings themselves are holy. This is a man, you cannot help thinking, who has never done anything for gain. This man had to do these things or die. This is a man who is desperate, and at the same time full of love. He is trying desperately to embrace the world with this love which nobody appreciates. And, finding himself alone, always alone and unacknowledged, he is filled with a black sorrow.

He was trying to explain it to me the other day as we stood at a bar. It's true, he was a little under the weather and so it was even more difficult to explain than normally. He was trying to say that what he felt was worse than sorrow, a sort of sub-human black pain which was in the spinal column and not in the heart or brain. This gnawing black pain, though he didn't say so, I realized at once was the reverse of his great love: it was the black unending curtain against which his gleaming pictures stand out and glow with a holy phosphorescence. He says to me, standing in his little hotel room: "I want that the pictures should look back at me; if I look at them and they don't look at me too then they are no good." The remark came about because some one had ob-

358

served that in all his pictures there was an eye, the cosmological eye, this person said. As I walked away from the hotel I was thinking that perhaps this ubiquitous eye was the vestigial organ of his love so deeply implanted into everything he looked at that it shone back at him out of the darkness of human insensitivity. More, that this eye had to be in everything he did or he would go mad. This eye had to be there in order to gnaw into men's vitals, to get hold of them like a crab, and make them realize that Hans Reichel exists.

This cosmological eye is sunk deep within his body. Everything he looks at and seizes must be brought below the threshold of consciousness, brought deep into the entrails where there reigns an absolute night and where also the tender little mouths with which he absorbs his vision eat away until only the quintessence remains. Here, in the warm bowels, the metamorphosis takes place. In the absolute night, in the black pain hidden away in the backbone, the substance of things is dissolved until only the essence shines forth. The objects of his love, as they swim up to the light to arrange themselves on his canvases, marry one another in strange mystic unions which are indissoluble. But the real ceremony goes on below, in the dark, according to the inscrutable atomic laws of wedlock. There are no witnesses, no solemn oaths. Phenomenon weds phenomenon in the way that atomic elements marry to make the miraculous substance of living matter. There are polygamous marriages and polyandrous marriages, but no morganatic marriages. There are monstrous unions too, just as in nature, and they are as inviolable, as indissoluble as the others. Caprice rules, but it is the stern caprice of nature, and so divine.

There is a picture which he calls "The Stillborn Twins." It is an ensemble of miniature panels in which there is not only the embryonic flavor but the hieroglyphic as well. If he likes you, Reichel will show you in one of the panels the little shirt which the mother of the stillborn twins was probably thinking of in her agony. He says it so simply and honestly that you feel like weeping. The little shirt embedded in a cold pre-natal green is indeed the sort of shirt which only a woman in travail could summon up. You feel that with the freezing torture of birth, at the moment when the mind seems ready to snap, the mother's eye inwardly turning gropes frantically towards some tender, known object which will attach her, if only for a moment, to the world of human entities. In this quick, agonized clutch the mother sinks back, through worlds unknown to man, to planets long since disappeared, where perhaps there were no baby's shirts but where there was the warmth, the tenderness, the mossy envelope of a love beyond love, of a love for the disparate elements which metamorphose through the mother, through her pain, through her death, so that life may go on. Each panel, if you read it with the cosmological eye, is a throw-back to an undecipherable script of life. The whole cosmos is moving back and forth through the sluice of time and the stillborn twins are embedded there in the cold pre-natal green with the shirt that was never worn.

When I see him sitting in the armchair in a garden without bounds I see him dreaming backward with the stillborn twins. I see him as he looks to himself when there is no mirror anywhere in the world: when he is caught in a stone trance and has to imagine the mirror which is not there. The little white bird in the corner near his feet is talking to him, but he is deaf and the voice of the bird is inside him and he does not know whether he is talking to himself or whether he has become the little white bird itself. Caught like that, in the stony trance, the bird is plucked to the quick. It is as though the idea, bird, was suddenly arrested in the act of passing through the brain. The bird and the trance and the bird *in* the trance are transfixed. It shows in the expression on his face. The face is Reichel's, but it is a Reichel that has passed into a cataleptic state. A fleeting wonder hovers over the stone mask. Neither fear nor terror is registered in his expression—only an inexpressible wonder, as though he were the last witness of a world sliding down into darkness. And in this last minute vision the little white bird comes to speak to him—but he is already deaf. The most miraculous words are being uttered inside him, this bird language which no one has ever understood; he has it now, deep inside him. But it is at this moment when everything is clear that he sees with stony vision the world slipping away into the black pit of nothingness.

There is another self-portrait—a bust which is smothered in a mass of green foliage. It's extraordinary how he bobs up out of the still ferns, with a more human look now, but still drunk with wonder, still amazed, bedazzled and overwhelmed by the feast of the eye. He seems to be floating up from the paleozoic ooze and, as if he had caught the distant roar of the Flood, there is in his face the premonition of impending catastrophe. He seems to be anticipating the destruction of the great forests, the annihilation of countless living trees and the lush green foliage of a spring which will never happen again. Every variety of leaf, every shade of green seems to be packed into this small canvas. It is a sort of bath in the vernal equinox, and man is happily absent from his preoccupations. Only Reichel is there, with his big round eyes, and the wonder is on him and this great indwelling wonder saturates the impending doom and casts a searchlight into the unknown.

In every cataclysm Reichel is present. Sometimes he is a fish hanging in the sky beneath a triple-ringed sun. He hangs there like a God of Vengeance raining down his maledictions upon man. He is the God who destroys the fishermen's nets, the God who brings down thunder and lightning so that the fishermen may be drowned. Sometimes he appears incarnated as a snail, and you may see him at work building his own monument. Sometimes he is a gay and happy snail crawling about on the sands of Spain. Sometimes he is only the dream of a snail, and then his world already phantasmagorical becomes musical and diaphanous. You are there in his dream at the precise moment when everything is melting, when only the barest suggestion of form remains to give a last fleeting clue to the appearance of things. Swift as flame, elusive, perpetually on the wing, nevertheless there is always in his pictures the iron claw which grasps the unseizable and imprisons it without hurt or damage. It is the dexterity of the master, the visionary clutch which holds firm and secure its prey without ruffling a feather.

There are moments when he gives you the impression of being seated on another planet making his inventory of the world. Conjunctions are recorded such as no astronomer has noted. I am thinking now of a picture which he calls "Almost Full Moon." The *almost* is characteristic of Reichel. This *almost* full is not the almost full with which we are familiar. It is the almost-full-moon which a man would see from Mars, let us say. For when it will be full, this moon, it will throw a green, spectral light reflected from a planet just bursting into life. This is a moon which has somehow strayed from its orbit. It belongs to a night studded with strange configurations and it hangs there taut as an anchor in an ocean of pitchblende. So finely balanced is it in this unfamiliar sky that the addition of a thread would destroy its equilibrium. This is one of the moons which the poets are constantly charting and concerning which, fortunately, there is no scientific knowledge. Under these new moons the destiny of the race will one day be determined. They are the anarchic moons which swim in the latent protoplasm of the race, which bring about baffling disturbances, angoisse, hallucinations. Everything that happens now and has been happening for the last twenty thousand years or so is put in the balance against this weird, prophetic cusp of a moon which is traveling towards its optimum.

The moon and the sea! What cold, clean attractions obsess him! That warm, cosy fire out of which men build their petty emotions seems almost unknown to Reichel. He inhabits the depths, of ocean and of sky. Only in the depths is he content and in his element. Once he described to me a Medusa he had seen in the waters of Spain. It came swimming towards him like a sea-organ playing a mysterious oceanic music. I thought, as he was describing the Medusa, of another painting for which he could not find words. I saw him make the motion with his arms, that helpless, fluttering stammer of the man who has not yet named everything. He was *almost* on the point of describing it when suddenly he stopped, as if paralyzed by the dread of naming it. But while he was stuttering and stammering I heard the music playing; I knew that the old woman with the white hair was only another creature from the depths, a Medusa in female guise who was playing for him the music of eternal sorrow. I knew that she was the woman who inhabited "The Haunted House" where in hot somber tones the little white bird is perched, warbling the pre-ideological language unknown to man. I knew that she was there in the "Remembrance of a Stained Glass Window," the being which inhabits the window, revealing herself in silence only to those who have opened their hearts. I knew that she was in the wall on which he had painted a verse of Rilke's, this gloomy, desolate wall over which a smothered sun casts a wan ray of light. I knew that what he could not name was in everything, like his black sorrow, and that he had chosen a language as fluid as music in order not to be broken on the sharp spokes of the intellect.

363

In everything he does color is the predominant note. By the choice and blend of his tones you know that he is a musician, that he is preoccupied with what is unseizable and untranslatable. His colors are like the dark melodies of César Franck. They are all weighted with black, a live black, like the heart of chaos itself. This black might also be said to correspond to a kind of beneficent ignorance which permits him to resuscitate the powers of magic. Everything he portrays has a symbolic and contagious quality: the subject is but the means for conveying a significance which is deeper than form or language. When I think, for example, of the picture which he calls "The Holy Place," one of his strikingly unobtrusive subjects, I have to fall back on the word enigmatic. There is nothing in this work which bears resemblance to other holy places that we know of. It is made up of entirely new elements which through form and color suggest all that is called up by the title. And yet, by some strange alchemy, this little canvas, which might also have been called "Urim and Thummim," revives the memory of that which was lost to the Jews upon the destruction of the Holy Temple. It suggests the fact that in the consciousness of the race nothing which is sacred has been lost, that on the contrary it is we who are lost and vainly seeking, and that we shall go on vainly seeking until we learn to see with other eyes.

In this black out of which his rich colors are born there is not only the transcendental but the despotic. His black is not oppressive, but profound, producing a *fruitful* disquietude. It gives one to believe that there is no rock bottom any more than there is eternal truth. Nor even God, in the sense of the Absolute, for to create God one would first have to describe a circle. No, there is no God in these paintings, unless it be Reichel himself. There is no need for a God because it is all one creative substance born out of darkness and relapsing into darkness again.

Autobiographical Note

I WAS BORN in New York City December 26, 1891 of American parents. My grandfathers came to America to escape military service. All my ancestors are German and come from every part of Germany; the family is scattered all over the world, in the most remote and outlandish parts. The men were mostly seafarers, peasants, poets and musicians. Until I went to school I spoke nothing but German and the atmosphere in which I was raised, despite the fact that my parents were born in America, was German through and through. From five to ten were the most important years of my life; I lived in the street and acquired the typical American gangster spirit. The 14th Ward, Brooklyn, where I was raised, is particularly dear to me; it was an immigrant quarter and my companions were all of different nationality. The Spanish-American war, which broke out when I was seven, was a big event in my young life; I enjoyed the mob spirit which broke loose and which permitted me to understand at an early age the violence and lawlessness which is so characteristic of America.

My parents were relatively poor, hard-working, thrifty, unimaginative. (My father never read a book in his life.) I was well cared for and had a very happy, healthy time of it until I had to shift for myself. I had no desire to earn a living, no sense of economy, and no respect for my elders or for laws or institutions. I defied my parents and those about me almost from the time I was able to talk. I left City College a few months after I entered it, disgusted with the atmosphere of the place and the stupidity of the curriculum. Took a job in the financial district, with a cement company, and quickly regretted it. Two years later my father gave me the money to go to Cornell; I took the money and disappeared with my mistress, a woman old enough to be my mother. I returned home a year or so later and then left for good, to go West. Worked in various parts of the country, mostly the southwest. Did all sorts of odd jobs, usually as a ranch hand. Was on my way to Juneau, Alaska, to work as a placer miner in the gold fields, when I was taken down with fever. Returned to New York and led a roving, shiftless, vagabond life, working at anything and everything, but never for very long. I was a good athlete and trained every day of my life for about five years—as though I were going to enter the Olympic games. I owe my excellent health to this early Spartan regime, the continuous poverty in which I have lived, and the fact that I never worry. I lived recklessly and rebelliously up to my thirtieth year, was the leader in everything, and suffered primarily because I was too honest, too sincere, too truthful, too generous.

Was forced to study the piano at an early age, showed some talent and later studied it seriously, hoping to become a concert pianist, but didn't. Gave it up entirely, my motto always being "all or nothing". Was obliged to enter my father's tailoring establishment, because he was unable to manage his affairs. Learned almost nothing about tailoring; instead, I began to write. Probably the first thing I ever wrote was in my father's shop—a long essay on Nietzsche's *Anti-Christ*. Usually I wrote letters to my friends, letters forty and fifty pages long, about everything under the sun: they were humorous letters, as well as pompously intellectual. (I still like writing letters best of all!) At any rate, I didn't think then that I would ever be a writer—I was almost afraid to think such a thing.

When America entered the war I went to Washington to work as a clerk in the War Department—sorting mail. In my spare time I did a little reporting for one of the Washington papers. I got out of the draft by using my head, came back to New York again and took over my father's business during his illness. I was always an out and out pacifist, and still am. I believe it is justifiable to kill a man in anger, but not in cold blood or on principle, as the laws and governments of the world advocate. During the war I married and became a father. Though jobs were plentiful at that time I was always out of work. I held innumerable positions, for a day or less often. Among them the following: dish-washer, bus boy, newsie, messenger boy, grave-digger, bill sticker, book salesman, bell hop, bartender, liquor salesman, typist, adding machine operator, librarian, statistician, charity worker, mechanic, insurance collector, garbage collector, usher, secretary to an evangelist, dock hand, street car conductor, gymnasium instructor, milk driver, ticket chopper, etc.

The most important encounter of my life was with Emma Goldman in San Diego, California. She opened up the whole world of European culture for me and gave a new impetus to my life, as well as direction. I was violently interested in the I. W. W. movement at the time it was in swing, and remember with great reverence and affection such people as Jim Larkin, Elizabeth Gurley Flynn, Giovanitti and Carlo Tresca. I was never a member of any club, fraternity, social or political organization. As a youngster I had been led from one church to another—first Lutheran, then Presbyterian, then Methodist, then Episcopalian. I later followed with great interest the lectures at the Bahai Center and the Theosophists and New Thoughters and Seventh Day Adventists and so on. I was thoroughly eclectic and immune. The Quakers and the Mormons impressed me by their integrity and sincerity—and by their self-sufficiency. I think they make the best Americans.

In 1920, after serving as messenger and stool pigeon for the company, I became personnel director of the Western Union Telegraph Company, N. Y. City. I held the job almost five years and still consider it the richest period in my life. The scum and riff-raff of New York passed through my hands—well over a hundred thousand men, women and boys. During a three weeks' vacation, in 1923, I wrote my first book—a study of twelve eccentric messengers. It was a long book and probably a very bad one, but it gave me the itch to write. I quit the job without a word of notice, determined to be a writer. From then on the real misery began. From 1924 to 1928 I wrote a great many stories and articles, none of which were ever accepted. Finally I printed my own things and with the aid of my second wife I sold them from door to door, later in restaurants and night clubs. Eventually I was obliged to beg in the streets.

Through an unexpected piece of fortune I was able to come to Europe, in 1928, where I stayed the whole year, touring a good part of the continent. Remained in New York the year of 1929, again broke, miserable, unable to see a way out. Early in 1930 I raised the money to return to Europe, intending to go direct to Spain, but never getting any farther than Paris, where I have remained since.

In addition to the book on the messengers, which I wrote in three weeks, I completed two novels while in America, and I brought with me to Europe a third one, which was unfinished. On finishing it I offered it to a publisher in Paris who promptly lost it and then asked me one day if I were sure I had ever given it to him. I had no carbon copy of the book—three years' work gone up the flue. I began *Tropic of Cancer*, which is announced as my "first" book, about a year after landing in Paris. It was written from place to place on all sorts of paper, often on the backs of old manuscripts. I had little hope, when writing it, of ever seeing it published. It was an act of desperation. The publication of this book, by the Obelisk Press, Paris, opened the door to the world for me. It gave me innumerable friends and acquaintances, from all over the world. I still have no money and I still do not know how to earn a living, but I have plenty of friends and well-wishers, and I have lost my fear of starvation, which was becoming an obsession. I am now absolutely at one with my destiny and reconciled to anything which may happen. I haven't the slightest fear about the future, because I have learned how to live in the present.

As for influences . . . The real influence has been life itself, the life of the streets especially, of which I never tire. I am a city man through and through; I hate nature, just as I hate the "classics."

I owe a lot to the dictionary and the encyclopaedia which, like Balzac, I read voraciously when I was a youngster. Until I was twenty-five I had scarcely read a novel, except for the Russians. I was interested almost exclusively in religion, philosophy, science, history, sociology, art, archaeology, primitive cultures, mythologies, etc. I scarcely ever looked at a newspaper—and I have never read a detective story in my life. On the other hand, I have read everything in the field of humor which I could lay hands on—there is precious little! I liked Eastern folk lore and fairy tales, especially Japanese tales, which are full of violence and malevolence. I liked writers like Herbert Spencer, Fabre, Havelock Ellis, Fraser, the older Huxley and such like. I was widely read in the European drama, thanks to Emma Goldman—knew the European dramatists before the English or the American. I read the Russians before the Anglo-Saxons, and the Germans before the French. My greatest influences were Dostoievski, Nietzsche and Elie Fauré. Proust and Spengler were tremendously fecundating. Of American writers the only real influences were Whitman and Emerson. I admit to Melville's genius, but find him boring. I dislike Henry James intensely, and absolutely detest Edgar Allan Poe. On the whole I dislike the trend of American literature; it is realistic, prosaic and "pedagogic"; it is written down, to please the lowest common denominator, and it is good, in my opinion, only in the realm of the short story. Men like Sherwood Anderson and Saroyan, who are poles apart, I consider masterful and the equals of, if not superior to, any European, in this realm. As for English literature, it leaves me cold, as do the English themselves: it is a sort of fish-world which is completely alien to me. I am thankful to have made a humble acquaintance with French literature which on the whole is feeble and limited, but which in comparison with Anglo-Saxon literature to-day is an unlimited world of the imagination. I owe much to the Dadaists and Surrealists. I prefer the French writers who are un-French. I think that France is the China of the Occident, though decidedly inferior in every way to the real China. I think France is the best place in the Occidental world to live and to work, but it is still far from being a healthy, vital world.

My aim, in writing, it to establish a greater REALITY. I am not a realist or naturalist; I am for life, which in literature, it seems to me, can only be attained by the use of dream and symbol. I am at bottom a metaphysical writer, and my use of drama and incident is only a device to posit something more profound. I am against pornography and for obscenity—and violence. Above all, for imagination, fantasy, for a liberty as yet undreamed of. I use destruction creatively, perhaps a little too much in the German style, but aiming always towards a real, inner harmony, an inner peace—and silence. I prefer music above all the arts, because it is so absolutely sufficient unto itself and because it tends towards silence. I believe that literature, to become truly communicable (which it is not at present), must make greater use of the symbol and the metaphor, of the mythological and the archaic. Most of our literature is like the text-book; everything takes place on an arid plateau of intellectuality. Ninety-nine percent of what is written—and this goes for all our art products—should be destroyed. I want to be read by less and less people; I have no interest in the life of the masses, nor in the intentions of the existing governments of the world. I hope and believe that the whole civilized world will be wiped out in the next hundred years or so. I believe that man can exist, and in an infinitely better, larger way, without "civilization."

HENRY MILLER.

HENRY MILLER was born in Manhattan in 1891, and attended elementary and high school in Brooklyn where his family moved when he was one. The rest of his education has been informal, acquired through wide reading and through travel. His first published book, *Tropic of Cancer*, appeared in Paris in 1934, although he had written many stories and two novels before that time. He lived in France for ten years, returning to the United States at the beginning of World War II after he had made an eight months' trip through Greece which resulted in *The Colossus of Maroussi*. In the early 1940's with the American artist, Abe Rattner, Miller made a cross-country tour of the United States which is recorded in *The Air-Conditioned Nightmare* and *Remember to Remember*. Mr. Miller settled in Big Sur, California, in 1945. In 1958 he was elected to membership in the National Institute of Arts and Letters, and in 1961 was awarded a special citation of the Prix International des Editeurs on the occasion of the coming publication of *Tropic of Cancer* in the United States and Italy. Mr. Miller no longer lives in Big Sur, but is still a resident of California.

BOOKS BY HENRY MILLER
published by NEW DIRECTIONS

THE AIR CONDITIONED NIGHTMARE
An account of a three-year trip through the United States. Paperbound.

ALLER RETOUR NEW YORK
An exuberant, rambling letter to Miller's friend Alfred Perlès describing his visit to New York in 1935 and return to Europe aboard a Dutch ship.

BIG SUR AND THE ORANGES OF HIERONYMUS BOSCH
Henry Miller here describes the earthly paradise he has found on the California coast and the devils, human and natural, which have threatened it. Paperbound.

THE BOOKS IN MY LIFE
A candid and self-revealing journey back into memory, sharing with the reader the thrills of new discovery that a lifetime of wide reading has brought to an original and questioning mind. Paperbound.

THE COLOSSUS OF MAROUSSI
A travel book about Greece. "It gives you a feeling of the country and the people that I have never gotten from any modern book." (Edmund Wilson.) Paperbound.

THE COSMOLOGICAL EYE
A miscellany of representative examples of Miller stories, sketches, prose poems, philosophical and critical essays, surrealist fantasies, and autobiographical notes. Included are several sections from *Black Spring*, together with the famous story "Max." Hardbound and paperbound.

THE HENRY MILLER READER
A cross-section designed to show the whole range of Miller's writing—stories, literary essays, "portraits" of people and places—interlarded with new autobiographical comments by Henry Miller. Edited, with an introduction, by Lawrence Durrell. Paperbound.

HENRY MILLER ON WRITING
Passages on the art and practice of writing chosen from all of Miller's books, brought together by Thomas H. Moore, co-founder of the Henry Miller Literary Society, with Miller's active collaboration. Paperbound.

REMEMBER TO REMEMBER
Miller continues his examination of the American scene, in essays and stories, and finds men capable of resisting the dehumanizing pressures of civilization. Hardbound and paperbound.

THE SMILE AT THE FOOT OF THE LADDER
This touching fable tells of Auguste, a famous clown who could make people laugh but who sought to impart to his audiences a lasting joy.

STAND STILL LIKE THE HUMMINGBIRD
A collection of stories and essays, many of which have appeared only in foreign magazines or in small limited editions now out of print, reflecting the incredible vitality and variety of interests of Henry Miller. Hardbound and paperbound.

THE TIME OF THE ASSASSINS
A study of Rimbaud that is as much a study of Miller and has throughout the electric quality of miraculous empathy. Paperbound.

THE WISDOM OF THE HEART
A rich collection of Miller's stories and philosophical pieces, including his studies of D. H. Lawrence and Balzac. Paperbound.

New Directions Paperbooks—A Partial Listing

For complete listing request free catalog from
New Directions, 80 Eighth Avenue, New York 10011

†Bilingual

For complete listing request free catalog from
New Directions, 80 Eighth Avenue, New York 10011

†Bilingual